ILLUMINATIONS

BY THE SAME AUTHOR

From Hell (with Eddie Campbell)
Lost Girls (with Melinda Gebbie)
Voice of the Fire
The League of Extraordinary Gentlemen
(with Kevin O'Neill)
Unearthing (with Mitch Jenkins)
Providence (with Jacen Burrows)
Cinema Purgatorio (with Kevin O'Neill)
Jerusalem
Moon and Serpent Bumper Book of Magic
(with Steve Moore, John Coulthart and others)

ILLUMINATIONS

ALAN MOORE

BLOOMSBURY PUBLISHING
NEW YORK • LONDON • OXFORD • NEW DELHI • SYDNEY

BLOOMSBURY PUBLISHING
Bloomsbury Publishing Plc
50 Bedford Square, London, WC1B 3DP, UK
29 Earlsfort Terrace, Dublin 2, Ireland

BLOOMSBURY, BLOOMSBURY PUBLISHING and the Diana logo are trademarks of Bloomsbury Publishing Plc

First published in Great Britain 2022

A catalogue record for this book is available from the British Library

ISBN: HB: 978-1-5266-4315-5; TPB: 978-1-5266-4316-2;
WATERSTONES SIGNED EDITION: 978-1-5266-4356-8;
WATERSTONES EXCLUSIVE EDITION: 978-1-5266-6056-5;
EBOOK: 978-1-5266-4314-8; EPDF: 978-1-5266-4312-4

2 4 6 8 10 9 7 5 3 1

Typeset by Integra Software Services Pvt. Ltd.

Printed and bound in Great Britain by CPI Group (UK) Ltd, Croydon CR0 4YY

MIX
Paper from responsible sources
FSC® C171272

To find out more about our authors and books visit www.bloomsbury.com and sign up for our newsletters

CONTENTS

HYPOTHETICAL LIZARD

Half her face was porcelain.

Seated upon her balcony, absently chewing the anaemic blue flowers she had plucked from her window garden, Som-Som regarded the courtyard of the House Without Clocks. Unadorned and circular, it lay beneath her like a shadowy and stagnant well. The black flagstones, polished to an impassive lustre by the passage of many feet, looked more like still water than stone when viewed from above. The cracks and fissures that might have spoiled the effect were visible only where veins of moss followed their winding seams through the otherwise featureless jet. It could as easily have been a delicate lattice of pond scum that would shatter and disperse with the first splash, the first ripple …

When Som-Som was five, her mother had noticed the aching beauty prefigured in her infant face and had brought the uncomprehending child through the yammering maze of night-time Liavek until they reached the pastel house with its round black courtyard. Yielding to the tug of her mother's hand, Som-Som dragged across the midnight slabs with the echo of her footsteps whispering back to her from the high, curved wall that bounded all but a quarter of the enclosure. The concave façade of the House Without Clocks itself completed the circle, and into its broad arc were set seven doors, each of a different colour. It was at the central door, the white one, that her mother knocked.

There was the sound of small and careful footsteps, followed by the brief muttering of a latch as the door was unlocked from the other side. It glided noiselessly open. Dressed all in white against the whiteness of the chambers beyond, a fifteen-year-old girl stared out into the dark at them, her eyes remote and unquestioning.

The garment she wore was shaped to her body and coloured like snow, with faint blue shadows pooling in its folds and creases. It covered her from head to toe, save for the openings that had been cut away to reveal her right breast, her left hand and her impenetrable, mask-like face.

Staring up at the slim figure framed in its icy rectangle of light, Som-Som had at first assumed that the girl's visible flesh was reddened by the application of paint or powder. Looking closer, she realised with a thrill of fascination and horror that the skin was entirely covered by small yet legible words, tattooed in vivid crimson upon the smooth white canvas beneath. Finely worded sentences, ambiguous and suggestive, spiralled out from the maroon bud of her nipple. Verses of elegant and cryptic passion followed the orbit of her left eye before resolving themselves into a perfect metaphor beneath the shadow of her cheekbone. Her fingers dripped with poetry.

She looked first at Som-Som and then at her mother, and there was no judgement in her eyes. As if something had been agreed upon, she turned and walked with tiny, precise steps into the arctic dazzle of the House Without Clocks. After an instant, Som-Som and her mother followed, closing the white door behind them.

The girl (whose name, Som-Som later learned, was Book) led the two of them through spectrally perfumed corridors to a room that was at once gigantic and blinding. White light, refracted through lenses and faceted glassware, seemed to hang in the air like a ghostly cobweb, so that the shapes and forms within the room were softened. At the centre of this foggy phosphorescence, a tall woman reclined upon polar furs, the cushions strewn about her feet embossed with intricate frost patterns. The glimmering blur of her surroundings erased the wrinkles from her skin and made her ageless, but when she spoke her voice was old. Her name was Ouish, and she was the mistress and proprietor of the House Without Clocks.

The conversation that passed between the two women was low and obscure, and Som-Som caught little of it. At one point, Mistress Ouish rose from her bed of white pelts and hobbled over to inspect the child. The old woman took Som-Som's face lightly between thumb and forefinger, turning the head in order to study the profile. Her touch was like crepe, but surprisingly warm in a room that gleamed with such unearthly coldness. Evidently satisfied, she turned and nodded once to the girl called Book before returning to the embrace of the furs.

The tattooed servant left the room, returning some moments later bearing a small pouch of bleached leather. It jingled faintly as she walked. She handed it to Som-Som's mother, who looked frightened and uncertain. Its weight seemed to reassure her, and she did not resist or complain as Book took her lightly by the arm and guided her out of the white chamber.

Long minutes passed before Som-Som realised that her mother was not coming back.

There was Khafi, a nineteen-year-old dislocationist who, lying upon his stomach, could curl his body backward until his buttocks were seated comfortably upon the top of his head while his face smiled out from between the ankles. There was Delice, a woman in middle age who used fourteen needles to provoke inconceivable pleasures and torments, all without leaving the faintest mark. Mopetel, suspending her own heartbeat and breath, could approximate a corpse-like state for more than two hours. Jazu had fine black hair growing all over his body and would walk upon all fours and only communicate in growls. And there was Rushushi, and Hata, and unblinking Loba Pak …

Living amidst this menagerie of exotics, where the singular was worn down by repeated contact until it became the commonplace, Som-Som was afforded a certain objectivity.

Without discrimination or favour, she spent the best part of her days observing the animate rarities about her, wondering which of them provided a template for what she was to become. Eavesdropping upon Mistress Ouish and her closest associates, patiently decoding their under-language of pauses and accentuated syllables, Som-Som had determined that she was being preserved for something special – special even amidst the gallery of specialties that was the House Without Clocks. Would she be instructed in the art of driving men and women to ecstasy with the vibrations of her voice, like Hata? Would Mopetel's talent of impermanent death become hers? Smiling as she accepted the candied fruits and marzipans offered by her indulgent elders, she would study their faces and consider.

Upon her ninth birthday, Som-Som was escorted by Book to the dazzling sanctum of Mistress Ouish. Her parched smile disquieting with its uncharacteristic warmth, Mistress Ouish had dismissed Book and then patted the wintery hides beside her, gesturing for Som-Som to sit. With what looked like someone else's expression stitched across her face, the proprietor of the House Without Clocks informed Som-Som of what might be her unique position within that establishment.

If she wished, she would become a whore of sorcerers, exclusive to their use. Henceforth, only those cunning hands that sculpted fortune itself would have access to the warm slopes of her substance. She would come to understand the abstracted lusts of those who moved the secret levers of the world, and she would be happy in their service.

Kneeling at the very edge of the bed of silver fur, Som-Som had felt the world shudder to a standstill as the old woman's words rolled about inside her head, crashing together like huge glass planets.

Sorcerers?

Often, sent to fetch some minor philtre or remedy for the older inhabitants of the House Without Clocks, Som-Som's errands had taken her to Wizard's Row. The street itself, shifting and inconstant, full of small movements at the periphery of her vision, presented no clear or consistent image that she could summon from her memory. Some of its denizens, however, were unforgettable. Their eyes. Their terrible, knowing eyes …

She pictured herself naked before a gaze that had known the depths of the oceans of chance in which people are but fishes, a gaze that saw the secret wave patterns in those unfathomable tides of circumstance. In her stomach, something more ambiguous than either fear or exhilaration began to extend its tendrils. Somewhere far away, in a white room filled with obscuring brilliance, Mistress Ouish was detailing a list of those conditions that must be fulfilled before Som-Som could commence her new duties.

It seemed that many who dealt in the manipulation of luck would themselves leave nothing to chance. Before such a sorcerer would enter fully into physical congress with another being, the inflexible observation of certain precautions was demanded. Foremost amongst these were those safeguards pertaining to secrecy. The ecstasies of wizards were events of awesome and terrifying moment, during which their power was at its most capricious, its least contained.

It was not unknown for various phenomena to manifest spontaneously, or for the name of a luck-invested object to be murmured at the moment of release. In the world of the magicians, such indiscretions could be of lethal consequence. The most innocent of boudoir confidences, if relayed to an enemy of sufficient ruthlessness, might yield a dreadful harvest to the incautious thaumaturge. Perhaps he would be plucked from the night by cold hands with unblinking yellow eyes set into their palms, or perhaps a sore upon his neck would blossom into purple, babyish lips, whispering delirious obscenities into his ear until all reason was driven from him.

The intangible continent of fortune was a territory steeped in hazard, and she who would be whore to sorcerers specifically must also undertake to be the bride of Silence.

To this end, Som-Som would be taken to a specific residence in Wizard's Row, an address remarkable in that it could only be located upon the third and fifth days of the week. Here, the child would be given a small pickled worm, ochre in colour, revealing the greyish-pink mansion of her soul to the fingers of one who abided in that place, a physiomancer of great renown. At this juncture, the Silencing would commence.

Connecting the brain's hemispheres there existed a single gristly thread, the thoroughfare by which the urgent neural messages of the preverbal and intuitive right lobe might pass to its more rational and active counterpart upon the left. In Som-Som, this delicate bridge would be destroyed, severed by a sharp knife, so as to permit no further communication between the two halves of the child's psyche.

Following her recovery from this surgery, the girl would be granted a year in which to adjust to her new perceptions. She would learn to balance and to pick up objects without the benefit of stereoscopic sight or depth of vision. After many bouts of tearful and frustrating paralysis, during which she would merely stand and tremble, making poignant half-completed gestures while her body remained torn between conflicting urges, she would finally achieve some measure of coordination and restored grace. Certainly, her movements would always possess a slow and slightly staggered quality, but if directed properly, there was no reason why this dreamlike effect should not in itself be erotically enhancing. At the end of her year of readjustment, Som-Som would have a cast taken of her face, after which she would be fitted with the Broken Mask.

The Broken Mask was not so much broken as sliced cleanly in two. Made of porcelain and covering the entire head, it would be precisely bisected with a small, silver chisel, starting at the nape of the neck, traversing the cold and hairless cranium, descending the ridge of the nose to divide the expressionless lips forever. The left side of the mask would be taken away and crushed to a fine talcum before being thrown to the winds.

Prior to the fitting of the Broken Mask, Som-Som's head would be completely shaved, the scalp afterwards rubbed with the foul-smelling mauve juices of a berry known to destroy the follicles of the hair so that there could be no regrowth. This would at least partially ensure her comfort during the next fifteen years, in which time the mask was not to be removed unless the slowly changing shape of her skull made it uncomfortable. In this eventuality, the mask would be taken from her head and recast.

Covering the right side of her head, the flawless topography of the Broken Mask would be uninterrupted by any aperture for hearing or vision. The porcelain eye was opaque and white and blind. The porcelain ear heard nothing. Concealed beneath this shell, their organic counterparts would be similarly disadvantaged. Som-Som would see nothing with her right eye, and would be deaf in her right ear. Only in the uncovered half of her face would the perceptions be unimpaired.

By some paradoxical mirror-fluke of nature, those sensory impressions gleaned from the apparatus of the body's left side would be conveyed to the brain's right hemisphere. And there, due to the severing of the neural causeway that had connected both lobes, the information would remain. It would never reach those centres of cerebral activity that govern speech and communication, for they were situated in the left brain, a land now irretrievably lost beyond the surgically created chasm. Her eye would see, but her lips would know nothing of it. Conversation that her ear might gather would forever go unrepeated by a tongue ignorant of words it should shape.

She would be blinded, but not exactly. Her hearing would remain, after a fashion, and she would even be able to speak. But she would be Silenced.

Within the flattering opalescence of her white chamber, Mistress Ouish concluded her descriptions of the honours which awaited the stunned nine-year-old. She rang the tiny china bell that signalled Book to the room, terminating the audience. Stumbling over feet made suddenly too large by loss of circulation, Som-Som allowed the tattooed servant to lead her into the startling, mundane daylight.

Poised upon the threshold, Book had turned to the blinking child beside her and smiled. It wrinkled the words written upon her cheeks, rendering them briefly illegible, and it was not a cruel smile.

'When you are Silenced and can reveal their conclusions to no one, I shall permit you to read all of my stories.'

Her voice was uneven of pitch, as if she had long been unpractised in its application. Raising her ungloved and crimson-speckled hand, she touched the calligraphy upon her forehead, and then, lowering it, lightly brushed the lyric spiral of her breast. Smiling once more, she turned and went inside the house, closing the white door behind her, an ambulatory pornography.

It was the first time that Som-Som had even heard her speak.

The following day, Som-Som was escorted to an elusive residence where a man with a comb of white hair, which had been varnished into a stiff dorsal fin running back across his skull, gave her a tiny, brownish worm to chew. She noted that it was withered and ugly, but probably no more so than it had been in life. She placed it upon her tongue, because that was expected of her, and she began to chew.

She awoke as two separate people, unspeaking strangers who shared the same skin without collaboration or conference. She was conveyed back to the House Without Clocks in a small cart lined with cushions. She rattled through the arched entranceway and across the gargantuan inkblot of the courtyard, and all that had been promised eventually came to pass.

Twelve years ago.

Seated upon her balcony, her half-visible lips stained blue by the juices of the masticated blossoms, Som-Som regarded the courtyard of the House Without Clocks. Unrippled by the afternoon breeze, the black pond stared back at her. Here and there upon the impenetrably dark water, fallen leaves were floating, motionless scraps of sepia against the blackness.

Surely, if she were to topple forward with delicious slowness towards the midnight well beneath her, she would come to no harm? Dropping like a pebble, she would splash through the impassive jet of the surface, a tumbling commotion of silver in the cold, ebony waters surrounding her. Up above, the ripples would race outward like pulses of agony throbbing from a wound. They would break in black, lapping wavelets against the courtyard walls of the House Without Clocks, and then the waters would once more become as still as stone.

Down below, kicking out with clean, unfaltering strokes, she would swim beneath the ground, out below the curved walls of the House Without Clocks, out under the City of Luck itself, and into those unchartered, solid oceans that lie beyond. Diving deep, she would glide amongst the glittering veins of ore, through the buried and forgotten strata. Darting upward, she would flicker and twist through the warm shallows of the topsoil, surfacing occasionally to leap in a shimmering arc through the sunlight, droplets of soil beading in the air about her. Resubmerging, she would strike out for the cool solitude of the clay and sandstone, far, far beneath her …

Someone walked across the surface of the black water, wooden sandals scuffing audibly against its suddenly hardened substance, crunching through leaves that were quite dry. Unable to sustain itself before such contradictions, the illusion melted and was immediately beyond recall.

One side of Som-Som's face clouded in annoyance at this intrusion upon her reverie, half her brow clenching into a petulant frown while the other half remained uncreased and indifferent. Her single visible eye, one from a pair of gems made more exquisite by the loss of its twin, glared down at the visitor passing beneath her. Unnoticed upon her balcony, she studied the interloper, struck suddenly by some quirk of gait or posture that seemed familiar. Her left eye squinted slightly as she strained for a better view, deforming the symmetry of her bisected face into a mirthless wink.

The figure was slender and of medium height, swathed in gorgeous bandages of red silk from crown to ankle so that only the face, hands, and feet were left unwrapped. The delicate line of the shoulder and arm seemed unmistakably female, but there remained something masculine about the manner in which the torso joined with the narrow, angular hips. Walking unhurriedly across the courtyard, it paused before the pale yellow door that lay at the rightmost extremity of the House Without Clocks. There the figure hesitated, turning to survey the courtyard and giving Som-Som her first clear glimpse of a painted face at once strikingly alien and instantly recognisable.

The visitor's name was Rawra Chin, and she was a man.

During the years of her service within that drifting environment, her perceptions of the world limited by her condition and by the virtual confinement that was its effective result, Som-Som had nonetheless contrived to reach a plateau of understanding, an internal vantage point overlooking the vast sphere of human activity from which the Broken Mask had excluded her. This perspective afforded her certain insights that were at once acute and peculiar.

She understood, for example, that quite apart from being a limitless ocean of fortune, the world was also a churning maelstrom of sex. Establishments such as the House Without Clocks were islands within that current, where people were washed ashore by the tides of need and loneliness. Some would remain there forever, lodged upon the high-tide line. Most would be sucked away when the ebb of the waters came. Of these fragments reclaimed by the ocean, few would ever again reach land, and if they did, it would not be in those latitudes.

Rawra Chin, it seemed, was an exception.

Som-Som remembered her as a wide-boned and awkward boy of fourteen whose employment at the House Without Clocks had commenced when Som-Som was already in the fifth year of her service. Despite the flatness and breadth of her face and the clumsiness of her deportment, Rawra Chin had even then possessed some rare and indefinable essence of personality, animating the uneasy frame of the adolescent boy and lending her a beauty that was disturbing in its effect.

Mistress Ouish, long skilled in detecting that pearl of the remarkable that is concealed within the oyster of the ordinary, had noticed Rawra Chin's distinct yet elusive charm when she decided to employ the youth. So, too, did the clientele of the House Without Clocks, with numerous merchants, fishermen and soldiers proclaiming her their especial favourite, asking after her whenever they should chance to visit that establishment.

The common bond shared by all those who admired this charisma within Rawra Chin was that none of them could precisely identify it. It remained a mystery, concealed somewhere within the oddly disparate components of her broad and starkly decorated face, hovering at some imaginary point of focus between her hasty pencil-line of a mouth and her widely spaced eyes, overwhelmingly tangible, eternally ungraspable.

Som-Som, one of two people within the House who had come to know Rawra Chin closely, had always been inclined to the belief that her charms originated in the emotional depths of the nervous and hesitant lad herself, rather than in some fluke of physique or physiognomy.

There was a restless melancholy that seemed to inform everything from the youth's stance to the way she brushed her hair, so long and soft, so golden it was almost white. There was also the occasional icicle glitter of fear in those eyes, which had too great a distance between them for prettiness but just enough for beauty. These disparate threads of personality were woven into a design that gave the overwhelming impression of vulnerability. As to the precise nature of that vulnerability, Som-Som had no more idea than the most brief and casual of Rawra's adoring customers.

Often, she had come to sit and drink tea with Som-Som upon her balcony to pass the time between engagements, a diversion popular with many of the inhabitants of the House Without Clocks. Due to the singularity of Som-Som's impairment, they could reveal their longings or resentments without fear. Rawra Chin would visit her during the long, dull mornings, seeming to delight in the thin floral infusions and the opportunity for one-sided conversation.

It seemed to Som-Som that she had contributed little to these often intimate discussions, having no confidences that she was able to share. Since the side of her brain that governed speech had known nothing but darkness and silence for several years, the best that it could offer conversationally was a string of inappropriate and disconnected fragments, half-remembered impressions and anecdotes relating to the world that Som-Som had known before the Silencing.

Confusing matters further, Som-Som's verbal half could not hear and was forced to make interjections without knowing whether the other person had finished speaking. Thus, while Rawra Chin would be engaged in a vivid description of what she hoped to do once her employment at the House Without Clocks was ended, Som-Som would startle her by saying, 'I remember that my mother was an unlikeable woman who rushed everywhere to get her life over with the sooner,' or something equally obscure, followed by a long silence during which she would stare politely at Rawra Chin and sip her floral infusion through the left corner of her mouth.

Though at first disoriented by these random pronunciations, Rawra Chin grew accustomed to them, waiting until Som-Som had finished her non sequitur before resuming. The continuing presence of these bizarre ejaculations did not seem to lessen Rawra Chin's enjoyment of their conversational interludes. Som-Som supposed that her real contribution to these talks had been her simple presence.

Her function was that of a receptacle for the aspirations and anxieties of others, but this never became oppressive. She enjoyed the exclusiveness of these glimpses into the way that ordinary life was conducted. The fact that people would relate to her things that went unvoiced even to their lovers gave Som-Som a perspective upon human nature more true and comprehensive than that enjoyed by many sages and philosophers.

This gave her a measure of personal power, and she took pride in her ability to unravel the many and varied personas that presented themselves to her, laying bare the essential characteristics that were concealed beneath their façades of affectation and self-deception. Rawra Chin had been Som-Som's only failure.

Like everyone else, she had been unable to give a name to that rare and precious element upon which the bewilderingly attractive adolescent had founded her identity.

On the other hand, Som-Som had been able to construct a relatively complete picture of Rawra Chin's aversions and ambitions, however superficial these appeared without an understanding of her more fundamental motivations.

Som-Som knew, for example, that Rawra Chin did not intend to make a lifetime's vocation of prostitution. While she had heard similar avowals from most of the occupants of the House Without Clocks, Som-Som sensed a determination in Rawra Chin that was iron-hard, setting her appraisal of the future apart from the rather sad and much-thumbed fantasies of her fellows.

Rawra Chin often assured Som-Som that she would one day be a great performer travelling the globe, transporting her art to the masses by way of a celebrated company of dramaticians such as the Torn-Stocking Troupe, or Dimuk Paparian's Mnemonic Players. The less aesthetically demanding acts of pantomime that she was called upon to perform each day behind the pale yellow door of the House Without Clocks were merely a clumsy rehearsal for the innumerable thespian triumphs waiting somewhere in her future.

The pale yellow door gave access to that part of the house that was given over to romantic pursuits of a more theatrical nature, its four floors each housing a single specialist in the erotic arts, linked by a polished wooden staircase that zigzagged up outside the house from courtyard level towards the grey slate incline of the roof.

In the topmost chamber lived Mopetel, the corpse-mime. Beneath her lived Loba Pak, whose flesh had an unusual consistency that enabled her to adjust her features into the semblance of almost any woman between the ages of fourteen and seventy. Rawra Chin lived on the second floor, acting out mundane and unimaginative roles for her eager male clientele, but compensating for this with her charisma. On the first floor, immediately beyond the pale yellow door, there lived a brilliant and savagely passionate male actor named Foral Yatt, whose talent had been subverted into a plaything by the many female customers who enjoyed his company. It was with Foral Yatt that Rawra Chin had become amorously entangled.

Foral Yatt was the subject of a great number of those balcony conversations, conducted through the motionless fog of warm vapour that hung above their tea bowls. While Rawra Chin spoke animatedly, Som-Som would sit and listen, breaking her silence intermittently to remark that she remembered the colour of a quilt her grandmother had made for her when she was an infant, or that a brother whose name she could no longer call to mind had once knocked over the pot-boil and badly scalded his legs.

The heart of Rawra Chin's anguish concerning Foral Yatt seemed to lie in her knowledge that if she were to achieve her ambition, she must leave the intense and darkly attractive young actor while she progressed to greater things. She confessed to Som-Som that though in private she and Foral Yatt would make their plans as if they would quit the House Without Clocks together, pursuing parallel careers in the outside world, Rawra Chin knew that this was a fiction.

Despite the fact that Foral Yatt's raw talent dwarfed her own to insignificance, he possessed neither the indefinable appeal of Rawra Chin nor the remorseless drive that would propel him through the pale yellow door and into the pitch and swell of that better life that lay beyond. Adding masochistically to her anguish, the wide-faced boy also felt troubled by the fact that she was using her nearness to Foral Yatt to study the finer points of his superior craft, storing each nuance of characterisation, each breathtakingly understated gesture, until that point in her career-to-come when she might use them. Having purged herself for the moment of her moral burden, Rawra Chin would sit and stare miserably at Som-Som, waiting for some acknowledgement of her dilemma. Long moments would pass, measured in whatever units were appropriate within the House Without Clocks, until finally Som-Som would smile and say, 'It was raining on the afternoon that I almost choked on a pebble,' or 'Her name was either Mur or Mar, and I think that she was my sister,' after which Rawra Chin would finish her tea and leave, feeling obscurely contented.

Despite her tormented writhings, Rawra Chin had eventually summoned sufficient strength of character – or sufficient callousness – to inform Foral Yatt that she would be leaving him, as she had been offered a place in a small but critically acclaimed touring company by a customer who happened to be the merchant without whose continuing financial support the company could not survive.

Som-Som could still remember the ugly playlet that the two estranged lovers had performed in the courtyard of the House on the morning that Rawra Chin was to leave. The players paced across the flat black stage – seemingly oblivious to the audience above that watched with boredom or amusement from their balconies – as their angry accusals and sullen denials rang from the curving courtyard walls.

Foral Yatt pathetically followed Rawra Chin around the courtyard, almost staggering beneath the weight of the dreadful, unexpected betrayal. He was a tall, lean man with beautiful arms, his dark and deep-set eyes brimming with tears as he trailed behind Rawra Chin, an unwanted satellite still trapped within her orbit by the irresistible gravity of her mystique. The fact that he kept his skull shaven to a close stubble to facilitate the numerous changes of wig required by his customers only added to his air of desolation.

Rawra Chin remained a measured number of paces in front of him, occasionally directing some pained but dignified comment over her shoulder while he ranted, incoherent with hurt, raging and confused. Som-Som suspected that she was in some oblique way enjoying this abuse from her former lover, that she accepted his tirade as an inverted tribute to her mesmeric influence over him.

Eventually, when desperation had driven Foral Yatt beyond all considerations of dignity, he threatened to kill himself. Pulling something from the small pouch that he wore at his belt, the distraught young actor held it aloft so that it glittered in the morning sunlight.

It was a miniature human skull, fashioned from green glass and holding no more than a mouthful of the clear, liquorice-scented liquid that it had been designed to contain. No more than a mouthful was required. These suicidal trinkets could be purchased quite openly, and it was impossible to determine how many of Liavek's more pessimistically inclined citizens carried one of the death's-heads in anticipation of that day when life was no longer endurable.

His voice ragged with emotion, Foral Yatt swore that he would not be deserted in so casual a manner. He promised to end his life if Rawra Chin did not pick up her baggage and carry it back through the pale yellow door to their chambers. They stared at each other, and Som-Som had thought that she perceived a flicker of uncertainty dance across the widely spaced eyes of Rawra Chin as they moved from Foral Yatt's face to the skull-shaped bottle in his hand. The instant seemed to inflate into a massive balloon of silence, punctured by the sudden rattle of hooves and wheels from beyond the courtyard's arched entrance, signalling the arrival of the carriage that was to take Rawra Chin to join her theatre troupe. She darted one last glance at Foral Yatt and then, picking up her baggage, turned and walked out through the archway.

Foral Yatt stood transfixed at the centre of the huge black disc, still with one flawless arm raised, clutching its cold green fistful of oblivion. He stared blankly at the archway as if expecting her to reappear and tell him it was all some ill-considered hoax. From beyond the encircling walls there came the jingle of reins, followed by a slow clattering and the creaking of wood and leather as the carriage moved away down the winding streets of the City of Luck. After a pause, during which it seemed that he would never move again, the actor slowly and falteringly lowered his arm.

Three floors above him, realising the abandoned lover wouldn't kill himself, one of the denizens of the House Without

Clocks pursed her shiny black lips discontentedly and made a clucking sound before retiring to her quarters. Hearing the sound, Foral Yatt tilted back his grey-stubbled skull and stared up at the watchers in surprise, as if previously unaware of their scrutiny. His eyes were full of miserable incomprehension, and it was a relief to Som-Som when he lowered them to the black tiles at his feet before walking slowly across the courtyard towards the pale yellow door, the glass skull now quite forgotten in his hand.

Scarcely a handful of months elapsed before news began to work its way back to the House Without Clocks of Rawra Chin's dizzying success. It seemed that her elusive charisma was able to captivate audiences as easily as it had once enthralled her individual customers. Her performance as the tragic and infertile Queen Gorda in Mossoc's *The Crib* was already the talk of Liavek's intelligentsia, and rumor had it that a special performance for His Scarlet Eminence was being considered.

Such talk was generally kept from the inconsolable Foral Yatt, but within the year Rawra Chin's fame had spread to the point where the embittered young actor was as aware of it as anyone. He seemed to take the news of her stellar ascent with less resentment than might have been anticipated, once the initial despair of separation had lifted from him. Indeed, save for a coldness that would creep into his eyes at the mention of her name, Foral Yatt made much of his indifference to his former lover's fortunes. He never spoke of her, and those less insightful than Som-Som might have supposed that he had forgotten her altogether.

Now, five years later, she had returned.

In the courtyard beneath Som-Som's balcony, Rawra Chin turned to face the pale yellow door, a resigned slump in her shoulders. She lifted one hand to knock, and there was a sudden dazzling scintillation that seemed to play about her fingers. It took Som-Som a moment to realise that Rawra Chin had chips of some reflective substance pasted to her nails. The afternoon was hushed, as if holding its breath while it listened, and the sound of Rawra Chin's white knuckles upon the pale yellow wood was disproportionately loud.

Seated high above on her balcony, Som-Som found that she wanted desperately to call out, to warn Rawra Chin that it was a mistake to return to this place, that she should leave immediately. Silence, massive and absolute, surrounded her and would not permit her to make the smallest sound. She was embedded in silence, a tiny bubble of consciousness within an infinity of solid rock, mute and grey and endless. She struggled against it, willing her tongue to shape the vital words of warning, knowing as she did so that it was hopeless.

Below, someone unlocked the pale yellow door from inside and it creaked once, musically, as it opened. It was too late.

Som-Som's balcony was situated upon the third floor, the adjacent living area being one of four contained behind the violet door at the extreme left of the House Without Clocks' concave front. Thus, as she sat upon her balcony and gazed down at Rawra Chin, she could not see who had opened the door. She supposed that it was Foral Yatt.

There was a surprisingly subdued exchange of words, following which the crimson-wrapped figure of the celebrated performer stepped inside the house and beyond Som-Som's vision. The pale yellow door closed with a sound like something sucking its teeth.

After that, there was only silence. Som-Som remained seated upon her balcony staring down at the pale yellow door with mute anguish in her one visible eye while the sky gradually darkened behind her. Finally, when the moment of her urgent need for a voice was long past, she spoke.

'I ran as fast as I could, but when I reached my mother's house, the bird was already dead.'

Since the closing of the yellow door, no word had been spoken in the rooms that lay immediately behind it. Foral Yatt sat in a hard wooden chair beside the open fire, amber light flickering across one side of his lean face. Rawra Chin stood by the window, her vivid crimson darkening to a dull, scab-like burgundy against the failing light outside. Uncertain how best to gauge the distance that had arisen between them, she watched the play of firelight upon the velvet of his shaven skull until the absence of conversation was more than she could endure.

'I brought you a gift.'

Foral Yatt slowly turned his head towards her, away from the fire, so that the shadow slid across his face, and his expression was no longer visible. Rawra Chin immersed one chalk-white hand in the black fur of the bag she carried, from which it emerged holding a small copper ball between the mirror-tipped fingers. She held it out to him and, after a moment, he took it.

'What is it?'

She had forgotten how captivating his voice was, dry and deep and hungry, quite unlike her own. Calm and evenly modulated, there remained a sense of something watchful and carnivorous lurking just beyond it, pacing quietly behind the accents. Rawra Chin licked her lips.

'It's a toy … a toy of the intellect. I'm told that it's very relaxing. Many of the busiest merchants I know find that it calms them immeasurably after the bustle of commerce.'

Foral Yatt turned the smooth copper sphere between his fingers so that it gleamed red in the glow of the fire. 'What's so special about it?'

Rawra Chin took a step away from the window, her first tentative movement towards him since entering the House, and then paused. She let her black fur bag drop with a soft thud, like the corpse of an enormous spider, on to the empty seat of the room's other chair. A certain establishing of territory accompanied the gesture, and Rawra Chin hoped she had not overstepped in her eagerness. Foral Yatt's face was still in shadow, but he did not seem to react adversely to the wedge-end represented by the bag dozing before the hearth. Encouraged by this lack of obvious rebuke, Rawra Chin smiled, albeit nervously, as she replied to him.

'There might be a lizard asleep inside the ball, or there might not. That's the puzzle.'

His silence seemed to invite elaboration.

'The story goes that there exists a lizard capable of hibernating for years or even centuries without food or air or moisture, slowing its vital processes so that a dozen winters might pass between each beat of its heart. I am told that it is a very small creature, no bigger than the top joint of my thumb when it is curled up.

'The people who make these ornaments allegedly place one of the sleeping reptiles inside each ball before sealing it. If you look closely, you can see that there's a seam around the middle.'

Foral Yatt declined to do so, remaining seated, his back towards the fire, holding the ball in his right hand and turning it so that molten highlights rolled across its surface. Though an impenetrable shadow still concealed his expression, Rawra Chin sensed that the quality of his silence had changed. She felt whatever slight advantage she had gained begin to slip away. Why wouldn't he speak? Unable to keep the edge of unease from her voice, she resumed her monologue.

'You can't open it, and, and you have to think about whether there really is a lizard inside it or not. It's to do with how we perceive the world around us, and when you think about it, you start to see that it doesn't matter if there's a lizard inside there or not, and then you can think about what's real and what isn't real, and …'

Her voice trailed off, as if suddenly aware of its own incoherence.

'… and it's said to be very relaxing,' she concluded lamely, after a flat, dismal pause.

'Why did you come back?'

'I don't know.'

'You don't know.'

It was as if her words had hit a mirror, rebounding back at her full of new meanings and implications, warped out of true by some fluke of the glass. Rawra Chin's fragile composure began to crumble before that flat, disinterested voice.

'I … I don't mean that I don't know. I just mean …' She looked down at her pale, well-kept hands to find that she was wringing them together. They looked like crabs mating after having been kept in the dark for too long. 'I mean that there was no real reason for me to come back here. My work, my career, it's all too perfect. I have a lot of money. I have friends. I've just completed my role as Bromar's eldest daughter in *The Lucksmith* and everybody will talk about me for months. For a while, I do not have to work. I can do whatever I want. I didn't have to come back here.'

Foral Yatt remained silent, the firelight behind his shaven head edging his skull with a trim of blurred phosphorescence as it shone through the stubble. The copper ball turned between his fingers, a miniature planet rolling from day into night.

'It's just that … this place, this house, it has something. There's something inside this house, and it's something true. It isn't a good thing. It's just a true thing, and I don't know what the name of it is, and I don't even like it, but I know that it's true and I know that it's here and I felt, I don't know, I felt that I had to come back and look at it. It's like …'

Rawra Chin's hands seemed to pluck and squeeze the air before her, as if the words she required were concealed beneath its skin, and by probing she could guess at their shape. Separated now, the blanched crustacean lovers lay upon their backs, feebly waving their legs as they expired upon some unseen shoreline.

'It's like an accident I saw … a farmer, crushed beneath his cart. He was alive, but his ribs were broken and sticking through his side. I didn't know what they were at first, because it was all such a mess. There were a lot of people gathered 'round, but nobody could move the cart without hurting him even more than he was hurt already.

'It was summer, and there were a lot of flies. I remember him screaming and shouting for somebody to beat the flies away, and an old woman went out and did that for him, but until then nobody had moved, not until he screamed at them. It was horrible. I walked by as fast as I could because he was suffering and there was nothing anybody could do, except for the old woman who was beating the flies away with her apron.

'But I went back.

'I stopped just a little way down the road, and I went back. I couldn't help it. It was just so real and so painful, that man, lying there under that terrible weight and screaming for his wife, his children; it was so real that it just cut through everything else in the world, all the things that my luck and my money have built up around me, and I knew that it meant something, and I went back there and I watched him drown on his own blood while the old woman told him not to worry, that his wife and children would be there soon.

'And that's why I came back to the House Without Clocks.'

There was a long hyphen of silence. A copper world rotated between the fingers of a faceless and unanswering god.

'And I still love you.'

Someone rapped twice upon the pale yellow door. For a moment there was no movement within the room save for the illusion of motion engendered by the firelight. Then Foral Yatt rose from the hard wooden chair, still with the fire at his back and his face in eclipse. Crossing the room, ducking beneath the blackened beams that supported the low ceiling, he passed close enough for her to raise her hand and brush his arm, so that it would be thought an accident of passage. But she didn't.

Foral Yatt opened the door.

The figure on the other side of the threshold was perhaps forty years of age, a large and strong-boned woman with raw cheeks who wore a single garment, a tent of smoky grey fur. It covered the top of her head, with a hole cut away to reveal the face, and then its striking, minimal lines dropped away to the floor. There was no opening in the fur through which she might extend her hands, which suggested to Rawra Chin that the woman must have servants to do everything for her, the feeding to her of meals not excluded. Even in the world that Rawra Chin had known over the previous five years, such arrogantly flaunted wealth was impressive.

As the inopportune visitor tilted back her head to speak, the flickering yellow light caught her face, and Rawra Chin noticed that the woman had an amber blemish, unpleasantly furry-looking, which covered almost her entire left cheek. The woman had obviously attempted to conceal it beneath a thick coat of white powder, with little success. The discoloration remained visible through the make-up as if it were a paper-thin flatfish that swam through her subcutaneous tissue, its dark shape discernible just below the clouded surface of her face.

When she spoke, her voice was distressingly loud, her tone strident and somehow abusive.

'Foral Yatt. Dear Foral Yatt, how long? How long has it been since I saw you last?' Foral Yatt's reply was professionally polite, coolly inoffensive, and yet delivered at such volume that Rawra Chin winced involuntarily, even though she stood several paces behind him. It came to her suddenly that the fur-draped woman must suffer from some defect of hearing.

'It has been two days since you were here, Donna Blerot. I have missed you.'

A wave of hotness washed over Rawra Chin, cooling almost instantly to a leaden ingot in her stomach. Foral Yatt had a customer, and she must leave him to his labours. Her disappointment was so big she could not admit that it was hers. She resolved to leave immediately, hoping to keep it one step behind her until she could reach her own rooms in a lodging house on the far side of the City of Luck. Once she was safely behind closed doors she would let it have its way with her, and then there would be tears. She was reaching for her bag, sleeping there in its chair, when Foral Yatt spoke again.

'However, it is not convenient that I should see you tonight. A member of my family has come to visit.' Here he gestured vaguely over his shoulder towards the stunned Rawra Chin. 'And I regret that you and I must let our yearnings simmer untended for one more day. Please be patient, Donna Blerot. When finally we meet together, you know that our union will be the sweeter for this postponement.' Donna Blerot turned her head and gazed past Foral Yatt at the slim, crimson-swathed figure that stood in the flamelit room, almost like a flame herself within the gaudy wrappings. The dame's eyes were frozen and merciless, boring into Rawra Chin for long instants before she turned them once more towards Foral Yatt, her expression softening.

'This is too bad, Foral Yatt. Simply too bad. But I shall forgive you. How could I ever do otherwise?'

She smiled, her teeth yellow and her lips too wide.

'Until tomorrow then?'

'Until tomorrow, dearest Donna Blerot.'

The woman turned from the door and Rawra Chin heard the slow, derisive clapping of her wooden sandals as she walked back across the black courtyard. Foral Yatt closed the door, sliding the bolt across. The sound of the bolt's passage, metal against metal, was electrifying in its implications, and Rawra Chin shuddered in resonance. The actor turned away from the closed portal and stared at her, his face brazen in the fire-glow. His face seemed less chiselled and gaunt than she had remembered it. His eyes, conversely, were so riveting and intense that she knew her recollection had not done them justice. Across a chamber so filled with swaying clots of darkness that it seemed like a ballroom for shadows, they stared at each other. Neither spoke.

He walked towards her, pausing only to set the small copper globe upon the polished white wood of his tabletop before continuing. His pace was so deliberate that Rawra Chin felt sure he must be aware of the tension that this deliciously prolonged approach kindled within her. Unable to meet his gaze, she lowered her lashes so that the quivering light of the room became streaks of incoherent brilliance. Her breathing grew shallow, and she trembled.

The warm, dry smell of his skin enveloped her. She knew that he was standing just before her, no more than a forearm's length away. Then he touched her face. The shock of physical contact almost caused her to jerk her head back, but she controlled the impulse. Her heart rang like an anvil as his fingernail traced the line of her jaw.

The ingenious arrangement of bandages that was Rawra Chin's costume had a single fastening, concealed behind a triangular black gem in a filigree surround that she wore upon the right side of her throat. The pin pricked her neck as Foral Yatt withdrew it from the blood-red windings, but even this seemed almost unbearably pleasant to her in that aching, oversensitised state. She lifted her gaze and his eyes swallowed her whole. With his hands moving in languid, confident circles, he began to unwind the long band of brightly dyed gauze, starting from her head and spiralling downward.

Free of the confining wrap, her thick hair tumbled down upon her white shoulders. She gasped and shook her head from side to side, but it was not an indication of denial. A wave of thrilling coolness crept down her body as progressively more of her skin was exposed to the drafts of the room. It moved across her belly and down to the angular and jutting hips, over the shaven pudenda and past the jumping, half-erect penis. It continued down her thighs and on towards the rush carpeting, where the unravelled wrappings gathered in a widening red puddle about her feet, as if her naked flesh bled from a dozen imperceptible wounds.

He nodded his head to her once, still without a sound, and she knelt upon the floor at his feet, her knees pressed against the tangle of fallen bandages so that they would leave a faint lattice of impressions upon her skin. Closing her eyes, she allowed her head to sink forward until it came to rest against the seat of the chair in which she had placed her bag an eternity before. Its luscious dark fur and the hard wood were equally cool against her burning cheek.

Behind her, a single brief chime, Foral Yatt's buckle dropped unceremoniously to the rush matting. Upon an impulse, she allowed her eyes to open, their gaze drifting across the chamber, drinking in the moment in all its infinitesimal detail. On the other side of the room, the copper ball rested upon the tabletop where Foral Yatt had placed it. It was like the freshly gouged eye of a brazen speaking-head, such as certain personages in Wizard's Row were reputed to possess.

It stared back at Rawra Chin, glittering suggestively, and all that came to pass behind the pale yellow door was reflected impartially, in perfect miniature, upon the convex surface of that lifeless and unblinking orb.

Later, lying flat upon her stomach, with their mingled sweat drying in the hollow of her back, Rawra Chin allowed her awareness to float tethered upon the margins of wakefulness while Foral Yatt squatted naked by the fire, adding fresh coals to the fading redness that had burned low during the preceding hour. The air was heavy with the intoxicating bouquet of semen, and each of her muscles slumped in blissful exhaustion.

Still, something nagged at her, even in the sublime depths of her sated torpor. There was yet something unresolved between the two of them, no matter how eloquent their lovemaking may have seemed. It was barely a real thing at all, more a disquieting absence than an intrusive presence, and she might have ignored it. This, however, proved more than she could bear. It was a cavity within her that must be filled before she could be complete. Though reluctant to send ripples through the calm afterglow of their congress, eventually she found her voice.

'Do you still love me?' This was followed, after a hesitant beat, by, 'Despite what I did to you?'

She turned her head so that the right side of her face rested against the interwoven rushes. He crouched before the fire with his back towards her as he carefully arranged cold black nuggets atop the bright embers. His skin glistened, a yellow smear of watercolour highlight running down the side towards the fire. She followed the line of his vertebrae with her eyes to the plumb-line-straight crease that bisected the hard buttocks, adoring him. He did not turn to her as he replied.

'Is there a lizard asleep within the ball?'

Taking another piece of coal in a hand already blackened by dust, Foral Yatt placed a capstone atop the dark pyramid in the scaled-down hell of the fireplace. Nothing more was said behind the pale yellow door that night.

The following morning, Rawra Chin visited Som-Som and took tea with her, as if the five-year hiatus in their ritual had never existed. She recounted a string of anecdotes from her career, then paused to sip her infusion while Som-Som informed her that her mother had once closed a door, and that it had once been dark, and that once she had been unable to stop coughing. Rawra Chin's smooth re-entry into the bizarre rhythms of their conversation did much to eradicate any distance between the two that might have flourished in their half decade of separation. Even so, it was not until the interlude approached its conclusion that the performer felt comfortable enough to broach the subject of her resumed relationship with Foral Yatt.

'I won't be staying here forever, of course. In another month or so, I must begin to consider my next role, and it would be impossible to do that here. But this time, when I leave, I believe I shall take him with me. I'm rich enough to keep him until he finds work of his own, and it seems ridiculous that someone with his talent should be wasting it upon …'

Her hands performed a curious movement that was part theatrical gesture and part genuine involuntary revulsion. It was as if they were retching with violent spasms that shuddered out from the slender throat of the wrist and on towards her fingertips, where ten mirrors shivered in the cold morning sunlight.

'… upon ugly, sick old women like that terrible Donna Blerot. He deserves so much better. I could look after him, I could find work for him, and then perhaps neither of us would need to come back to this place ever again, not even just to look at it. Don't you think that would be a good idea?'

Som-Som sipped her floral infusion through the corner of her mouth and said nothing.

'I think we can do it. I think that we can love each other and be together without anything going wrong between us. It was only my ambition that pushed us apart before, and I've fulfilled that now. Things can be just as they were, only somewhere else, in a better place than this.'

Rawra Chin looked so thoughtful, sucking the dazzling tip of her right index finger so that it made a small and liquid popping sound when she pulled it from between her lips. She did this twice. Behind her, birds wheeled above the diverse skyline of Liavek. When she spoke again, her voice had assumed a puzzled tone.

'Of course, he has changed. I suppose we've both changed. He's very quiet now, and very … very commanding. Yes, that's it exactly. Very commanding.

'It's wonderful, I'm not complaining at all. After all, those are his chambers and he's being kind enough to let me stay there for the next couple of months so that I don't need to keep up my rooms at the lodging house.

'I don't mind doing whatever he wants. I think, you know, I think it's good for me in a way, good for how I am as a person. Since my career broke out of the egg, nobody has told me what to do. I think that's spoiled me. It doesn't feel right, somehow. Not when people just defer to me all the time. I think I need someone to—'

'A sticky head looked out from between the cow's legs, and I screamed.'

Som-Som's interjection was so startling that even Rawra Chin, accustomed to such utterances, was momentarily unnerved. Blinking, she waited to see if the half-masked woman intended to make any further comment before continuing. 'I'm having my clothes sent over from the lodging house. I have so many beautiful things, it hardly seems fair. Foral Yatt says that he will store my wardrobe, but he does not want me to wear the more exotic creations while I am with him. He prefers plainer things.'

Rawra Chin glanced down at the clothing she was dressed in. She wore a simple blouse of grey cotton and a skirt of similar material. Her white-gold hair swung about her narrow shoulders and sparked life from the dusk-coloured fabric with its contrast. It lay against her blouse like wan torchlight reflected on wet, grey cobbles. Evidently satisfied with the novel restraint and subtlety of her costume, she raised her lashes and smiled across the tea bowls at Som-Som.

'But enough of my affairs and vanities. Which side of luck have you yourself walked these five years gone?'

The divided face stared back at her with its one live eye. No one spoke. Over the City of Luck, great scavenger birds dipped and shrieked, so that it sounded as if babies had been torn up from the earth and dragged wailing into the oppressive dome of the sky.

On the fifth day after her arrival, Rawra Chin appeared upon Som-Som's balcony wearing breeches of leather with a stout length of rope looped about the waist as a belt. She did not refer to this reversal of her sartorial tendencies, but after that Som-Som never again saw her in a skirt and supposed that this was due to Foral Yatt's austere influence. The performer seemed also to forgo the application of face paint and the wearing of all jewellery save for a simple band of unadorned iron, which she wore upon the smallest finger of her left hand. The ten slivers of mirror were long since vanished.

Two weeks after her return, Foral Yatt persuaded Rawra Chin to shave off her hair.

Sitting with Som-Som the following morning, she would break off from her trail of conversation every few seconds and run one incredulous palm back from her temple and across the stubble. Her talk had a forced gaiety, and there was something nervous and darting within her eyes. Som-Som realised with some surprise that Rawra Chin no longer seemed attractive. It was as if her charisma had leaked out of her, or been sheared away as ruthlessly as the spun sunlight of her hair.

'I think, I think I look better like this, don't you?'

Som-Som said nothing.

'I mean to say that it, well, it makes such a change. And I think it will do my hair a service, after it grows back. The colourings I use had made it so brittle, a new head of hair will be such a relief. And of course, Foral Yatt likes it this way.'

The casual delivery of this last phrase was belied by an evasive glance and an air of restless self-consciousness.

'I mean, I understand how it must look, how it must look to people who don't know him, but …' One hand rasped lightly across her skull in a single, backward motion. '… But the way that I dress is important to him; the way I look, it's so important to him, the way that I look when we make love.'

Som-Som cleared her throat and told the performer the name of the street where she had lived before the night when her mother had led her out by the hand, through the noise and towards the Silence. Rawra Chin continued her monologue without acknowledging the interjection, her eyes hollow and sleepless with their gaze still fixed on the grubby tiles.

'He's changed, you see. He wants different things now. And, and I don't mind. I love him. I don't mind what he wants me to do. I even like it; sometimes I like it for myself and not just for him. But the fact, the fact that I like it, that's something that frightens me. Not frightens me, really, but it's as if everything is changing and moving under my feet, and as if I'm changing too, and I feel as if I should be frightened, but I'm not. It's so easy, just slipping into it. It's so easy just to let it happen, and I don't mind. I love him and I don't mind.'

From the dilated pupil of the courtyard, someone called Rawra Chin's name. Som-Som turned her gaze to the flagstones below, puzzling for a moment over the stranger who stood there before she was able to reconcile the familiar face with the unplaceable gait and manner, finally resolving these disparate impressions into Foral Yatt.

Rawra Chin had spoken the truth. Foral Yatt had changed.

Standing beneath them, looking up with one hand raised to shield his eyes from the sun, the bar of shadow cast across his features did not conceal the change that had come over them. The actor seemed less lean. Som-Som supposed that this was in part due to Rawra Chin's wealth supplementing his income and his diet.

His clothing, too, was noticeably different from the sombre and functional raiment that he had appeared to favour. Foral Yatt wore a long tunic, its blue so deep and vibrant that it bordered upon iridescence. A wide orange sash was wound twice about his waist, and the billowing pants that he wore beneath were orange also, a fragile, mottled orange, almost white in places. His feet were naked and exquisite, much smaller than Som-Som would have expected them to be. Something glittered, a sparkling fog about the toes.

'Rawra Chin? Our meal is almost prepared.'

His voice had altered, too: lighter, a patina of melody imposed upon its assured tones. And there was something else, something which above all was responsible for the striking change in his aspect, something so obvious that it escaped Som-Som completely. Rawra Chin murmured an apology as she made ready to leave, not bothering to tie up any loose ends remaining from her conversation with Som-Som. As was her custom, she reached out and squeezed Som-Som's wrist to let the half of her brain that was cut off from sight or sound know that her visitor was leaving. In response, the half-masked woman lifted her gaze until it met Rawra Chin's. When she spoke, her voice was filled with a sadness that seemed to have no bearing upon the content of her speech.

'I do not think that the food was so good, back then.'

Rawra Chin's lips twitched once, a helpless little facial shrug, and then she turned and ran down the narrow wooden stairs that led to the courtyard below, where Foral Yatt awaited her.

She joined him there and they exchanged a snatch of dialogue that was too low for Som-Som to hear before making their way towards the pale yellow door. Som-Som craned her neck to watch them go. Just before they passed from her sight, she identified the single glaring quirk that had so transformed the young actor.

Running along his brow in an uneven snowline, curling around the topmost rim of his ears, Foral Yatt's hair was starting to grow out.

On the fifteenth night after her arrival at the House Without Clocks, something occurred behind the pale yellow door that gave Rawra Chin her first glimpse into the darkness that had been waiting for her for five long years. She went indoors to share her evening repast with Foral Yatt just as the sun was butchering the western horizon, and before morning, she had seen the abyss. She was not to comprehend the immensity of the hungry void beneath her for some three days further, but that first shattering look was the beginning. It was as if she dropped a pebble into the chasm that awaited her and listened for the splash. When three days later the splash had still not come, she knew that the blackness was bottomless, and that there was no hope.

On the earlier evening, however, when she walked through the pale yellow door with the sunset at her back and the rich aroma of the pot-boil hanging before her, this shadow was yet to fall. It seemed to her that all her anxieties were containable.

They ate their meal quickly, the two of them facing each other across the blanched wood of the table, and then Rawra Chin cleared away what debris there was while Foral Yatt retired to his bedchamber to prepare for the business of the evening ahead. Rawra Chin, scraping an obstinate scab of dried legume from the lip of his bowl, wondered idly what she would find to amuse herself tonight during the hours when her presence behind the pale yellow door was not required.

On previous nights she had walked down to the harbour. Watching the moon's reflection in the iron-green water, she had tried to wring some cooling trickle of romance from her situation.

With an abbreviated cry of pain and surprise, she looked down to discover that she had split her nail upon the nub of dried and hardened food. Her nails were a ruin, she thought, all of them bitten and uneven, many of them split or with raw pink about the quick. She wondered how long it would take for them to regain their former elegance, and as she did so, she ran her other hand back over her razed scalp without being aware of the gesture.

Foral Yatt called to her from the bedchamber and she went to see what he wanted, wiping her hands upon the coarse grey fabric of her shirt as she trudged across the rush matting.

Stepping through the door of the chamber, she was puzzled to discover that Foral Yatt had retired to bed, rather than preparing for the evening's duties. He lay upon the rough cotton of the sheets with his eyes half closed and his hands resting limp upon the patches of dyed sackcloth that formed the counterpane.

'I cannot work this evening. I am ill.'

Rawra Chin's brow knotted into a frown. He did not look discomforted nor was his voice unsteady or less masterful, and yet he said that he was sick. It was as if he meant her to understand that this was a lie but to respond as if it were irrefutable truth. Searching within herself, she discovered, with only the briefest pang of surprise or disappointment, that she did not mind. She accommodated the fiction, because that was the easiest thing to do.

'But what of Mistress Ouish? There have been other nights lately when you have not worked. A room not in use is a drain on her resources. Others have been dismissed for as much.'

Mistress Ouish, though now blind and close to death, was still the dominating presence at the House Without Clocks. Even Rawra Chin, who had not been employed at that establishment for five years, regarded the old woman with alloyed respect and fear. From his blatantly spurious sickbed, Foral Yatt spoke again.

'You are right. If no work is done here tonight, it will be the worse for me.'

He raised his lowered lids and stared directly into Rawra Chin's eyes. He smiled, knowing that to smile altered nothing between them. The masquerade was accepted by mutual consent. His voice dry and measured, he continued.

'That is why you must do my work for me.'

It was as if there were some sudden dysfunction within Rawra Chin's mind that rendered her unable to glean any sense from Foral Yatt's words. 'That', 'must', 'do', 'work' – all of these sounded alien, so that she was almost convinced that the actor had coined them upon the spot. She ran the sentence through her head again and again. 'That is why you must do my work for me.' 'That is why you must do my work for me.' What did it mean?

And then, recovering from the shock of the utterance, she understood.

She shook her head and in her horror still had room to be surprised by the absence of soft hair swinging against her neck. Barely audibly, she said, 'No.' But it didn't mean 'I will not'. It meant 'Please don't'.

But he did.

Donna Blerot took her hand (his hand?) and pulled it up beneath the fur tent so that it came to rest upon the dampness between the disfigured woman's thick legs. Beneath her single outer garment, the dame was naked, flesh damp and solid like dough.

Later, burying herself in the woman's body as Donna Blerot sprawled back across the table, gasping noiselessly like a fish upon a slab, Rawra Chin looked down at her and saw the abyss. The bell of grey fur had ridden up to reveal the body beneath, so that it now covered Donna Blerot's face, birthmark and all. For a lurching instant, the woman looked like a drowned thing washed up on the coastline of the Sea of Luck, a sheet already covering the puffy, fish-eaten face.

Fighting nausea, Rawra Chin shifted her glance so that it came to rest on her own body, luminous with sweat, plunging mechanically forward, jerking back, thrusting and withdrawing like a gauntlet-manikin worked by the hand of another. She regarded the jutting hardness that grew from her own loins and wondered how it was that she could be doing this thing. She felt no desire, no lust for the deaf woman and her bucking, heaving desperation. She felt nothing but shame and horror. How could her body sustain such ardour in the face of that abomination?

Later still, Donna Blerot kissed Rawra Chin and left, closing the pale yellow door behind her. The performer sat naked in one of the wooden chairs, elbows resting upon the tabletop before her, face concealed behind her hands as if behind the slammed doors of a church. The memory of the matron's kiss was still thick about her lips. It had seemed as if a fat and bitter mollusc were attempting to crawl into her mouth, leaving its glistening saliva trail across her chin. This imagery slithered out of her mind and down her throat, until it dropped into her stomach. There was a faint, warning spasm and Rawra Chin tortured herself with an image of their hastily devoured meal from earlier that evening. The gelatinous, half-melted skirt of fat trailing from the grey-pink fingers of meat …

Struggling silently to keep from vomiting, she did not hear Foral Yatt leave his bedchamber until he was standing just beside her.

'There. Was that so bad?'

Startled by his voice, Rawra Chin moved one hand so that only half of her face remained concealed, and opened her eyes. She was looking down at the floor, and she could see nothing of Foral Yatt above the knee without moving her head, which seemed an unendurable prospect.

His feet were as white as the flesh of almonds.

Fixed to each of the toenails was a tiny mirror. Suspended beneath the surface of ten miniature, glittering pools, Rawra Chin's reflections stared back at her, insects drowning in quicksilver.

Rising unsteadily from her seat and pushing past Foral Yatt, Rawra Chin staggered to that chamber set aside for bathing and the performance of one's toilet. Lava rose in her throat, flooding her mouth, and she was sobbing as she emptied herself noisily into a chipped and yellowed handbasin. Drained, she gagged upon emptiness until the convulsions in her gut subsided, and then raised her head to look at the room about her through a quivering lens of tears.

Something caught her eye, a green blur twinkling from atop the chest where Foral Yatt kept his soaps and perfumes and oils. Rawra Chin wiped her eyes with the blunt edge of one hand and tried to focus upon the distracting blot of emerald. It was a fixed point on which to anchor her perceptions, still reeling in the wake of her nausea. Gradually, the object swam into definition against the damp gloom of the washroom.

Tiny glass sockets stared at her, unblinking. Behind them, within the translucent green brainpan, unguessable dreams marinated within cerebral juices that smelled of liquorice.

Rawra Chin stared at the skull full of poison. It stared back at her, its gaze concealing nothing.

Time passed in the House Without Clocks. On the eighteenth night following her arrival, Rawra Chin fell to the darkness. That which had only licked and tasted her now distended its jaws and took her at a bite.

She was drunk, although it would have happened had this not been the case. Miserable over the dinner table, she had taken an excess of wine in the hope of numbing the pangs of self-loathing. The alcohol served only to muddy her anxieties, making them slippery, more difficult to apprehend. She stood framed in the open doorway with one hand upon the pale yellow wood, looking out at the deserted courtyard, drinking great ragged lungfuls of autumn air. It did nothing to still the buzzing that droned inside her head, a dismal hive somewhere between her ears. Gazing at the indifferent black flagstones, she understood that she must leave. Leave Foral Yatt. Leave at once and return to the soothing babble of her wardrobe boys, the comforting dreariness of committing endless lines to her memory. If she did not go immediately, she would be trapped forever, crushed beneath the hulking farm wagon of circumstance, screaming for someone to brush away the flies. If she did not go immediately …

From the chambers behind her, Foral Yatt called her name.

She looked up from the wide obsidian pond; there reared the archway, with Liavek beyond it.

A note of mounting impatience discernible in his voice, Foral Yatt called again.

She turned and walked back into the house, closing the pale yellow door behind her. He was in the bedchamber, as had become customary since the evening when Rawra Chin had been called upon to service Donna Blerot, her first knowledge of a woman. She supposed that Foral Yatt had summoned her to order a repetition of that occasion, and for an instant she savoured a fantasy of refusal, but not for longer than that.

'My love? Would you light the lantern for me? It is so dark in here.' Foral Yatt's voice, altering since Rawra Chin's arrival in that place, had moved into an other stage of its metamorphosis. Softened to a deep velvet, it seduced rather than commanded. Her fingers struggled with the flint for a second before the tinder caught, and then she lifted the flame to the wick of the lantern. A bubble of sulphurous yellow light expanded and contracted within the chamber, wavering until the flame grew still and its light clear. Rawra Chin turned from the lamp, white-hot maggots engraved upon her retinas by the brilliance she had brought into being. Foral Yatt lay upon his side on top of the patchwork counterpane, supporting himself upon one elbow, fingertips lost in the tight blond curls at his temples. A wide band of blue cosmetic colour ran in a diagonal line across his face, overlaying the left side of his brow, sweeping down across the left eye, the bridge of the nose, the right cheek. A narrower band of red, little more than a single brushstroke, followed its upper edge over the ridges and hollows of his smooth, sculpted features, terminating beneath the right ear.

He was wearing one of her costumes.

It was a gown, long and violet, gathered in extravagant ruffs at the shoulders so that the arms were bare. The collar was high, reaching to the point just above the bulge in Foral Yatt's throat, and below that the material was solid and opaque until it reached a demarcation line just beneath the breastbone. From there, the dress seemed to have been slashed into long strips that trailed down to the ankles, every second violet ribbon having been cut away and replaced by a panel of coral pink twine, knotted into snowflake patterns through which the skin beneath was visible. There were mirrors upon his toes and fingers.

Entering through a chink in the wall, with a sound like a child blowing across the neck of a narrow jar, a breeze disturbed the perfumed air and caused the lantern flame to stutter. For a moment, armies of light and shadow rushed back and forth in quick-fire border disputes. The shadows gathered within Foral Yatt's eye sockets seemed to flow across his cheek like an over-spill of tar before shrinking back to pool beneath the overhang of his brow. He smiled up at her through lips fastidiously stained a rich indigo.

'I had to come back. I couldn't just leave you here.'

The second word in each sentence was stressed in a lush and affected manner, so that even as Rawra Chin struggled to make sense of the actor's words, so too was she striving to identify that quirk of inflection, maddeningly familiar and yet beyond the grasp of her recall.

'But … what do you mean? You haven't been anywhere. You …'

Rawra Chin could feel something bearing down upon her, coming towards her with a hideous speed that froze the will and made evasion unthinkable. It was like stories she had heard concerning eclipses when men would see the giant moon-shadow rushing towards them across the land, a vast planet of darkness rolling over the tiny fields and pastures with a speed that was only comparable to itself. Standing there in the scented chamber, she understood their terror. The shadow world was almost upon her. Another moment and she would be crushed beneath its endless, inescapable mass.

From the bed, Foral Yatt spoke again. The pattern of emphasis within his speech continued to dance just beyond the fringes of recognition, mocking and unattainable.

'I left you. Don't you remember? I left you because it was so important to me that people should know my name. I know it must have seemed unfair to you, but you were only ordinary, and I am a special creature. I have something rare in me, a unique charm that men have not words to describe, and though I loved you deeply, deeply, it was my duty to expose the treasure that I am to the world and all its people. Surely this is not beyond your comprehension?'

Quite suddenly, Rawra Chin knew where she had heard the voice that Foral Yatt was using. The dark planet crashed upon her, and she was lost.

'But all of that is done with, now. Now, people everywhere know my name and are drawn like moths to the fire within me, whose nature only I can put a name to. Now I am complete, and I am free to love you once more. I adore you. I worship you. I love you, love you more than anything in the world save for celebrity. But …'

The parody was unspeakably vicious, undeniably accurate. Having identified the voice, Rawra Chin could do nothing more than accept the cruel mirror image of the face that accompanied it. Nailed by the black weight of a phantom moon, she could only watch as Foral Yatt exposed all the conceits, the inanities, the small evasions that were the components of her existence. The young man lounged upon the bed, touching a shimmering constellation of fingertips to the blue of his lower lip in a pantomime of anxiety and indecision. Looking up at Rawra Chin, his long lashes flashed an urgent semaphore pleading for sympathy while his jaw trembled beneath the burden of the words unspoken in the mouth above. Finally, when he had drawn out his melodramatic hesitation to the snapping point of absurdity, the words spilled out in a breathless cascade.

'… But do you still love me?'

He paused, blinking twice.

'Despite what I did to you?'

In one corner of the room, the idiot child began to blow across the slender neck of its jar, and the patterns of light and shade within the chamber convulsed.

Rawra Chin, adrift upon a lurching ocean of nightmare, heard a voice speak in the distance.

'Is there a lizard asleep within the ball?'

The voice was so deep and masculine that she assumed it must belong to Foral Yatt, except that Foral Yatt's voice wasn't like that any more. Whose, then, could it be? When the answer came, her senses were too brutalised to ring with more than the dullest peal of despair. It was her voice. Of course it was her voice.

On the bed, Foral Yatt smiled and flopped languidly on to his back. The smile he wore belonged to Foral Yatt rather than to his grotesque and pointed lampoon of Rawra Chin, but when he spoke, it was with her accents.

'Perhaps I am a ball. Perhaps the unfathomable quality that men perceive in me is a lizard, coiled within me, its material reality questionable, its effects upon the mind undisputed.'

Their eyes were locked, their awareness of each other fixed in that moment of mutual understanding that has always existed between snakes and rabbits. Licking his indigo lips, Foral Yatt luxuriated in the taste of the long instant preceding the stroke of grace.

'Shall I tell you the name of my lizard? Shall I tell you the name of that thing that makes me vulnerable, makes me loved, worshipped, celebrated?'

Knowing the answer already, Rawra Chin shook her head violently from side to side, but was unable to make the slightest sound.

'Guilt.'

There. It had been said. He knew. The lantern flame quivered. The shadows charged and then fell back, regrouping for their next assault.

'You see, it is vital to what I am. It is the hurt that drives me, and without it, I am nothing. Oh, my love, I feel so ashamed of all the misery that I have brought you.'

Standing at the foot of the bed, swaying, the wine of their supper now bitter in her belly, Rawra Chin became confused as the layers of meaning began to fold in upon each other, blossoming into new shapes like a toy of artfully creased paper. Was Foral Yatt describing feelings of his own or mimicking those agonies that he perceived in her? Did he genuinely feel remorse for the venomous charade that he had perpetrated? At the centre of the fear and confusion that tore through Rawra Chin like a hurricane, a nugget of resentment began to form, cold and bright in the still heart of the cyclone.

How dare he apologise? How dare he plead for understanding after this insufferable pageant of debasement? The anger grew within Rawra Chin as she gazed icily down at the figure on the bed, the yielding and defenceless line of the body beneath the slatted violet gown gradually becoming as infuriating as the wheedling of that unbearable little-girl voice.

'Can you forgive me? Oh, my love, you seem so stern. How thoughtless I was to injure you in such a dreadful, careless fashion.'

Foral Yatt sat up and reached for Rawra Chin with imploring arms, pale as they emerged like swans' necks from the ruffs at the actor's shoulders. His eyes pleaded for release from the apparent agonies of self-flagellation that he was enduring, and his blue lips mouthed inaudible half words of explanation and apology, puckering as if for a kiss of absolution.

With as much force as she could muster, Rawra Chin struck him across the mouth with the back of her hand, smearing the blue lip dye over his cheek and her knuckle.

The dry smack of the blow and the bark of pain from the actor rebounded back at them from the cold stone of the walls. Foral Yatt fell back, covering his face and rolling on to his side so that he lay curled upon the patchwork with his back to Rawra Chin.

Struck suddenly by the sight of his curving spine, visible through the dishevelled violet fringes of his gown, Rawra Chin found that the anger in her heart was matched by a sudden pressure at her loins as a burgeoning erection reared against the restricting hide of her ash-grey breeches. On the bed, Foral Yatt nursed his mouth and began to weep. Almost of their own volition, fingers that felt suddenly numb and overlarge moved towards the knot in her rope belt, where it pressed in a hard fist of hemp against Rawra Chin's stomach.

She raped him twice, brutally, and there was no pleasure in it.

When it was done, she understood the damage that she had done to herself and began to sob noiselessly, in the way that men do, sitting there upon the edge of the counterpane with her shoulders shuddering in silence. Foral Yatt lay on the bed behind her, staring at the far wall. Rawra Chin's seed had dried in a small, irregular oval on the plucked alabaster flesh above his right knee, a tight puckering of the skin beneath the thin, clear varnish. He picked at it absently with mirrored nails and said nothing.

The wick of the lantern grew shorter, until finally it guttered and died. Thus could the passage of hours be measured, there in the House Without Clocks.

'I had no right. No right to treat you like that …'

'Please. It doesn't matter.'

'Will you stay? Will you stay here with me?'

'I can't.'

'But … what am I to do if you go? There is no reason for you to leave.'

'There's my work. My work and my career.'

'But what about me? You're leaving me trapped here, don't you see? I'll never get away now. Please. I'll do anything you want, but don't leave me here.'

'You should have thought of that before you took your revenge.'

'Oh, please, I said that I was sorry. Can't you think of what we were to each other and forgive me?'

'It's too late, my love. It's far too late.'

'I won't let you go. I won't let us be separated again.'

'Please. I don't want a scene. What happened last time was so embarrassing.'

'Oh, don't worry. I won't make any fuss at all.'

'Good. Now, I must send one of the House-waifs to order my carriage for the morning and arrange to have my wardrobe moved back to the lodging house.'

'Won't you leave me anything? Please. Let me keep the violet gown.'

'No.'

'Don't you see what you're doing to me? You're taking away everything! How has this happened?'

'Don't be naïve. We are in the City of Luck.'

'Here, you speak to me of luck? I am no longer sure that luck exists. Is there luck, or is there only circumstance without form or pattern, a senseless wave that obliterates all before it?'

'Is there a lizard asleep within the ball?'

Seated upon her balcony, absently chewing the anaemic blue flowers she had plucked from her window garden, Som-Som regarded the courtyard of the House Without Clocks.

A carriage had arrived outside the curving walls with the first shafts of dawn, some short while ago. The half-masked woman had realised that Rawra Chin must be leaving the House to return to her fabulous existence in the world beyond its seven variegated portals.

Since Rawra Chin had originally spoken of her stay at the House in terms of months rather than weeks, Som-Som supposed that it was the dark undercurrents flowing between her and Foral Yatt that had prompted this unannounced departure. She wondered if the performer would call upon her to say goodbye before she left, and felt a pang of sadness at the thought of their separation.

Countering this regret, there was a tremendous relief. Som-Som was glad that Rawra Chin had not allowed herself to become a prisoner of the terrible gravity that the House possessed, and for this reason alone, she hoped that luck would take the performer far beyond those walls that curved like grey, embracing arms.

The sound of the pale yellow door opening was jewel-sharp in the silent morning, and Som-Som leaned out from her balcony to watch the elegant, crimson-bandaged figure step out on to the cold black flagstones, where the chill of the night had left a faint dusting of frost.

To Som-Som, who had not enjoyed the perception of depth since her ninth year, it seemed that a self-propelling droplet of blood had leaked from a pale yellow gash in the skin of the House to roll across the frost-flecked black disc of the courtyard, trickling slowly towards the arch on the opposite side. Occasionally, a two-dimensional white hand became visible, depending upon the perspective, a cream petal bobbing briefly to the surface of the red blot before vanishing again.

As the bead of crimson progressed across the yard, it became something that a person without her affliction would recognise as a human being. The figure paused at a point halfway across the courtyard and turned, tilting back its head to gaze directly at Som-Som, as if it had been aware of the half-masked woman's scrutiny since first setting foot outside the pale yellow door. From out of the redness, a face swam into view.

Foral Yatt stared up into Som-Som's eyes, both the one that blinked and the one that could not.

His expression seemed furtive for an instant, tinged with a guilt that Som-Som found disturbingly familiar, and then he smiled. Long seconds passed unrecorded while their eyes remained locked, and then he turned and continued across the wide circle of jet, passing out through the high stone archway.

After a moment there came the sound of reins snapping, followed by a rattle of hoof upon cobblestone as the carriage horses roused themselves and cantered off down the winding thoroughfares of Liavek, where the scent of a hundred simmering breakfasts hung reassuringly between the huddled buildings.

Som-Som sat motionless upon her balcony, her gaze still fixed upon the point where Foral Yatt had stood when he'd turned and looked at her. His smile remained there, an after-image in her mind's eye. It was a smile of a type that Som-Som had seen before, and which she recognised instantly.

It was a wizard's smile. It was the expression of a luck-shaper who had finally achieved a satisfaction long postponed. For an unquantifiable time, Som-Som did not move. A blank expression was frozen on to her face so that those divided features regained a semblance of unity, the living half transformed to porcelain by her bewilderment.

Standing suddenly, she upset her chair so that it toppled to the balcony floor behind her. She moved rapidly, with an odd jerkiness. All of the training and discipline that had disguised her difficulties of locomotion were cast aside as she ran down the narrow wooden steps and across the rounded yard.

The pale yellow door was not locked.

Rawra Chin was seated at the table, rigid and upright in one of the straight-backed chairs. She seemed to be staring at two objects that rested on the white wood of the tabletop, barely distinct in the smoky dawn light. Approaching the table, Som-Som peered closer, squinting the eye that still possessed the ability to do so.

One of the objects was a plain copper ball that meant nothing to her. The other item seemed more like an egg with the top cleanly sliced off.

Except that it was green.

Except that it had empty, staring sockets and a lipless smile.

She noticed the odour of liquorice at the same moment that she realised Rawra Chin had not breathed since her arrival in the chamber.

It was not a physical horror that propelled Som-Som backward through the pale yellow door, gasping and stumbling, shoved out into the courtyard by the immensity of what lay within. Neither was it an aversion to the presence of the dead. The whore of sorcerers is witness to worse things than simple mortality during the course of her service, and suicides at the House Without Clocks were frequent enough to be unremarkable. Certainly too frequent to engender so violent a reaction in one whose customers had, upon occasion, transformed into beings of a different species or entities of churning white vapour at the moment of their greatest pleasure.

Neither was it entirely a horror that preyed upon the mind, nor wholly a revulsion of the spirit. It had no shape, no dimension at all that she could grasp, and that was the fullest horror of it. A monstrous crime had been committed, an atrocity of appalling magnitude and scale that somehow remained both abstract and intangible. Having no perceivable edges, its monstrosity was thus infinite, and it was this that sent Som-Som reeling out backward into the cold, black courtyard.

She wanted to scream at the indifferent windows of the House Without Clocks, still shuttered against the morning light while those beyond enjoyed whatever sleep they had earned the previous evening. She wanted to cry out and wake the City of Luck itself, alerting it to this abomination, perpetrated while Liavek looked the other way, unsuspecting.

But of course, she could say nothing. The enormity of what had occurred remained locked within her, something scaly and cold and repugnant inside her mind, which could never be seen, never be touched or spoken of to another. Curled in the unreachable dark behind the porcelain mask, it basked, beyond proof, beyond refute.

Hardly there at all.

NOT EVEN LEGEND

In my experience, if a jilky is involved, it usually gets put down to a mains explosion.

When Merelda finally made her exclamatory arrival at the CSICON get-together – she'd parked up by the old covered market and had puffed the length of Fetter Street before remembering that the ring binder with all her suggestions was still in the back seat, which was classic her – most of the others were already there. The estate agents' street door was on the latch, and after navigating an unlit front office to the larger conference room beyond, she'd plunged into the jovial pre-meeting chatter and spent an agreeable five minutes air-kissing hello to everybody.

At the central table's end, she spotted fidgety and lightly stubbled Marcus Clarke, founder of the Committee for Surrealist Investigation of Claims Of the Normal, babbling enthusiastically to a lugubrious David Watkins. Watkins, always the most soberly dressed at the paranormal study group's bi-weekly meetings, was branch manager at Chalcombe & Bentine, this being why the CSICON crowd had access to these after-hours premises. Awkwardly taking off her rain-specked coat, Merelda waved to her teacher friend Emma, who was mad on cryptids and was seated at the other end from Dave and Marcus. Various unwieldy conversations dangled from the leather-scented air and clattered like atonal wind chimes. Brian Appleby, Tall Brian, was proselytising about ghosts with Adriana, that goth media-studies lecturer who only joined, like, a few weeks ago or something. Brian Taylor, Little Brian, was nowhere about for the third meeting in a row, but then Merelda figured him and his wife – Sandra, was it? – were still getting used to the new baby.

So, about ten people. Not bad. Errol Meeks was offering a domestic anecdote concerning his new boiler that made everybody laugh and feel obscurely guilty that there weren't more black guys in the group. Carl with the foreign last name, something-vich, sat closest to the door, looking unhappy. For some reason, there was a rolled length of carpet propped against the empty chair beside him, and Merelda thought he might have said that he was moving house soon. It was probably to do with that. His glum expression, on the other hand, was probably to do with Alison Macready, who was looking daggers at him from the table's Dave and Marcus end, where she was sitting in a huddle with her friends and upstairs neighbours, Steve and Sheila Denton. Carl and Alison had been an item for the previous eighteen months or so, which meant their break-up at the last meeting had been accompanied by a bit of an atmosphere. Uncomfortable, but these things happened.

With her coat draped on her forearm like a toreador, Merelda made a halting circumnavigation of the table, pausing to exchange a word or two with everyone before she got to the unoccupied chair next to Emma. Actually, tonight might prove quite lively, with the big debate Marcus had scheduled, over a proposed change of direction, both for CSICON as a whole and for their quarterly small-press mag, *Interesting Times*. Sitting beside her friend, she asked what the young teacher thought of Marcus's 'uncharted waters' scheme, but Emma said she wasn't sure she really understood it and, changing the subject, showed Merelda a blurred shot of a purported chupacabra on her phone. The mumble of surrounding discourse fell away on a steep gradient, like in a cinema when the lights dip for the main feature, and Merelda guessed the meeting proper was about to start. She couldn't wait.

I left it as long as I could and then made my excuses. As I stepped into the wind and drizzle, I heard somebody behind me shout, 'Hey, hang on. You forgot your … thing.' From what I'd been told back two weeks hence, this would have been right around the point at which the jilky had dilated both its lateral spills. Of course, nobody understood exactly what it was, but they'd have had some time – a second or two, at the most – to individually understand exactly what it wasn't. You might think that I'd be taking quite a risk with such a drastic clean-up exercise, but not in my experience.

He nodded and made intermittent grunts at everything that Marcus said because he liked the chap, known him for years, but to be honest, David had misgivings about this whole 'new direction' thing. Surely the group was all right how it was, although he didn't feel that he could just come out and say that. David was uncomfortably aware that he was CSICON's oldest member and he didn't want the others to think that he was opposed to new ideas, set in his ways or 'square' in any sense. Did people still say square? He didn't know, and mournfully accepted that this made him even squarer.

Marcus bobbed his number-one cut excitedly now as he warmed to his subject. 'I mean, people who report phenomena, they generally report things in existing categories. What about, though, what about if somebody encountered something where we didn't have a category; where we didn't even have a word? How would you go about reporting that? You wouldn't, would you? There must be a thousand cases where …' David let his attention wander to the rest of the Surrealist Investigators, mumbling clumps of rhubarb spread incongruously around a polished table more accustomed to Chalcombe & Bentine's orderly appraisals of the housing market. There was a commotion over by the door as voluble Merelda Jacobs blustered in, complaining about leaving something in her car and having to walk back down Fetter Street 'through all the rain' to fetch it. Well, whose fault was that? Across the room, directly opposite Carl Wasowiec and his teetering stack of old newspapers, Brian

Appleby was obviously trying to chat up the new girl, Adriana, with his outsized Adam's apple going up and down grotesquely like a yo-yo. David sighed, albeit inwardly.

Perhaps Marcus was right. Perhaps CSICON was overdue for some sort of a shake-up. He thought back to when the pair of them had got the whole thing going, what, three years ago now, in 2016? That was back during David's rough patch after Anne had left him – she was Leave, he was Remain – when he'd realised just how few friends he had and jumped at any opportunity for conversation. He'd known Marcus since the noughties, when the younger man had been a client and they'd discovered that they were both long-time readers of *Fortean Times*. Following Anne's departure, Marcus dropped by maybe twice a week to have a beer or several and keep David company. It had been on one such occasion that Marcus had floated the idea of a paranormal studies group 'but with a sense of humour', whereupon David had drunkenly suggested they could gather in the spacious conference room at work – and three years later, here they were. David supposed, if he was honest, that he'd privately been hoping he might meet some eligible women, but that hadn't been the case. He'd had his hopes up about leggy Sheila Hall until, apparently from out of nowhere, she'd got married to Steve Denton. Was he any better than poor Brian Appleby when it came down to it, disguising loneliness behind a jabbering tirade about the Enfield poltergeist?

Beside him, Marcus called the group to order, and went into his arm-waving pitch for 'studying the negative space in phenomenology', whatever that might mean. The evening had begun.

As I said earlier, a Whispering Pete's emotional life takes some getting used to: although I'd not met her prior to that night – and obviously she hated me – for my part, I was mostly thinking about all the sex that we were going to have, and how pretty her eyes were. And, yes, I was feeling guilty about her; about the lot of them. I know it makes no rational sense when this was the first time that I'd laid eyes on them, but it was the last time that they'd lay eyes on me. The last time that they'd do a lot of things. Though I accept it's pretty much impossible for me, I tried to see things from their point of view, and that's why I felt sorry for them. I knew when I met them two weeks' time ago, it wouldn't seem so bad, but I still wanted to give them a while together on what was, from their perspective, their last night. I didn't get up and leave straight away, is what I'm saying here. I'm not a monster.

This was definitely the last meeting she was coming to. She'd made her mind up at the point where, halfway through twatsplaining all about the restless dead, that stringy Brian guy had asked her if she'd ever seen the movie that Timothy Spall had been so good in. He'd a copy up at his place and if Adriana ever fancied popping round to watch it …

Now she thought about it, this whole CSICON set-up hadn't really been what she was looking for, which was, essentially, material for her master's thesis, 'Paranormal Subculture and the New Right'. The problem, she conceded, was with her: she'd not been honest with them when she joined. She'd let them think that she was studying psychic phenomena, when in fact she was studying the people who were studying that stuff: people like them.

Up at the top end of the table, the bald English teacher who was obviously gay continued with his energetic monologue. The main thrust of the argument, if Adriana had it right, was that instead of seeking vampires, flying saucers, yetis, Loch Ness monsters and a lot of other things that probably weren't real, the group should look for evidence of things that nobody had ever said existed in the first place. 'I mean, everybody understands what ghosts are.' Well, no, actually, they didn't. 'What we should be looking for are things that have been previously invisible to us.' Which, if you thought about it even for a moment, obviously included ghosts. Basically, not an academic.

Adriana, carefully avoiding eye contact with the unduly lanky table-tilter to her left, allowed her artificial lashes to brush briefly over the remainder of the group. Next to the gushing and gesticulating teacher sat the estate agent who was old enough to be her dad, but even more depressed and angry-looking. Further down, across from her, the Polish guy was making sure that everybody saw the gleaming high-tech speaker system he'd apparently just bought, while at the table's other end, the fifty-something redhead who'd arrived late made a big deal about flipping through her ring binder and tutting loudly. Next to her sat the short blonde girl who was always wearing jumpers borrowed from a boxset Scandi noir – the one that Adriana thought was possibly another teacher – and then there was Errol, a few empty seats away on Adriana's right. Errol was CSICON's sole stab at racial diversity and, by coincidence, about the only one whose name she could remember.

None of them were much use for her purposes, in that none of them were particularly right wing. She'd do better coming at the problem from the other end and infiltrating the English Defence League, keeping her ears open for a mention of Atlantis or the Hollow Earth. Transferring her laconic chewing gum from one cheek to the other, Adriana doubled her resolve, and knew without a shadow of a doubt that when the group assembled in a fortnight's time, she wasn't going to be there.

Anyway, when finally I got to the October night in question, I did what the mormoleen had sleepily and snugly reminisced about, which, from the mormoleen's perspective, had of course already happened: I arrived at the smart premises comparatively early, where I found the jilky waiting for me in the alley just off Purser's Row. There was a covered manhole in the shadows from which I presumed the jilky had emerged, and which it would use to make its departure when the matter was concluded. I'd not visited the area before, but there had been a street map in that clipping from the local paper I'd cut out, the day after tomorrow. I'd be coming here a lot over the last three years, apparently. The intermittent rain meant hardly anybody was about, though with the evolutionary psychology thing that I mentioned, it would have made little difference if they had been. I mean, when I walked the jilky to the offices, we bumped into someone with a receding hairline who appeared to know me. One of my acquaintances-to-be, no doubt. Glancing towards the jilky, he smiled sympathetically and said, 'Laundrette night, eh? Yeah, I know that one.' It was literally that easy.

It transpired that other than the balding fellow and another man who seemed to work there at the place, we were the first arrivals. We went in and found ourselves a pair of seats, so I could nod to all the unfamiliar faces as, in ones and twos, they turned up for the meeting. The one sticky moment was when an attractive brunette wearing tight jeans and a fake fur jacket – beads of rain were hung from the acrylic hairs like diamonds – practically spat at me when she walked in with two friends and I offered a non-committal smile of greeting. Turning pointedly away without a word, she and the couple she'd arrived with went and sat up in the big room's furthest corner. This, I reasoned, must be Alison, who I'd been looking forward to meeting since learning of her in the diary that I fill in every night, so that it's there for me to have already read the day before. The way she saw things, two weeks earlier, for no apparent reason, I'd ended a passionate relationship that had been going on more than a year, so she had every reason to despise me. In two weeks' time, I was going to behave appallingly.

Errol was well distracted, to be honest, and his full attention wasn't on the pep talk Marcus was delivering, but even so, he wasn't sure he liked the sound of this whole 'new direction' thing. The only reason Errol was in CSICON – OK, not the only reason, nearly all the people there were really nice, but the main reason – was that it gave him an outlet for his illustration and cartoon work in the little magazine they put out, *Interesting Times*. All right, there'd only been four issues in three years, but Errol had done all the covers and interior spot illos. He was getting better all the time; might even soon be good enough to have a stab at turning pro and jacking in the shift work at the care home. The thing was, all Errol's work for *Interesting Times* was based upon familiar stereotypes – vampires and ghouls and black-eyed aliens – particularly the cartoons. If CSICON was now dumping the spontaneous human combustion and the anal probes in favour of something that nobody had ever previously imagined, what was he supposed to draw?

Amongst his various distractions, number one was obviously the plastic washing-up bowl in his boiler cupboard. It was there to catch the slow but steadily accumulating drips from the new boiler until his mate Paul the Pipe could come and have a look at it on Friday. But the bowl was only so big, and would fill up in around four hours to the point where it was slopping over. Errol had been training himself to wake in the middle of the night and empty it into the bath, so that it wasn't pissing through the kitchen ceiling when he came down in the morning. He'd performed this ritual before he'd left for Chalcombe & Bentine's around an hour before, and thought that it should last until he got home later, but you never knew. Returning to a flooded downstairs loo would be the worst imaginable way that Errol could wrap up this Thursday evening, so the possibility was weighing heavy on his mind.

The other things distracting him were relatively minor, and were, in the main, related to his fellow CSICON members. That new woman, Adriana, sitting to the left of him, she had some kind of scent on that he didn't like at all – a heavy, choking lavender that made him want to sneeze and go to sleep at the same time. Then, right across the table was the gold-framed painting Carl had brought in, which was frankly horrible and might have been a picture of a badly deformed horse. Or something. Worse than both of these in the distraction stakes, however, was Merelda Jacobs at the table's bottom end, continually fussing with her bloody binder, muttering under her breath at every minor inconvenience and making the whole evening about her, as usual. Errol didn't even like her name.

He tried to focus on Marcus's monologue, which at that moment was concerned with 'entities that our taxonomies have made us blind to'. Errol wasn't all that confident about his understanding of 'taxonomies', and couldn't see how things that we were blind to made for decent gag cartoons.

On second thoughts, it looked more like a sofa than a horse, but was so badly painted that you couldn't tell. Merelda Jacobs made what turned out to be the first in a miniseries of exasperated sighs, and in his head, the water in the washing-up bowl crept insidiously towards the plastic brim.

That's not to say my life's without its unexpected treats. For instance, after slogging all the way through 2020, I was honestly taken aback by my giddy euphoria on reaching Christmas 2019, after years of lock-down and disruption. Everybody else looked miserable about December's general election and resultant Tory landslide, whereas I was wide-eyed, marvelling at everything as if I'd just stepped into fairyland. Just seeing people shaking hands and hugging, or in tight-pressed, surly crowds on public transport was surprisingly emotional, which isn't me at all.

To be fair, I was also looking forward very much to having sex again, after that long, dry period in isolation. As I said, we Whispering Petes are mostly in it for the sex, and if my disappearing diary was to be believed, I was about to embark on a fruitful and protracted period of serial satisfaction stretching to the 1980s, by which time I'm an unusually experienced teenager. In order to commence my sexual salad days, though, I was first apparently obliged to go through with this whole depressing business in town centre, as reported by the clipping in my emptying scrapbook. From the diary, it appeared that in the last week of October, I'd be calling in at my friend Trudy's place, to chat with her about what I'd be doing/had already done upon Thursday the seventeenth. Naturally, Trudy's one of the concealed people herself. Trudy's a mormoleen. She does what mormoleens do.

And, it has to be said, I fall for it every time: I went to bed on Halloween and had a terrible night's sleep, as if I'd eaten an amphetamine and coffee sandwich just before retiring. Waking on the morning of the thirtieth, I spent the whole day groggy and unrested, sort of jet-lagged, until early evening when I paid my scheduled visit to the mormoleen. Her house was on the Granby estate to the west of Calderford, a dingy and unprepossessing residence, whereas the neighbour's front porch was a madness of unnecessary DIY, exactly as you might expect from someone living next door to a mormoleen. Wearing her customary smug and dreamy smile, Trudy invited me indoors.

As per the diary, I already knew a jilky would be there, so I knew what to look for. And besides, I'd already encountered one in 2035 through my not-yet-wife Mila. When I entered Trudy's living room, I spotted the guitar case and knew straight away what I was looking at: as if a mormoleen would ever have the energy to learn an instrument. I nodded amiably at the guitar case and received a brief flutter of colour in reply. Nobody knows what jilkies are, because nobody's ever really seen one. They exploit the way human perception has evolved, always selecting for survival value over accuracy, so that most of what we see is a simplistic glyph rather than what is really there. Jilkies cannot be simplified, and so the mind, in desperation, makes up something else to fill the sudden gap in its reality. As far as anyone can tell, they feed upon the energy released when a molecular bond is disrupted. And while I'm no expert, this particular guitar case seemed unusually plump and contented, sprawling there on Trudy's sofa. I sat in the armchair opposite.

The mormoleen began at once to languidly assure me that what I'd done had been necessary; almost heroic. She said that I'd told her in September how the study group I was monitoring had decided to consider strange phenomena outside existing categories, and would have to be shut down. The whole concealed community, she purred, were grateful for the action that I'd taken with the jilky, and had I seen the piece in the Thropshire Herald*? I reminded her that I'd been looking at it in my scrapbook for the next few decades, though I guessed it would be vanishing sometime during the last two weeks. She gave a lazy laugh and said I was a wonder. Just as always, I drank in the flattery and soon felt all charged up about myself and my forthcoming already accomplished mission. That's a mormoleen. That's how they operate. Everyone likes their company because they leave you energised and bursting with enthusiasm, when what's really going on is that they're drinking your ability to calm down and relax. It's like they siphon other people's serotonin and then wallow in it, always with that drowsy grin. That's why I hadn't slept the night before, but that didn't occur to me till I was striding home from Trudy's, full of vigour and exhausting self-importance. Fucking mormoleens.*

At least she'd given me the details of what I was in for in a fortnight ago's time, although I can't say I was looking backwards to it.

… and then, right, as if to rub her face in it, there were the helium balloons. Like he was throwing a kids' birthday party.

As if he was celebrating, and this just after her blue surprise on Tuesday. She wanted to scream; she wanted to burst into tears; she wanted to stand up, halfway through Marcus and his waffle about thinking the unthinkable, just walk across the room and break the bastard's nose. She couldn't understand how they had come to this.

She'd met him when she'd joined the group, back in the spring of 2018, and not long after she'd moved into the ground-floor flat downstairs from Steve and Sheila, who had hooked up at the group before they married and suggested Alison should come along one evening. She supposed they meant well, knowing she was on her own and maybe hoping she might meet somebody – which, of course, she had. She gave the pair a sideways glance as they sat between her and Marcus, holding hands and very publicly in love. She hadn't told them yet, about the test. She wanted to throw up.

That first night, eighteen months ago, he'd been so sweet and tender. Even in the urgent heat of the encounter, there'd been something in his manner that suggested an endearing sadness. He'd been so fond and attentive, it had almost been as if they had been saying goodbye rather than hello. The sex had been incredible. She'd never had a lover who'd seemed so familiar with her body and its needs, right from the very start. Her throat tight, she admitted it: she'd thought he was the one. Even the pained and guilty looks he'd sometimes give her – more towards the end of their relationship than at the start, now that she thought about it – she had written off as possibly prenuptial jitters. When he'd asked if they could talk, two weeks back, she'd pathetically assumed that he was maybe going to propose. He wasn't. And then, icing on the cake, there was the news two days ago.

She didn't know what she was going to do – about the baby, about anything. She didn't even know if she should tell him. She'd been planning to, to stage the full dramatic soap-opera showdown, although what would that achieve? The way he'd greeted her when she came in, it was as if they'd never met before. As if all of the breathless moments that they'd shared had never happened, or that it was only her they'd happened to. They were like strangers, was that what he was saying? Well, OK. Message received. At least, she thought, she understood her situation clearly now.

Except for the balloons.

What that means is, I'm one of the concealed people ordinary humans share the planet with. We're what a man called Donald Rumsfeld will apparently refer to in about eighteen years my time as 'unknown unknowns'. We don't show up in folklore, since we've all got different strategies by which we can avoid attention, and this is most probably the reason we've survived for so long, undetected and undreamed of. There's perhaps two or three dozen separate species of concealed people in the world, although in the UK you only tend to find Snapjackets, jilkies, mormoleens and Whispering Petes. I don't know any Snapjackets to speak to – to be honest, they're repulsive little insect-vegetable hybrids that can camouflage themselves as nearly anything and eat domestic pets – but mormoleens and jilkies I find tolerable in small doses. We all have a sort of understanding whereby we don't mess with other concealed people, although mormoleens are too laid-back to let this bother them unduly.

As for Whispering Petes, the reason that nobody knows we're here is that, from any biological perspective, we're completely ordinary human beings. It's just that our consciousness is travelling the other way through time. This happens not in the moment-by-moment sense, where we vomit our milk and cornflakes into cereal bowls before going to bed at seven in the morning – I don't think that we could function that way – but more in the day-by-day sense. We wake up on Sunday morning, have the day the right way round and go to bed that night, but when we wake up the next day, it's Saturday. If our lives were a book, you'd read the last page first, and then the second-to-last page, and so on. This has several advantages, although relationships are difficult, at least to start with. Which can be a problem, because intimate relationships are pretty much a Whispering Pete's major preoccupation. Snapjackets do what they do so that they can ingest terriers; jilkies feed on a specific kind of energy; the mormoleens are, I don't know, insomnivores or something; while we Whispering Petes are largely in it for the sex.

Nobody has the first idea why we're called Whispering Petes, when we don't whisper and don't seem to have more Petes than any other demographic group. I mean, something like 58 per cent of us are women. There's a theory that we get the name at some point in the distant future, like, say, the twenty-third century, and that it's been transmitted to the past as an oral tradition passed down from one generation to the next through normal Whispering Pete genealogy.

As an example, in my own case, my first memories are of my deathbed in the summer months of 2059, as a drugged and muddled eighty-two-year-old surrounded by autonomous machines. My first coherent recollections, on the other hand, are of a calm and sunlit private ward in Aberdeen. Sitting beside my bed was a beautiful dark-haired woman in her seventies, and a handsome young man of barely thirty. Both were smiling at me. 'Welcome to the world,' she said. 'You are Carl Wasowiec, and you're a Whispering Pete.' This was my wife, my darling Mila, and our son Jan, who had memories reaching to the twenty-second century. The two of them were Whispering Petes as well. It was a nice way to undie.

Those early, elderly years were idyllic. All of us felt younger, stronger every day, although it still seemed strange when Jan reached childhood with more life experience than either me or Mila, and all three of us knew, to the hour, where things were heading. I remember one occasion when Jan was a strapping six-year-old. Mila was staring at him, shaking her exquisitely made head incredulously. 'Look at you! How are they ever going to get you into me?'

Jan was unborn in 2028, and Mila found her sudden, bulbous pregnancy a thoroughly unpleasant shock, although across the previous next nine months it dwindled to a much-missed nothing. We had unprotected sex over the dining table as a kind of wake. Then, two years before later, it was time for me and her to meet, in 2026, at one of the street parties thrown to celebrate the end of the pandemic years. Mila and I weren't celebrating, though. We wept a little, and made love, and fell asleep staring into each other's eyes on the next pillow, then we both woke up in empty beds the day before, and that was the last time we saw each other.

After that I went into that miserable stretch of lockdowns, false dawns, riots and pandemonium, where my romantic life consisted of coarse fantasies about the supermarket girls delivering my groceries. During that period, I mostly occupied myself with looking through my many diaries and scrapbooks to see what I had in store for me once the pandemic waves reached their concluding point of origin in 2020. Even I sometimes feel a bit haunted by my diaries: dozens of them at the start, all filled with my handwriting and describing things that hadn't happened to me yet. What I do, every night I write about the day I've had, and then when I wake up, that entry will have disappeared, along with the entry preceding it – which I wouldn't be writing until later on that evening. I've skimmed through most of them, back to the childhood that it appears I'll be having in Gdansk, during all the upheavals of the 1970s. It's an eventful life. In ten years ago's time, I get to meet my mum and dad, before the motorway collision in 2009 that delivers them to me.

One of the most intriguing things, however, something that I thought about a lot in lockdown, was a clipping in the 2019 scrapbook that I'd had unyellowing in my diminishing collection for some forty years. It had been cut out from the Thropshire Herald, *Saturday, 19 October, and the headline read* TEN DEAD IN UNEXPLAINED TOWN CENTRE TRAGEDY.

The article concerned an extirpated paranormal studies group, of which it seemed that I was going to be a member – I was mentioned in the piece as having not attended the fateful event in question due to being incapacitated by a migraine. Clearly 2019 me was lying through my teeth, because I don't get migraines. This suggested I would be involved in what was going to happen, though the scale of the disaster meant that I wouldn't be working on my own. From the toned-down descriptions of the scene, it sounded as if I'd be in attendance with a jilky.

By cross-referencing with my 2019 diary, I was able to learn more. The group, which it appeared that I was going to belong to until 2016, would apparently be thinking of commencing a new area of study which might threaten the concealed people with exposure. That, it seemed, would be my motivation for the disassembly of ten human beings. As for the morality – well, for a Whispering Pete, there isn't any. There's just things we're definitely going to do, and how we feel about it doesn't make a scrap of difference. This is our existence, working backwards through a diary that's already written, from romance to massacre, not having any choice or say in anything.

'So, in conclusion, then, I hope I've made you think about the things we might be overlooking. Wonderful things, which might be right there under our noses.' Marcus risked a sidelong look at David. Was he getting *any* of the subtext, Marcus wondered? 'I just think it's so important that, as individuals, we feel free to explore beyond the limits and the categories we impose upon ourselves.' Oh, for God's sake. Could he sound any more like he was chatting someone up? It must be obvious to everybody in the group, except the person that it was intended for. 'We should stop dwelling on a past that never worked out how we hoped it would, and open ourselves up to new experiences.' David was just sat there, staring glumly into space, and clearly hadn't caught the reference to moping over Anne.

'It's just, I think, there comes a time for all of us when we've got to move on and perhaps, I don't know, try something new?' From the doubtful expressions on the other members' faces, Marcus could already see that they weren't really into his change-of-direction thing, although that didn't bother him. He wasn't really into it himself. It was just there to camouflage the things he had to say to David. Marcus had been borderline obsessed since David had arranged the purchase of his current house in 2007; had been there offering sympathy when David's hateful gammon wife had waddled off after the EU referendum. Those bachelor evenings round at David's, sipping beer and listening to David's dreary 10cc collection, talking about *Fortean Times* – there'd been so many nights when Marcus had been sure something was going to happen, but it never quite did.

'Anyhoo, that's about it. I hope I've got you all excited and eager to try out some new possibilities. If you've got anything you want to say to me, then come and see me later on when I can make myself available.' Was that too Kenneth Williams? Not for David, evidently. He was still gazing morosely at the ceiling. Well, for God's sake, what had Marcus been expecting? That they'd wait for everybody to go home, and then shag on the conference table?

Instead, everyone just sat there looking a bit awkward. Alison Macready seemed as if she was about to say something, but then Carl Wasowiec stood up and ducked his head as if he was embarrassed or uncomfortable. Had Marcus's talk been that bad? Wasowiec said, 'I'm sorry, everybody, but I've got to go. I'm looking forward to getting to know you all.' And what, pray tell, was that supposed to mean? Before anyone got a chance to ask, Carl hurried straight out through the door that he was sitting by and left the pile of variously coloured laundry he'd brought in with him just teetering there on its chair. There was the sound of Chalcombe & Bentine's poorly oiled street door opening, and Errol Meeks looked baffled and called out, 'Hey, hang on. You forgot your … thing.' But there was no reply.

For Marcus, who could judge a fellow by his laundry, the precarious stack of clothing was a puzzle. All the different patterns, all the colours. Now he studied it more closely, there were … at the sides, it looked like pockets hanging inside out, that had elaborate paisley linings. And then – what was going on? – spilling out from these gaudy apertures, there was some kind of tinsel, except—

My name's Carl, and I'm what's called a Whispering Pete.

LOCATION, LOCATION, LOCATION

Bedford approached perfection.

Angie checked the dashboard clock. It was a bit before ten-thirty on that final Sunday morning, with no people on the streets and, other than her own, no moving vehicles. All things considered, an unusually pretty August day.

Progressing eastward down deserted Mill Street, the subdued purr of the Astra's engine seemed almost embarrassing against an otherwise uninterrupted silence, like some noisy child she had unwisely taken to a funeral. She made a right turn into Castle Road before she reached the looming church spire of St Cuthbert's, indicating only out of habit. There was nobody behind her.

Sunrays fell in columns, beautifully dappling the pavements and parked cars outside the John Bunyan Museum as she passed it on her right, the mottled light resulting from that last day's atmospheric circumstances. Angie's weather app, for once, had been entirely accurate: 'The heavens shall be made a sea of glass, like unto crystal, wherein seven candlesticks shall be displayed.' Essaying a smooth curve into the Castle Road's main stretch, she only counted four of these – baroque, floating immensities that made the stomach flip to look at them – but had no doubt the other three were lost from view, somewhere behind the tall trees rising at this end of Newnham Road.

She made an effort to ignore the sky, just as she did her best to screen out all the other troubling elements of that eventful weekend – through a single-minded concentration on her duties as the charitable trust's executor. The beneficiary of the bequest, back in town after a long period away, would meet her at the property in a few minutes for a viewing and a handing-over of the keys and necessary documents. She had no clear idea of her career arc after that, nor where she saw herself in twelve months' time.

Parking a short walk from the Albany Road junction, Angie noticed that one of the red-brick terrace houses on the street's far side still had a sun-bleached Brexit Party poster in its downstairs window. Was it really just the end of last year when all that stuff had been going on, with half the population busily anticipating world's end while the other half prepared for paradise? Above the Castle Mound and hidden river to the south, there was a beast that had a lion's head, plus six wings crammed with heavy-lidded and incurious eyes. This surely was the worst possible outcome, one where absolutely everybody turned out to be right. Sighing resignedly, she climbed out of the car.

It was a glorious day. Its air was clean and fresh, with, on the breeze, a menthol redolence that she identified as incense, perhaps eucalyptus. Also, once outside the Astra, her discovery that the pervasive hush was laced with distant birdsong made the enterprise seem less intimidating, although only slightly. Over the far end of Castle Road, off to the east, a second towering eminence presided, this one with a bull's head but the same six wings, folded around it like enormous fans, the same indifference in their thousands of unblinking eyes. The birds were nice, though.

Still a few yards from the Albany Road turning, she was briefly startled by her first sight of the client, glimpsed across the box-cut privet bordering the corner house. Standing in the middle of the road in front of his new residence, he had his back to her and appeared to be contemplating the allotments on Albany Road's far side, directly opposite his garden gate and white front door, both for the moment closed against him. Though she'd done her best to banish any preconceptions, he was nothing like what she'd expected. Not so tall, for one thing. Perhaps fleshier. He had on a rust-coloured summer jacket worn with matching slacks and what seemed to be Air Max trainers. Mousy collar-length hair with blond tips and highlights, something like a mullet. He was vaping, sipping intermittently from a stylised gold fountain pen as he surveyed the straggling allotments.

Confident now that her navy trouser suit and near-homeopathic trace of make-up had been the correct decision, Angie called a breezy greeting as she tick-tocked into Albany's deserted quiet.

'Um … hi. I'm guessing you're my half past ten, to see the house? I'm Angie, from Carstairs & Calderwood. I hope you haven't been here long.'

He turned to her and smiled, slipping the vape pen into his breast pocket.

'Oh, no, only a few minutes. I arrived a little early, anyway. Wanted a bit of time to wallow in nostalgia, I suppose, and get a feel for how the place is now. It's nice to meet you, Angie.'

He stuck out his hand which, when she shook it, felt completely ordinary. Firm, dry, confident, without electric shocks or noticeable curing of her mild sciatica. Seen from the front, he wasn't a bad-looking man, but there was no resemblance to the publicity pictures. Not so young, for one thing, perhaps early forties or late thirties? As in her appraisal from the rear, there was a certain chubbiness about his face, clean-shaven save a tidy sticking-plaster patch of neckbeard at an interval beneath the chin. The T-shirt he had on below his russet sports coat said, 'I may be old, but at least I got to see all of the best bands.' A Rolex. One pierced ear that had a small gilt hoop in.

'So, what should I call you? Is there something that's the proper thing to say – "Your Highness" or "Your Majesty"? I don't know much about all this. I don't want to be rude.'

He looked down at himself self-deprecatingly, and laughed.

'Well, I suppose I must look like a Jez in this kit, mustn't I?'

Laughing herself, Angie began to like him.

'Jez it is. Shall we go in?'

Turning their backs upon the fenced-off vista of the yellowing allotments, they made their unhurried way towards the corner house, number eighteen. Both commented admiringly on how the slate roof rose into a modest turret over the bay windows, neither seeing fit to mention the colossal form of yet another beast that reached into the crystallised blue skies above it. This one, in addition to the sextuple eye-studded pinions, had a man's head. Its receded hair and gormless look reminded the solicitor of her ex-husband, Derek, and she wondered briefly where he was right now, along with everybody else. Then Jez unlatched the wrought-iron gate and they proceeded up a short brick path to the front door, recessed beneath a porch that had 'THE ARK' embossed in neat black characters above it. Fishing in her bag, she handed him the keys to heaven's kingdom, with Carstairs & Calderwood's distinctive logo on the plastic fob, and two by two they entered.

In the hallway, dust motes ventured glittering pirouettes through shafts of sunlight slanting from a window halfway up the stairs, and a grandfather clock measured eternity in thudding millimetres. Seeming at least not displeased by first impressions, the new owner paused to study a framed print that hung on the sedately papered left-side wall, above a fussy little table with a vase of artificial flowers. Viewed across the client's well-tailored shoulder, Angie could make out the portrait of a somewhat bird-faced older woman dressed in a white robe and bonnet, seated with a hefty Bible open on her lap against a solemn umber background. Pursed lips almost smiling, but a carefully curated worry in the painted eyes. Here the prospective resident glanced back at Angie, nodding to the picture with a fond expression.

'It's Joanna Southcott, bless her cotton socks. I don't expect she had it easy.'

Forehead creasing, Angie made a clean breast of her ignorance.

'I'm sorry, I'm afraid I don't know anything about her. Was she one of the four women who began the Panacea movement? I think I read that the leader was from Bedford. Is this her?'

He shook his head. His eyes, she thought, had something of the look that she recalled from Sunday School, although greatly diluted. Warm and brown, they weren't so much repositories of suffering and anguish as of some long-standing disappointment or frustration.

'No. Joanna was a Devon lass, brought up in Gittisham. This was, what, middle of the eighteenth century, something like that? A footman tried it on when she was a domestic servant, and then, when she wasn't having any, made out she was going mad. Gaslighted her, essentially. She joined John Wesley's crew in Exeter, where they persuaded her she was a prophetess. Next thing you know, she's telling everybody that she's the Woman of the Apocalypse, the pregnant girl clothed in the sun, from Revelation. She flogged paper seals, twelve bob a throw, that guaranteed a place in heaven for twelve thousand dozen people. Everybody name-dropped her, from William Blake to Dickens.'

Here the first-time homeowner returned his sympathetic gaze to Southcott's portrait, scratching at the palm of one hand absent-mindedly as he wrapped up his anecdote.

'When she was sixty-four – this would have been 1814 or thereabouts – Joanna made it known that she was up the duff with Shiloh, the messiah that gets talked about in Genesis. She had a due date sometime in October, but, well, obviously, nothing happened and she went into what her supporters called a trance, by which, presumably, they meant a coma. Anyway, she died on or around my birthday. Then, a century thereafter, pretty much exactly, you had Mabel Barltrop and her well-heeled single woman pen pals, cooking up the Panacea Society from Southcott's teachings, there on the low slopes of World War One. I'm sure most people thought of Southcott and the Panaceans as delusional old trouts, but here we are.'

He shrugged apologetically, and as if by some unspoken agreement, Angie opened the first door that led off from the hallway on the left as they came in. Together they went into the antimacassar still of the end-terrace property's impeccably preserved front room.

A dark green carpet covered varnished floorboards, almost to the parlour's edges, bearing a symmetrical design of fronds and curlicues that Angie thought resembled a disquieting hybrid between humming tops and jellyfish. The freshly laundered nets and velour curtains were tied back to either side, framing a view of the allotments opposite, which didn't look quite as scorched and neglected as she'd thought them at first glance. Beyond the waist-high fencing, she could make out bud-bedizened saplings and a bush that dripped with portly blackberries, although the bull-headed enormity still standing on the east horizon tended to draw most of her attention. Jez was trying out a massive horsehair sofa and examining the glass-doored china cabinet, where the glazed faces of Edwardian women stared out from commemorative plates. She was directing his attention to the decorative mouldings up above the picture rail when she glimpsed motion from the corner of her eye, and turned once more to look out of the window.

Outside, something terrible was scuttling along Albany Road.

Recoiling, her protesting senses tried to frame what she was seeing as machinery, as some kind of construction vehicle, ingeniously articulated, moving without wheels, but … no. No, that wasn't it at all. It was alive. It was an insect, a huge locust bigger than a bus that picked its way in the direction of the river, the precise typewriter movement of its sickeningly thick legs turning Angie's stomach. On the meaty hind limbs were erectile hairs like radio antennae, bristling and grotesque. The weight and textures of its lamp-black body – glistening gristle, lacquered chitin – had a terrible immediacy that dispelled her last feeble attempts to read the creature as a CGI effect, the way she'd handled the glass stratosphere with its unnerving weather front of beasts and candlesticks. This was, incontrovertibly, a giant bug as real and physical as the allotment gate it stalked past, or the blue composting bin that stood beyond. And then she realised, with a lurch, that even this dreadful analysis was just a self-protective screen, an effort to prevent herself from understanding what was really there. It wasn't a giant bug – or at least, not entirely. It was much, much worse than that.

At the monstrosity's rear end, curling up from the rustling black lacework of its folded wings, was the fatal and beckoning finger of a scorpion's tail, plump and segmented, terminating in a shellacked talon with a viscous bead of poison drooling from its tip. However, more disturbing yet were the additions to the locust's front extremity, which Angie had not taken in before this moment of lucidity: raised up before it like a begging dog were two crustacean pincers, and between these, sprouting from the insect's thorax, was a human head. Its inky hair hung in lank curtains, drawn back to reveal the sallow features as the horror craned its neck to right and left, scanning the empty street ahead for obstacles or prey. The jaw was dislocated or deformed, accommodating as it was a radiator grill of outsized teeth, the blood-caked sabres of a hungry jungle predator. It rolled its angry, unforgiving eyes, mad with the hideous truth of what it was. Angie became aware that she was hyperventilating.

As she watched the awful thing creeping away downhill to the embankment, she noted that Jez now stood beside her, watching with her. He'd recovered the e-cigarette from his top pocket and drew on it thoughtfully, turning his gaze to the transfixed solicitor with what seemed genuine concern.

'I'm sorry. I've not given any thought to how all this must look to normal people, have I? Here's you, weathering what must be a demanding brief with such professionalism that it hasn't once occurred to me: you must be terrified. Please don't be. None of this is what it looks like.'

Angie let him lead her to the ancient tan settee, where he sat on the other end and waited for her to stop shaking, the vape stick now back in his breast pocket.

'L-Look, I know this is none of my business and I don't want to step over any lines, but if this isn't what it looks like, then what is it? Are you telling me that wasn't an enormous locust with a man's head and a scorpion's tail crawling along Albany Road just now?'

The Panacea Trust's sole beneficiary stared at the coelenterate flourishes of the deep emerald carpeting. He shifted on the couch's creaking leather and appeared almost embarrassed.

'No. I mean, yes, that was a giant locust. It was real. This is all real, but … well, you shouldn't feel intimidated by it, all the things with lion's heads and what have you. They're just symbols manifested in a certain order, like the letters in a word or sentence. It's a sort of language.'

Angie was beginning to feel rather small and sorry for herself, which made her cross.

'Well, if it is, it's language that's impenetrable and designed to frighten everybody.'

She was sure she'd gone too far. It wasn't her place to critique the client, and especially not this one. Anxiously, she waited for his brow to cloud in thunderous rebuke, and was surprised when all he did was beam and look delighted with her.

'Yes! That's it right there! As a solicitor, you know the kind of language that I mean.'

She thought this over for a while before she spoke.

'You mean contractual language?'

He could not have been more pleased. He clapped both hands against his thighs enthusiastically. The gesture seemed old-fashioned, practically Dickensian; the sort of move a public schoolboy from the 1940s might pick up in imitation of their Latin teacher.

'You're bang on. Contractual language. That's exactly what it is, deliberately intimidating and unfathomable. The man-headed locusts and bull-headed men, the slaughtered lamb with seven eyes and seven horns – these are all clauses and subclauses and disclaimers in a legal document. And yes, I know, we've got to bring all this archaic nonsense up to date and make it more accessible. Some of this terminology, the images and symbols that it's drafted in, are pre-Sumerian. That's not the way to run a modern business. I kept telling everybody, but …'

He trailed off, peering glumly at the morning glories on the ornamental fireplace surround. Out in the hallway, the grandfather clock continued its dull listing of the seconds, underscoring the dejected pause. Angie considered what he'd said, determined to keep this professional and not to relapse into paralysing awe. The bit about the seven-eyed dead lamb had startled her, simply because she hadn't witnessed that particular celestial vision yet, and didn't much like having to imagine it. Similarly, she had an uncomfortable suspicion that by 'business' he meant 'universe', the implications of which made the soles of her feet cringe and tingle, like when she saw someone in a film balanced precariously on a high window ledge. It was a thought you could fall into, and your fall would never stop. He was still staring at the floral tiles around the hearth. She felt she ought to say something.

'This contract … it's been in place for some time, then, and is just now coming into force? So, what are its conditions? What does it relate to? If this is all confidential stuff that you don't want to talk about, that's fine. Just say, and I'll shut up.'

He offered her a weak smile in response, and Angie saw the tiredness in his eyes.

'No. To be honest, it's nice having somebody to moan to. I don't get to unload very often. What this contract is about, it's all the fiddling details of the handover. Our legal people have been quibbling about the wording for, what, fifty years or more? "That needs a comma. That needs a huge wine press spurting blood. That needs a human-headed locust." All right, fifty-something years, it's longer for you than it is for us, but still. That's more than half a century we've been in business limbo without proper management, and that's not counting nearly two millennia of inactivity before that. It makes us look stagnant as a company, doesn't it? That's not the message that we should be putting out.'

Angie was having trouble keeping up.

'Sorry, but I'm still not getting this handover that you mentioned. What is it that's being handed over, and to whom?'

He looked taken aback, as if he'd thought that fact too obvious to warrant mention.

'Well, the company. The business. With the former chief executive passed on, the whole lot comes to me. You've no idea how long I've waited for this, feeling like an idler with no proper job, but now it's here … I don't know. It's a big responsibility, but I expect I'll manage.'

'So, the former chief executive …?'

'My dad.'

After some several moments without blinking, she processed what he was telling her and was surprised to feel a desolated lurch, right at her very core. She'd always thought she was an atheist.

'He's dead?'

The client sighed and nodded, scratching at his palm distractedly. She understood that this was all still raw, still recent, something he was dealing with, that fifty-odd years might be just a week or two where he was from. Staring down at his trainers planted on the writhing emerald carpet, he continued in a quizzical and distant tone, as though he spoke more to himself than Angie.

'Funnily enough, it happened only a few months before they ran that headline in *Time* magazine. I mean, I see now it was just coincidence, a fluke of the statistics, but it put the wind up everybody just the same. Of course, my dad, he'd been on his last legs for centuries, just getting worse and worse, but you know what it's like. Somehow you think they'll always be there.'

Angie felt that she should pat his shoulder, but she left it too long and decided not to.

'So, the immortality …?'

Jez snorted.

'Well, there's clearly no such thing. How do you know that you're immortal, unless you get to the end of time and haven't died? You're probably just very long-lived, aren't you? Naturally, Dad being Dad, he's going to assume that he's immortal, even when he's haemorrhaging stars and coughing up black matter. That last thousand years, no kidding, he could barely get up from the throne. We told him he should see somebody, get it looked at, but he'd take no notice. He was one of those; thought he knew everything. And now he's gone, and I'm in charge of ... well, all this.'

He gazed disconsolately into some internal void for a few moments, then seemed to recover his composure, offering Angie a pained smile that bordered on a grimace.

'Ah, well. That's enough of that. Shall we get on with showing me around the house?'

Next off the hallway to the left, the living/dining room was bigger than the parlour, though perhaps it got less direct light. There was a polished hardwood table you could see your face in, and a complement of straight-backed chairs that Angie thought might have been Regency, with a repeated fleur-de-lis motif in their upholstery. The white-gold carpet looked like a steamrollered ghost.

A near-sarcophagus-sized sideboard stood against the north wall, china knick-knacks crowded at its ends in order to accommodate the worn and corner-blunted packing case that rested in the centre. Roughly three feet wide and two feet high by one foot deep, its blemished boards seemed held together by the doubled lengths of twine in which the box was bound. A luggage label, creased and jaundiced, was affixed up top with something written on it in a trembling hand, too small for Angie to make out. The almost black of a Box Brownie photograph, the box's shabby presence dominated what was otherwise a tidy and impeccably presented space. Her client gently ran his hand across the object's battered surfaces, twanging its taut strings playfully.

'So this is it, then. This is the society's panacea against crime and banditry, along with sadness and perplexity. Not much to look at close up, is it?'

Angie grudgingly allowed that Bedford had most likely seen the last of crime and banditry, and that despite the disappearance of its population, she was not particularly sad – perhaps because her doctor had prescribed anti-depressants at around this time last year – but she was certainly perplexed.

'What is it?' She recalled that Revelation said something about a book with seven seals, but didn't think a box tied up with string was mentioned anywhere. Jez grinned, nodding towards the hall.

'This is her box, Joanna Southcott's. When she died, she left it sealed up with instructions saying it was only to be opened by two dozen bishops, at a time of gravest national emergency. What Mabel Barltrop, Rachael Fox, Kate Firth and Helen Exeter were doing from the twenties onwards was petitioning the government to convene four-and-twenty bishops, so that they could open Southcott's treasure chest. I'm not entirely sure the Church of England even had twenty-four bishops by that point, but Mabel and the others weren't much bothered by the technicalities.'

Here the incoming tenant lifted the container in both hands to test its weight before putting it down again. Though cumbersome, it clearly wasn't heavy. Angie asked the obvious question.

'And does anybody know what's in it?'

Turning from the sombre package and towards the room's west-facing window, the solicitor's last ever client raised his eyebrows speculatively and pressed his lips into a doubtful pout.

'Depends who you believe. According to the Panaceans, it's Joanna Southcott's prophecies of the apocalypse in 2004 – and, OK, sixteen years out, but across the centuries, that's still not bad. What muddied up the waters, though, in 1927 this so-called psychic investigator, Harry Price, he claimed he'd found the box and had it opened. Said that it was empty except for some unimportant papers, a horse pistol and a lottery ticket. Naturally, the Panacea Society claimed that the box Price opened was a fake or a mistake. They had the real thing here in Bedford, they insisted, and would carry on petitioning to have its mysteries revealed. You've got to hand it to them, haven't you, for sticking to their guns? I mean, this was a group made up almost exclusively of well-off single women, living in an England that was near enough *The Handmaid's Tale*.'

They were both standing by the window now, gazing across the house's generous back garden at the fenced grounds of the Panacea Museum in Newnham Road, the sideboard and its indeterminate collection of debris or prophecy behind them. Angie turned to face her client, incredulous.

'You know about *The Handmaid's Tale*?'

'Well, only the first season.' He gave her a slightly guilty look. 'I haven't read the book.'

Outside, an oddly diffused sunlight powdered the rear lawn of number eighteen, a bright rectangle enclosed by tall leylandii of a neatly manicured viridian. Beyond that, other than the back of the museum and the stand of trees on Newnham Road, not much was visible from Angie's limited perspective. There was very little sky on view, though she supposed that the gargantuan figure with six wings and Derek-her-ex-husband's head was still there in the west, morosely overseeing Bedford's day of judgement. Angie at last put her finger on the one thing troubling her about this situation – other than the obvious, which was everything.

'I think there's something I'm not understanding here. How can you be so normal? I don't mean, "Oh, you're a big celebrity and yet you act so ordinary." I'm not complimenting you about your common touch. I'm saying you watch boxsets, you wear trainers and naff T-shirts, and you've even got a Bedford accent. And yet you're apparently the son of something inconceivable that made the universe. How is it even possible we're standing here talking about *The Handmaid's Tale*?'

He looked hurt.

'You don't like the T-shirt?'

Angie struggled to come up with a response that didn't involve her immediate damnation.

'Look, the T-shirt's fine. My brother Craig had one just like it, but this is exactly what I'm having trouble with. Why are you dressed like somebody I might bump into at Games Workshop? Why should you care if I like your T-shirt? This can't all be for my benefit. I'd have been just as happy if you'd turned up in the robe and sandals you wore last time. I know it's not intended, but this is actually a bit confusing and upsetting. Sorry.'

Plump face growing serious, the client nodded in acknowledgement.

'Yes, well, how you see me isn't how I am, but then, the robe and sandals version wasn't either. It's not some hypnotic screen that I'm projecting, some illusion to spare you the alien horror of my true state; nothing sinister like that. To be quite honest, it's just human evolutionary biology. Mankind's developing perceptual apparatus has consistently selected, sensibly enough, for practical survival value over accuracy. A true, comprehensive understanding of, say, a ferocious jaguar might well diminish a human's ability to run away at the first glimpse, effectively eliminating such complete perceptions from the gene pool. How you see and hear things is a bit like simplified computer icons, or the way you read that map of London's tube stations – you know the map bears no resemblance to any geographical reality, but if you follow the convenient fiction of its coloured lines, you'll reach your destination. That's much like how you perceive me. How your species perceives everything.'

Despite beginning to wish that she'd never raised the issue, Angie did her best to take this in.

'So, nothing's ever been the way we thought it was, that's what you're saying? When I see you looking like a normal guy, in normal modern clothes, that's just a kind of shorthand for something I wouldn't have the language to conceive of or describe? And when I hear you talking about everyday things in contemporary English, with a Bedford accent, then it's just some nonsense I'm inventing to hold my made-up reality together?'

Once again Jez nodded, neckbeard wobbling to the beat.

'Yeah, pretty much. Except it isn't nonsense, and you're not inventing it. It's more like an approximation of what's happening, a translation into human terms that are at least distant equivalents and thus might be of use to you. For instance, when you hear me talk about my dad, he's not my dad. He isn't even "he". I'm not his son. It's more like the relationship between a sentient meta-algorithm and a number value that the algorithm has spontaneously generated. Understandably, the average non-algorithmic man or woman has problems relating, but if it's presented as a father-son arrangement or a corporate handover, they'll have a way to comprehend the changes that are going on.'

He turned back to the window and the sunlit grass beyond, features relaxing into what she thought might be a playful smirk.

'Of course, the only thing that none of this applies to is my Bedford accent. That's completely how it sounds. I spent a lot of time in Bedford growing up. Shall we go out and have a butcher's at the garden?'

This was so abrupt that Angie found herself accompanying her client through a 1930s time-capsule kitchen to the property's back door before she thought to ask him what he meant about his Bedford upbringing. Amused, he paused between a dreadnought gas stove and a bottomless stone sink to qualify his puzzling assertion, smiling sheepishly.

'I'm sorry. I was kidding … although not entirely. It's true I remember Bedford from way back, before I manifested physically, but that was a Precambrian Bedford. There were mudslides, there were geysers, but they didn't have a noticeable local accent. That's just me being a dick.'

Although the answer would no doubt be mind-destroying, Angie asked her question anyway.

'Why were you in Precambrian Bedford?'

There was a refrigerator opposite the stove, which Angie's client opened and briefly inspected before making his reply. The fridge was humming and its light worked, indicating that there was still electricity, although she didn't quite see how there could be. Jez issued a grunt of moderate approval as he let the weighted door swing shut.

'Sometimes the old man let me visit him at work, back then when he was setting up the business. During the Precambrian, his workshop was just up the road, northeast of here. I think Transition Cycles is there now. I used to sit there in the corner with a bag of sweets and watch him do all the gene-editing and that.

He'd swear and kick things when he made a typo, got his guanine mixed up with his adenine, but I was only, what, three or four million, typical kid, so I just thought it was a laugh. I realised later that Dad was dyslexic, but back then, in the Precambrian … you have to understand it was a different time. We didn't have the same awareness about learning difficulties, and so he was half-way through production on marsupials before anybody noticed anything was wrong. But anyway, yeah, I know Bedford from when Dad was doing the preliminary work on Eden.'

Angie blinked five times in quick succession, then repeated the last word of his boyhood nostalgia back to him in a flat tone, without hope or enthusiasm.

'Eden.'

'Well, he had to put it somewhere, so why not? I think John Bunyan must have had an inkling, but the Panaceans hit the nail almost exactly on the head: they said that Eden had been situated in number eighteen's back garden, just outside. Which one of these keys that you gave me is the one to the back door?'

As if dazed by a theological concussion, Angie mutely indicated a brass mortice key attached to the Carstairs & Calderwood calligraphy. After a moment's fumbling and a comment that the lock could use some WD-40, the door opened and they both stepped out into the mentholated morning air. Her view no longer cropped by the rear windows of the property, she glanced up at the double-glazed sky and immediately forgot about the Eden shock-reveal that had so recently transfixed her.

'Jesus Christ!'

She hadn't meant to say it. Angie clapped her hand across her mouth in horror and stared wide-eyed at the client, cringing in apology. Jez shook his head and waved one chubby palm in her direction, chuckling as he brushed aside the faux pas.

'No, don't worry. Blasphemy, it's not even a misdemeanour these days, is it? I use that expression all the time, like when I finally got to see the company accounts. And in the case of that stuff going on up there, I'm in complete agreement. I mean, Jesus Christ.'

They stood together at the top of the brick steps that led down to the garden proper, necks craned back as they regarded the uproarious skies directly overhead.

Against the blue glass of the upper atmosphere, appalling mile-high spectres were suspended like Magritte trombones, two forms that faced each other in a stalled tableau of violent opposition. One was female and extremely pregnant. With the other it was difficult to say. The gravid female figure seemed to have more altitude, her anxious features angled down towards the couple in the garden. Angie thought she recognised the face but, in her holy terror, couldn't say where from. The woman had an upturned crescent moon beneath her naked feet. She wore a constellation of twelve stars as a tiara, and the garment that she clutched in disarray about her was too bright to look upon, a rag of crumpled plasma clinging to her parted legs and swollen belly, as though torn white-hot from off the sun. She had the faraway translucency of watercolour, and she looked afraid.

The creature hovering beneath her had its crimson back turned on the world and the observers far below, a boiling storm of beaded blood or rubies. Muscles big as counties knotted in its shoulder blades and buttocks, chilli-red with salamander frills. Its quadruped anatomy hunched forward to assail the woman and her unborn offspring, sticky highlights glinting from a rolling snakeskin hide and the meniscus of its arched spine helping, from that vantage, to conceal the fact it had too many heads.

These cyclopean bodies hung there over Bedford, asteroids perpetually falling so that Angie thought them motionless, a frozen film still of industrial scale, until she saw that both were moving imperceptibly in glacial slow motion, as though through a different sort of time where legendary things were always and forever happening. The sun-clad woman's lips began contorting to a scream, unhurried as an opening flower. Although more thin and tremulous than she remembered it, the fortyish solicitor at last retrieved her misplaced voice.

'The woman, that's … is that Joanna Southcott?'

The incoming owner had resorted once more to his vape stick, sucking on it thoughtfully as he surveyed the lurid *Weird Tales* cover up above through narrowed eyes, with his expression that of a Victorian explorer. A bit pompous, Angie noted. Was he trying to impress her?

'Yeah, you're right, but it's Joanna as a younger woman, or at least, that's how you're seeing this bit. Obviously, it was how she saw herself, clothed in the sun and in her last trimester. She was pretty, wasn't she? I'm guessing this is what was in her mind when she lost consciousness after her phantom pregnancy. This is Joanna Southcott's coma-dream.'

He sipped the vape again, exhaling arabesques of fragranced steam, then looked at Angie.

'Yeah, it's just contractual language, but if an uneducated eighteenth-century serving girl with premonitions somehow gets a glimpse of it, she's going to be all kinds of messed up. Stands to reason. And of course, most of this terminology, this imagery, it's unbelievably hostile to women. Come on – we don't need to watch this. I'd much sooner you were showing me the garden.'

The vape went back in its rust-coloured breast pocket as the client descended to the lawn with Angie following, her eyes fixed on her shoes that navigated the uneven brickwork of the steps. She thought that if she could just learn the trick of never looking upward, she might yet get through this without losing any marbles. Following him out on to the level baize and limiting her gaze to the surrounding hedges, she resolved to stick with her initial strategy of focussing upon the job in hand.

'Well, this is it. The ground from here to the museum is part of the property, so it's all yours. It's big for a backyard, admittedly, but I'd have never thought that this was Eden if you hadn't said.'

He raised an eyebrow, jacket striking an appealing contrast with the dark green hedge beyond.

'Oh, sorry, no, this wasn't Eden. Probably I didn't put it very well, but what I said was, this is where the Panacea Society ladies *thought* Eden had been, and they were only out by a few dozen yards. The actual garden was just slightly further east, across Albany Road from the front door.'

She had a sudden mental image of the world's new chief executive as she'd first seen him, standing with his back to her and his new property, supping his vape pen and serenely gazing over …

'Those allotments? That was where the Book of Genesis took place?'

The bridge of his nose corrugated in a minimalist shrug.

'Well, sort of. But the thing with Genesis, it's hardly a first-hand account. How could it be? I think that it was written halfway through the Book of Kings, something like that. They took a garbled version of the story, as leaked by some babbling prophet in a lotus-stupor, then they altered that to make it all a metaphor for when Nebuchadnezzar kicked the Israelites out of Judea and burned down their temple. So, that bit about the angels with the fiery swords was just a more poetic way of saying Babylonian soldiers. The real Eden story happened here in Bedford, just over the road. The rest is bollocks. Although, to be honest, angels really do have fiery swords.'

Angie, who'd been reflecting on the first time she'd heard Dylan's 'Gates of Eden' and had not imagined them as waist-high chain-link, found that she was shocked by Jez's mild profanity. Of course, after a moment's thought, she saw that her reaction was ridiculous: if someone was omnipotent, then they must surely have the power to utter the word 'bollocks'. In companionable silence, they trod ponderously about the shaved lime rectangle. She couldn't think of anything further to say or ask concerning Eden's local origins. As they turned back once more towards the rear of number eighteen, her eye level never venturing above the brick stairs and the open garden door, she changed the subject to what she hoped was a less contentious matter.

'I suppose that you'll be opening the box, the one you showed me, with Joanna Southcott's prophecies inside?' Angie resisted the temptation to look up and see how Southcott's airborne younger self was doing with her labour pains. 'I mean, I know you won't be able to convene the bishops like she wanted, and it's probably a bit late to be opening it now, with this already going on, but I'd have thought that you'd at least be curious about it. I know I would.'

They reclimbed the steps to the back door. He shrugged his nose again, rather dismissively.

'No, I don't think so. I'd prefer to let it stay a puzzle, like Schrödinger's cat. It's Schrödinger's apocalypse, how's that? I mean, the actual contents of the box are bound to be a let-down, aren't they, after all this build up? What if it was just the pistol and the ticket for the lottery, like Harry Price insisted? That wouldn't be very satisfying, would it? Wouldn't be much of a revelation, even for a boxset season ender. You'd want something jaw-dropping, something impossibly dramatic that racked up the tension and left everybody hanging, desperate for the next instalment. Frankly, I don't see whatever's in Joanna's box as having *Killing Eve* potential, unless ...'

Halfway up, he stopped and turned to Angie, face lit up by what had just occurred to him.

'I know! What I'd do, if all this was the last episode of the whole series, I'd have me – that is, my character – I'd have me letting you, your character, open the box herself, if that was what she wanted. I'd perhaps have us joking around about the subject for a while and making light of it, you know, to lull the audience into a false sense of security. A sort of misdirection. Anyway, your character, we have her opening the box. Perhaps she feels that it's an honour. Would she feel that? Or, I don't know, she's a modern woman, so perhaps she feels it's just a joke? It doesn't matter. Main thing is, she undoes all the strings – perhaps there's seven of them, like the seven seals – and opens it. Inside there's just a lottery ticket and a horse pistol, how Harry Price described it. Massive disappointment! You can see it in her face. I'm thinking close-up, from below.'

Angie suppressed a shiver. Was it starting to get chilly, out here in the sun-drenched garden? What she wanted, more than anything, was to step back into the kitchen. It was so close, the back door ajar like that, but her client was caught up in his increasingly unnerving Vince Gilligan narrative.

'So, both of us, our characters, are in the living room with the box open on the table and inside it nothing but the ticket and the pistol. You, your character, you're really disappointed, but you reach into the box and you pick up the lottery ticket for a closer look, and it's just that. It's just a lottery ticket. It isn't even ticket number six-six-six or anything. And then you turn it over.'

Reaching the denouement, his light voice grew low and gravelly, as though recounting a ghost story or an urban legend, the bit where they look round and the hitchhiker has disappeared.

'And on the other side, in spidery and faded writing, it says, "Take the gun and shoot him through the head, or he will end humanity." There's your reaction shot, just your stunned face, then bang, black screen, theme music, maybe something by Nick Cave, end credits. What do you think?'

Angie was terrified, unable to prevent herself imagining the scene, the dreadful choice. What would she do? And what did he mean, telling her a story like that? Was that what was going to happen? Was this some preliminary game before she went to hell? She knew she probably deserved it. When she'd slept with Trevor from the office, her and Derek were still technically a married couple, so that was adultery. She wished she'd never done it; had wished that she'd never done it even during the six minutes when she was actually doing it. Trevor was hideous. 'Take the gun and shoot him through the head, or he will end humanity.' What would she do? The client was staring at her in dawning concern as finally he registered the shock and panic in her headlight-frozen eyes.

'Oh, look, I'm sorry. I'm an idiot. That sounded really creepy, didn't it? And threatening. I didn't mean it to, I promise. I watch too much television, and I'm shit at conversation with real people. And with you, I mean, you're handling all of this so well, and I suppose that I was trying to say something entertaining, something that you'd think was funny. The last thing I wanted was to come across as scary. Please forgive me. You must think I'm an enormous twat.'

He was so earnestly contrite that Angie felt immediately reassured – embarrassed, even, by her sacrilegious fugue of a few moments earlier and the fact that she'd misread him so badly. She gave a relieved sigh and self-conscious giggle almost simultaneously, so that he'd see that she'd been frightened but was game enough to laugh it off. The tension broken, they continued back towards the house.

'No, I won't think that you're a twat if you don't think that I'm some bag of nerves who's not up to the job. I was just shocked by what you said, by the idea of it, which I suppose means that it would make a good season-ender after all. You can't help wondering what the character would do.'

Jez was already at the back door, going in. 'What do you think she'd do?'

Angie considered. 'Well, she wouldn't do it, would she? Look, if it's an early nineteenth-century horse pistol, it would more than likely blow up in her hand and take her eye out. Quite apart from that, I don't see that she's got a motive. I mean, "shoot him or he'll end humanity"? And what would that accomplish? I was up at half past eight this morning, and humanity looked like it had already ended. Everybody's gone, apart from me. Apart from her. So, no, she wouldn't do it.'

Before following her client back into the stubbornly anachronistic kitchen, Angie risked a last squint at the sky. Although still awful, it was nowhere near as bad as she'd expected. The vast, pregnant woman that she'd found the most upsetting element of the scenario – titanic and yet frighteningly vulnerable – was now greatly reduced in size, having retreated to a safe remove, gradually dwindling into the noon-blue heights. The lunar sickle under her bare feet was now about the same size as an ordinary daytime moon. Did that mean that the woman with Joanna Southcott's face was now in space, in orbit? Angie felt relieved on her behalf. She was well out of it.

The ghastly red thing, a clenched butcher's fist of hate and malice, was still just as big as when she'd last looked, floating in approximately the same posture with its winged back mercifully turned towards her. The wings were now spread spectacularly, where before she'd barely registered them, scalloped kites with wet pink membrane stretched between umbrella ribs of bone. Beneath each lifted sail there hung a seething cloud, the black of a scabbed wound, both cumuli dissolving at their edges into sanguinary specks that rose to stain and stipple the azure. Her eyes adjusting to the distance, Angie at first took the slowly moving flecks for swarming insects, then perhaps some species of large bird; a flock of liquorice flamingos. After several seconds' observation, though, there was no way around it: they were crimson angels, rising in whatever the collective noun for such a breed might be, a murmuration or a murder. An unkindness.

Now she had her eye in, it was evident that these ascending flakes of clotted blackness weren't the only aerial phenomena abroad in the meridian skies. From higher up, from the vicinity of the withdrawing star-crowned woman, there descended a precipitation of white dots, a talcum dusting settling through the stratosphere towards the dark arterial spatter spraying up to meet it from below. She understood that this was the opposing team. Realising that she'd paused, the client took a few steps back to Angie's side, peering up glumly at what she was peering at.

'Yeah, this is the big fight scene coming up, with the red dragon's angels and the angels of the Lord. It looks like a cup final, but it's more like wrestling – the dragon is the heel, so he'll be going down. It's really just the contract's small print, with a long list of penalty clauses and what have you, but it gets a bit Sam Peckinpah in places. To be honest, I think we'd be better off indoors until this lot are done with all the smiting. You can show me the upstairs.'

Throughout the brief excursion, the four six-winged beasts had kept to their positions at the compass points, mute and impassive, like adjudicators, or the corner posts of an ethereal boxing ring. Angie and Jez went back inside, and Jez locked the back door behind them.

'Huh. I don't know why I bothered doing that. Not when it's like you said, and there's nobody left except you. Force of habit, I suppose.'

They made their way back through the atavistic kitchen. In the hall the seconds were still falling like lead shot from the grandfather clock, and Angie asked the client if there was genuinely no one left on Earth but her. There at the bottom of the stairs, he stood and thought about it.

'No. No, it's just you. Everyone else is … well, you've heard about the Rapture? It's a bit like that, except it isn't just a thing for all the fans – the Christians – or for people who've not coveted their neighbour's ass or anything like that. It's everybody. Good, bad or indifferent, atheists and Mormons, Satanists and Buddhists, Moslems and Jehovah's Witnesses, the lot. Actually, "Rapture" is an out-of-date expression. In today's terms, think of it as "everybody's information has been instantly uploaded to the cloud". Except for yours, of course. The seraphim in legal said we had to retain one decent solicitor to represent the Panacea Charitable Trust, in order to keep all of this legitimate.'

The client began to mount the stairs and Angie followed him, considering what he had said. From what she'd gathered, there was still some ambiguity about her own position. With this mind-numbing transaction finally concluded, would her further services be necessary, or would she be 'instantly uploaded to the cloud', something which, frankly, didn't sound ideal? She couldn't think of any way to raise the issue when the answer might reduce her to a pleading wreck and spoil what had, until then, been a well-conducted lawyer/client interaction. Best, perhaps, to change the subject.

Halfway up the staircase was a small, north-facing window which, she realised as she passed it, looked down on to Castle Road. She couldn't see the Astra from this angle, although over on the street's far side she could make out the faded Brexit Party poster that she'd noticed earlier, still languishing behind its glass in the deserted terrace. A stray idea occurred to her.

'I don't suppose that you kept up with Brexit, or had any thoughts about it?'

He continued his ascension, which on this occasion went no further than the upstairs landing.

'Well, in my experience, you give the ballot to a mob of populists and nine times out of ten the vote goes to Barabbas. Or the golden bull-calf. That was the will of the people, wasn't it?'

Unable to think of a credible rebuttal, Angie joined him on the landing. Here they started with a cursory inspection of the bathroom, very tasteful in mint-green and ivory. The bath itself was one of those claw-footed items that she'd only previously seen in picture books or films, and which she'd always found vaguely unnerving – a Hieronymus Bosch life form to accompany the walking helmets and crawling hot-water bottles. There appeared to be no shower, and while she didn't raise the issue, Angie wondered if, with just the tub, this would present the client with bathing difficulties. Having read some of the literature, she wasn't sure if he could displace water in the normal way or if he'd have to lounge there on the steaming surface, high and dry.

She was sure that none of the fervent matrons of the Panacea Society had ever, in a century of ownership, once used that bath or flushed that sacred toilet.

They continued from the bathroom to the property's rear bedroom, overlooking the back garden. No doubt reasoning that the returned messiah would be organising very little in the way of sleepovers, this had at some point been converted to a study. An Edwardian writing desk was set by the west window with its view of the museum in Newnham Road, while the remaining walls were decked in bookshelves, floor to ceiling. It was very cosy, although Angie didn't know why an omniscient being would have need to study anything. Her client stood perusing his new library, his hands deep in his pockets as he read the embossed spines without discernible enthusiasm.

'This is my suggested reading list, then? This is what they thought I'd enjoy flipping through on rainy afternoons? There's nothing here but books about me and my dad, as if I'm Frank Sinatra Junior or somebody. I mean, who does that? Who wants to read all about their fucking awful upbringing, or how their dad was always going into one and smashing the place up? There's no crime fiction, there's no science fiction, nothing here by anyone who's black or Asian. And for saying there were never more than one or two blokes in the Panacea Society, there's nothing here by women. If you walked into a bookshop and this was their catalogue, you'd walk straight out again. I'll probably get rid of them as a job lot and then have a flat-screen installed. That's more me, if I'm truthful.'

Angie ran her hand across the writing table's varnished wood, its glinting leather and the plump, soft paper of its blotter; reassured herself that this was still a solid world, for all that it kept bleeding into dream. From this reaffirmation of reality, she glanced up at the window and was nonplussed to discover that, in August, it was snowing. Fat white flakes fell lazily through blazing sunshine, although as she watched, her mind corrected this initial error of perception. Obviously, it wasn't snowflakes. It was feathers, some of them on fire. Jez joined her by the antique bureau.

'That'll be the debris from the angel-holocaust that's going on above us. You can see why I suggested that we come indoors before we got the Full English Gomorrah. It's like this for the next hour or two now. Nothing I can do about it, I'm afraid.'

Outside the window in the distance, sizzling through the swansdown blizzard, there were intermittent shooting stars, blazing parabolas that plunged like crippled Spitfires on to Bedford. Angie speculated that these were slain angels, burning up as they passed through Earth's atmosphere. They watched this phosphorous precipitation for a while, and then she and her client returned along the landing for a look at the front bedroom, where there was a bit more light.

'Oh, this is nice.'

Angie agreed. It was nice. The wallpaper was blue coronets on misty pink, the brass bed buffed to gold beneath a counterpane of white chenille. On the rococo dressing table a glass jar of potpourri was resting on a doily, gently perfuming the air with lavender and rose. Thick claret curtains were held back by brocade ties to either side of the bay windows, and out through the pristine nets, charred plumage and meteoritic angel-corpses rained down on the neighbourhoods around Albany Road. The beast with a bull's head still kept watch from the east, unflinching as a bored Buckingham Palace sentry, even when the flaming casualties appeared to fall directly on its immense bovine face.

It took her quite some time to register that the allotments on the road's far side were nowhere near as meagre as they'd seemed when she arrived. This was perhaps because the proper verdant glory of the fenced enclosure had been unapparent from ground level and was only noticeable from above, but from above the modest acreage was a vision of fertility. How had she missed those half a dozen sturdy trees, or overlooked those scoliotic canes bowed by tomatoes big as stop lights?

Thinking to remark on this, she turned and found Jez watching her with an uncomfortable expression, brow and lipline writhing as though in the throes of some inner predicament. She asked him what was wrong, which only seemed to make whatever it was worse.

'Look, I don't want to … no. No, it's a bad idea. Forget it.'

Unsure what it was she should forget, she pressed him further. He groaned and looked authentically miserable.

'Angie, I know how this is going to sound. We've got a huge power gradient here and I'm not trying to abuse that, OK? You can tell me to get lost, you can say no, and nothing is conditional on that. It won't change how much I respect you for the job you've done today. It won't change our relationship. It's just, you're the first woman that I've had a decent conversation with in getting on two thousand years. I'm desperate for you not to think this is some Harvey Weinstein thing, but would you be offended if I asked about the possibility of having sex with you? It's OK if you're offended, that's completely understandable. I'm sorry, this is unprofessional. I shouldn't have said anything.'

She looked at him, and for the first time recognised in his tormented eyes a little of the man in all the paintings. He was a good-looking chap – not handsome like the men in her occasional sex fantasies, but streets ahead of all the specimens she'd slept with in real life. He was no Trevor, put it that way. As for going to bed with him, she couldn't think of any reasons not to. He seemed likeable, and with her future still uncertain, this might be her last fling. Seriously, who was going to sniff at rolling in the hay with mankind's saviour, even if he'd admittedly just disappeared mankind? Who would pretend they'd ever had a better offer? Now that she'd allowed herself to think about it in such terms, this was kind of a sexy situation, with the whole house, the whole planet, to themselves.

'No, don't apologise. I think I'd like that, what you said. And no, somehow I don't feel pressured. Can we do some kissing and stuff first?'

Face flooded with relief and gratitude, he stepped towards her, wrapped his arms around her. He was warm and yielding, and his scent was like wood shavings and fresh laundry.

'Of course we can. Kissing and sex and all of that, it's literally the only good thing about being in a body made of flesh. The rest of it just hurts. Angie, you smell so good. This is amazing.'

Then her tongue was in his mouth, and their hands moved like those of virtuosos on the keyboard of the other's spine. Kissing turned everyone into a teenager, and clearly neither Angie nor her client were an exception. They caressed and fondled, making noises of appreciation down their noses as they tenderly undressed each other, blind and voiceless, their lips suction-locked together and their eyes closed. Only when she was down to her bra, the blouse and jacket somewhere on the carpet with her kicked-off shoes, did Angie think of something and break off the increasingly heated contact.

'Just a minute.'

Padding to the window, she unfastened the elaborate ties and pulled the wine-dark drapes together with a jingling swish of curtain rings. She knew that the bull-headed titan and his thousand-eyed wings weren't deliberately staring at her tits, but it was creepy and off-putting all the same. Having the blinds drawn made her feel less like she was in some unusually ecclesiastical *Confessions* film. With this accomplished, Angie and her client carried on where they'd left off.

In minutes, both were naked and their osculation had grown frantic. She had nipples that were sucked to rubber thimbles and his hot erection in her palm. Those fingers on his right hand, usually depicted raised in benediction, were inside her, blessing juices into holy water. As their conjoined stumble led them inexorably towards the bed, like a conflicted pantomime horse, Angie realised that in the gloaming of the curtained bedchamber, his head was glowing faintly with its own diffuse and milky radiance. Nothing too bright or dazzling. You wouldn't notice it in normal daylight.

It was pretty good, the sex. Excellent, even. He was thoughtful and attentive at all times, and when he asked if he could lick her out, his face was that of an incredulously happy puppy. Conscientious to a fault, he made sure she had one orgasm in the bank before he moved into an unsurprising missionary pose on top of her, careful to reassure her over any contraceptive worries.

'It's all right, you won't get pregnant. Mum and Dad weren't just from different species, they were from entirely separate ontologies, so technically I'm like a mule. I'm sterile. I can't reproduce.'

They fucked enthusiastically while smouldering angel carcasses dropped screaming on to Bedford all around them. He delayed his climax until Angie's second one so they could come together, something that she'd always counted as a minor miracle, and yet it left her feeling shallow for having expected something more; perhaps something transcendent, with a spiritual dimension. Or if not transcendent, at least dirtier. Speaking objectively, it was the best shag that she'd ever had, and if the special effects left her disappointed, then she knew the fault was very probably with her. Her and the numbing, spectacle-addicted culture that had sculpted her desires and needs. She was too modern.

Afterwards they lay together side by side and talked, their conversation punctuated by sounds of collision as fatalities from the war overhead impacted with the nearby avenues. He seemed to want to talk about his parents, and as Angie listened, she ran one magenta fingernail across his ribs, pausing to trace the contour of what she at first believed to be an appendectomy scar.

'I wish that I could have done more for my mum, the stuff she'd been through. My conception was the last thing anyone would call immaculate. You'll notice that the PR stories in the Bible don't say anything about consent. And when they say she was a virgin, in that place and time that means she was about fourteen. I can't even imagine what it must have been like, an all-powerful iterative equation, violently imprinting a genetic sequence on some helpless child who lacked the senses to perceive it properly. All the time I was growing up, she only mentioned it the once. From what I gathered, she experienced it as a sexual assault by an enormous eight-winged seagull. That detached look that she has in all the iconography is post-traumatic stress disorder. It destroyed her.'

He asked Angie if she minded that he vaped, and when she said she didn't, he hopped briefly from beneath the covers to retrieve his e-fag from the crumpled jacket on the floor. She had to admit that his bum was lovely. Back in bed, he drew a lungful of fruit-flavoured fog before continuing.

'Dad was a nightmare, basically, and worse when he'd been drinking. Yeah, I know, it wasn't really drinking, that's just what you're hearing as a close equivalent to what I'm saying. What it was, was prayer. Prayer got him hammered. That's not why he made humanity, but it was certainly an unexpected bonus. His behaviour got more and more erratic, and then finally he fell into a sort of feedback loop: people would pray, he'd get drunk and annihilate a town or two, which would make all of the survivors pray, and so on. He thought he was hiding it, but everybody knew. I mean, you take the Book of Job. It's obvious that he's completely rat-arsed, and that Satan talks him into beating someone up, as if he was some two-pint Tyson spoiling everybody's Friday night. What could we do? It's not like anyone was going to stage an intervention.'

Angie ventured an amusing anecdote about her own dad, who had been a type compositor when that profession still existed, with a passion for real ale and sixties vinyl, but this thread of conversation didn't seem to take off or go anywhere. They talked for a bit longer, until the downpour of angels outside sounded as if it was over, and then Jez asked Angie if she fancied any lunch.

They didn't bother getting dressed. They left their clothing scattered on the bedroom floor, as though by some mute understanding that the age of people wearing things was over. The world and its dress code were no more. Downstairs, Angie sat comfortably naked in the dining room while Jez fussed in the kitchen, with her gaze continually drawn back to the dark lumber of Joanna Southcott's box, squatting there on the sideboard like an unexploded New Testament time bomb. From the next room, Jez called through to ask her if she wanted wine with dinner, and if so, would Pinot Grigio be OK? He'd looked through all the cupboards without finding the wine glasses so this would, unfortunately, be served up in dainty little teacups. Angie said she didn't mind.

The food turned out to be a beautifully prepared portion of sea bass each, with an accompaniment of still-warm artisan bread rolls. The fish was perfect, falling off the fork, and the fresh bread steamed when she cracked the crust. By this juncture of her unusually eventful day, Angie decided that she found the nudist dining weirder than the paranormal nature of her lunch companion. She supposed she was acclimatising. Sipping hesitantly from the child-sized chinaware, she was surprised by just how good the wine was, if a bit close to room temperature. Thinking about it, she was even more surprised that the abstemious Panacea

Society had thought to put away a bottle or two for the home's new owner to enjoy on his return. When she remarked at this to Jez, he stared at Angie blankly for a second, fork paused halfway to his mouth, then realised her misapprehension.

'Oh, what, this? This isn't from the Panacea Society. I got this from the tap. That's why it's not properly chilled. If I'd thought earlier, I could have filled a jug and stuck it in the fridge.'

She chewed this over with the sea bass – which, now that she thought about it, was just as unlikely an ingredient for the charitable trust to have provided as the wine. The business in the kitchen with Jez doing all the prep work had been theatre, she saw now; a performance for her benefit to make the meal seem less uncanny. She was fairly certain that if she went out into the kitchen, the gas oven would be stone cold. He'd just waved his hand or summoned angels, hadn't he? Deceitful, although probably well meaning. It was good grub just the same, and very filling. Neither of them finished it.

When he had cleared the plates and cutlery away, they sat and treated themselves to a second doll's-house cup of transubstantiated Pinot Grigio. Angie was uncomfortably aware that her job here at number eighteen was concluded, and that it would only be good manners to leave shortly and allow the client to get on with his day. It seemed like a good time to raise the matter of her prospects.

'I suppose I should be getting off soon. Is it all right if I stay in Bedford, or should I prepare to be uploaded to the cloud?'

He looked hurt that she'd even had to ask.

'The cloud? No. Not unless you want to be. I'm told it's very nice, in a nirvana sort of way, with the white light and bliss and everything, but frankly, we'd expected you to stick around the town here. You're the other party's legal representative, and so the company's obliged to take your satisfaction very seriously. Besides, how would it look if I let you show me the house, then went to bed with you, and then had you disintegrated? Also, from a practical perspective, all our legal people were appointed by my dad. There might well come a time when I need independent counsel. No, you stay wherever you feel comfortable. As far as I'm concerned, the whole of Bedford's yours.'

Which seemed a generous gratuity. She thanked him and his company for their consideration, and the chat moved smoothly on to other matters, mostly season three of *Killing Eve*. They both agreed that Jodie Comer had been brilliant, although Jez maintained that he was personally getting a bit tired of made-up charismatic psychopaths. Eventually they lapsed into an easy silence and she noticed that he was once more scratching his palm distractedly. She figured it was time for her to go.

He walked her to the front door, where the hallway clock informed her that it was only a minute or two after half past one, as if minutes and hours were still a thing. She didn't bother to collect her clothing from upstairs, even the jacket with her keys and mobile in its inside pocket. It wasn't that sort of planet any more. Nude on the doorstep, they exchanged a fond kiss and both wished each other luck, before the client went back inside and Angie turned to find out what was left of Bedford, now that it was hers. The orange bricks of the front path were warm beneath her feet.

At the front gate she lingered to assess her options. While she'd thought originally to pick up her car from Castle Road around the corner and then drive back to her flat, that didn't seem to be the way that things were going. Cars and homes, like mobile phones and clothing, had already begun to feel slightly retro; a bit last Saturday night, before the advent of a billion-year-long Sunday.

Angie stepped out on the sun-baked pavement of Albany Road and latched the gate behind her. There were dozens of singed feathers shifting in a listless breeze along the gutter, and what looked to be an outsized lump of coal that rested, smoking, in the middle of the street. Beyond that, on the far side of the road, the low fence that had previously bounded the allotments now enclosed a miniature deciduous forest, full of thirty-year-old trees that hadn't been around at half past ten that morning. Most of them appeared to be in fruit, and choirs of birds perched on already overburdened boughs, relinquishing the wildflower tangle of the ground below to drifting bees and at least three species of butterfly. Outside the bolted gate of the transformed allotments stood a man with wings, who Angie estimated to be at least nine feet tall. His chest was puffed out and his hands were clasped behind his back. He had a number-one cut, white robes, and a sword with a blue-hot acetylene flame for a blade that somehow hung from his rope belt without setting the robes on fire. Security.

The beatific bouncer, turning his shaved head at intervals for deadpan glances up and down Albany Road, appeared to have no interest in the naturist solicitor. Taking this as an indication that she wasn't the angelic bruiser's primary prey, Angie stepped out on to the grey macadam and began to cross towards him. Pausing halfway, she identified the charred material at the road's centre as a huge incinerated torso, one of the supernal combatants that hadn't burned away completely in the atmosphere before it hit the streets of Bedford. There was nothing left save for a blackened ribcage with a yard-long sternum, a Gothic accordion, steaming and defeated. Wondering if the aerial slaughter was entirely over, she looked back at the house and the marvel-haunted skies above it.

The hallucinatory dogfight was concluded, with its casualties and contrails cleared away to ready the high cirrus stage for what appeared to be the headline act: it was equestrian after a fashion, featuring a skimpily clad bareback rider and her steed, although this crawled rather than cantered. Angie recognised the painfully slow mount as the red dragon that had been trolling the pregnant woman earlier, reduced here to a seven-headed beast of burden at the whim of its capricious mistress. Two or three of the vermillion creature's near-motionless craniums were thrown back in resentful snarls, as it progressed across the firmament at a real-time clay animation pace. Sprawling along its back, insouciant as a Tory Leader of the House, what Angie understood to be a deified ancient Iraqi sex worker lifted her gem-encrusted grail in a sardonic toast to heaven.

Sumptuous body insufficiently concealed by gossamers of red and purple, only the colossal wanton's painted eyes betrayed her age, which made the furthest nebulae seem barely adolescent. Her expression was that of a former Pinewood beauty, dragging the iconic costume out of mothballs yet again and wearily reprising a career-defining scene at her nineteenth comic convention. Little wonder she was knocking back the Saints' Blood. Angie speculated as to the contractual language that the sacred harlot represented, and concluded that this must be something like a wax seal or a signature, down at the bottom of the document's last page. Conceivably the beast-and-woman combo was a corporate logo, possibly a mascot, an over-elaborate MGM lion. With an unexpected pang of sympathy for both these veteran performers, Angie turned away and carried on across Albany Road.

On the far pavement, the impossibly tall sentry guarding the allotments' west gate – a twelve-footer, she decided, seen from closer up – ruffled his feathers self-importantly at her approach. He looked her up and down disinterestedly, as though contenting himself that she had nowhere to conceal weaponry or vodka, and then gave her a perfunctory nod.

'Yeah, you're all right, love. Go on in.'

His voice was like a hurricane ten miles away. Until that moment, Angie hadn't really planned on entering the paradisiacal allotments, but hadn't specifically been planning not to. Now that the imposing doorman raised the prospect, she could see it had advantages: if she'd ruled out returning to her car or flat, then she was going to need some manner of accommodation, and here looked as promising as anywhere. Plus, the Light of the World was living just across the street, and it might be nice having somebody she knew around the neighbourhood, someone she might run into as he set out for his morning walk along the Great Ouse, or whatever his routine turned out to be. She entertained the fleeting thought that one night he might ask her over to watch season four of *Killing Eve*, before remembering that there wasn't going to be one. Oh, well. Angie thanked the angel and then, sliding back the bolt that was the low gate's only fastening, she stepped into the jungle.

Like a Tardis or an acrimonious divorce, it seemed much bigger from inside than out, and it smelled lovely; a bouillon of everything. Closing the gate and setting out through lush grass for the nearest shady arbour, she took stock of her divine surroundings with their frankly unbelievable biodiversity. Parrots splashed Rousseau colours on the woodland's canopy while tangerine-furred foxes rustled through the orchids carpeting its floor. Moving with a magnificent deliberation through a distant stand of elms, she thought she saw a tiger, and against the suede mahogany of Angie's forearm trickled a sole ladybird, bright as a shaving cut. Coiling around a branch above her was something she took for an exotic vine that had a curious metallic sheen, glinting and coppery. All of it tingled.

Angie barely noticed she'd acquired a retinue of iridescent turquoise dragonflies that hovered in formation at her brow, a shimmering seven-pointed diadem. Strolling unhurriedly between the fruiting trees, she used her tongue to dislodge a recalcitrant fibre of sea bass from her front teeth, noting as she did so the persistent tang of her recent fish dinner flavouring her mouth. It was a pity that her client hadn't thought to offer her dessert, some sweet indulgence that would cleanse her palate and allow her to more thoroughly appreciate the tastes and perfumes of her Castle Road arcadia.

The final woman, then, there in the garden, faintly peckish.

COLD READING

In the old black and white plate, the shadow on the left of the ghost's face uncurled its legs to scuttle for the margin and the cluttered desk beyond. I shrank back in my seat and no word of a lie, I genuinely felt it. It was over in a second when I realised it was just a garden spider come indoors out of the cold, what had been camouflaged against the dark bits of the photo, but I really felt that sort of tingle up the spine that all my clients go on about, so I know what they're saying. I can empathise with them. It's not all acting.

Actually, to be perfectly honest, I think nine times out of ten, it's that gives us what I suppose you'd call a supernatural feeling: something turning out to not be what you thought it was. I can remember I was only six or seven when I saw my first and only ghost. I was with Mum and Dad in the lounge of a seaside pub at night, standing there glued to the glass doors and gawping out into the dark, not thinking of anything in particular. Just then I saw this man walking across the car park of the pub away from me. He wasn't any colour. He was all washed out and grey, and then I realised there were parts of him that I could see through. I could see the scrubby strips of grass, the bollards, and the drooping lengths of chain that closed the car park in through the black folds and shadows of his jacket. I thought, 'It's a ghost! I'm really seeing one!' And then – and this was the most frightening bit – it turned its head and looked straight at me. It had got two blurry faces, one of them just slightly offset from the other, and it smiled in at me through the glass from out there in the night, and then it spoke my name. It's like, I saw its lips move, but I heard its voice as if it was right next to me, rather than outside in the car park. It said, 'Ricky? Would you like a Fanta?'

Obviously, it was my dad, standing behind me in the lounge with his reflection superimposed on the dark outside. The business with two faces turned out to be caused by double glazing, but just for a second there, you know? I'd thought it was a ghost and that it proved all of the stories that I'd heard from other kids at school. I think it made me cry, and when I explained why – about the ghost and everything – Dad told me off and said I was like an old woman, getting taken in by all that superstitious rubbish. Always very level-headed was my father, and I probably take after him in that respect, although I never really liked him much. I was much closer to my mum, but then that's very often how it is with boys, especially an only child. When Dad passed on, I suppose Mum was my first audience, as well as being my most willing and my most appreciative. She thought the world of me, my mum. She gave a little gasp and filled up when I did his voice and said, 'I always loved you, Irene.'

Knowing Dad, it was a safe bet that he'd never told her that in life, and when I saw the comfort that I'd brought that woman, my own mum, that's when I knew I had a gift. That's when I knew what Ricky Sullivan had been put on this Earth for. Oh, there'll always be the unbelievers and debunkers in the papers, on the telly or what have you, and it does, it makes me angry when they say people like me are cold, unfeeling, just taking advantage and all that. I'm sorry, but if they could see the happiness in people's faces, if they really thought about the service me and others like me are providing, giving people strength to get on with their lives when they've just lost a loved one, well, they couldn't say the things they say. I'm sorry, they just couldn't. I don't have to justify myself.

I mean, do I believe all of the things that I tell people? In my heart, I can't say that I do. But then, what about priests? You can't tell me that all of them believe every last word of what they preach, but do they get called 'ghouls in cardigans' or 'Vincent

Price, but camp'? No. No, they don't. That's because people recognise all of the reassurance and the comfort that religion brings to people, and it doesn't really matter if it's true or not. Or doctors, it's like doctors when they say that a placebo – that's like, what, a sugar pill? – that a placebo can work wonders without any side effects, but that they can't prescribe them 'cause of all the medical red tape and ethics, health and safety, all that business. That's me. I'm a spiritual sugar pill, but I do people good. I'm sorry, but I touch their lives.

And yes, I suppose you could say that I've done very well out of it, got the mortgage on this house paid off last year, but that's not what I do it for. It's not the money. How can I explain? It's more the gratitude, the look on some poor widow's face and knowing that you've helped them. That, to me, what can I say? That look's worth more than gold. That's my reward, right there.

Although this place *is* very nice, it must be said, with the old-fashioned furniture and all the books, the angel figurines along the mantelpiece, all that. It's mostly for the clients' benefit, same as the New Age music I've got on. It reassures them, makes them feel as if they're in safe hands. No, no, it's very comfortable. It's very cosy, especially now that the clocks have gone back and we've got these cold nights. If I peer out of the window at the park across the road, it looks like one of them old-fashioned fogs tonight, where you can hardly even see the trees. It just makes me feel all the warmer, with the central heating turned up, standing here in this new cardigan that one of my old ladies knitted for me. Said I hadn't charged enough for all the happiness I'd brought her, bless her, and she knew that I liked cardigans. A lovely lady. No, when I was little, what I liked best were the rainy, windy nights when I could lay tucked up in bed and think about all of the people out there in the cold, so that I could feel even snugger by comparison. I'm lucky in that that's what my whole life's like these days, very snug. Snug by comparison, you might say. Ah. There goes the phone. The landline, not my mobile, although even I have trouble telling them apart because the ringtone's very similar.

'Hello, there. You've reached Ricky Sullivan – the angel's answering service. This is Ricky speaking. So, how can I help you?'

'Um, hello. My name's Dave, David Berridge. Look, I've … well, I've lost somebody, y'know, recently, and I was just … I don't know. To be honest, I've been in two minds about if I should ring you up or not. I've never really been much of a one for all this, no offence, and I don't even know if they'd approve, the person that I've lost …'

Just judging from the accent, he's a local man, probably lower middle class and in his, what, his forties? Early fifties? He sounds lost, as if his life's just fell to bits and nothing makes sense to him any more. He's calling out for help, and I've already heard enough to know that as clients go, this one is classic Ricky Sullivan. You can tell quite a lot about a person just from speaking to them on the phone. I'm writing down his full name on my jotter even as I'm talking to him.

'Mr Berridge, let me stop you right there. I prefer it if vessels of light … that's what I call my clients … if vessels of light don't tell me anything about themselves before they come in for a consultation, if that's what you should decide to do. That way I get a clearer reading of their aura, without any preconceptions, and it's fairer on them. What I always say is, if a person has a genuine psychic gift, why should you tell them everything? They should be telling you! That way, you can judge for yourself if I'm the real thing or not. That's only fair. We do get a few con men in this business, and that's why I insist that the special people who've been brave enough to seek my help are treated properly and given credit as intelligent adults. I'm sorry, but that's just the way I am. Now, if you should decide to come in for a consultation, that'll be just fifty pounds, or it's a hundred for a house call. No need to bring any money with you, you can pay me when you get the invoice in a week or two, and only if you think that what I've done in contacting your loved one's worth that much.'

I used to ask less, but I found that people are more likely to believe in something if they've paid more for it. Mr Berridge, he sounds half convinced already, though his manner's very shaken and uncertain. I expect that he's been through a lot. He ums and ahs a bit and then asks if he can come to the house and have a consultation, perhaps later, around eight or so? I tell him that's fine, and that he can call by earlier if he likes, I shall be in all evening. It's a little touch, but it makes everything feel more relaxed and casual. It puts people at their ease and makes them feel as though they're in control of things, and that's important when you've had a loss.

He thanks me and hangs up, and right away I fish out the old iPhone and call up the local paper's website, scrolling through the last two weeks' obituaries before I find the name that I've got scribbled on my notepad. 'Berridge, Dennis, beloved brother of David, uncle of Darrell and Josephine, passed away quietly at home, November blah blah blah', and after that there was one of those poems that they must get from a book, like Best Man's speeches. I'm not criticising. People are entitled to their feelings, obviously, but I just think it's tacky and it's inappropriate, I'm sorry but I do, especially when it's about something as personal as someone's death.

So, anyway, a brother, then. I check and see if Mr Berridge is on Facebook, and it turns out I'm in luck. Just reading through the updates and then following links to a few other sites, I've pretty soon got all the information that I need to make a good impression on the client when he turns up. From what I'm reading here, they weren't just brothers, they were twins. It's hardly any wonder David Berridge sounded so shook up. They say they often share a psychic link, do twins, and when one of them dies, it must be terrible. I can remember Ronnie Kray, the gangster, when he died and it said in the paper that his brother Reg had sent a wreath he'd made out 'to the other half of me'. It must be dreadful, losing somebody so close. You'd be so vulnerable. Still, on the bright side, it makes all my prep work easier, only having the one birthdate to remember and with a good many details of their upbringing in common. And it says here they're identical, so David's Facebook photo will do me for Dennis, too: a very bland face with fine, mousy hair that's going grey and starting to recede; a light dusting of freckles on the nose; lacklustre eyes and a slight overbite that makes his mouth look rabbity. He doesn't look as if he's got much to him, to be frank about it, although I suppose it might be a poor choice of photograph. That's why I always make sure Jenny – she's my press girl – I make sure that she runs all the pictures by me before sending them out anywhere. I don't want any more of me with that little moustache I used to have. I mean, I've never looked like Vincent Price, that's just ridiculous, but where's the sense in giving people ammunition? Anyway, clean-shaven I look younger.

Oh, now this is interesting. Dennis Berridge had a blog, apparently. Hmm. Flicking through the recent entries, I'm afraid I have to say … oh, now, that's very negative. That's very harsh … I have to say he doesn't sound like someone that I'd have got on with. In the science stream at school, then working as a physics teacher until it all got too much for him and he took an early retirement this last April. He sounds like a very bitter man. He starts off ranting about the Americans, the Christians, how they're saying that the Bible should be taught alongside evolution in schools. Well, I don't see what's wrong with that, with putting both sides of the argument. Oh, here we go. It's Richard Dawkins this and Richard Dawkins that. There's all the old stuff about homeopathy, how can it work with the dilution and the rest of it, and I expect … yes, here we are. 'Why isn't Doris Stokes keeping in touch more often since she died? Surely she still has books to push?' That's low. I'm sorry, that's just low. I mean, the woman's dead and she can't answer back. Show some respect, that's all I'm saying.

Thinking back, that must be what his brother meant when he said that he didn't know if the departed would approve of him consulting me. No, no, I'll bet he wouldn't. I'll bet Dennis would regard that as a bitter irony, the thought of someone like me having the last laugh. Wouldn't he just?

I memorise all the important details … a Great Dane called Benji that both twins were soft on when they were eleven, things like that … and then I smarten up the front room for when

Mr Berridge calls. There's not much that needs doing, just some little touches to create the proper atmosphere. I put the dimmers down a whisker and then light a joss stick. I'm not sure what kind of incense it is technically. It's that sort that smells a bit pink, if you know what I mean. I put a couple of my most impressive ghost books on the coffee table. There's the Elliott O'Donnell *Haunted Britain* where the spider gave me a fright earlier, and a great big thing full of airbrushed angels, both just lying casually around, as if I read them all the time, when actually I'm not what you'd call a great reader. Even *Haunted Britain*, I just got it for the pictures, really. They're very impressive at first glance. You take the monk: 'PLATE II. PHOTOGRAPH OF A NOTORIOUS SOMERSET GHOST'. It's a proper what I call old-fashioned spooky apparition, manifesting on the well-lit landing of a fancy house in Bristol. Only when you've looked at it a minute or two do you notice how the light that's falling on the monk is coming from a different side to everything else in the picture, so that you can tell it's a double exposure. And of course, you have to ask yourself what the photographer (a Mr A. S. Palmer, it says in the caption) would be doing setting up his camera and his lighting kit to take a picture of an empty stretch of landing. Still, like I say, it's effective if you only catch a glimpse of it.

Was that the doorbell? With the background music that I've got on now, *Rainforest Sounds*, there's some bits where it's very tinkly, like – what are they called? – wind chimes, and it's difficult to tell if someone's at the door or not. It's only half past seven so I shouldn't think it's time for my vessel of light yet, although I did say he could come early if he wanted. Even out here in the hallway, I can't make out if there's anybody there outside the frosted glass. It's probably just shadows from my hedge, but I expect I'd better check and see, in case it's …

'Hello. Sorry, didn't mean to startle you. Would you be Mr Sullivan?'

God, Ricky, get a grip. First it's a spider, and now this. I've heard of being highly strung and sensitive, but this is being an old woman like your dad said. Still, I make a good recovery.

'Yes. Yes, I am. I'm Ricky Sullivan, lovely to meet you. I hope you've not stood here long, only I had some music on and wasn't sure if I could hear the bell or not. You must be Mr Berridge.'

He's just like his Facebook picture, except he's a bit more drawn and crumpled-looking since he had that took, a bit more haggard, which is the bereavement, I expect. He's standing framed there in the open doorway, letting all the cold in. He looks up and manages a weary little smile, bless.

'Mr Berridge, yes, that's right. And no, I'd only just turned up. I hadn't even had a chance to ring the bell. You must have had one of those feelings that you fellers have.'

Well, there's a stroke of luck. He's half convinced and he's not even in the door yet.

'Oh, well, it's not much, but there's times when me having a God-given gift can come in handy. Anyway, come in the warm. We'll see what I can do to help you, shall we?'

He sidles in past me, still with that self-deprecating smile, and I shut the front door behind him. It's that cold outside that you can feel it in the hallway, even with the heating up. There's no wind, and the fog's just hanging there like rubbed-out smudges on a pencil drawing. He goes through into the front room and sits down upon the sofa without taking his long mac off, which gives the impression that he's not anticipating staying very long. Well, we'll see about that. I take the chair opposite.

'Mr Berridge, can I just say that when you walked in, I got a very strong impression. Stronger than I usually pick up off of my regular vessels of light. You've recently been separated from somebody, am I right? Not just somebody close, but someone who was so close to you that I can't even imagine what it must have been like. No, no, let me finish. I'm getting a letter "D" and what I think might be a name? Denzel? Is that right? Wait a minute … no. That's not right. No, it's Dennis. Definitely Dennis. And the picture that I'm getting … no, that must be wrong. That can't be right. I'm sorry, Mr Berridge, but I think I'm going to have to let you down. I must be having an off night. I'm trying to get a picture of your loved one, but all I can see is … well, it's you, basically.'

Oh, yes. That's got his attention. He looks up into my eyes, with that same rueful little smile, and shakes his head in wonderment.

'It's my twin brother. That's who I've been separated from. I've got to say I didn't know if I should come to visit you like this, but, well, you're living up to all my hopes and expectations. So, can he say anything, my brother? Is there any message that he's got for me?'

I'm sorry, but I can't resist it, not when I've read all that rubbish on his brother's blog.

'Yes. Yes, there is. I'm not sure I can understand it properly, but I think Dennis wants to say that he was wrong. Does that make any sense? I'm sensing that he never thought there'd be an afterlife, and that he might have had some harsh words about those of us who do. Is that an accurate impression that I'm passing on? He's saying he wants to apologise, and he knows better now. He says it's wonderful, the place he's in. He's telling me that he's been reunited with old friends. He says to tell you he's with … Benjamin, or Benji? Is that right? Is that somebody that you used to know?'

To tell the truth, I threw that last bit in just on an impulse, but I've hit the jackpot, so to speak. He's filling up. He's staring at me and his eyes are wet. The little smile he had is gone.

'Benji was … he was a Great Dane that we had when we were kids. Both of us loved him. But then, you know that already. Mr Sullivan, to think that you could bring up a beloved childhood pet like that … you're truly unbelievable. If I had any doubts about what kind of man you were before I came to see you, they're all gone. And what you said, how Dennis was always so sure that there was no life after death and having to reluctantly admit that he was wrong, that all rings very true as well. That's very much what Dennis used to be like. Very much the cold-eyed rationalist. It must have took him by surprise, his current circumstances, but if I know him, he'd see the funny side as well.'

The little smile's come back again. I'm not a one to brag, but I think we can chalk up this one as a victory for Ricky Sullivan. I'm wondering if I offer a cup of tea and biscuits, perhaps we can chat about his brother for a while and then I'll see him out, ching, fifty quid, but no, he's off again.

'Am I correct in thinking that you said you'd do a house call for a hundred pounds? I wasn't certain earlier that it would be the proper thing to do, but like I say, that business about Benji, you've convinced me. You're the right person to do this with. I mean, surely you'd get a clearer message, wouldn't you, if we were in the actual house where Dennis lived?'

I'm nodding from the point where he mentioned the hundred pounds. Well, I must say, I hadn't thought this sounded very promising when David Berridge rang up earlier. He sounded so nervous and hesitant I wasn't even sure that he'd turn up, but listen to him now, after he's had a dose of what I call the Ricky Sullivan effect. He's like a different person. He's more confident. It's like he's made his mind up. I think that's a measure of the magic I bring to a situation, just my personality.

'Well, yes, I'm sure that it'd make things clearer. More vibrations with a visit, obviously. Were you after making an appointment, or was it tonight that you were thinking of? I mean, I don't mind. With the bookings I've got coming up, tonight would actually be quite convenient.'

Meaning it's better from my point of view if we go now while he's still feeling the enthusiasm, rather than giving him time to change his mind. But no, he's nodding. He looks eager.

'No, tonight is good. Tonight is perfect. It's not far. We could be there in twenty minutes.'

This is turning out to be a very profitable evening. For the house, I've still got plenty of material I haven't used, their parents' names and so on, so I can give him his money's worth. I can give him a proper visitation. I wonder if I dare do his brother's voice? It's a safe bet that they'd sound very like each other, but you never know. His brother might have had a stammer or a lisp or something. We'll see how it goes, play it by ear. He stands up from the sofa with his hands still jammed deep in his raincoat pockets … he's not took them out the whole time that he's been here. He must be feeling the weather even worse than I am … and I take my scarf and leather coat down from the peg out in the hall so I can let us out. It cost a lot, the coat, but you should see it on. It makes me look much taller and much more mysterious, like somebody from out *The X-Files* or *The Matrix*.

I shepherd him out the door, and while I lock it after us, I hear the phone go. It might be another client, so my natural impulse is to pop back in and answer it, but no. I'll let it go. The answerphone will pick it up, and anyway, if I'm that interested, I can always call the landline when I'm out and see who left a message. When I put my keys back in my pocket, I have a quick fumble and make sure I've got my mobile, safe inside a kiddie's knitted bootie, which is what I keep it in. I turn round and venture a breezy, 'Right, shall we be off?' But David, Mr Berridge, is already out the open front gate and away along the street, so that I have to hurry to catch up with him.

Oh, but it's bitter out tonight. It strikes right at you through your cardigan. I don't think that I can remember a December quite as cold as this since I was little. It's the kind of cold that takes you back, and with the fog, it's dreadful. I'd forgotten, but it has a smell to it, does fog. It's like damp smoke or something; it's less of a smell than it's a miserable musty feeling in your nose. And there's a sort of cold burn in your airways when you breathe it. To be honest, I'll be glad to get the stuff with Berridge over with so I can get back home. It's, what, just after eight now? Twenty minutes there and twenty back, another twenty for the business, I could probably be back in time for *QI*. I'll admit, the humour isn't always to my taste, but you can find out all these interesting little facts, like how the sea slug's actually a form of cucumber, if I remember right. Isn't that fascinating? If only these sceptics, all these types like Mr Berridge's late brother, if they could just open up their eyes and see how marvellous and inexplicable God's wonders really are, like with the nature and that, then perhaps they wouldn't be so smug and certain when it came to voicing their opinions. Because that's all that they are, opinions. None of us can really know for certain, can we, what awaits us on the other side? I must say, I wish Mr Berridge would slow down a bit. Still, he's keen. That's the main thing.

We walk down the road beside the park and then cross that dual carriageway that's at the bottom end. It's funny, but for saying that it's so near Christmas, there's hardly a soul about. Must be the weather, keeping them indoors. Or the recession. People always look so worried and so tense this time of year. It's very stressful, isn't it, trying to live up to everybody's expectations? Not that I find it a problem, Christmas. To be honest, I always look forward to it. I mean, ever since my mother passed, I haven't really anyone to buy for, so it's not a great expense. I know that for some people it's a lonely time, and that it's when you get most of the suicides and that, but speaking personally, I always find I get a little bulge in clients and consultations around January, so it's an ill wind and so forth.

There's kebab-shop neon and occasionally a set of headlights burning through the fog. We walk along by the dual carriageway for a few minutes, then we cross another main road that runs off downhill. I'm too puffed keeping up with him to make much of a go at conversation, but it's not like there's an awkward silence. We're just eager to get where we're going, for our different reasons. He's thinking about his brother and I'm thinking about Stephen Fry and that hundred and fifty quid.

You know, in all the years I've lived where I am now, I've never had much cause to come down this way previously, and never as far as this. It's what I think of as one of the rougher neighbourhoods, where most of it's all tower blocks but where you'll get the odd building going back to Cromwell's time or even earlier. I don't know why they don't just pave it over, put a precinct up or something, with some nice pavement cafés. It's probably the riff-raff down here with their tenants' rights and everything that's stopping it from happening. I know that this sounds awful, but if we have a bad winter, what with all these cuts, it might thin out some of the obstacles around these parts and end up being the best thing that's ever happened to the district. There. I'm sorry, but I've said it.

If you want the honest truth, I think it's areas like this that are the real ghosts, aren't they? Mouldy old things, dead things from hundreds of years ago that have no right to still be making an appearance in the present day, with all their creaking woodwork and their rattling chains. These terrible young men with their pale, undernourished faces and their hoodie tops, like apparitions, like the monk in Mr A. S. Palmer's photograph. Shrieks in the night and phantom bloodstains on the paving slabs outside a takeaway that will have disappeared by the next afternoon, it is, it's like a Gothic novel. And just like a ghost, a neighbourhood like this will hang around for centuries with all its flapping rags and its depressing atmosphere. It's an accusing presence, making everyone feel guilty about things that happened before most of us were born. It's not our fault if people were too lazy to make something of themselves and find a better place to live. Leave us alone.

Oh, look at that. A great big lump of dog's mess on the pavement. That's disgusting. I'm lucky I spotted it, what with the fog. If Dennis Berridge had to live round here, all I can say is that he can't have been much of a physics teacher. Or perhaps he was, but never got on in the education system as it is now. Either way, it must have made him bitter that somewhere like this was all he could afford. Reading his blog, I sensed he was a very angry man. You'll often find that people who say nasty things about spiritual healers – which is how I see myself – you'll often find that it's their own frustrations and their failures that they're really cross about, deep down inside. His brother David here, though, seems much more contented in himself, more open-minded and more likeable. Walking a pace or two ahead, he turns and glances back across his shoulder at me with his funny smile that, frankly, in the useless lamplight that they have down here, is looking a bit ghastly. Doesn't look like a vessel of light, let's put it that way. But you must remember that he's had a blow, the poor soul.

'Not far now. Dennis's house is just along the end here.'

Well, thank God for that. If we'd have had to go much further, I think I'd have wanted rabies shots. I'm sorry, but I would. This street we're on, it's like a terraced row with little badly kept front gardens, most of them with the gates hanging off or missing altogether. David takes a right turn up the pathway of a pebble-dashed affair and I follow behind him. The house looks to be in a better condition than the other properties along here, although not by much. It's shabby, and the paint's all peeling off round the front doorway, but at least its windows aren't smashed in and patched with plasterboard like that house that we just passed two doors down. Someone had drawn a willy on its wood fence with black spray paint and it had, you know, the stuff, the droplets coming out the end. Who wants to see that? They've got ugly minds, some people. Ugly minds.

'I'll tell you what, I'll just check round the side to see that all the windows and back door are still all right since Dennis died. He kept a key under that flowerpot, next to the front doorstep there. Let yourself in, and if they've cut off the electric, there's a big torch in the passage, just inside the door.'

This is a bit irregular but, still, a hundred pounds. I have a job finding the plant pot in the dark and then my fingertips are that cold that they're numb, so that I've only just unlocked the door and found the torch that Mr Berridge mentioned when he's back from his inspection, standing there behind me. I can't see his face in this light, but I know he'll have that weary, gormless smile showing his rabbit teeth, that little overbite he's got. I switch the torch on and it throws a puddle of tea-coloured light along the passageway, so I can see the bottom of the stairs. I think that's … no. Is it? I think that's the old-fashioned stair rods showing, brass ones like they used to have. That's shameful. You're not telling me a science teacher couldn't have afforded to splash out on fitted carpets?

Mr Berridge slips in past me, and I notice he leaves me to shut the door behind us, thank you very much. Born in a field, as my mum used to say. Not that shutting the door has made a scrap of difference to the cold. If anything, it's colder indoors than it was outside and there's that smell, the smell of other people's houses. With the better sort of residences you don't notice it, they all just smell of Glade or something – mine does – but in poorer people's houses, you can smell all the fish fingers and the dirty socks going back years, like it's accumulated in the furniture. I try the light switch in the hall, but nothing happens. I doubt that the council would cut somebody's electric off so soon after they'd died, so probably what happened was he hadn't paid his bill. I think it's better if I hurry things along a bit, get to the business, so to speak. I don't want to spend too long here.

'Well, now, this is very atmospheric, Mr Berridge. Very atmospheric. I can almost feel Dennis's presence, as if he were right here next to me. I sense that he's concerned about you, worried that you're suffering needlessly over his death. He's saying that he doesn't want you to be hurt.'

I angle up the torch beam from where it's been playing over the unappetising wallpaper and the chipped skirting board and there they are, the goofy teeth and mournful smile as he considers.

'Yes, that sounds like Dennis. We were always ever so protective of each other, being twins. If either of us were in any trouble or had someone picking on them, then the other would be on it like a ton of bricks. Dennis particularly. Out of us two, Dennis was always the bloody-minded one.'

Why am I not surprised? Anyone who can fume for pages about chiropractors and the like is hardly likely to be someone normal who just lets things go. I'm frankly glad I never met him. He sounds like a nightmare.

'He sounds like a lovely, very caring man. Just let me ask you, was there a possession or an object Dennis was especially attached to, something I could touch? I find it often makes the contact stronger, that's all. It could be a favourite pair of slippers or a record he was fond of. Literally, it could be anything. Just something so I can make a connection with him.'

There's the smile again. It's probably the torchlight bouncing round this narrow passageway, but it looks almost pitying, or even condescending. Oh, it's very cold in here. It's icy.

'Well, if you want something so you can connect with Dennis, I think if I popped upstairs a minute I might come back with the very thing. Go in the living room and make yourself at home.'

He turns and walks towards the stairs, then he looks back at me, and … no. No, his voice is very faint and I can hardly make it out. He's asking if I'd like … don't know. A cuppa? Is he offering to make a cup of tea? I shake my head, smiling politely.

'No, no, I'll be fine. You go ahead and I'll wait in the living room.'

He turns and walks up the stairs very casually for saying there's no lights on, although obviously he's more familiar with the place than I am. I'm guessing he's spent a lot of time here.

I push the door open and I sweep my torch around the living room. God, this is a depressing little hole for somebody to spend their final years in. There's three bookshelves, mostly science and science fiction from the look of it, and there's no television. Two sagging armchairs with one each side of an old three-bar fire. I've not seen one of them in years. Upstairs I can hear Mr Berridge walking back and forth as he looks for whatever piece of sentimental tat he's going to bring back down for me to go into my Vulcan mind-meld with. It'll be Richard Dawkins' autograph, I shouldn't wonder. If he's going to be a while, then I suppose I could risk sitting on one of the chairs and rest my feet after that walking. I hope he's not long. It's twenty-five to nine already and I'm going to miss the start of *QI* unless Mr Berridge gets a move on. Sitting in the dark like this, well, it's not how I like to spend my Friday evenings, put it that way.

Oh, hang on, there was that call I had when I was just locking the front door, wasn't there? While Charlie Boy's upstairs having a weep over his brother's keepsakes, I can at least check on that and see if there's another client in the pipeline. Honestly, my fingers, fishing out the bootie with the iPhone in from my coat pocket, they're half frozen. If it gets much colder they'll be falling off.

Dialling the number and the suffix that connects me to the answerphone takes ages. Clump-clump-clump upstairs, the footsteps through the ceiling. Thinking back, it didn't sound like 'cuppa', what he offered me when he was just about to go up. It was more like 'phantom' or a word like that, except that doesn't make … ah! Here we are. The girl's voice tells me I was called at eight o'clock and then there's the long pause before it plays the message.

Fanta. That's what he said. 'Ricky? Would you like a Fanta?' But why should he …?

'Mr Sullivan? I'm sorry, this is David Berridge. Listen, I've been talking to my wife and, well, I'm sorry, I've had second thoughts about coming to see you. I don't think it's anything that the departed would have wanted. I'm sorry to cancel the appointment and I hope I haven't, like, put you about or anything. Anyway, thanks again, and sorry. Um, you take care. Bye. Bye …'

What? Is this … is he playing a trick or something, calling from upstairs, just some mean joke to make me … no, he didn't call. It's me who called, what am I thinking? It's the landline, isn't it? The landline at my house. I called and it said eight o'clock and he was with me then, outside my gate. There must be, I don't know, there must be something that explains this – calm down, Ricky – something I've not thought of, and in just a minute I'll be laughing at how daft I am. Because if David Berridge, if he rang at eight to call it off, if he's still sat at home, then …

Up above me on the landing there's a creak. Somebody's coming down the stairs. I'm sorry.

I'm so sorry.

THE IMPROBABLY COMPLEX HIGH-ENERGY STATE

It was the best of times; it was the first of times. In that initial femtosecond of it all – and if a femtosecond lasted for a second then a second would last thirty million years or so – in that bolt-upright quantum startle, with the whole idea of past still in the future, everything was perfect.

Clattering out of blank nothing, there eventuated an exquisitely contrived arrangement of what might have been translucent lacquer tiles. Lacking a medium to carry sound, the clattering was purely visual. Without scale, the toppling tiles were unimaginably massive or infinitesimal. Impossible, of course, to speak of shape or colour in the blank and empty run-up to those qualities, but the emergent form had something like the perfume of geometry, within its spin a premonition – more a taste – of clear, cold pink in mixed-state oscillation with the rich blue of a peacock's shoulder. By its very nature, it was beautiful beyond compare. This incomparability was also true for the duration of the subatomic instant in which these preliminary phenomena occurred: still yet to reach the smallest measure of chronology, it felt like it went on forever.

The event, arresting and unprecedented, not yet even on the brink of substance, had instead for its material what could be called an eidolon of light, an optimistic diagram for energy and matter. Having thus spontaneously generated a precursor to solidity and with it a primordial object, the insensate mathematic force that had unwittingly precipitated ontological eruption seemed compelled to run through every plausible contingency of structure, as the cascade of increasingly elaborate surfaces crashed silent into being. In a fabulous kaleidoscope dilation, there were steam pavilions, tessellated runways, grand Alhambras, spectral lidos, avenues, concourses, corridors of an incalculable stature, opening and closing and unfolding like a schoolchild's paper oracle. Spontaneously germinating kiosks blossomed into Futurist cathedrals, ripened into unimaginable cities that were iterated to the limits of the gradually swelling moment. Abstract architectural logic shimmered, radiant with manifest contingency. Although an arithmetical inferno beyond definition or description, this quickly evolving situation was as close to heavenly as anything would ever get.

Characteristically, the aforesaid initial object, exponentially accumulated and incessantly self-complicating, implied – and indeed, necessitated – an initial subject. From the fizzing symmetry, as multiplying stadia unpacked themselves from empty vacuum everywhere about, a rumour of submicroscopic particles converged with highly ordered randomness upon a striking new configuration, a fortuitous stylistic breakthrough with a shocking absence of straight lines. Back then, of course, in the euphoric algebra of that first femto-blink, improbability was not yet even possible. As choreographed accident, untrammelled by unlikelihood, the scrum of proto-atoms and incipient molecules collided into a foreshadowing of organism. Now – and there was only now – suspended at the centre of a stately void whose inner eggshell surface was embroidered with basilicas, there coalesced a self-possessed ellipsoid of uncertain size. Lit by the same inflection of pink/blue as its progressively elaborate surroundings, glistening and crenellated with a fractal tracery of creases, this primary entity was what would be eventually referred to as a Boltzmann brain.

The Boltzmann brain, sentient life extemporaneously formed from subatomic happenstance, inevitable consequence of a non-finite universe, as per the thought experiment of nineteenth-century physicist and theoretician Ludwig Boltzmann was, in that fast-breeding and surprisingly well-regimented paradise before statistics, no less probable than any other outcome. Nonetheless, from the brain's own barely congealed perspective, its existence was an unbelievable surprise.

Born into a condition of black silence that, lacking the notions of both sound and whiteness, was not even understood as such, the disconcerted prototype of consciousness became at first uneasily aware that it existed, then aware of that awareness – and with these initial principles in place, thus was philosophy invented, as was solipsism. Relatively quickly – if it's possible to speak of quickness in that femto-splinter of beginning – the emergent locus of cognition, slippery and blind, developed a hypothesis as to what might be going on, an opening stab at what in later eras would be called reality.

Blithely originating reason, the brain reasoned that if it existed, as appeared to be the case, it seemed conceivable that there might be some broader pasture of existence somewhere for it to do its existing in. Furthermore, while incidentally creating the activity of noticing things, the brain noticed that its speculations with regard to a potentially wider field of being must have necessarily arrived at some point following its earlier feat of noticing; the moment it had noticed it existed. Through this inference of a sequential nature to events and its conjectures on the possibility of a location, the detached cerebrum, still in the traumatic processes of being born, construed both time and space. It was, clearly, on something of a roll.

Giddy with genesis, the Boltzmann curiosity next posited that its just recently deduced continuum might not be the black, solitary emptiness it seemed. In the brain's own hastily crystallised opinion, an alternative hypothesis pointed to an existence in which there existed various other points of information signalling their nature, but with no means of registering these imagined signals, the blue/pink electrified blancmange remained oblivious to everything. If only the almost material form it sensed that it possessed could be augmented by some kind of apparatus sensitive enough to note the least perturbance, the most subtle fluctuation in whatever medium this preliminary business was all taking place.

Although without scale in its own terms, by the standards of the present day, the entire rapidly developing continuum inhabited by the cerebral fluke of probability was smaller than the most elusive quanta, and was thus susceptible to quantum principles. For instance, the observer effect – that with time would be employed by Werner Heisenberg – was, in an infinitely tiny nascent universe with only one observer, more dramatic and immediate by several factors, and no sooner had the singular observer made its observation than the blurry fog of almost-particles surrounding it began to congeal into visibility and form by way of a protuberant new structure on the brain's anterior upper bulges. This new shape, ghostly at first but rapidly accruing definition, was essentially a conical construction not dissimilar to a witch's bonnet of soft felt, the point pushed down inside the pointed crown to form a deep concavity. The novel ornament was thus at once both penile and vaginal in its contours, slumping forward to depend from the brain's 'brow' much like the luminous appendages that would one day be worn by lanternfish.

From the sensory-deprivation-tank perspective of the Boltzmann thought experiment, this vaporous growth process was experienced initially as a vague, non-specific tingling sensation. This was still, however, a sensation; something which had not existed previously and was, therefore, to be marvelled at. The brain was thus already lost in wonderment before the organ sprouting from its frontal lobe developed a lush carpeting of hairs, or filaments, on its exterior and interior surfaces, millions of individual cilia suddenly quivering with information as the freshly minted nightmare of perception thundered unannounced into the black and solitary silence of creation's first inhabitant. Which, we may freely speculate, was quite a thing.

A militant chrysanthemum of mosques and locomotives swelled out from a centrally located nowhere, filling almost instantly the floating brain's new-found field of awareness, even as more recent, contradictory wonderlands expanded up from the arrangement's previously hidden interstices to replace it: sword lagoons, wedding-cake icebergs, stilt panopticons, and so endlessly forth.

And talk about loud. The furry cone that drooped from the front upper surface of the Boltzmann brain like a damp hat had simultaneously allowed the advent of the earliest spectator and the earliest listener, which meant that the vibrations flooding the emergent femto-cosmos could be meaningfully described as sound. Though in the main, this could be typified as oceanic and inchoate white noise, there, in that initial flicker of untrammelled probability, the hiss and crackle would occasionally resolve itself into brief snatches of contingent symphony or accidental aria. The whole incessant and hallucinatory eruption into being was accompanied by possibilities of music; by the jingles, hymns and heavy metal of a billion yet-to-happen worlds. Randomly permutated voices likewise trilled and soared between the budding marvels of that flickering blue/pink Creation, outcries of innumerable speculated physiologies or vocal apparatuses, with somewhere in amongst the happenstantial glossolalia and trickling cadence a precursory idea of language.

Awestruck by the billowing extravagance and struggling to assimilate its first experience of an experience, the floating brain came, not unreasonably, to associate these random sonic outbursts with whatever visual aspect of the spectacle its bristling and indented fore-sprout happened to be pointed at. By these means, purely as a way to inwardly both classify and categorise the incoming information, a cacophonous vocabulary was achieved. To offer an example, a brief trumpet fanfare in C major was associated with what looked like a pincushion of conjoined chess pieces, although only pawns and bishops. Meanwhile, a colossal fountain that produced a spray of stylised duo-decapods was represented by the sharp-edged tinkle of a shattering bottle. Mostly nouns to start with, then, though soon acquiring noisy verbs and even a few adjectival screams, bleats or explosions.

Utilising its own improvised syntax and grammar, it determined that the type of sonic cluster representing discrete entities could be referred to as a noun – something like the word 'minimal' pronounced through a harmonica – while each distinct activity engaged in by these entities, all of the manifesting, toppling and whizzing, could be called a verb – a sound effect resembling a large quadrupedal mammal falling down a flight of stairs. Accompanying this latter coinage was the brain's dismaying realisation that it was itself a noun that had no verb attached: in all the seething metamorphic panorama spread before its new-found scrutiny, it was the only thing not visibly involved in an activity; the only object not engaged in manifesting, toppling or whizzing.

Observing that, with its manifestation already accomplished, most other verb activities apparently involved some form of movement, it attempted to imagine an appendage useful to that end. Once more exploiting Heisenbergian indeterminacy, as with its flaccid sensory apparatus, it was able to produce from the surrounding soup of proto-particles a vaporous posterior plume that rapidly congealed to a whip-like flagellum with articulated vertebrae, some twenty-five times longer than the brain itself and coloured a pale gentian.

Instinctively attempting an experimental shimmy of its splendid new extension, the brain found itself propelled some distance forward from its prior position, which, as the only place that it had ever previously known, had been its birthing point. The Boltzmann speculation gloomily concluded that the probability of again occupying this precise spatial location must be vanishingly small, and in this way provided the initial rough sketch for nostalgia before once more flexing its new tail and rocketing away into the overboiling foam of form, a sapient spermatozoon. With a rapid rotary action swiftly proving to be most efficient, the trial spinal streamer functioned rather like an egg whisk, stirring up an effervescent contrail of minuscule bubbles from the fluid medium through which it travelled, the clear albumen of space-time.

Over melting terraces and recombinant palisades, through glassy tunnels like the bore of some tremendous wave, between the scything ocean-liner blades of an immense electric fan, the brain torpedoed, with its wake of froth, into the strobing pink and blue of everywhere. It soared exhilarant above metallic ornamental gardens that had threatening bladed topiary and, oh, the cryptic miracles it witnessed, the orchestral havoc that it heard. Many were its adventures during this, its headstrong youth: the laughing chandelier affair; the incident of the self-referential obstacle; that sobering episode with the winged maisonettes; a rhombus avalanche; and the quickly obsessional advent of numbering, to name but five. It planed alone down avenues gone exponential, and reflected, for the first and last time that this would be possible without self-consciousness or irony, that in all of its explorations it had made significant discoveries about itself.

The brain had learned, for instance, that it had a tendency to waver between recklessness and trepid overcaution. It had haltingly deduced a periodic table of its own responses, with preliminary elements like paranoia and bewilderment already set in place, leaving suggestive gaps for as-yet-undiscovered substances, such as ennui or lechery. Having met the absurd futility of what appeared to be a massive self-dismantling roundabout with an obscure forerunner of amusement, it had postulated the conceivable existence of a sense of humour somewhere in the swelling cosmos, but at length accepted, with some disappointment, that it didn't have one.

On a more pragmatic and less self-absorbed front, Boltzmann's thought experiment had learned that it could skilfully vibrate the follicles coating the surface of the sensor-cone, worn on its prow like a ship's figurehead, and, in the way that modern microphones can also serve as speakers, could rebroadcast audial and visual impressions by precisely reproducing the vibrations which accompanied said content's first reception. Acoustically this sounded like an early synthesiser, while the visual transmissions were delivered as a hologram-style bubble that contained the expressed scene in miniature, much like a pictographic cartoon speech balloon, albeit realised in three dimensions.

Following this innovation, the preliminary creature's passage through the burgeoning geometries that flared and flickered all about it was accompanied by glittering snow-globe utterances, suspended in its frothy wake at irregular intervals; jewel-like vignettes, each wrapped in its accompanying soundtrack; eerie trailers advertising a forthcoming animated feature. With its bridal train of purpling surf bedizened by these drifting image-opals, the augmented Boltzmann brain continued its exploratory cruise into the stupefying formal overgrowth, the ghastly premonition of a tourist lost in that unfathomable Eden.

Wriggling down algebraic arcades for shelter during a brief but intense monsoon of flutes, the brain used this involuntary period of inactivity to invent indoor play. Experimenting with the willed vibration of its sensory filaments, it realised that it was not solely forced to reproduce the sights and sounds it had experienced, but that it could create new visions and disaster-symphonies from its own rapidly developing imagination, non-existent noises made by things that hadn't happened. Thus, with the cessation of the woodwind downpour, it once more set forth across the pastures of amok manifestation, but now with a necklace string of lies and artworks at its back amidst the nearly violet spume. Eternity's first monster splashed and frolicked, glorying in its singularity and its unique abilities.

Finding the second brain, then, was a dreadful shock.

It happened during the initial entity's traverse of several huge typewriter-like constructions that were fused, ingeniously, to comprise a marvellous emporium of pecking, plunging characters and punctuation. Hanging roughly at the central point of this arrangement was what the by-now-experienced voyager at first took for a fault with its own sensory equipment: a blurred area of its visual field shaped like an egg and made, apparently, from fog. Suspecting that its optical protrusion was becoming cataracted in some way, the Boltzmann daydream stopped dead in its fizzy tracks in order to examine this ghostly anomaly at closer quarters.

On inspection, the new thing proved to be a phenomenon in its own right, rather than the anticipated optic flaw. It was a vaporous ellipse, a tendrilled smoulder gathering shape and slippery texture as it curdled towards substance. Noting a resemblance between the object's misty composition and the similar particle fog that it had witnessed while materialising its own bone-chain of a tail, the brain haltingly comprehended that this must be how it had appeared, when it first coalesced into awareness from the riotous quantum broth. Rapidly adding free-floating unease and existential dread to its evolving periodic table of responses, the brain realised with a start that it was looking at the birthing process of another individual like itself. Confirming this unsettling apprehension, the inchoate cloud shook off the last vestiges of its former fuzziness and twinkled into pin-sharp focus with a sticky glister on its lobes, its crenellated folds. It was, beyond all doubt, another brain. Lacking for audiovisual organs or a method of propulsion, the perplexing new arrival hovered there in the ongoing rush of architectural generation, insensate and motionless. It didn't even know it was a noun.

The universe's former sole inhabitant here twitched its trailing length of spine in a display of agitation or, to use the brain's own terminology, element eighty-three. This worrying turn of events, it knew, necessitated some wrenching adjustments to its formative vocabulary and worldview. Foremost amongst the great many philosophical anxieties that this occurrence represented was the hitherto unknown and therefore unexamined question of identity, a thing which, until that point, as the former lone inhabitant of anything, it hadn't really felt a need to contemplate.

This upset would require additions to the brain's internal language system, some sort of pronoun to describe itself as separate from any other brain that happened to drop by, and possibly a different pronoun to refer to this unwelcome upstart that, to its unpractised sensor-hump, seemed smaller, less attractive and less charismatic than itself. Admittedly, its concept of 'attractive' was not very much advanced from 'non-repulsive', while charisma was seen only as a lack of dismal unimportance, but nevertheless, the Boltzmann horror was increasingly persuaded to its own scornful appraisal of this relatively dull and ugly interloper. It seemed possible that more than pronouns would be needed to distinguish between the original brain and this dreary dwarf successor.

Perhaps some kind of identifying label process could be implemented, something that went beyond simply 'Boltzmann brain' and managed to convey a sentient being's status and significance, its unique personality? This process, it conceived, should be named naming. Warming to the idea, it contrived to fashion from its memory of sounds and syllables an appellation wonderful enough to represent itself, and while it felt that the sound sequence 'Panperule' held all of the requisite awe and grave magnificence, there was still something missing. In a flash of inspiration, it inaugurated the definite article – a soft implosion – as the indicator of a given thing's uniqueness and pre-eminence. The Panperule. It had a ring to it. There could be any number of intruding brains, but none of them could ever be The Panperule.

Feeling much better for its acquisition of an impromptu identity, The Panperule turned its attentions once more to the other brain that bobbed before it, blissfully oblivious. So, what was to be done about it, this anonymous blob that was nowhere near as large or interesting as The Panperule? Unnoticed, great brick chimney stacks assembled themselves into an immense industrial sea urchin somewhere overhead while the first Boltzmann brain assessed its various options, racked with indecisiveness (element nine). The course requiring the least effort on The Panperule's part would be simply to ignore the new arrival and continue on its foaming violet way, though it conceded this might lead to greater difficulties later on. What if the new brain in its turn evolved a way of sensing its environment, of moving through it, acting on it? What if it should come to the absurd conclusion that this self-inventing funfair of existence was in some way the new brain's domain, not realising that it was instead for the convenience of The Panperule? Might that not lay the ground for future conflict?

After some deliberation, a more elegant alternative became apparent. Since the new brain was not presently observing anything, the Heisenbergian loophole could still be exploited. Theoretically, this would allow The Panperule to alter the latecomer's proto-substance as it had its own, with sensory awareness and mobility within its gift. Much better that the gate-crasher be taught this bursting universe according to The Panperule than formulate a rival worldview of its own, and better yet to have the new brain feel indebtedness (element thirty) from the outset, rather than element eighty-seven, animosity, or forty-two, resentment. As an afterthought, the senior brain decided that it would at first bestow only the wilting quiff of sensory equipment, leaving the bone tail, and thus the chance to swim away, until after The Panperule felt that its introductory lessons had been properly absorbed.

With that resolved, it concentrated on the smeared potential smouldering about the junior entity, quantum scintilla hesitating over what to be. This focussed observation by The Panperule began instantly to collapse the wave of probability into a thin spray of the actual, and the more developed brain looked on with interest as an indistinct smog of hypothesis reduced to one specific form. Seen from the modern point of view, this process most resembled slowed-down footage of an aspirin dissolving in a glass of water, but played in reverse. Superpositioned particles in powdery suspension gathered frothing substance as they streamed towards a point immediately above the younger brain, where a faint stippled outline of the slumping and indented forehead bonnet was teased into view, then gradually coloured in with semblance and solidity. It was perhaps a little smaller than The Panperule's own hunch-brain mound of sound and vision, as this seemed most natural and appropriate. Unfinished, naked, functionally useless without its follicular embellishments, the newly fashioned sensory tumour came with rolling blue/pink highlights in its snakeskin sheen before these were obscured by spreading blotches of quivering filament, sensitive suede upholstery that swathed the neurologic polyp's inner and external surfaces in carnival sensation. Once again, this coat of individually vibrating hairs could possibly be seen as less luxuriant than the glossy coiffure that The Panperule had lavished on itself but, in that sparsely populated femto-moment, seen by whom?

As riptides of perception, luminous and howling, crashed into the black and solitary silence of the second brain's awareness, all its fibres stood on end, much like those on the backbone of a threatened cat. Some several thousand of the delicate erectile quills shrilled and vibrated, one upon another, and The Panperule was startled by the high-pitched and protracted signal, plainly of distress (element forty-three), with which the foundling greeted its first glimpse of glorious existence: it was screaming, and this was by definition primal. Puzzled by the vehemence of this reaction when its own attainment of sensation had elicited only mute awe (element one) and stunned bewilderment (element two), The Panperule did not consider that the newcomer's initial vision of reality contained The Panperule itself – a disembodied brain crowned with a shivering beehive hairstyle, skeleton propeller dangling beneath it like the downstroke of a horrifying question mark – as a predominating foreground feature. It could only conclude that this second Boltzmann fluke was rather highly strung, and inwardly congratulated itself on its earlier decision not to furnish the new brain with means of locomotion or escape.

Waiting until the fledgling had exhausted its paroxysm of terror, with the frightened ululations at last dwindled to an apprehensive hush, The Panperule commenced its tutelage. This was accomplished by the generation of ellipsoid information beads, speech bubbles, glass-egg utterances that contained both image and identifying sound, so that the captive/pupil could be taught the rudiments of language, although as the only such existing then, that language would of course be Panperule. As if to illustrate the egocentric nature of this process, the first glinting word-globule emitted was a heavily idealised portrait of the senior brain, a huge Halloween tadpole, with attached to it the sampled thighbone-trumpet fanfare that was, onomatopoeically, the sound-group 'Panperule'. After the hundred or so repetitions of this image-bauble thought sufficient to embed it in the understudy's memory, the lesson moved on to the many other monumental nouns, the restless verbs, the decorative face-powder adjectives, the somehow accusatory pronouns and inflection-shifting punctuation. This took quite a while. From the perspective of the non-consenting student, born from nothingness into a secondary-education language class, it took eternity.

Once the indoctrination was complete and the now educated secondary brain was relatively fluent in Panperule, there followed a short session for questions and answers. While translation from a mode of speech composed of moving pictures and accompanying random noises can be only inexact, the femto-verse's opening conversation is approximately reproduced hereunder:

'What is all this highly structured stuff that's going on? I'm terrified (element ninety-five)!'

'Why, my young disciple, this is simply what existence looks like when it all comes pouring out of nowhere. When you've lived as long as I, it will seem commonplace and even disappointing.'

'I'm still terrified, but now I'm also intellectually intimidated (forty-four) and envious (thirteen). Although I'll almost certainly recall your oft-reiterated name forever, I must ask, who are you, and how did you come to be?'

'The Panperule, The Panperule, I am The Panperule! I am a marvellous collision of unlikely pseudo-molecules that happened into being with the advent of this thundering and tumbling cosmos, and before me, nothing was. The Panperule!'

'I remain ninety-five-stricken, but this is now tinged with (one) awe, and (three) paranoia. Am I to deduce from your previous speech-trinket that you are, by implication, the self-made creator of this existential torrent; this suspiciously well-organised exploding whirligig?'

'It would be false if I did not deny that that was not the case. The Panperule!'

'Are you then my creator also? Please forgive my incredulity – it is but that your semblance is, to a trifling degree, somewhat unsettling (seventy-one).'

'As I have clearly said, it is hardly erroneous to refute that I am not this posited almighty being. I am, with great certainty, The Panperule, adorned by the most cataclysmic adjectives, and in my own exquisite image have I made you!'

This last crystalline pronouncement, which contained The Panperule's first use of the term 'you' in reference to the newly hatched brain, was accompanied by an unflattering representation of the younger Boltzmann organism which, until that moment, had not had the least idea of what it looked like. What it looked like was a crumpled lump of offal that was entering puberty, and though it did not go on for as long, the screaming this time was perhaps more plaintive and despairing (sixty-four). When the lament at last subsided to a hyphenated trail of tinkling pearls that were equivalent to hiccups or else snuffles, the apprentice entity, afflicted now by a tremendous loss of self-esteem (eleven), haltingly resumed brainkind's first awkward and uncomfortable attempt at dialogue.

'I'm sorry. It was just rather a shock to see myself in that condition … but I notice that I am not wholly in your image, lacking as I do one of those flexible nether extensions that appear to help with moving, gesturing and other verb activities. Could you provide for me an osseous flail of my own, in your capacity as manufacturer of all things that exist?'

'We'll see. For am I not The Panperule?'

'That is the firm impression that I am incessantly receiving. May I ask if, in addition to the hoped-for train of knucklebones, I am to have an aural label of my own, a name by which you might informally refer to me?'

The Panperule weighed up this proposition as a murmuration of titanic windmills, vanes a spinning blur like aeroplane propellers, droned across the panoramic spread of miracles behind it. In the end, the elder apparition grudgingly selected a one syllable cross-section from a harp glissando, unaware of its coincidental similarity to the much later terrestrial English boy's forename.

'You shall from this moment forth be known as Glynne.'

'I am The Glynne, then?'

'No. No, you're just Glynne.'

A short while after this exchange, the swarm of windmills now replaced by crackling foil marigolds of equal size, The Panperule relented and rewarded Glynne with the requested knobbly tail-bone, strenuously observed into demi-material existence and only a little more discoloured, spindly, and feeble than its maker's own. While this intentional disparity was largely motivated by no more than boundless vanity (fourteen), it was also a practical consideration born out of The Panperule's concern that Glynne might view the gift of motion as an opportunity to wriggle off and hide: with the new body part consisting of, essentially, a length of knotted string that trailed from Glynne's hindquarters in the style of goldfish excrement, The Panperule was confident that any such absconding could be hunted down successfully within a body length or two. In the event, however, this precaution proved unnecessary, Glynne being intimidated by the whole incarnated-existence thing and anxious to remain in the proximity of blue/pink space-time's self-proclaimed creator.

Thus was the impending universe's first relationship commenced; its first romantic fable, its first drama and its first long con. The exploits of The Panperule and Glynne – which in their glassy speech balloon recounting by the former were a predecessor to the broadside ballad – would be sung exultantly throughout the furthest reaches of the bustling cosmos, by The Panperule and Glynne, although chiefly The Panperule. There were hair-raising anecdotes of how The Panperule's heroics had saved Glynne from, chronologically, a life without the benefit of education, a stampede of maddened octahedrons, brick moths, what was possibly a violent gang war between libraries and boutiques, a candlestick tornado, and a dangerous clockslide.

Obviously, it wasn't all adventure. There were memorable frolics, gambols, idylls, romps, and games of chase in glades of monumental corkscrew. There were epic conversations or, more accurately, interrupted monologues that literally twinkled with The Panperule's paperweight epigrams. There were companionable silences, as when they both observed the spectacular setting of an intricately folded origami sun, and for a moment, the spine-tips of the two brains would coil about each other hesitatingly, as though by accident. During the time they'd spent together, amidst all the frisking and the fun, The Panperule had slowly come to see Glynne in a different light. The smaller stature of the younger creature now seemed less stunted inferiority than it seemed slender or agreeably petite. Sometimes The Panperule would notice how appealing Glynne's perceptual pompadour looked now it had grown out a little, or would gaze transfixed at the accelerated sinuous wriggle that Glynne had acquired to compensate for having a considerably shorter tail. Why had it never noted previously the aesthetically beguiling contours of Glynne's plump occipital lobes, as seen from the rear? How had it overlooked the adolescent brain's endearing speech impediment, the way that Glynne extruded audiovisual crystals that were less ellipsoid than they were cylindrical? The Panperule, both intrigued and alarmed by these unprecedented feelings, teetered unaware upon the brink of lechery (seventy-eight), or even love (one hundred and eleven).

The inevitable consummation happened in the deep, mauve-shadowed valleys of a king-size ornamental ladies' fan, where the hallucinatory couple drifted recreationally. The Panperule gently directed their discussion to a philosophical consideration of the sensory experience itself, moving by increments to a debate on methods by which this experience might be pleasurably enhanced. Without directly saying so, The Panperule strongly insinuated that, as supreme being, it was generously offering Glynne initiation into the most sacred mystery of all creation. Glynne – coquettishly, as it seemed to The Panperule – affected to be unsure what exactly was being proposed, practically begging the more knowledgeable brain to employ bottled film-clip language that was more explicit and direct, even more crude, the little tease. Above the great fan's stiffly folded ridges floated laundry cloudbanks, lavender light dappling on crease and wrinkle, on unravelled cirrus threads.

'It can be shown, empirically, that conscious and perceptive beings such as we are space-time's prime phenomena, and therefore fully realising our perceptual potential is a holy duty and an existential obligation, wouldn't you agree? Oh, Glynne, the gelatinous lustre on your come-hither parietal flank drives me crazy! We know that the vibration of our sensor-filaments permits both sight and hearing, while when these aforesaid hairs vibrate on one another, this allows our fishbowl phraseology and pictographic discourse. Glynne, I'll bet you've got the tightest little hippocampus. By extrapolation from our metabiological design, we may deduce, then, that the ultimate perceptual experience is that induced by one sentient individual vibrating their sensory follicles against those of another. Baby, let's get freaky, you and me. As for the practicalities of this exchange, it would appear most natural for the younger party to float upside down, above and facing their more venerable co-participant. Glynne, you're so hot, I'm worried that I'll prematurely shower you with shiny beads of moving light and music! It would seem mechanically expedient at this juncture for the inverted junior brain to tense its sensory protrusion and next introduce it to the open and relaxed concavity in the detector-wimple of its more mature and worldly colleague. Oh, Glynne, stick your ear stalk in my hairy eyehole and I shall not lose respect for you! The Panperule!'

While not without misgivings, Glynne was, relatively speaking, a newcomer to existence, with no reason to suppose that what space-time's self-styled creator had suggested was not something commonplace and wholly normal. Carefully perusing what amounted to a three-dimensional instruction manual in The Panperule's suspended dialogue bubbles, Glynne rose to the recommended elevation and obligingly proceeded to turn upside down. In doing so, the Boltzmann ingénue observed that the surrounding cosmos, full of endlessly reiterated symmetries, looked much the same whichever way up one happened to be. Having attained the correct orientation, Glynne attempted to tense their perceptual forelock as The Panperule had stipulated, finding that the subsequent compression made the organ denser, slightly narrower, and possibly a little longer. After glancing to confirm that the presumably experienced older brain was in the right position just below, with its sensory toupee suitably dilated and unclenched, Glynne apprehensively inched forward to accomplish the required insertion, all the while expecting only darkness and abrupt curtailment of sensation. On that issue, Glynne could not have been more wrong.

The Panperule, for its part, had developed a cerise cast to its colouration and was trembling excitedly at frequencies that generated a distinct subsonic hum. Receptor-cowlick gaping and relaxed, the universe's firstborn shivered, several hundred thousand smart-hairs bristling in anticipation as they measured the approach of Glynne's fibrous and sensitive baguette. Unable to restrain itself, The Panperule lunged forward for a sort of skull-free headbutt, hairstyle yawning like a dislocated python as it swallowed that of the inverted youngster, almost to the gleaming pseudo-scalp provided by Glynne's frontal lobe, and then—

And then a firework show involving beetle carapace and nebula; involving squeal, bleat and full orchestration as both individuals' neural filaments fired randomly, shrilling against each other, back and forth, a strenuously bowed crescendo on a pre-organic violin of sparks and voices. Gasping cryptic art-house movie clips with inappropriate scores, the shuddering abominations squashed their coifs together furiously in a fugue of mutual, mixed-media sensation. Lubricated by a sweat of light and music, they exhilarated in the strobing slide-show rush of tessellated goldfish, blancmange demolitions and a landslide of sound-bite non-sequiturs, the bursts of imagery and noise occurring rhythmically, with an accelerating tempo. Growing more accomplished in this very satisfying new activity, the pair experimented daringly: Glynne was the first to shyly wonder just what it might feel like to rotate his signal-monitoring mohawk rather than just move it in and out, commencing with a single brain roll that gave the cerebral adolescent's hirsute growth a solitary turn inside that of The startled-but-appreciative Panperule, like a repulsive pencil in a histrionic sharpener. So moved by the manoeuvre was the senior Boltzmann cheese-dream, it insisted Glynne continue this delicious clockwise circling motion while The Panperule commenced a complementary rotation in the opposite direction. They quickly discovered that the faster this was done, the more delirious and titillating the resultant riptide of berserk perception. Soon the two were spinning in the manner of a Catherine Wheel, bony flagella flung out by the centrifugal force and whipping up a radiating halo of aerated pink/blue microbubbles to surround their loud and dazzling consummation, their ridiculous debauch.

Beginner's luck permitted them to simultaneously attain to a climactic and convulsive state of rapture, a point at which the chaos of input overwhelmed the duo's capacity to process further data. There was an obliterating flash of something that they didn't know was white, a double thundercrack as whirling spine-tips snapped through the prelude to a sound barrier, and then a falling away from each other, enervated and both panting murmur-diamonds. There ensued a period of recovery. When dignity and the preceding air of scholarly composure were sufficiently restored, The Panperule vibrated up a lengthy glass-egg monologue describing the communion with Glynne in luridly embellished terms, originating both the lovers' sonnet and pornography.

Now there began a golden era, or at least an era of a richer pink, a deeper blue. The liberating intimacy of their recent shared experience effected profound changes in The Panperule's view of existence; shifts in how it saw itself and, as importantly, how it saw Glynne. The senior intelligence now understood that prior to finding and accessorising its young protégé, life had been incomplete. It realised that the entire fast-breeding expanse of creation could have only been contrived as perfect backdrop scenery for the erotic passions of The Panperule and Glynne, an arbour of incessantly erupting form where to conduct their legendary trysts and amatory gyrations, their salacious meeting of the minds. It was as if the whole continuum, born to perfection, was contriving to improve on that already flawless state by first providing a svelte younger playmate for The Panperule, and then a means by which this tousled youth could drive the more full-bodied and mature brain past the brink of ecstasy (seventy-seven). The immaculate world, multiplying in its bounty all around them, was made truly Paradise by the advent of Glynne and the unending entertainment that Glynne represented. The unprecedented feelings that this thought engendered in The Panperule could be viewed as a loose equivalent of horniness, or free-floating arousal (ninety-one).

All in all, the situation showed a marked improvement that would reinforce The Panperule's slowly congealing philosophical position. In an as-yet-unimagined nutshell, this revolved around the notion that existence – being a phenomenon entirely engineered for the convenience of The Panperule – had an inbuilt direction, which was that things would, of physical necessity, get better, better yet, continually better, a perfection with no top to it, perfection escalated without end. The Panperule privately named this principle Thermo-never-die-namics, the idea that energy was like a party that might start out quiet and reserved but would warm up as it progressed. This satisfying, or at least self-satisfying, teleology would come eventually to have pivotal significance, but for the moment it served to provide The Panperule's increasingly lascivious advances to the maybe underage brain with a justifying philosophic gloss. The sky, it seemed, was barely the beginnings of the limit.

The initial femtosecond of existence was at this point roughly halfway through, and in that blissful afternoon The Panperule and Glynne excursed with libertine abandon. Through Arcadian meadows of car-aerial that swayed and whispered in a Brownian breeze the pair disported themselves, shameless in the endlessly expanding pleasure garden that was theirs alone. At every opportunity, the couple would put into practice the delightful new sport they'd invented, turning coital cartwheels above hybrid structures caught at an implausible halfway point between boxing glove and jukebox. They would roll together, sticky with found footage and industrial noise, and in their gooey pillow talk they would refer to this enthrallingly indecent pastime by the pet name [STACK OF CROCKERY DROPPED IN AN ECHO CHAMBER], a verb best transliterated as 'clattersmashtinkling'. The Panperule clattersmashtinkled Glynne without surcease, both vertically and horizontally, from a libidinous variety of angles. If the mood was right, The Panperule would sometimes start on top and be the partner doing all of the compressing and inserting. In their meta-rut, they rattled the inflating aerodromes and stained the ever-dropping fire escapes of Heaven with their documentary ejaculate. Unsupervised, they gloried in their wanton freedom, though Glynne not so much, and scarce an instant passed but that The Panperule exulted in this unimprovably licentious universe, seemingly made for just the two of them.

It was around then that they happened on the other brains, one and a quarter hundred of them.

Blind and mute without their hairpiece augmentations, they hung in a cube formation, five by five by five, a school; a squadron; a flotilla; glinting like fresh mackerel. None of them knew the other ones were there, suspended in their ordered rows, oblivious as commuters. They were situated, tailless and thus motionless, in a void area between gargantuan duelling gyroscopes. However, owing to The Panperule and Glynne's then ongoing preoccupation with a bout of heavy petting and their oblique angle of approach, the floating block of newly formed brains didn't really register until the shrieking and tonsorially entangled couple were on top of them. There was a moment of stunned silence that went on for far too long before The Panperule remembered that it was supposed to have created everything. Not keen to be diminished in Glynne's sensor-follicles, The Panperule went for a rather unconvincing save along the lines of, 'See, Glynne, the incredible surprise gift I have fashioned for you on our anniversary! The Panperule!' Which anniversary, of course, remained unspecified.

From this point on, The Panperule was improvising frantically, though careful to sustain its aura of omniscient calm. When Glynne enquired what it was meant to do with all these brains, the senior organism haltingly explained that the new creatures were meant as a peer group for the young apprentice, friends of Glynne's own age, that kind of thing. In an extemporaneous afterthought, The Panperule announced that it would generously allow Glynne to modify these new companions, and endow them with the sensate wigs required for them to learn the rudiments of spoken Panperule. It hinted that Glynne should regard this time-consuming task as a promotion, given that the youngster would be blessed with the extraordinary power to bring things into manifested form with only forceful observation. That Glynne had in fact owned this ability right from the outset was not mentioned.

Luckily, thanks to the careful grooming of The Panperule, naivety was Glynne's foremost defining quality. After a fairly slapdash lesson in applied manifestation from its lover and immediate superior, Glynne set industriously to work, imagining perceptive haircuts into being on the hovering platoon of inductees. Following The Panperule's instructions, Glynne at first provided the insensible recruits with only bare protuberances, thus far unadorned by their plush of receptive cilia. In this way, the whole one hundred and twenty-five of them could simultaneously receive their rug of quivering antennae, and so get all the preliminary wailing over with at once.

Predictably, when Glynne came to this part of the procedure, the effect was deafening. More unexpectedly, the vocal mass hysteria was also oddly moving. Floating there in front of the assembled screaming brains as though a medalled tyrant overlooking a parade, The Panperule found itself stirred by all those frightened voices lifting in a unison of terror; the appalled diapason of that trauma choir. Although initially annoyed by this intrusion on the hanky-panky it had so enjoyed with Glynne, The Panperule could see how having many Glynnes as subjects – an extended fan base, if you will – might be to its considerable benefit. As a significant improvement on conditions that seemed optimal already, this accorded nicely with the doctrines of Thermo-never-die-namics and The Panperule's own personal philosophy regarding its ongoing incremental betterness. When the sheer pandemonium of some ten dozen newborn minds in horrible distress at last subsided into intermittent sobs and sniffles, space-time's first self-satisfied panjandrum glided forward eerily to make its presentation. As was customary, this commenced with getting on a thousand repetitions of the blown-glass glyph and hunting-horn acoustic that identified The Panperule. The second word in the vocabulary, 'Glynne', by contrast, had reiterations that were barely into double figures.

The tutorial on this occasion went on for much longer than it had done during Glynne's indoctrination, with there having been so many new experiences, and therefore new bubble-words coined, in the intervening time. Another reason that the lesson overran would be The Panperule's decision to include additional material after the language course was over, almost in the way of bonus extras. First, the captive audience were treated to a recitation that reprised 'The Ballad of The Panperule and Glynne' in all its many, many stanzas. Next there came what might be termed a blooper reel, wherein the sparkling speech-ellipsoids captured moments when Glynne had done something wrong, or had come close to injury in an amusing way. The final and most controversial feature was a perhaps over-vivid explanation of the term 'clattersmashtinkling', illustrated by a crystal-ball recording of that special first time for The Panperule and its considerably younger brainfriend, single quotes or commas in attempted soixante-neuf. This test run for a sex tape was, by virtue of The Panperule's prescient grasp of media, viewed by everybody in the universe. The trapped spectators, to be fair, had no idea what they were looking at. A stag film broadcast to a crèche, a pink/blue movie, it elicited only confusion (twenty-seven), nausea (twelve), and fear (nineteen).

The following question-and-answer session was a lively one, especially with Glynne's outstanding stint as moderator. The major conundrums of existence – how did it come into being; does it have a purpose; why is there sentient life; what's that thing over there, somewhere between a dead snake and a Teddy boy? – were all cleared up quite early on in the exchange, their single answer being several further repetitions of 'The Panperule'. This wasn't even monotheism, as that term would imply some manner of imaginable alternative. The fleet of student brains seemed to accept their subordinate roles as readily as Glynne had done, reasoning that this set-up must just be the way existence was and having nothing at hand to compare it to. The Panperule's supremacy established, the discussion moved on to a clamorous demand for tails, and also a surprising number of requests for supplementary information on clattersmashtinkling.

With this out of the way, when work conditions and some basic standards of behaviour had been established, Glynne commenced the allocation of the spinal flails. Even with five of these materialised at once, a column at a time, this was a lengthy process that was highly reminiscent of a Ford assembly line, and thus of fascism. Once outfitted with tailbones, each successive quintet of new converts was encouraged to assemble a short distance off, still in their vertical formation, and in this way reconstruct the group's original cubic assemblage as Glynne's ministrations deconstructed it. This was because The Panperule had taken quite a shine to the impressive discipline of the arrangement, which had something of the marching band about it – albeit realised in three dimensions and with Boltzmann brains that did not march but only wriggled. It may have been this military aspect, or at least some premonition of that bearing, which inspired The Panperule's management style once Glynne had done the necessary work and the entire platoon was mobilised.

Chattering and excited, the freshly augmented pups were understandably keen to try out their new flagella, though The Panperule insisted that this be enacted in an orderly and even stately manner. To this end, the one hundred and twenty-seven extra-cranial grotesques embarked upon a long theatrical tour of the endlessly expanding provinces. While maintaining their relative positions in the cube, the congregation of sapient hamburgers squirmed forth across mutating pastures with The Panperule up at the front of the procession, followed by the royal consort: Glynne had been pressed into service as a combination of drum majorette and orchestral conductor, bone tail swishing metronomically, leading the box-shaped brain armada through 'The Ballad of The Panperule and Glynne' in an ambitious polyphonic remix.

The resultant sound – an oceanic swell of anguish – was forerunner to the later choral compositions of Gyorgy Ligeti, although more apocalyptic. As with a receding tide before a great tsunami of despair (sixty-four), it rang out through the cascading ironing boards and cuckoo clocks of space-time as the terrifying choir continued with its outing. Naturally, the expelled speech-lozenges from such a vocalising multitude were quickly in the hundred thousands and soon after that the millions, a polluting backwash of spent karaoke ornaments, yet still the hideous fleet sailed on. The Panperule was, as expected, having the most perfectly amazing time, and if left to its own devices would have seen this bedlam pageant carried on for the remainder of eternity. Glynne, being more attuned to rumblings of dissatisfaction in the ranks, eventually suggested that they'd best soon call a halt, preferably at some meaningful destination that might justify the whole dispiriting ordeal.

Creasing its frontal lobe into a frown, The Panperule belatedly accepted that a destination would have been a good idea, but also understood that now was not the best time to admit this. A confession of that kind would surely undermine the aura of omniscience, the air of deity on which its pantomimed imperium depended. Improvising furiously, it confided in its deputy that, by a marvellous coincidence, the nondescript terrain that they were then approaching was indeed their journey's end. Here Glynne responded, in a furtive whisper of miniature language-globules, that the area ahead seemed to be no more than a levitating wilderness of cyclopean doughnuts. Making it up on the spot, The Panperule declared that the apparently dull neighbourhood was actually the precise centre of existence, well aware that this pronouncement would be near impossible to verify. Since Glynne did not immediately ridicule this claim, The Panperule went further and explained that the unprepossessing but historically important site would make an excellent location for a novel institute of learning, the concept for which had lately crossed the older creature's naked mind. In literally floating the idea to Glynne, The Panperule strongly implied that their continuum could not be thought of as a proper universe without a reputable university.

At once intrigued and taken in by this, Glynne brought the marching minds to a dead stop, though tactfully allowing them to finish the verse of the ballad they were halfway through. Surprisingly, the rumbles Glynne had taken for dissatisfaction did not end with the parade, suggesting that they were instead a product of the background ambience. When this was brought to the attention of The Panperule, it was declared that these reverberations were most likely aftershocks resulting from The Panperule's original act of creation. This caused Glynne to point out that the rumblings were not gradually fading as might be expected but, if anything, were growing subtly stronger. Issuing a sharply pointed speech-ellipsoid which implied a tone of mounting irritation with the younger brain, The Panperule retorted that according to the well-established principles of Thermo-never-die-namics, everything just went on getting even better, even bigger, all the time, and that included aftershocks. It added, rather waspishly, that Glynne's apparent ignorance of basic science only demonstrated the necessity for educational establishments, such as the hub of academic excellence lately put forward by The Panperule. The implication, clearly evident, was that the sooner Glynne and the new workforce built their required campus, then the sooner they'd be liberated from the need for idiotic questions.

Glynne, it's fair to say, was not best pleased by this high-handed attitude, but wasn't going to risk a confrontation with the thing that had allegedly created space-time. Thus was born passive aggression: taking on instinctively the role of union representative, Glynne stipulated that their new brain-army should be given individual names before they set to work constructing this legacy project of The Panperule's. When these demands were met with an ellipsoid splutter of affronted indignation from the universe's unelected management, Glynne countered with additional conditions, such as clauses guaranteeing rest and recreation periods for the newly formulated proletariat, insinuating that there would be no clattersmashtinkling of any kind until these issues were resolved.

Following this robust exchange of views, The Panperule grandly announced to the still-hovering cube of press-ganged cerebellums that they were to be rewarded with both names and holidays for their forthcoming labours on a fabulous academy, to be known as The Panperuleum.

The naming ceremony was brisk and efficient, bordering, in Glynne's opinion, on perfunctory. All one hundred and twenty-five names were a monosyllable, fractional samplings of much longer sounds, and all of them commenced with the same phoneme, which was 'gl'. So there were Glack, and Glod, and Glimp, and Glert, and also many whose names were coincidental homophones for later English words, like Glue, Glow, Glove, Glide, Gloat, Glum and at least three Glares, though all with different spellings. Glynn suspected that The Panperule associated short names that began with 'gl' – names like Glynne's own – with pitiful inferiority. That said, the newly christened lower ranks seemed more than happy to be given even rudimentary identities. With names, they at last had a self to inflate, be infatuated with, deceive, or justify. A name, being almost a quality, was something to be proud of; something one could think superior to other names and which thus made all sorts of satisfying prejudices possible. For instance, later, once the brains had been released from their cubic formation, Glynne would note their tendency to congregate only with brains whose names had the same vowel sound as their own. Glynne also observed, while in conversation with Glytte, Glig and Glimp, that brains whose names contained an 'oo', like Gloot and company, were generally indolent, untrustworthy and avaricious. This was a purely aesthetic judgement, but also the only form of racism that was then readily available. Although, in Glynne's defence, it was a very different time.

After the glut of appellations had been handed out, including one for Glut itself, The Panperule once more ran through its vacuous charade of granting the amassed Boltzmann militia an ability to manifest through observation, which they already unwittingly possessed. The brains were then permitted to relax their hexahedron, which allowed an opportunity to fraternise and chatter while The Panperule and Glynne designed the proposed universal university, though frankly it was mostly Glynne. The rookies revelled in their shore leave while the higher ranks were in discussion, with the entry-level entities jiggling everywhere and eagerly attempting glassy, bulbous conversation when there really wasn't much as yet to talk about. The limited number of topics dominating these first stabs at dialogue were, in descending order, a debate on what that rumbling was and how come it was getting louder; some deliberation as to Glynne's degree of perceived hotness; and a general agreement that all brains who had a different vowel sound in their names were fat and ugly. These initial discourses were typically concluded when the subject of clattersmashtinkling came up, it being soon discovered that to talk about the practice led, almost inevitably, to the practice of the practice. Space-time, all too quickly, rang from end to end with a prolonged concerto of dropped crockery.

No matter how quaint or appealing such a seething orgy of aroused flagellant brains might sound upon first hearing, for The Panperule and Glynne it was a gruesome inconvenience. While they were trying to concentrate upon their architectural intentions (or at least while Glynne was), everywhere about them was the thrust and squelch of copulating comb-overs. Mathematically, the horde of virginal participants had signally increased the number of erotic permutations possible, with more scope for perversion. Polyamorous arrangements seemed particularly popular, with many of the rockabilly seats-of-consciousness convening threesomes, whirling in a horrid Manx triskelion of untrammelled lust. There were also some foursomes, although these configurations bore unfortunate resemblance to self-molesting swastikas. The all-encompassing debauch looked dreadful, countless plugs of hair circling unseen bathtub plugholes, and it sounded like a raunchy landslide. Nothing in this was conducive to municipal design.

The Panperule's initial blue-sky visualisation for the mooted place of learning had been hugely disappointing, even to The Panperule: a number of that region's monstrous floating doughnuts piled up like a stack of tyres or lumpy oil drum, it would have lent an already barren zone the aura of a city-limits junkyard. When Glynne tactfully suggested making some minor improvements to the elder thing's original design, The Panperule was more than happy to sit back and watch the unrestrained brain-on-brain action that continued all around. Arcing ejaculations of speech-droplets went off here and there amongst the heaving proto-bodies, like timed fountains. Though most congress tended to be homophonic, between those whose names shared vowel sounds, there quickly emerged a heterophonic subculture that found a frisson in what oos and ees and aas could do for one another. This became immediately fashionable, although there remained a general consensus that clattersmashtinkling with anyone called Glup, Glum, Glug, Gluph, Glut, Glud or the like was tantamount to bestiality – which doesn't mean it wasn't going on.

Observing this erogenous phantasmagoria transacted in the flickering pink and blue, The Panperule found that it was becoming unendurably aroused. Sensing that Glynne was currently immersed in planning and would not appreciate advances of that sort, The Panperule experimented with alternatives. It soon discovered that if the indented tip of its fun-fur proboscis were turned outside-in, so that the sensory cone was curled up into its own cavity, The Panperule was quite good at clattersmashtinkling itself. Admittedly, the act seemed somewhat dull and repetitious without the sensory input of a partner, but was an improvement over not clattersmashtinkling at all. At least, this was The Panperule's opinion. Glynne, attempting to design space-time's first school despite the continuing brain-debauch and The Panperule having invented masturbation, saw things differently. For one thing, what The Panperule was doing was supremely unattractive to an onlooker, much like a woolly mastodon somehow inhaling its own hairy trunk. Rotating its perceptual cilia in a despairing eye-roll, Glynne returned to work amidst the hovering ellipsoid diagrams.

The rumbling continued, but by this point everyone was used to it.

Eventually, in the faintly sordid and wholly exhausted aftermath, when everybody in the start-up universe apart from Glynne was drifting limp and spent amongst a trillion rose-and-cornflower bubbles and used speech balloons, the urban planning was completed. Waiting for the six-score disembodied libertines and their auto-erotic generalissimo to rouse from their disreputable torpors, Glynne expelled a polite cat's-eye marble cough to attract the post-coital crowd's attention, then explained the technical specifications of their new academy.

The outer structure would be made from three of the tremendous floating doughnuts. Two of these, vertically oriented, would be fused together, intersecting at right angles to each other, with the third hoop, horizontal in orientation, looped around them like a waistband. Skeletally spherical, this basic outline would then be adorned by the mass-observed materialisations of the wriggling freshers. Crucially, the sphere's hollow interior was to be fitted with a cube of six amphitheatres, turned inward and facing one another to create a global lecture space without an up or down. There would be tunnel entrances at top and bottom, with four more at the cardinal points of the horizontal ring, where it intersected with the pair of upright circles. All in all, in both its beauty and utility, it was a bold and very modern statement that possessed great dignity.

The Panperule described this triumph of design as 'doughnuts stuck together', thus implying that the idea was entirely of its own devising. It went on to suggest minor tweaks, including a slight flattening of the proposed sphere, plus the addition of an observation-sculpted tail and sensory kiss-curl so that the academy would, in effect, be a gigantic statue of The Panperule. Nobody liked this concept save The Panperule but, as is frequently the way, this was the version that was pink-and-blue-lit and immediately implemented.

Twenty six-brain work gangs laboured on the edifice, relentlessly observing it into existence, supervised by Glynne and five appointed foremen, one from each of the main vowel sounds. This took quite a long while. Much like any building site, the undertaking also turned out to be loud and messy. In their swooping, staring squadrons, each one half-a-dozen strong, the muscular young Boltzmann beefcake strived and sweated sound effects through rolling clouds of quantum dust that crusted mauve on sticky lobes. From the remove of an unused free-floating toroid, an unsightly pharaoh checking progress on a deformed sphinx, The Panperule surveyed this vista of cerebrospinal toil that was pre-reminiscent of the great Russian constructivists, clattersmashtinkling itself to near unconsciousness while doing so.

The uproar of construction, for a time, drowned out The Panperule's glass gasps of self-inflicted ecstasy and even masked the gradually increasing background rumble. Meanwhile, space-time elsewhere carried on as normal: getting bigger; ticking through its femto-lifespan; vomiting its careless, ceaseless prodigies and permutations. Brobdingnagian harps, trilobites, cooling towers and anchor-bouquets were amongst the only nameable components of this ongoing eruption into form, at least from a modern perspective. It need not be said that all of these spontaneously generated shapes were much more interesting and magnificent than the distressing effigy that the brain workforce was then in the process of erecting – a sideshow exhibit in a jar, displayed in company with masterpieces.

Finally, The Panperuleum was finished, to the satisfaction of The Panperule alone. So pleased was the eponymous dictator/deity by the dimensions of this loathsome idol, that it failed to notice how the quiff-tip of the graven image was turned inwards, pleasuring itself. This subtle touch – The Panperule forever wanking at the alleged centre of the universe – had been devised by an increasingly resentful Glynne, and executed by the deputy director's phonetically sympathetic cohort Glytte, Glig, Glimp and Glock, that last of which chose to identify as an entirely different vowel sound. As the proto-university's first term commenced, Glynne's clique looked on with carefully suppressed amusement as the influx of collegiate brains filed solemnly into the multi-oriented auditorium beneath a semblance of their demiurge, captured eternally in flagrant self-abuse.

This palaeo-academic era, while it lasted, was largely congenial, aggressively erudite and crushingly monotonous. This was because The Panperuleum employed only one lecturer and taught only one subject, that being Thermo-never-die-namics. Worse, the single lecturer appeared not to have fully thought this self-invented theory through, and offered only a few heavily opinionated anecdotes in its support. Chief amongst these was the oft-repeated notion that the rumbling – by now loud enough to render many of the lectures unintelligible – was merely an aftershock being all that it could be, in a universe of everlasting self-improvement. Typically, The Panperule would make a rambling presentation of these same ideas, over and over, followed by the customary session of questions and answers, before calling for a recess. These break periods, during which socialising and, inevitably, much clattersmashtinkling were allowed, were demarcation points as critical as dawn or dusk in that unvarying bluish-pink continuum. They were also the only thing that made the academic life remotely bearable, all that prevented more of the assembled students from becoming restless and politically radical than there already were.

Glynne could not help but notice that the frequent calls for recess offered ample opportunity for the sole lecturer's philandering amongst the student body, many of whom seemed inordinately flattered by their creepy principal's advances. There would regularly be a dozen or so scholars that competed for The Panperule's attention, always floating in those spaces closest to the lectern, teasing up their sensory extensions into ever more outrageous styles and flirting openly in the question-and-answer intervals. They made Glynne sick, with their pretended understanding of and interest in Thermo-never-die-namics, their sycophantic tittering each time The Panperule attempted an ellipsoid joke. Apparently, it only knew the one, this being a display of something stupid, actual or invented, that Glynne was reputed to have done. In fact, 'the Glynne joke' in its many variations had become so widespread that a number of the students had suggested glassy dissertations on the subject, their preposterous sound-library voices ringing in The Panperuleum's deranged acoustics.

During recess periods, The Panperule would make itself available for one-on-one tuition with whichever simpering cerebellum had been fluttering their cilia most invitingly, these episodes invariably taking place off-campus, usually in the vicinity of the leftover levitating doughnuts. On one such occasion, Glynne suggested that the eager-to-please Glock should follow lecturer and student to establish the validity of these extracurricular excursions. Unsurprisingly, when the culturally appropriative hanger-on reported back to what it called its 'vowelies' – Glynne, Glytte, Glig, Glimp and company would shudder visibly whenever Glock used this expression – it regurgitated a long-lens ellipsoid image of The Panperule lewdly frolicking with glee, and, coincidentally, with Glee: off on the so-called dark side of the nearest hovering toroidal lump, master and pupil made 'the beast with two brains'. Endlessly repeated in Glock's paparazzi loop, The Panperule and Glee entwined their spinal tails as an obscene caduceus; mashing their hairy fascinators one against the other in delirious abandon. With a hardening hippocampus, Glynne gazed coldly at this pitiful and grubby assignation, the unsightly older brain making a fool of itself with the squeaking juvenile. Glynne didn't excrete so much as a single cut-glass word, but all of its companions, even Glock, knew that the second-in-command was both resentful and humiliated (forty-two and fifty). Glynne was literally bristling.

It was a story old as time, which was to say less than a femtosecond.

The inevitable confrontation happened at the start of summer term, although in accordance with the principles of Thermo-never-die-namics they were all summer terms. The rumbling sound was so pronounced by this point that the bulbous declarations of The Panperule were necessarily the size of glass dirigibles, in order to be heard above the thunderous reverberations. The bore of The Panperuleum's entrance tunnels had been widened so that these spent conversation-globules could more easily be swept into the outer void by students made to serve as Boltzmann janitors, yet still the garrulous detritus tended to accumulate in corners of the multiplanar auditorium, shimmering and jingling unappealingly.

The Panperule had just concluded a meandering account of how Thermo-never-die-namics implied that the classic Glynne joke would just keep on getting funnier and funnier the more it was repeated, then called for a session of questions and answers with its furry sensor lecherously pointed at the giggling front-row students. It was here that Glynne and a tail-picked team of phonetic cronies made their entrance, shimmying into position between lecturer and audience with cerise suds everywhere. In the immediate apprehensive silence, while The Panperule contracted its receptor cone into a perplexed squint, Glynne volunteered a carefully considered question.

'For whom can this perpetually improving universe be said to be improving?'

The Panperule, taken aback by Glynne's enquiry, blustered a long stream of floating ornaments to the effect that space-time was continually getting better from its own perspective, and that surely this must be the same for everyone and everything. Aware that this could be seen as a flimsy argument, The Panperule fell back on the increasingly loud rumble as supporting evidence, then ended with a flourish of arch rhetoric by asking if Glynne had a more convincing theory. Glee, Glam, Gloop and all the other fawning teacher's pets were tittering already at their tutor's classic put-down, and agreeing that this ill-planned intervention took the whole Glynne joke to the next level, when the deputy brain dipped its velvet prong in an affirming nod.

'Yes, I believe I have. It seems to me that this existence, far from constantly improving on perfection, is in no small measure getting worse. As evidence, I too would cite the mounting volume of the rumbling noise that makes our discourse pointless and inaudible, that forces us to cough up speeches like translucent zeppelins. How does this, in any sense, improve our situation?'

Reeling from this heresy, its sense-aperture hanging slack with disbelief, The Panperule here accidentally loaned weight to Glynne's proposal by exclaiming, 'What?'

In audiovisual bubbles now inflected with a heavily ironic tone, Glynne condescendingly reprised those opening remarks, then went on to make matters worse by calling into doubt the customary explanation for the worsening grumble of eternity.

'I put it to you that, rather than high-spirited aftershocks, it is more likely that these sounds are instead the fore-rumble of some cataclysm yet to come.'

Spluttering incoherent image-beads, The Panperule loudly insisted that this absurd notion contradicted the established tenets of Thermo-never-die-namics, and at this, Glynne merely nodded.

'I contend that it is well past time for Thermo-never-die-namics to be superseded by a more substantial theory of my own devising. I contend that our improbably well-organised continuum is in fact degenerating, with the advent of self-aware creatures actively contributing to that decline: putting a bunch of brains in charge of space-time is, quite evidently, a disastrous idea.'

The omnipresent rumbling was briefly challenged by the incredulous murmur of the students as they tried to comprehend

Glynne's radical new train of thought. The Panperule anxiously noted that Glee, Glam, Gloop, Glow and Gleam – its fan club/harem – were all gazing gooey-haired at Glynne, using the tips of their spine-tails to toy coquettishly with their luxuriant forelocks. From The Panperule's perspective, none of this was going well. As space-time's self-described creator dithered over how best to subdue the insurrection, Glynne calmly continued its incendiary monologue.

'My theory states that our unlikely universe will shift to a condition of continual collapse, perhaps commenced by whatever catastrophe is presaged by these current rumbles. This slow disintegration will eventually end when our continuum is stripped of all complexity; of life, and form, and energy; unburdened of the many tropes that comprise its existence. This un-tropic state, inevitable, unavoidable, I have named Untropy.

'Further to this, I can predict with confidence that in whatever eras of the cosmos follow, signs of Untropy will be so commonplace they will establish my conjecture as a universal fact. Indeed, these later ages will be so immersed in Untropy, in all existence running down to frigid, black disorder, that our world will only be imaginable by assuming that the universe began in a high-energy state of near infinite complexity, as a logical opposite of its eventual end in cold, and dark, and utter disarray: in Untropy. And other than the implication that The Panperule will no longer be tangling tonsures with cheap floozies up on the leftover doughnuts, I'm afraid I really can't see frozen nothingness as an improvement.'

Though the by-now-sensor-splitting rumble drowned the odd word here and there, everyone caught the gist. Some of the more highly strung brains fainted, floating quiff-down and unconscious in amongst their gaping colleagues. Glee and Gloop applauded by slapping their undersides together. It may have been this final indignity that drove The Panperule to its unfortunate reaction.

Howling, 'Glynne! The Panperule! That's quite enough! The Panperule!' in a speech-glob big as a double-decker

Hindenburg, The Panperule lifted its skeletal flagellum up above the shivering hairpiece in the manner of a not-yet-extant scorpion. Before it had the time to fully understand what it was doing, the infuriated elder lashed out with a bone whip in the general direction of its smirking deputy. The crack as the tail's flexible tip broke a prototype sound barrier was like an atom bomb, audible even through the all-consuming seismic background noise.

Intended as a reprimanding slap, the narrow tail end caught Glynn squarely on the frontal lobe and smashed the younger brain to pseudo-molecules. Glynne's twitching tail, no longer anchored to a central cortex, fell unhurriedly into the depths or heights of the stunned auditorium.

The Panperule was as surprised as anybody. Having only just invented homicide, it had been previously unaware of the brainform's alarming vulnerability. With this in mind, it was already starting to materialise a hard, protective carapace around its softer parts, an armour plating in metallic blue that left only the hairpiece and the tail exposed. The student brains, still numb with shock and watching Glynne's remains tumble away from them into The Panperuleum's immense concavity, did not immediately notice what The Panperule was doing. When they did, they quickly realised there was nothing stopping them from modifying their own forms in the same way.

It was immediately a quasi-biologic arms race. Now adorned with frightful morning stars that turned each thrashing tail into a mace and chain, both Glytte and Glig launched themselves at The Panperule in a consuming lust for vengeance (one hundred and fifteen). Fortunately for the startled tyrant, a still-loyal squad of 'ee'-named brains that had evolved a sort of belly-mounted crossbow intervened between The Panperule and his Glynnist attackers. Bolts of bone fizzed through the fluid atmosphere on bubbling trajectories, blasting a fatal hole through Glig but giving Glytte the instants needed to evolve a more robust defensive shell, a metal-plated galleon with two rows of cannon poking through its gun ports on each side.

The femtosecond was within a hair's breadth of its end; the rumbling a hair's breadth of its crescendo. Wriggling away from the engagement's epicentre to a safer vantage point, The Panperule was disconcerted by how rapidly the incident was escalating, how this in its turn drove the advance of military technology into a murderous fast-forward blur. Elsewhere in the university-turned-battlefield, the homophonic triplets Glare, Glheir and Glhey're had modified themselves with buzz saws before slaughtering a gang of diphthongs that had only managed catapults. The much-maligned brains with an 'uh' sound in their names meanwhile extruded petrol engines, biplane fins and sub-machine guns, settling scores with the more privileged vowels that denigrated them as brutish and promiscuous. The Panperuleum's vast interior became now a Hieronymus Bosch firefight, scarred by arcs of funeral-black smoke as Glup or Glug went down in flames. It was a Boltzmann blitz, and everywhere the steel-jacketed combatants streaked through a hail of cannonballs and cluster-bombs, performing haphazard lobotomies on one another as they went.

The rumbling was now visible, and everything was shaking. Ugly cracks began to race across the concave inner surface of The Panperuleum, just as Glytte sprouted guided missiles and attained a nuclear capability. You couldn't see for bits of brain.

'Clattersmashtinkle,' thought The Panperule, approximately and belatedly.

Somewhere hydrogen was happening, and it was all downhill from there.

ILLUMINATIONS

He'd never have abandoned past for future in the first place, if it hadn't been for her. She'd lured him from his sandcastles, and told him that the grown-up world was ice cream. They'd walked up a beach of years together, getting good jobs/house and two kids/older, then she'd left him in the drizzle on tomorrow's seafront, when its long-postponed amusement park was in sight just ahead, and all his strings of coloured bulbs had gone out one by one.

He's looking at the album, the black pages mourning childhood summers. Silvery triangles of antique gum and his late parents' spit, commemorating photo hinges long since fallen out, or squares of absence as the old book loses, one by one, its memories. A remaining image has an unknown little girl in the grey gradients of its background, stepping gingerly along a shoreline of the previous century, with all four foot of her reflection caught there in the film of brine beneath her flinching toes.

His former wife had not only called off their times to come, but cancelled their times fled into the bargain. Based on mutual misperception, all the moments he'd thought he remembered had become unreal, or only real to him, a dream erased on waking. Most of who he'd been was gone, leaving a gaping hole that he'd been trying frantically to stuff with photographs, newspaper clippings, anything; a gutted scarecrow with a sportscoat where he'd had a chest.

Turning the pages, heavy with incarcerated light, he looks long on a better world, sadnesses edited away by the Box Brownie's limitations: in the glazed emulsions of its memory, nothing is happening indoors, or after dark, or in the rain. The only month is August and the only fortnight factory. His mum and dad are squinting, holding a flat hand to shadow-stripe their eyes like sailors looking out for land, smiling both, happy just to be in Welmouth and no longer dead.

The pair of them had changed tense, gone from is to was, during his rubble years that followed the divorce, children replaced by weekly voices on the phone. He'd first lost his retired bus-driver dad, of a failed heart, then six weeks later his increasingly deaf mother, grief-distracted, run down by a number twenty-seven that she'd not heard coming. There followed her sparse funeral, the mourners' sympathy so recently depleted, and then later the house clearance; the discovered books of photographs.

Him and his mum are both in swimming costumes, sitting damp on towels behind a flapping windbreak, the white dunes around them mohawked spiky black by grass. He's eight with a side-parting, fiddling with a plastic bucket, Mum expressionless as she unscrews the thermos. Seawater is glittering, beaded on elastic-captured cleavage, and he feels the ghost of his off-picture father's momentary lust fluttering briefly under the gloss finish, batting against the long-lost lens.

Become a family of one, a no-such-thing, he'd not known who or what he was. He'd searched all over for the missing man – home, work, pub, internet – attempting to retrieve a version of himself he recognised, all the time looking like a bad identikit in his own bathroom mirror. Then, sat in his parents' disappearing parlour, finally he'd found the grinning, gap-toothed nipper riding a giant snail of painted fibreglass through fifty years ago, and he'd thought, '*There* he is!'

Thin lines of sand, chalk-dusting flagstone seams along the prom, and in the background rises Pleasureland, with helter-skelter spire and monster wheel and plunging track past its pretended castle gates. Dad stoops to give him something on the threshold, either coming out or going in, and through an entrance tumorous with balloons you can see snail cars, watchful louts, ghost corridors, skirts lifting in the funhouse gust; unnerving premonitions of adulthood, painted all in 1967's ashen palette.

Was that mollusc ride the last time he'd been unconditionally happy? He found himself thinking about Welmouth all the while, and the east coast resort town's props and scenery set-dressed his dreams. He thought he should perhaps go back there for a day out, a weekend, and in this way arrest his life's now unrequired forward momentum. Every day he'd bravely re-enlisted in the human struggle with tomorrow, but, as its big guns came out, he planned a staged withdrawal into yesterday.

Each snapshot is a moment's snakeskin moult, and begs an awful question: that break in the cloud, that street, that afternoon, those walk-on extras, where have they all gone? Why is there no investigation? These dead children, paddling bony in the surf, how do they come to be pressed flat in weighty volumes, with the colours all squeezed out of them? He broods like a TV detective, nagged by the cold case that never felt right, taping overexposed faces to his cranial whiteboard.

He'd reached his decision on a week in Welmouth by unnoticeable increments, so that he didn't consciously know he was making it. There'd been a brochure here, a bus timetable there, the blokes at work with mouths that said, 'Yeah, that sounds nice,' and eyes that thought it was a bad idea. Nobody mentioned midlife crisis to his face, but the eyebrow telepathy was deafening. No longer needing photographs, he formed his memories now as rectangles in shiny black and white.

The shingle glistening as the wave withdraws, and footsore women in sharp-cornered glasses staring undecided at the rides. The eight-foot heads of then ubiquitous comedians erupt from poster stars above the Hippodrome, their names and catchphrases in plump, enthusiastic printing that anticipates the audience. Fingers of melting soft-whip dribble on a cone's soggy embossing, and a starfish, dead and petrified, sits in a seaside bucket of tap water for six months awaiting its revival.

It wasn't a revisit then, but an obsessive recreation. He'd booked for a week at South Becks caravan park, but it was called

Ocean Vista now. Deciding to go the whole second-childhood hog, he'd got his ticket for an early morning coach ride out to Welmouth, even though there were much more convenient and quicker ways to get there. He reluctantly accepted that a *Beano Summer Special* for the journey would have been grotesque, and anyway, he didn't know if they still did them.

Here's his father – a demob suit, clean shirt open at the collar – as he trades outdated army banter with the Woodbine-smoking coach driver, heaving their suitcases into the bus's secret side compartment. Here's the rounded wall of Southwich castle on the way there, same route every year, taken through finger-printed window glass, with him, Mum and the camera spectral in reflection. He sits with his mum, an only child. His father and an over-jolly stranger share the double seat in front.

The four-hour journey had been horrible, mostly on motorways of relatively recent manufacture. He'd sat through closed lanes and LED predictions of delay, his fellow passengers having retreated into earphone-induced catatonia that he had at last understood the need for. Southwich had been bypassed altogether. Its still-standing castle, evidence that lost days had existed, was made hypothetical, and the revised approach to Welmouth went without a first heart-bursting glimpse of distant sea.

At a coach depot open to enormous sky, short-back-and-sided boys with wooden barrows wheel the luggage to a bus stop for two bob. From there his family ride along the breezy front to South Becks. Here's him and Mum, his Vimto and her shandy, perched on deco brickwork in the Admiral Nelson's forecourt while his father saunters down to the camp's paper shop to get their caravan keys, dangling from behind-the-counter pegboard, sunlight slowly bleaching Kodak ads.

This time the coach went straight to Ocean Vista, and the full scale of his error punched him squarely in the face. The Disneyesque holiday franchise had remade South Becks into a cloned resort with nursery stylings and a 'Splash Lagoon', where students dressed as marine animals prowled the reception area, looking for victims to cheer up. For half an hour, he'd waited to check in by the red lollipop that designated his specific caravan block, and begun to realise his mistake in coming here.

He runs ahead between the hummocked vans, tin loaves irregularly spaced on threadbare grass. A rare interior shot looking towards light-flooded windows down at the far end, him and his mum to either side across a central table, her with glasses on and crossword, him with a Ray Bradbury paperback, *The Silver Locusts*. Curtains tied, restrained from the invading brilliance. In a peaked cap that he can't remember, the lad frowns and thinks about his Martian future in the far-off 1990s.

Following a handout map, he'd sulked through the obsessively neat grid of spacious mobile homes to 14A, which was essentially a long hotel room. All of its conveniences he took personally, as losses: modern plumbing vanished the camp's toilet block and its communal standpipes. Electricity erased the gaslight's whispering miasma. He knew these dissatisfactions were ridiculous. He warmed a ready meal he'd brought from home, then thought he'd spend his evening at the Admiral Nelson.

Holidays revolve about this handsome building at South Becks' north end. Its rounded balcony is the rear deck of a brick ship, panes of curved glass there in the bowed façade. Him and his parents sit, year after year, on a low outcropping beside the splintered trapdoor for deliveries, down from the pub's off-sales bar that does crisps and sweets. His mother rearranges a flower-patterned skirt across her knees while he interrogates a bag of Revels, weeding out the orange fondants.

The pub teetered derelict in gathering dusk. He stood bereaved and staring at steps cracked by weeds, at yard walls sagging drunk from the main building. Ocean Vista had bought up the Admiral Nelson and allowed it to disintegrate, pre-empting competition with the site's own-brand drinking establishments. He walked around it twice through settling dark without detecting any Double Diamond pulse, then slouched back to his van for supermarket wine and angry self-recrimination.

Back inside their creaky lozenge, his dad rattles matches, and gas fittings spill an underwater half-light. Sheets and blankets have transformed one of the built-in plastic sofas to his crackling bed, with him slid gleeful down inside as his mum twists the fixture's valve and switches on the night. Rain on the roof like drawing pins and sometimes muffled detonations from the upwind surf. He tumbles into sleep, and even his confusingly planned dream-rooms know they're somewhere else.

Next morning in the unfamiliar trailer he woke anxious, as if something dreadful had occurred the night before, although it hadn't. Breakfasting on smuggled cornflakes, he stepped out to see if the Admiral Nelson's plight might be alleviated by the light of day, but sunshine only made it worse. Half the pub was subsiding as though from a stroke, and its surprisingly unbroken eyes glazed at the empty beach across the road, dunes swaddled in protective chicken wire. He risked a stroll along the front.

With swimming costumes underneath their clothes, with towels and Tizer in a raffia shopping bag, the three of them slope down the concrete ramp on to the sands. First there's the glister of the shore, his father wearing outsized black trunks as he dunks his offspring shrieking in the breakers. Later on, they're up amongst the crumbling hillocks munching sandwiches, a paper Union Jack flown from his castle's bucket turret and cavalry-trim of crusted silicates down everybody's legs.

It was a good half mile beside the seawall into the town's centre, and the whole way he saw nobody on the mesh-bandaged beach. Rising colossal from the ocean seam beyond, stern pylons harvested the wind. Pale lamp posts towered at intervals with strands of unlit bulbs between them, beaded like saliva on a tensile thread of drool. Across a broad road, residential houses gawped at the remote horizon without recognition, as if Welmouth was unable to remember where or who it was.

He drags delighted behind Mum and Dad up King Street, a flamboyant main strip running uphill from the seafront. Here are brightly coloured racks of saucy postcards outside giant emporia of novelty and innuendo. Here, insistent men with thin moustaches, cameras and monkeys. They watch an impromptu demonstration of pink words hand-folded into sticks of rock, and at the top end there's Welmouth Palladium on one side, Louis Tussaud's indecipherable wax museum on the other.

Not yet ready to face Pleasureland or the amusement arcades further up, he'd crossed the road to King Street. Self-consciously seaside, this still looked enough like its old self to make erasures painfully apparent. Inappropriate cards had spread mammary wings and flapped away. Nothing was rude, not apes, not novelties, and local ices were displaced by national brands. The rock factory had gone, and taken Welmouth's sticky spirit with it. Then he saw the freeze-framed waxworks.

Waist-high in a shadowed corridor he wanders, hushed amongst the roped-off dead and their stiff conversations. Not-quite Khrushchev needles nowhere-near John Kennedy, and grown-up dukes and princes are still children here, like him. Uniformed wax attendants, then a living one that scares his mum. Chamber of Horrors, cringing from a rising damp of English murderers – Crippen, Christie, John Haigh and his acid bath, then, worst of all, the man hung by a steel hook through his stomach.

Paying his admission, he heard someone further in say, 'Well, I *think* that's Hitler,' and he laughed, knowing that here at least was genuine, old-fashioned disappointment, unchanged since he was a boy. The Beatles were a malformed Ringo and three Georges. Margaret Thatcher was the sole addition of the last five decades, and the downsized horror chamber had repurposed the hooked man to decorate a poorly conceived torture rack. Even the past's pain, he realised, was misunderstood.

King Street leaks into Welmouth's market, fish and flowers avalanching from its stalls, and accents that are breathed rather than spoken: 'Hhhary'alright?' Dad lugs their shopping to a walled pub yard just off the square, where they can have a drink and a sit-down before returning to South Becks. Here's him with a James Bond hat and mysterious smile, next to a potted shrub. He stands beside his dad to urinate in the gents' toilet, both made silent and uncomfortable by the graffiti.

After the strange reassurance of the waxworks, his perverse elation quickly dissipated on discovering that the market had shrunk to a forlorn veg stand and a place unlocking mobile phones. The square was edged with big-name chains, and he picked up more wine and food from Marks & Spencer's before choosing to walk back to Ocean Vista by a long road angling down towards the front, which he remembered once from real life and a dozen times from over-lit and yearning dreams.

He's thirteen, and his mum and dad have let him traipse back to the camp alone while they stay for another drink then catch the bus. He's got holiday money, and the back roads are where all the eerie second-hand shops are, the corner newsagents with paperbacks that he can't get at home. He finds a narrow place, all wood and windows, with used books and magazines in stacks, in heaps, in shoeboxes, and all their allergenic dust made into powdered gold by long, low sun. Everything shines.

He followed his uncertain memories back to the caravan site, and of course all the beguiling little outlets were no longer visible, if he was even on the right street, if they'd ever really been there. He was grateful, grudgingly, to find an Oxfam shop, and searched with barely suppressed desperation for some washed-up shards of debris from his foundered youth. Absurdly, all he purchased was an old transistor radio like the one his parents had, and, at the shopkeeper's suggestion, some new batteries.

It's there in nearly all the photographs: perched on the fold-out table at the bright end of the van; propped up between the slumped dunes, pouring Who and Kinks and Manfred Mann. In maroon plastic, it's the size and shape of a small handbag with a carrying strap on top. It has two buttons that select for long or medium wave, on/off and volume knobs, and a big dial for tuning, with a silvered speaker like a toy car's radiator grid. Pop voices underline the Welmouth sunshine.

Back in 14A, he snubbed the microwave and cooked his meal in the electric oven as a point of ideology. Depressed, he stayed indoors for the remainder of the afternoon and evening, drinking too much wine and getting angry when he found he couldn't tune the transistor radio properly. The big dial's hairline calibrations squealed between repeated, mournful foreign call signs, bursts of opera, and then, startlingly, irretrievably, a jingle for a pirate radio station closed down half a century before.

Yes, yes, he knows they're not real pirates, but he worships pirate radio, especially here on the coast where the reception's clearer. Caroline is good, but London's best with Tony Blackburn, John Peel, Kenny Everett, Dave Cash. He plugs a plastic acorn in his ear and listens to *The Perfumed Garden* after lights out, thrilling at the thought of DJs broadcasting from listing cabins out at sea, their playlists issuing from a transmitter on the masthead as a pulsing ring of cartoon lightning bolts.

Just 'Wonderful Big L' in electronically inflected tones, and then, though he sat twiddling drunkenly for hours, he couldn't find it. Clearly, he'd misheard or had an auditory hallucination, born of his increasingly disabling melancholy. At last he gave up and went to bed, partly resigned to not locating the right wavelength, partly afraid in case he did. Was this a breakdown? All night he jerked up from tiny nightmares, lost on waking, that nevertheless deposited unwelcome silts, black residues.

At twelve, he sees his dreams as just another district of his life, discusses them like real events with other kids. So many places overlap between their different sleep adventures – the same park, same school, same seaside holidays – that it seems natural to think of dreams as a persisting landscape, a geography. Imaginary Welmouth always there, in rearranged and misremembered avenues when he is elsewhere, thronged with short-sleeved phantoms even in the dead of winter.

He woke with his brain in rags, unsure for a long thirty seconds where he was, and then recalled the radio. Throughout breakfast he caught himself glancing at it apprehensively, and finally put it behind a cushion where he couldn't see it. Even then, he didn't want to stay indoors and keep it company, so he resolved upon another walk along the front, this time past the arcades to Pleasureland. After the flashback jingle, he'd begun to feel that Welmouth was concealing something from him.

There are other memories, pictures that nobody took. The girl his age, one leg in callipers and friends in tow, who propositions him when he's alone and playing in the sand bumps. The precocious local boy who fills him in on 'the white stuff that comes out where you wee', which leads him to confuse urinal cakes with semen. His first and only glimpse of a hydrocephalic child, pushed in a chair under cascading lights, the head impossible, the mother's eyes haughty and furious with love.

Self-aggravated, he stamped down the prom and, passing King Street, carried on. Across the road were the amusement palaces, strung in a flashing, avaricious strip but decorated now with characters from recent fantasy and horror films. He couldn't stand the world, and knew that if some politician – even Enoch Powell or Oswald Mosley – promised to relocate England to the 1960s, he'd most probably be voting for them like a shot. Perhaps fascism was always just weaponised nostalgia?

The seawall he skips along to Pleasureland, ahead of Mum and Dad, is strung with novelties. Sandblasted kiosks, ceilings veiled by a low-hanging fruit of buckets, spades and beach balls. There's a trampoline farm where the greenstick fractures wait around to happen, golf that's inconvenient but hardly crazy, and a model village where the inch-tall people frantically pretend there aren't bored giants everywhere. The pier, the roller rink, and then piped barrel-organ music, Doppler screams.

The miniature urban location spooked him by still unexpectedly existing, like the Radio London jingle. There'd been minor alterations, prurient and inappropriate with nude micro-adulterers on window ledges, although otherwise the open-air attraction was disturbingly unchanged. It was as though the future was avoidable on smaller scales. He thought of his two children, out of nowhere, and then hurried from the barely post-war Lilliput before he sat on its foot-tall town hall and wept.

There's more untaken photos: unidentifiable brown lumps ringed with white legs that screw themselves into wet sand, and jelly marbles like peeled grapes on the flat mirror of the tide-line. There's a bald man looking lost on the night boulevard who stares at him with frightened eyes, then runs away before he can alert his parents. At the Ripley's Odditorium, a murderously angry crocodile endures an extra brass hide of the pennies thrown by little boys, and waits years for its moment.

Exiting the model village, he found other odd survivals. Penny mechanisms had been rescued from the modernised arcades across the street and, trading a pound coin for pre-decimal currency, could still be played. Enthralled, he won a tube of sweets on the spring-loaded bagatelle, and hurt his wrist cranking tin jockeys to the finish line. Most startling, though, were clockwork tableaux under dusty glass, where misers and condemned men re-enacted endlessly their whirring punishments.

The seaside's witchcraft, that attracts and scares him, is inside these boxes. Papier mâché drunks with psoriatic paintwork jolt through cemeteries, assailed by pop-up skeletons. Usurers on minuscule deathbeds spurn retractable do-gooders rattling collection tins, and are next visited by peeling, sunburned Satans. In stiff fits and starts, the prisoner climbs to the tumbril, where a kneeling figurine is substituted. As the blade begins its fall, a pennyworth of light and motion is concluded.

From the dead games galvanised to twitching life, he stepped on to a daylit front, surprised by sunshine. He began to entertain the notion that his missing Welmouth might be flirting, teasing him with glimpses of a gone realm that was somehow still there, immanent, concealed. Perhaps the town was testing his devotion before showing him a magic door back to the place he needed it to be. In this dangerous frame of mind, he ventured out on to the boards of a reconstituted pier.

Peering through cracks into a dark of crash and foam, he knows that this floorboard peninsula exists but on the sufferance of the sea, and even at its iron rail, he feels precarious. A few yards from the mainland it's another country, having different rituals. Briefly unparented, he tries a What the Butler Saw machine, where photographs with nibbled edges topple past the viewing aperture, a monster flipbook, as a fluttering Edwardian drops her towel and steps self-consciously into the bath.

Safer and reinforced, the street on stilts had lost its air of rickety intrusion into plankton territories. The only enterprise of note was a historical exhibit advertised as 'Secret Welmouth', where he browsed an 1892 trunk-murder, a low-resolution sea serpent from 1947, and a curiously dull newspaper story of an unidentified male body washed ashore in August, 1966. He would have been on holiday there at the time, and reasoned this was why he'd read the uneventful clipping twice.

Some images developing in his interior darkroom might not be real photographs at all. Is this his father tutting at the *Welmouth Herald*, saying, 'Did you see where some poor bugger got washed up?' Does he remember paddling in the shallows, squinting puzzled at a distant crowd and ambulance up at the beach's farthest end, near Pleasureland? Or are these pictures counterfeits that place him closer to the morbid action? How much of his past life is a Photoshopped assembly, a director's cut?

He satisfied his sea-air appetite with cod and chips, large, from the fish bar at the pier's end. He licked slippery and steaming white flakes from his fingers, just as good as ever, and once more caught the elusive spoor of Welmouth as it should have been. Tracked up the strand in sightings of hand-lettered signs and bleached pavilions, this led only to the shock of the abandoned roller rink, its smooth expanse cracked now by thrusting fists of dandelion, the tannoy tower rusted and silent.

Welmouth spins about him, gold and blue, and in a crackling tin throat, 'All You Need Is Love' passes some brink where music is no longer separable from movement. Under whirling sky, in this Newtonian ricochet of children, there's no more to him than lyric glide. Mum stands at the perimeter, smile blurring by at intervals, a number on his clock face. As the song begins to fade, collapsing into other tunes, even back then he's made nostalgic by 'She loves you, yeah, yeah, yeah'.

Caught in a drift of roller skates, ex-missus and drowned strangers, Pleasureland was on him before he expected it. The turrets at its entrance stated flatly that his jet age was now medieval, while beyond them, painted-horse accompaniments and voices swirled in an acoustic maelstrom. Candyfloss and frying hot dog onions snagged olfactory fish hooks in his nostrils. He recalled his youthful sense of the amusement park as a colossal, single animal, and wondered if it would remember him.

Although he can't articulate the thought, he knows the seaside isn't real. The yearning winter daydream is the only Welmouth, the imaginary jailbreak from work, school, behaviour, and all but unbearable existence. The resort is only there as a suspension of the world and all its laws of what's allowed to happen. From the waxworks to the blondes on postcards, Welmouth's built from nothing else but inland fantasies. There rests its irresistible allure, and also its faint scent of hungry menace.

Past the gates, he was engulfed in stretched sound, sequenced light and families that floated by in straggly genetic clumps. Unchanged above, the giant wheel turned like time or fortune, and a rollercoaster alternated between ratcheted suspense and plunging terror, but there were omissions: no more mirror maze with people lost amongst themselves, no House where Fun was an upskirted wife. The ghost train had likewise been exorcised, though in truth Welmouth was all ghost train now.

He panics in the hallway of reflections and headbutts a self who's running in the opposite direction. The trick floor beneath him slides both ways, like memory, making forward progress difficult, and on the scary train his eyes are shut for the whole ride. Pleasureland's personality, he thinks, is jocular and spiteful with a cruel heart under its striped blazer. The big prize is unattainable, the children vomit excess motion, and in crystal cases leprous sailors can't stop laughing.

Shuffling in amongst the stalls, he didn't know why he had gone there or what he was meant to do. Bent-barrel rifle ranges had been done away with, and there were no longer ducks to hook. Paused at the top of the Big Wheel, he noticed a procession of Down's syndrome youngsters with their carer, trudging gravely on the beach below, their shadows lengthening behind them. It was later than he'd thought, and back on solid ground he was just heading for the exit when he found the snails.

Him and his mum and dad enact this slow tour every year, for want of any other family traditions. Pastel gastropods with lines that might be smiles on their vestigial faces, front half of each shell gone to allow for seating, they roll mounted on a track through grotto tunnels, out into the open air and the indifference of the public, unspectacular and yet dependable. The stiff antennae look like radio aerials, and he supposes that the metal rails they travel on are their silver calligraphies of slime.

Unable to resist, he bought his ticket from a very old man with a strawberry blemish under his left eye, who showed him to his steed and clunked the safety bar over his lap. Leaning across to do so, the attendant shared a carious, overfamiliar grin and said, 'Hhaaah, oy remember you, boy,' but before he could respond or ask the ticket-seller what he'd meant, the snail car was already moving off, into pink-lighted artificial catacombs with glistening mucous walls and oil-flavoured air.

They take the same ride every holiday, their crawling pilgrimage, until inside the twinkling passages he can no longer tell which year it is, or even if these annual excursions aren't all just the one year, happening again. Although there are still dates and days, the whole two weeks in Welmouth go on somewhere outside time, and have no consequences. Trundling with his parents in the ancient life form through synthetic caves, their offspring is pressed breathless between past and future.

Halfway down a mock-stone throat, it came to him that all of this had been a really bad idea, a spasm of bereavement and divorce. His almost faceless chariot took him, at its own excruciating pace, down corridors of his decrepit yesterday, on predetermined lines into the blind of an upcoming bend. He never should have come here, should have left it as an overexposed memory, but now it was too late. Points in the track ahead diverted him into a side shaft that he wasn't sure if he remembered.

In the photograph he's laughing on the snail, showing his overbite, but he's alone. And yes, of course he is, because his mum and dad must be outside to take the picture when the car emerges into daylight, but how can that be when he knows that they all three share the ride, each year the same? He feels for them beside him in the rattling pink gloom, but they're both gone. He's on his own, inching through twilight mines of recollection that are only his, and, other than himself, are empty.

There was something wrong, and his discomfort mounted with each yard of his advance into the glimmering sinus. He was almost certain that this unexpected branch line hadn't been there on his previous visits, but then lots of things that he felt sure of turned out not to be as he'd construed them. Up ahead, it looked like there were lighted alcoves set beside the track that he had definitely never seen before. Or had he? He began to feel extremely nervous, shifting in his seat, and tense.

In the first recess is a little girl, at first mistaken for those child-shaped Spastics' boxes once so commonplace, but this is different. There is still an iron brace imprisoning one leg, but this girl's older, twelve or thirteen, and is not soliciting donations. Standing in fine sand against a cloth of poorly rendered dunes and sky, she lifts her hem with one stiff hand to show the dusty, painted knickers. Flaking plaster lips curled to a knowing smirk, blind eyes smug with unmentionable secrets.

Stomach plummeting, he doesn't understand. Something has changed, here in the juddering shadows, and his situation seems now more uncomfortably immediate and real, thudding against his breast. He knows that things will only become more unbearable from here on, but he's trapped. He can't do anything to stop the ride and can't dismount; there isn't room. With its expression made inscrutable by the eroding years, his carriage drags him inexorably towards a second inset cavity.

Here, on floor papered to resemble paving slabs, its backdrop mimicking the seafront's night lights, sits the model of an infant suffering from something previously known as water on the brain, strapped in a reconstructed pushchair. The boy's skull is swollen to a thin skin bulb, the size of which exceeds that of the face below. Paused always at his trompe l'oeil kerb, the little figurine's expression holds a look of managed disappointment that shades into an appalling and unanswerable wisdom.

Deep inside, a part of him that fathoms more than he does starts a muffled screaming, hammering against the glass of his fixed stare. He hardly knows what's happening, only that it can't be, and there's nothing he can think or do that makes this less than shattering, even if he's not sure what's being broken. He reluctantly concedes that it can't be the snail that he hears whimpering, as they progress through subterranean pretence in the direction of what looks to be a last exhibit.

Face down in sand bright with blotted brine, the dead man's shape is soft and saturated, slumped so that a minnow-nibbled head points to the breakers airbrushed in its background. One shoe and accompanying sock are gone, and the revealed white foot is frightful, with black bits of grit embedded in the sodden, corrugating flesh. Around the corpse, inverted sepia saucers lazily rotate the pallid feelers ringing their perimeters, wilfully burying themselves like landmines.

He wants this to be a bad dream, an hallucination brought about by stress, because what else? Uneven walls crawl past in a rose glow, and he resembles one of the chewed-paper damned in their penny-a-go scenarios, creaking to bitter ends through clockwork purgatories. If he pretends that none of this has happened, he can go back to his caravan tonight and then tomorrow he'll go home, leaving his scare and the transistor radio behind. The car bumps through its exit, out into already fallen night.

How can he have been on the ride so long? As the snail stops, he looks for the old chap who'd so disquieted him on his way in, but the late afternoon shift's evidently over and a skinny young man with a quiff now helps him from the slithering vehicle. Spotting a blotch beneath the new attendant's eye, he reasons this must be the other fellow's son, ignoring his sure knowledge that birthmarks aren't generational. He hurries to the way out, through an altered fairground that he's trying not to register.

As he leaves Pleasureland, he gazes fixedly ahead, for his peripheral vision's crowded with things that aren't there. Bright duck-armadas barricade constricted straits, and on blurred balconies eye-corner underskirts blossom to squealing tulips in the updraft. Along skeleton-draped platforms, half-glimpsed passengers await commutes to nightmare, while in glass halls endlessly repeated apparitions meet in silent confrontation. Since he notices no LEDs, even the dark is the wrong sort.

Out between phony castle gates he blunders, heart still thumping and the night draft stippling bumps on his bare arms. He isn't so much thinking as colliding dodgems of incomprehension, and he startles at the overwhelming blackness of the seafront, sparse illuminations burning lonely on the sagging vine. A ginger-haired lad overtakes him, carrying a presumably just won stuffed toy, a lion-headed figure in a football outfit that he only narrowly contrives to keep himself from recognising.

Painfully protracted, at a snail's pace, it occurs to him that this is what he'd wanted. This is Welmouth as it was. Avoiding an ice-blue Ford Anglia, he finds himself on the arcade side of the avenue, across the road from the seawall and blacked-out beach. Moving against the frock-and-jacket current of an ambling crowd, he gapes in awful wonder at the puddled light around a cockle stand; at the huge billboard head of long-dead Jimmy Clitheroe, now playing at Welmouth Palladium.

The town was never flirting with him, didn't need to; it reeled him in using the hook and chain it had through his intestines. All the years he's thought it irrecoverable, it's been waiting here, a penny-plated crocodile. Spectra of coloured bulbs adorn his hairless crown, and from an isolate portable radio, a young Mick Jagger comments on the drag of getting old, as if it were a lifestyle choice. Coins sour the breath of the amusement parlours and his ears are ringing, distant fire alarms.

He sees them only yards ahead – the man, the woman and their little boy – stepping away into a dimly lit pub garden overshadowed by the Hippodrome. There's something in the couple's gait that stops him dead, the husband breezy with hands in his pockets, the wife lapping side to side like water. In their hard-to-place familiarity is something unaccountably alarming, then the twelve-year-old trailing behind them turns around to look at him, and he is speared by catastrophic understanding.

Shaking his head like a rear-window dog, he backs away before he's pointed out to the child's parents and makes all this worse. Breathing in sobs, he reels across the busy street between the Minis and the Vespas, hurdling from seawall to sand, unnoticed in the screaming need to get away from this fond horror, all these lights. Footfalls crunch damp beneath him in the panting black amongst the dunes, although ahead the running's smooth down to a crashing, drumbeat ocean.

When he wasn't there at work the Monday after and his phone was switched off, concerned colleagues calling at his flat reported no one home. His wife and kids were contacted, but had no clue as to his whereabouts. Eventually, police recovered some belongings, mostly clothes and an antique transistor radio, that the Ocean Vista people had retrieved from his deserted caravan. Though there were all the obvious speculations, his remains were never found, or, anyway, not subsequently.

WHAT WE CAN KNOW ABOUT THUNDERMAN

FOR KEVIN O'NEILL

1. (August, 2015)

Through the front window of Carl's Diner, Tuesday afternoon was bleeding out. Under a pimple-incubating light, amidst yellow Formica dulled by thirty years' ennui, the Supper Club of Infinite Earths squeezed into a family booth and put the many worlds to rights.

All four were writers, obviously – Jerry Binkle, Dan Wheems, Brandon Chuff and Milton Finefinger – since writers had much more invested in the finer points of comics continuity than, say, artists or colourists. Artists and colourists, as universally revered publisher's son-in-law 'Satanic' Samuel Blatz had oft expectorated, only had to draw the stuff you told them to and not go over any lines. They didn't need to know that it was just the 1940s Moon Queen who could turn herself to moonlight, or that energy-directing teenager Bronze Bolt was Thunderman's son from another timeline: didn't need to know, and, in the Supper Club's opinion, didn't truly care.

'It's like they don't see why the continuity's important. They're all, "So who gives a fuck if Mr Ocean's mom and dad came from Atlantis or Lemuria?", and I'm all, like, "Hello? The kid who you once were, pal, that's who gives a fuck. The kid who worshipped Mr Ocean, and who wanted to know everything about him, just so some asshole like you could come along in twenty years and change it all." All these revisions, what they're doing is they're making that fan knowledge that we worked so hard to learn into, almost, I guess, kind of a pointless waste of time.'

Dan Wheems and Milton Finefinger, feigning engrossment in their food, briefly locked eyes over the centrally positioned condiments. It was well known that 'Merry' Jerry Binkle, founder of this weekly gathering, was way too into Mr Ocean. Binkle had resigned from a high-paid position at American when they cancelled his *Ocean's Depths* miniseries after issue three, and was now back with Massive doing Beetle Boy and a whole bunch of contraindicated medicines.

His mouth still numb with novocaine from the dental appointment earlier, Wheems risked a lateral glance at famously impassive Brandon Chuff, seated beside him. Binkle was the oldest of the four men, but as editor-in-chief across town at American, Chuff was the Supper Club of Infinite Earths' senior member. As he sat and listened now to Jerry Binkle's remonstrations, Chuff was staring at the jaundiced tabletop with a quiet smile that meant, 'Well, I know better, but I'm too disinterested in what you're saying to correct you.' Wheems assumed that he was thinking back to the *Unending Brawl* crossover at American the summer before last, where, marking his own homework as the reboot's writer/editor, Chuff had revealed both Mr Ocean's jellyfish friend Fufu and his sidekick Ocean Kid to be false memories implanted by the Didn't Happener. Outside the diner, a profound blue gradient was established with, beyond the light pollution, a conjectured star or two.

Wearing the perma-smirk inflicted by Bell's palsy that made every utterance seem needlessly sardonic, Milton Finefinger, still stinging over the delays to his book *Union* caused by the Arvo Cake disaster, ventured here an interjection into Merry Jerry's enervating monologue. 'I heard how Sherman Glad came up with Mr Ocean when he visited a seafood restaurant called that once, in Boston. Of course, how Glad told it' – Milton's laugh was four snorts detonating somewhere near his sinuses, hnohh-hnohh-hnohh-hnohh, like that – 'he had this boyhood dream where he was drowning and got rescued by a strangely well-groomed merman. Now, that doesn't sound like what you'd call a *dry* dream, you know what I'm saying? Hnohh-hnohh-hnohh-hnohh.'

Jerry tucked his chin into his neck and crumpled an increasingly high forehead.

'Milton, you and I have had this conversation. As you know, in 1962, I interviewed Glad for my seminal fan publication, *Hooded Vigilante*. Visited his house, met his wife Gail and everything, when I was, like, this fifteen-year-old boy. It was when I asked how he'd come up with the Streak, Gold Eagle, Mr Ocean and the rest, that he made the since legendary statement that they'd come to him in dreams. He claimed the dreams had been transmitted from some other place, a parallel world or Ideal Platonic realm or something, where the things in Sherman's stories were all really happening. OK, that's maybe just a thing a writer tells a teenage fan, like "Santa's a real person" or whatever, but I thought he seemed sincere. And as for being gay, you wouldn't think that if you'd met Gail Glad when you were an impressionable youth. She was quite … memorable, if you know what I mean.'

Nobody did, exactly, but a reference to the since dead matron's boobs was their default assumption. With a sneer he couldn't help, Finefinger took another forkful of his Slippy Joe, which was an ordinary Sloppy Joe that had a quarter pound of butter melted over it. Dan Wheems attempted to pick up the conversation with an anecdote about either a character called S-Man, or, possibly, something about eczema: Dan's mouth wasn't working for some reason, so nobody understood a word that he was saying but kept on smiling and nodding as they waited for him to run out of steam.

Finefinger took a peek at Brandon Chuff, seated across from Binkle, wondering what was going through the mind of the ursine fan favourite as he gazed into the table's primrose sheen. From the ironic smile that played around Chuff's pursed lips, Milton speculated that he was most probably considering the fate of Sherman Glad. A pulp science fiction writer moonlighting in comics, Sherman had created many of American's best known and most enduring characters, but then in 1965 had tried, with other scriptwriters, to form a union. Needless to say, Glad and those other old guys were immediately fired, replaced as writers by an eager swarm of youthful comic fans who, grateful to be living out their boyhood dreams, seemed unaware or unconcerned that they were putting previously lionised creators out of work. Out went the grizzled 1950s hipsters like James Flaver, Edward Hannigan, and Sherman Glad, who'd made ends meet by grinding out genre-specific paperback pornography following his defenestration at American. In came the teenage/twenty-something King Bee and United Supermen enthusiasts like Jerry Binkle, Ralph Roth, David Moskowitz and Brandon Chuff. All said, Milton concluded, Chuff had no shortage of things to smile about.

Outside, through a front window that enclosed the scene as though within a panel border, up above the garment warehouse opposite, the sky was now a minimalist study by an artist unafraid of black space, with a dab or two of perfectly positioned white by which occluded forms might be deciphered. Telegraph poles. Wires and water towers. Cross-hatching in an alley's rotten yawn.

Amidst the yellow dazzle of the restaurant interior, a patient Jerry Binkle pushed his gold-rimmed glasses further up towards his barely there blond eyebrows.

'Dan, correct me if I'm wrong, but you seem to be talking about Esme? Esme Martinez?'

Dan Wheems gave two thumbs up and nodded vigorously, massively relieved that someone else could now pick up the thread of discourse and unburden him of the necessity for his slurred glossolalia. Celebrating this reprieve, the two-time Sammy Award winner (for his controversial run on Massive's *The Vindictives*) stuffed a largely unresponsive mouth with three more storeys of his High-Rise Burger, and left Binkle to unpack Wheems' unintelligible tribute to Esme Martinez.

Given that Dan's outburst had been prompted by Binkle's enthusiasm for Gail Glad, Jerry was fairly certain that its topic had been Esme Martinez's own physical attributes, which were considerable. A genuinely beautiful girl from Hispanic stock, Martinez was one of, at most, two or three women to have worked as artists in the industry as it was in the fifties and the sixties, slaving in a windowless room full of men, while getting pawed and putting up with it. Luckily, Jerry saw a way that he could get the conversation back on track without having to mention anything like that.

'Now, Esme – and as your gestures implied, Dan, she was a most pulchritudinous example of the more delicate gender – Esme was to my mind the best penciller that Mr Ocean ever had. Don't tell John Capellini that I said that, obviously, but all those years ago, when Mr Ocean was the back-up feature in *World's Best Adventure*, the stuff Esme could do in those little six-page stories was incredible! I mean, come on! "The Death of Fufu", anybody? Or the one where Mr O and Ocean Kid face off against the Mr Ocean of dimension thirteen who's, like, seventy feet tall with violet skin? People don't realise, all those characters still in the continuity today, like Hammerhead, or Lady Prilla of Lemuria, or places like the Oceanarium, those were all Esme's work; Esme's designs. I never ran into her back then, but Sol Stickman told me how he'd heard could be she was a lesbian.'

Milton Finefinger waved his overburdened fork dismissively. 'Sol Stickman said that about everyone who turned him down. That married woman in accounts with two kids, Linda? Lesbian. The female colourists? All lesbians. He even once said Mimi Drucker was a lesbian, which is like saying a piranha's vegan. Hnohh-hnohh-hnohh-hnohh.'

Everybody snickered except Brandon, who maintained his unassuming smile and his perusal of the daffodil Formica. Miriam Drucker was the VP at American, and though she clearly had enormous psychological and sexual issues, insufficient hetero-sexuality had never been considered one of them. Dan Wheems chewed thoughtfully on an especially recalcitrant slice of tomato, possibly from his High-Rise's brioche penthouse, and took a long sideways look at Brandon Chuff, hunching there next to him over an untouched plate of spicy wings.

Chuff's quirky little grin seemed now lascivious and, Wheems thought, faintly nostalgic. No doubt 'the respected *Blue Beam* and *United Supermen* auteur' (*Collectors' Fugue* #247, August, 1998) was reminiscing about all those famous New York comics-business orgies of the early seventies that Chuff and Binkle and their fellow fans-turned-pro had certainly attended. Gnawing with renewed determination on his gobbet of unyielding salad fruit, Dan recollected hideous anecdotes he'd heard over the years concerning these industrially lubricated get-togethers, drifting as he did so into a light trance of nightmare and arousal that was not entirely unfamiliar to the multiple Sammy recipient.

He masticated furiously, imagining the porno-Bosch tableaux that these assemblies of hormonal toddlers must surely have comprised: Pete Mastroserio, the up-and-coming editor at Banner Comics who'd moved to American around then, a moustachioed ground sloth that Dan Wheems could only picture, naked, as a limitless expanse of coarse-pored flesh, hairy and glistening, devoid of shape, or limbs, or orifices; Mimi Drucker, pre-analysis and dressed by all accounts in Moon Queen platinum wig, crescent headband, silver knee boots and coiled lunar whip, with her ecstatic cries presumably announced in that alarmingly deep voice she had; an even back then elderly Sol Stickman, like an unshelled turtle with his skin in hanging pleats, prehensile tongue plumbing the trachea of a front desk receptionist to a shrill soundtrack of contemporary disco favourites; a copy of *Exciting Comics* #1, disastrously left out of its protective Mylar bag and ruined by ejaculate.

Wheems shuddered. He'd entered the industry some ten years after that, with AIDS becoming part of the vocabulary, and such gatherings since relegated to an unimaginable fairy-story past. He was at once disturbed and envious regarding the much greater sexual opportunity enjoyed by older hands; the easy confidence with women that, it seemed, came naturally to company employees and freelancers of that stack-heeled vintage. Brandon Chuff, for instance, had until quite recently served as American's overstuffed casting couch, upon which an enthusiastic bounce or three might transform the successful applicant into proofreader on *Omnipotent Pre-Teen Militia*.

Well, that bulbous sliver of tomato wasn't giving up any time soon. Emerging from his horrible erotic reverie, Wheems noticed that one of the several small boys seated with a youngish woman in the next booth down – some kind of birthday party pizza treat, he fuzzily assumed – was staring at him with the ghastly and incredulous expression that Dan had become accustomed to from persons of that age range, without ever really understanding why he should elicit it. Closer to home, across the marigold veneer, Milt Finefinger was engaged in an almost indiscernible passive-aggressive struggle to the death with Jerry Binkle, who was volubly defending Mimi Drucker.

'Miriam, as I think she prefers, was a completely different person at that time, before the therapeutic breakthrough. And even back then, when she was in a vulnerable state, she totally re-energised American after the Metzenberger years. All the new titles and new talent that came in with her, you can't dismiss all that because of some behaviour that she couldn't help. I mean, I'm not a feminist, but if a man had acted out like Miriam did, nobody would have said a word.'

'Jerry, I think that if a male VP had dragged back every member of a *woman's* basketball team to his office so that he could bang them on his desk, somebody might have raised the subject. Anyway, those new books and new talents, what you're really saying is that Mimi, as she seems to call herself, cancelled *World's Best Adventure* and gave Mr Ocean his own book with you as writer and John Capellini as the artist. I mean, Dan here worked with Capellini on that *Junior Vindictives* thing for Massive, and that's how he told the story. Tell him, Dan. He's … Jesus Christ, Dan! What the fuck?'

From Finefinger's lopsided grin, Dan understood that this outburst was meant ironically, perhaps a jibe about the faintly colourless Wheems' utter lack of any startling unpredictability. He essayed a self-deprecating grimace in response, and as he did so noticed that the boy at the next table was still staring at him fixedly, but was now also weeping. Next, he spotted the undue amount of ketchup beaded on the yellow laminate, on his Ormazda T-shirt, on his cutlery, and on his hands. He realised that for the last five minutes, he'd been gnawing vigorously not at an unripe piece of tomato, but at his insensate bottom lip. Escaping under what his doctor later told him was unusually high pressure, Wheems' blood had gone everywhere. Appalled, he started up a sort of keening sound.

With all the 10 per cent red dot-screen draining from his dumbstruck features, Jerry Binkle didn't have the first idea what was going on. He'd never seen so much gore. This was worse than the notorious double-page spread in that *Rottweiler: The Blooding* special that the retailers had made Massive withdraw. What had just happened? Had Dan Wheems been shot? Had he been poisoned, something in that burger that worked just how poisons did in movies, with the victim spewing blood until the audience got the point? Jerry gaped, speechless, at Milt Finefinger beside him, but Finefinger seemed to find the gruesome spectacle an entertaining joke, still wearing that sarcastic leer.

Disgusted by his younger colleague's callousness, Binkle appealed to Brandon Chuff. If Chuff could move and let Wheems from the booth, perhaps this could be sorted out discreetly in the washroom? The distinguished editor-in-chief merely continued his unblinking contemplation of the tabletop, perhaps reflecting on the old days when the Comics Code Authority could drive publishers from the newsstands for depicting circumstances like their current one. Or possibly Chuff was still musing on the damage he'd inflicted on the Mr Ocean brand with that *Unending Brawl* atrocity. Or …

It was right around this point that everybody realised what the story was with Brandon Chuff.

To be entirely honest, this sudden collective understanding didn't help the situation any, and, in many ways, made matters worse. Dan Wheems, still dripping like a Halloween lawn sprinkler, having by then comprehended that he was trapped in his seat by the expired *United Supermen* scribe, massively compounded things by suffering a panic attack, at which point the traumatised kids with their maybe-mom at the next table started screaming. This attracted Jo, their thick-limbed and assertive waitress for the evening, and right after that came Carl, who ran Carl's Diner but was not the Carl referred to on the place's signage. It was a long story. Jerry Binkle fainted, and the outraged woman with the ululating children's birthday party called first the police and then, after a pause for thought, the paramedics. Dan Wheems, desperate to escape the booth, attempted to shove Brandon Chuff's inert mass out on to the white-and-yellow checked tiles of the diner's aisle, while Carl-but-not-the-signboard-Carl, suspecting that a body on the floor would in some undefined sense be a step too far, pushed from the other side in order to prevent this. The compression of their combined efforts caused Chuff's spectacles to fall into his spicy wings, and Jo the waitress slapped Milton Finefinger for what she perceived as his mordant insensitivity. Seen from outside the restaurant, this dreadful moment was enfolded by the nearly square front window's perfectly ruled frame with, presently, blue lights and lettered siren sound effects intruding from off-panel right.

But, anyway, so that's how Worsley Porlock got his editor-in-chief job at American.

2. (August, 1959)

1959, at the tail end of Eisenhower's incumbency, society was like a big, clean car there by the kerbside with its motor turning over but not really what you might call going anywhere. The decade, though eventful, registered as somehow indeterminate and nobody was sure of anything. Aged five, Worsley couldn't decide how he felt about Saturday. Was it his worst day, or his best?

The reason why it was potentially his worst was it was Saturday, right after lunch, when Worsley's dad would call by at the house to pick him up, so that the two of them could spend some time together. Worsley liked his dad OK, and sometimes they had fun, but the perennially anxious child had come to dread the weighted conversations, brief but stomach-churning, that his parents would unfailingly contrive on these occasions. The front doorbell would abruptly blurt its two-note warning chime, and then it was all Hi it's me and I can see it's you and that bare-knuckle timbre in their voices. Mom would grudgingly invite his father in while Worsley got his coat on, and there'd be a dogfight interchange above the radar of his ready comprehension. Is that perfume? I don't know, you tell me; is that Scotch? And then inevitably money, is this all, and Christ, Jean, what do you expect, I've told you there's no overtime.

When this exchange ended in bitter armistice, he and his dad would go out, sometimes to the park and once a ball game, but most often to a movie where they didn't have to think of things to say to one another. When they did talk, it was only ever, so, sport, did your mom have any visitors, and, well, there's Mrs Stevens from the place she works came round, and, yeah, but any guys, and, I don't know, I guess, and then a burning silence for a while.

The reason why it was potentially his best day was that after their excursion, be it to the penny arcades or a feature at the gently faded movie house, they'd always end up at Mr and Mrs Salter's five-and-dime store, two or three blocks from his mom's place. This, for Worsley, was a holy wonder. It was something in the smell the place had – newsprint, candy, floorboard wood and metal polish – or its tingling, inarticulable atmosphere; the falling talcum quality of afternoon light through the storefront's dusty glass, although back then he hadn't thought to differentiate between these separate phenomena. To him, it was all just the store and how it felt, which was cheap heaven down the street.

Ray Porlock, in his sandy pants and jacket and already looking like somebody in a creased old photograph, would every time approach the counter with a kind of carefree ranch-hand amble that Worsley had never seen his dad use anyplace but Salter's, like it was important Mr Salter see him as an easy-going cowboy without any clouds on his horizon. Mrs Salter, for some reason, never seemed to be around. The fortyish assembly worker always got a Coca-Cola for his son and a fresh pack of Camels for himself. He'd then pass the mom-contoured bottle, opened and with a wax-paper straw, to Worsley along with between a quarter and a buck, depending on how work was going. Him and Mr Salter, if there weren't too many customers, would then go to the far end of the counter so that they could talk and laugh about things while they had a cigarette together. His dad would call Mr Salter Ted, and Mr Salter would call his dad Joe, because he got a lot of customers and called them all that to save time. Their smoke hung in lassos of blue and brown and had a bitter smell that, from the parchment-coloured Camels packaging, Worsley assumed to be Egyptian. He would take his Coca-Cola and his money, seventy-five cents in this prosperous instance, to the store's other extremity down by the door where the sun smashed through the front window, long gold bars that broke to powder on the ballpoint pens and flashlight batteries and cards of darning needles.

Worsley's Coke was one homogenous experience – the fruited coffee taste, the sneezy carbonated sting behind the nose, the elegant sky-written white swoops of the lettering, the ghostly green tint staining the voluptuous glass hips – and was fulfilling physically, emotionally and psychologically, a vital part of his young life there in America. But for all that, it was the seventy-five cents that thrilled him to his crew-cut follicles.

The magazine rack rose away from him, cliff-face of an impossible new continent, its glossy journals and their marvellous calligraphies ignited to stained glass by pouring sunlight and made a religious vision. In the top-shelf dazzle at the crest were the unnerving catalogues of adult mystery, with names like *Spank* and *Cad* and *Spicy True War Stories*, covers wriggling with ladies who were coloured photographs or drawings but were always in their swimsuits or their underclothes, smiling with beach balls or else torturing the sweat-beaded GIs they'd taken prisoner. Beneath this mystifying and salacious pinnacle, in the display stand's middle reaches, was a scree of periodicals like *Saturday Evening Alert*, *Embittered Mechanic*, *Centrifugal American* and an issue of *Nutcase* with its mentally impeded mascot Wilbur T. Floyd dressed up as a beatnik on its beautifully painted front, these being less alarming than the magazines above but no more comprehensible. And then, down in the foothills at the bottom and thus perfectly positioned for the paediatric line of sight, there were three whole shelves which, electrifyingly, were totally devoted to that month's new comic books.

If the store's door was standing open on its cleverly devised brass elbow, if the breeze fluttered a colour-saturated cover, then they were like big exotic butterflies pinned for a natural history exhibit. Almost certainly by chance, the vertical arrangement of the books by different publishers, for Worsley, made the rack a smoothly graded spectrum of disinterest and barely understood desire: towards the store's front window on his left, Mr or Mrs Salter had arranged a stripe of jokey pamphlets from both Blinky Publishing and Bullseye Comics, with the former being the adventures of partially sighted high school student Blinky and his friends in *Blinky's Blind Dates*, *Blinky's Trips 'n' Tumbles* and *Blinky's Haunted Asylum* that had gags about voodoo and werewolves. Bullseye, on the other hand, from Worsley's five-year-old perspective, seemed to just put out a lot of stuff for little kids. There was *Obese Olivia*, *Stripe-Crazy Sue*, *Armed Combat Laughs with Gloomy Grunt* and *Aubrey Avarice the Tiniest Tycoon*, along with the infant mortality genre that seemed unique to Bullseye, like *Cardew the Spectral Child* and *Dead Stuff, the Tuff Little Zombie*.

Slightly to the right of these there was a three-shelf band of titles from the smaller companies that Worsley was inclined to take more seriously but still didn't really like: comics about everyday real things like cowboys, war and monsters. There were Banner Comics, turned out on a press normally used for cereal boxes and in consequence almost unreadable, printed with a potato on a fibrous, unrinsed dishcloth. Their insipid list included *Fighting Men in Love*, *Space Vet* and *A-Bomb Squirrel* for the less discerning younger reader. Under Banner came a line that didn't seem to even have an imprint, but upon inspection turned out to be from a company that had been called Punctual Comics in the 1940s, then became Goliath, and within a year or two would change its name to Massive. These, in 1959, were westerns such as *Tombstone Kid*, *Kid Derringer*, *Kid Cody* and *The Cactus Kid*, who seemed to shoot a lot of guys considering they were only kids, and then there were Goliath's mystery comics – *Journey into Strange*, *Tales of Astonishing*, *Abnormal Tales* and like that, that had giant monsters made of weirdly textured things like coal and wool and gas, with names like Zim Zam Zub or Klorg the Mushroom that Walked like a Man. They looked sort of intriguing, but the artists used a lot of black, so Worsley nursed a general suspicion that they might be meant for older boys than he, for unshockable nine- or ten-year-olds hardened by life, who wouldn't find Klorg sinister or harrowing, nor face his gilled, collagen-based monstrosity in their next several weeks of dreams.

At the store's other end, his dad and Mr Salter were still gabbing in their tangle of Egyptian smoke, and Mr Salter said so then the kid goes Lady if I put a penny in the slot and press the button will the bells ring, and his dad said yeah, yeah, that's a good one I gotta remember that and tell the other fellers on the line. Outside a truck backfired and faintly, down the street, someone's transistor radio was playing that one tune that Worsley liked, with how the floor fell out of this old guy's car when he put the clutch down, which, if Worsley understood the song correctly, had been caused by magic. Though, without a word for the gratification that he was deliberately delaying, he inched slowly to the right and didn't let his eyes fall on the treasure lode until he stood there right in front of it, could almost feel its toybox colours shining through his shirt and jeans.

American made comic books how they were obviously meant to be. They looked just right, and with that came the implication that the other companies were slightly wrong, or that they'd failed to meet the mark. While it was true American put out a lot of things that Worsley wasn't interested in – for instance, *Conquerors of Mystery*, *Our Unshaven Army*, *Henny Youngman* and their turgid *Perry Mason*, where the poorly drawn attorney looked like a failed cake with angry and accusing eyes – none of this mattered when they also brought about the flimsy miracles that now filled the boy's fixed, dilated gaze.

King Bee. World's Best Adventure. Exploit Comics. Thunderman …

Maybe two kids in Worsley's class would know who Blinky was, but everyone, even his mom, had heard of Thunderman. Thunderman had his own TV show, but he wasn't quite the same on that and couldn't do as much stuff, being just an ordinary actor guy and not the real Thunderman.

The real Thunderman was there in front of Worsley, and was there at several stages of his super-life at once, all inches from a five-year-old face that was underlit with wonder. Here was Thunderman in his own comic, where exposure to arch-adversary Felix Firestone's Random Ray seemed to have left the gold-and-purple costumed hero sporting the magnificent head of a Bengal tiger. Here was Thunderman when he was just a fair-haired kid of maybe twelve or so, imperilled by the similarly youthful Arcturan delinquent Anti-Matter Lad on the front page of *Thunderboy*, while simultaneously being sentenced by a jury of his fiftieth-century buddies, the Tomorrow Friends, there on the front of *Exploit Comics*. Here was Thunderman with King Bee and young pal Buzz in *World's Best Adventure*, matched against a tag team of their enemies the Droll and, once more, Felix Firestone. Sucking up more cola through the barber's-pole infinite spiral of his straw, Worsley considered Firestone's lack of confidence in his own criminal endeavours: during the purported genius's many six-page-long escapes from jail, he didn't even bother changing out of his grey prison uniform, as if he'd given up and knew there wasn't any point.

The man of storms, as his publishers sometimes called him, also featured in *Exciting Comics* (grinning while he arm-wrestled the Greek god Atlas); *Thunderman's Chum Teddy Baxter* (rescuing the junior news photographer from what the caption called 'The Planet of Doomed Baxters'); and *Thunderman's Girlfriend Peggy Parks* (staring appalled at the persistently endangered redhead's latest crazy transformation, with her lower body now that of a gigantic constrictor as 'The Python Peggy Parks'). Worsley was unsure in what sense the sneaky and suspicious radio reporter could be said to be Thunderman's 'girlfriend', when all that he did was catch her when she fell out of a window every other issue. But you'd never see him take her to a movie, or a dance, or put his hand under her skirt like Worsley had seen sometimes-uncle Paul doing with Worsley's mom last month, when it was Independence Day.

Away in Egypt down at the store's other end, his dad and Mr Salter were both talking in gruff voices like they understood things. Salter said he's gonna lose on TV he looks like a bum, we're gonna get that Boston toothpaste ad, and Worsley's dad said sure looks like it anyway, that's who my Jean is voting for I gotta feeling, and then Salter yeah, so anyway Joe how's that going, and then Dad it's pretty bad, and Salter ah she'll come around, and Dad no, no she won't. The two of them were wrapped around by floating yellowed gauze now, mummified in smoke.

Mouth momentarily filled with brown foam, Worsley regarded the remaining titles from American, the ones without Thunderman in. These were *King Bee*, who also starred in *Manhunt Comics* alongside a so-so character called Rocket Ranger, then an uninviting *Moon Queen* where they'd got her bound by her own silver whip to a grotesquely carven alien totem pole, and finally a book called *Comic Clarion Presents* in little letters on a scroll, with under that the Streak, a character – in a white costume and red boots with wings – that Worsley hadn't seen before. He drained his Coke down to the obscene noises at the bottom of the bottle, felt deliciously conflicted over which comics to spend his hot and sticky money on.

They were all so enticing, with their covers lit-up windows on to worlds of blazing satisfaction. All the pictures and the colours printed so much better on the shiny cover paper than they did on the insides, so that each one became a longed-for jewel, with skies of beautifully graded cyan, capes like banners, ochre Kansas dust. He loved the arcane cover furniture, the little disc up at the top left where it said American and Thunderman, the large serrated stamp at the top right that meant the issue was approved of by the Comics Code Authority, the glorious logos hurtling with speed lines or in chiselled platinum on brooding violet cumulus. They had a glaze, a lustre that was metaphysical.

He finally picked *Thunderman*, *King Bee*, *Exciting*, *Exploit*, *Manhunt*, *Thunderboy*, and thought he'd take a chance on *Comic Clarion* and the Streak because he liked the colour scheme, the white and red, like Japanese flags and Coke bottle caps. He solemnly transported his selection and the empty bottle with its sucked-flat straw across to Mr Salter at the counter, where he used up his leftover pennies on the five-cent box of second-hand old comics, not too creased or tattered, that was there beside the register. He chose a battered copy of *Alarming Adult Reverie*, one of Goliath's faintly sinister and bafflingly titled fantasy anthologies for children, where the cover-featured creature, Voom the Inexplicable, appeared to be made out of orange pine cones which made Worsley think he could most likely handle it. He stood on tiptoe so that he could pass his comics, his spent soda bottle and his seventy-five cents to Mr Salter, who called Worsley champ as he was ringing up the sale. The afternoon was humming like a dynamo.

His dad and Mr Salter had by this time stubbed out Egypt in a big glass Johnnie Walker's ashtray that was right there on the countertop. Its boozy late Victorian fop now strode through a volcanic fog of powdered ash with smudges on his monocle, and when you thought about it, Johnnie Walker was a sort of cartoon hero too, one every bit as famed and popular as Thunderman.

Then Worsley's dad, well I suppose we oughtta hit the road, then Mr Salter, take it easy Joe I'll see ya around, then Worsley and his dad walked the few blocks back to his mom's place without saying much. Ray Porlock, his son knew already, never had and wouldn't ever get to live a colourful, heroic life where he was always smiling, saving worlds and winking at the readers. His dad didn't have the right chin, the right attitude, or the right house inside a hollow mountain in the desert. There weren't any readers. None of this was his dad's fault, though Worsley couldn't help but feel that if Ray had just tried a little harder, then his parents might still be together and things would have been OK again. They walked home side by side with neither of them looking forward to arriving. Somewhere up above, a kind of rocket like a spiky iron bowling ball was shooting round and round the Earth that had a Russian dog inside it and was called a Spotnik. Over the tall buildings and the clouds and birds and aeroplanes, the Russian dog was maybe looking down right now on Worsley and his dad, and thinking that America was too sad to drop bombs on.

His mom met them on the doorstep and said did you have a nice time to his dad, but so you knew she meant she hadn't had a nice time and it was his dad's fault. Mom didn't invite his dad inside, but she made Worsley say goodbye and go indoors to take his coat off while the two of them had a hushed, angry talk out in the street. He heard his mom ask if his dad had taken Worsley to a bar, and heard his dad ask why his mom had to be such a bitch, but he was concentrating on *King Bee* #200, where there on the cover someone called Enigma Man challenged King Bee and Buzz in their own secret hideaway, the Hive. He seemed to know their true identities and everything. Guess who I am King Bee or I'll reveal your real name to the world. I just don't want him finding out that you're a lousy drunk. Great Lincoln's ghost who is Enigma Man and how does he know everything about us. Jesus Christ Jean you're a piece of work who's Paul who's

Bob you've got a fucking nerve. How can the droning duo save their secrets find out in The Puzzling Mystery of Enigma Man. You goddamned alcoholic failure go to hell just go to hell Ray. Approved by the Comics Code Authority. And slam.

When she came back into the room, she didn't say a word about what had just happened, nor did Worsley's dad get mentioned for the whole remainder of that Saturday. Which actually was a relief and certainly a whole lot better than the usual well what did he say about me, or the did he slur his words when he was talking did he smell of beer. As the late dark of August slumped on to Wisconsin, Worsley and his mom sat on the couch together and watched *Gunsmoke* while they ate two Swanson's TV dinners, with electric blue light crayoning their faces. After, they had lemon Jell-O and a can of plump mandarin orange segments that the label said came from Japan. Worsley liked *Gunsmoke*, and if it had only had more costumes, robots, masks and special powers, it would have been terrific. As it was, he liked how Marshal Dillon spent the better part of every episode reflecting on what was the decent thing to do. He also felt a great surge of affection for Miss Kitty that he thought perhaps was love, but didn't really know what this entailed, or what he and Miss Kitty might do if they were to meet up one day, except maybe she'd adopt him.

What decided it for Worsley and made Saturday his best day after all was what came afterwards, when he got sent upstairs to bed but was allowed to have his table lamp on and read for a while so long as he was quiet. When the long day was shut away behind his bedroom door, with all its adults and its other people, when he was here by himself then the whole world was Worsley.

He arranged the seven comics – seven and a half if you counted *Alarming Adult Reverie* – face up like giant fortune-telling cards upon his cosy maroon coverlet, then ordered them by inverse preference so he could read his worst one first and work up to his best one last. First up, it hardly needed saying, was *Alarming Adult Reverie*, an inch-long tear in its peculiar cover with the spindly, nervous-looking title lettering and an unsettlingly downbeat colour palette, stony greys and sombre navy in the background, reds and oranges that were more firelight than lollipop. Surprisingly, the stories on the inside, four of them plus a one-page text feature that he didn't bother reading, were all good and nowhere near as scary as their crumpled, threatening-vagrant cover made them seem. The story about Voom the Inexplicable, as an example, turned out to concern a guy who's always lying, saying he's related to the President and so on, so that no one likes him. Then he's caught by Voom the Inexplicable, who wants to invade Earth and asks this liar guy to tell him what defences Earth has got. The guy says we've got vanishing rays, moon-exploder missiles, skeleton gas and atomic daggers, so Voom says in that case he'll leave Earth alone, and everyone goes back to thinking that this guy's a lying jerk, and they don't know he's saved the world from Voom. To Worsley, this was more grown-up and realistic than another Felix Firestone jailbreak, though he couldn't have said why, exactly.

Next most worst was *Comic Clarion Presents* wherein, despite the austere ambulance appeal of that white-and-red suit, the Streak was kind of disappointing. Though the story was believable, with this mechanic guy who gets stuck in a cyclotron so light-speed particles colliding make him just as fast as them, the art was stiff and boring. The Streak looked so rigid when he ran that you'd think he was paralysed, and hardly capable of making it out to his mailbox for the morning paper, let alone nineteen times round the world in half a minute. Then came *Manhunt Comics*, where in the front story, King Bee's master-foe the Droll gives people special poison so that if they smile they die, then tells them jokes, but then the Rocket Ranger story at the back was something about earthquake-guns.

Exciting Comics next, then *King Bee,* where Enigma Man turned out to be King Bee and Buzz's trusted janitor Carruthers with his mind warped by a science-drink, then *Thunderboy*, then *Thunderman,* which usually he left until last as his favourite. This time, however, that much-coveted position went to *Exploit Comics*, which not only promised Thunderboy but also an appearance by his future best pals, the Tomorrow Friends. These, to Worsley's knowledge, had shown up just once before, some months ago, apparently to great reader response, when he'd concluded that the idea of a secret club of super-kids come from whatever century was just about the best thing ever.

First, stringing things out, he read the letters page, Exploit Enquiries, where some know-all kid in Iowa called Mervyn Clarke the Third was asking how come Thunderboy didn't go back in time and stop the alien war that destroyed Thunderland from happening. Worsley thought this was stupid, but in their reply, the editors said that it was a great idea, and that it could be one of their 'Unlikely' stories. These were stories that you didn't count as having really happened, because in them Thunderman did something real unlikely like, say, getting married, having kids, or dying. Worsley still thought Mervyn Clarke the Third and his idea were stupid.

Then he read the story in the back which, being *Exploit*, was most usually about Red Fox, who was a blatant copy of King Bee, with his boy partner Cub, his secret hideout called the Fox's Den, his Foxcar, and about a millionth of King Bee's appeal. This issue's offering did nothing to reverse the trend, and in fact introduced a manservant called Carrington.

And finally, the summit peak of Worsley's day, he read the Thunderboy adventure at the front, which surpassed all his expectations. Much to his relief, he soon discovered that the trial scene on the cover was only a test to see if Thunderboy was worthy to be a Tomorrow Friend, including the balloon where they said they were sentencing the barely teenaged hero to a hundred years' space-labour. The Tomorrow Friends, in their original appearance, had been four kids from a special school for super-children that existed in 4959 AD who'd formed a sort of super-gang or scout troop. The four founding members, Dust Damsel, Expanding Lad, Clock Kid and Sonic Girl, had seemingly picked up a fifth, Paradox Boy, between appearances, and now, with Thunderboy's surprise admission, there were six of them, all being friends in their dome-dwelling and jet-shoed tomorrow.

Worsley couldn't get enough of the Tomorrow Friends. For one thing, they were from the future, so they hadn't not existed yet and might one day be really real. He started to work out a plan, in which he'd write a letter to Expanding Lad or Clock Kid, telling them to come and pick him up at his mom's address in September, 1959. He'd have the letter put in a time capsule with a sign on that said Do Not Open for Three Thousand Years, and then sit back and wait for Clock Kid's flying hourglass to pop out of nowhere and collect him. If he got made a Tomorrow Friend, it would be like he had all these big brothers and big sisters that were the best family in the solar system, and they'd live together in a turquoise dome, and his name would be Thinking Boy because he thought so much.

He finished reading, then got out of bed and placed the seven-and-a-half new comics on the modest stack accumulating there beside the chest of drawers up in the corner. He had nearly twenty now. He climbed back underneath the covers, dutifully switching off the bedside lamp, and snuggled down into the silence and the black. After what seemed like a long time, he heard his mom talking to someone downstairs, on the phone it sounded like. Then, after that, he heard her and he didn't know if she was crying or else laughing at something somebody said on the TV.

And later, Worsley wasn't sure how long, he realised he'd done something really dumb and was now certain to be in a heap of trouble: though he couldn't recall all the details, he'd apparently got out of bed and walked the two or three blocks down to Salter's in the middle of the night, still dressed in his pyjamas. He was looking for the copy of *World's Best Adventure* that he wished he'd picked instead of *Comic Clarion Presents*. Salter's was open, but the lights were out and there was nobody around except for Mrs Salter, standing there behind the counter, staring at him and not saying anything. He realised she must work the night shift, which was why he'd never seen her in the day, and also that she was his mom's friend Mrs Stevens, and that Mrs Stevens was therefore a bigamist. Worsley looked for the copy of *World's Best Adventure* but it wasn't there, and all that he could find, alone save Mrs Salter-Stevens in the creepy moonlight, was a comic where the logo said *Thunderman Gone*. On the front cover, Thunderman was drunk and had a Johnnie Walker bottle in one hand, or maybe Johnnie Walker was there too and trying to help Thunderman stand up, it wasn't really clear. Stood on a doorstep over to the right was Peggy Parks, pointing at Thunderman and looking angry. Peggy Parks had got no clothes on, so that you could see her chest and where she'd got her little pee-pee hanging down, like he assumed that everyone had. Thunderman was saying This is quits and Peggy's speech balloon said You're too late for anything, which didn't quite make sense although he thought he could see what she meant. Worsley looked at the cover and knew that his life was spoiled. He also knew, all of a sudden, that the figure there across the darkened counter wasn't Mrs Salter, wasn't Mrs Stevens after all, and it was awful. It was awful.

So as Worsley whimpered in his sleep, up there over his head, over the bedroom ceiling and the roof tiles and the TV aerial, up near the moon, was where the Russian space-dog sat above the sky in judgement. It looked down on the United States and had its head on one side like they sometimes do, with eyes of caramel regret, and very likely nobody would ever know what it was thinking, because everything that it was thinking was in Russian, and in Dog.

3. (June, 2015)

It was the hottest night of a hot summer, and the long-discredited phlogiston theory of heat as a fluid substance had been resurrected in New York, convincingly. Hot air was pooled six inches deep above the sidewalks so that as he dragged his hefty wooden trunk in the approximate direction of the river, Arvo Cake was wading through lukewarm dishwater that he couldn't see.

Hell of a night. The smearing coloured lights and street cacophonies were an explosion at the Jolly Rancher's factory, a hurtling shrapnel of rear indicators and dim-looking girls with neon hair. Sweating and straining down the avenue, the tow rope rubbing a sore groove into his shoulder, Arvo was surprised to find himself blinking back tears, but, then, this was an awful thing that he was being made to do, to throw away something that he'd once loved, and none of this was fair.

Cerise had given him an ultimatum, about his collection. 'Either all this shit is gone, or I am.' And with women, anything they didn't happen to be interested in was shit, was Arvo right or was he right? He'd tried explaining to her – Christ, practically begging her – about how this wasn't just some comic book nerd thing, some nostalgia thing or how he couldn't let his childhood go; some lazy stereotype that feminists dreamed up. Now he was working at American and inking Byron James for the new *Union* book that Milton Finefinger was writing, his collection was all reference material now. But Cerise had just said, 'Nuh-uh,' a mannerism that she'd got from daytime television and she thought was cute. 'I mean it, Arvo. It's this shit or me.' And here he was.

It had to be, what, three, three-fifteen in the morning? So there were still assholes everywhere, except these were night-blooming assholes and more likely to be unhinged. One passed by him on a skateboard, sailing down the middle of the street while eating an enormous sub. Arvo hauled his trunk, scrape-bump, scrape-bump, past several hundred feet of all-night supermarkets and convenience stores, and every newspaper he saw had headlines about aliens or Elvis or some other junk that wasn't real, like he was in an information blackspot. What looked like a second- or third-generation bag lady was shouting at a barely conscious clerk about the AIDS in bottled water, and the manholes smouldered like inactive sewer-volcanoes, and scrape-bump, scrape-bump, scrape-bump.

Cerise, when he'd first met her, well, around that time she wasn't issuing so many ultimatums. She was shy and insecure about her weight back then, which, Arvo thought, was maybe how he'd got to score with her so easily after a lengthy list of previous disappointments. He'd not told her she was pretty, nor let on what an exciting shape she had, until she'd probably felt he was doing her a favour fucking her and, basically, he was. But then she'd changed, through reading books and articles in magazines, he thought it might have been. She'd started criticising what he said and how he acted, and the last few weeks the business about his collection had gone off-the-meter crazy. And now this. God damn it all, this wasn't what he wanted to be doing on a sweltering June night. Not when he'd got the last twelve pages (and a bit) of *Union* issue one to finish inking before next weekend.

The spillage of a million lights was splashed all over, making night into the radioactive ghost of day, a permanent electric dusk that smelled of farts and screams and hot dogs. Giant buildings crowded in and amplified the oven heat, reducing Arvo to an ant dragging an apple pip with their demoralising scale. Jelly bean prisms, car horns yelling, lens flare where there wasn't any lens. Getting the trunk over the street at crossings was an anxious business, just because the stop signs only gave you so much time and Arvo found himself forced to stoop down and pull the hardwood box by its brass handles, scuttling like a Universal Pictures hunchback.

But to get back to Cerise and how she'd lately started laying down the law. OK, technically it was her apartment. Technically. And yes, when he'd moved in, he'd said the graphic novels would be in her back room for a month or two at most until he'd figured out what he was going to do with them, but, hey, not everything works out as quick as we'd ideally like it to, or perfectly the way we want. Cerise would never comprehend that, Arvo ruefully accepted. Like most women that he'd known, the only comic that she'd ever read was *Blinky*, so she didn't understand the books that he liked, or why Arvo was so set on working in the industry. She didn't get it. Sure, her job at the insurance company was bringing in most of their income now, but in a month or two when *Union* was out, when it was getting all the cool reviews in *Comics Contemplator* and *Collectors' Fugue*, then it would be a different story. Then she'd see that he'd been right, but then, of course, Cerise being the way she was, he knew that that was never going to happen. She was never going to change, not now.

His whole collection. It was like she'd never really known him, never known what those books meant to him, or she could never have just said that: 'It's this shit or me.' To be quite honest, he was probably in shock about all this, now he was actually doing it. He'd put it off a day or three, after her ultimatum, but by then the state she'd got herself into with her demands, well, let's just say that wasn't getting any better, until it was pretty much unbearable just being in the same room with her. And so he'd at last resigned himself to trunk, and rope, and this unthinkable excursion. He loved his collection, and to him the whole ordeal had the proportions of a genuine Greek tragedy.

He wasn't really functioning the way he usually did. He'd known he'd be upset but, jeez, he never thought that it would be this difficult, with him not even thinking straight, and crying, and all that stuff. He was acting how he did in dreams. For instance, there'd been no conscious decision to head for the river, if that was indeed the way that he was going, and he didn't know what he was going to do, exactly, when he got there. Maybe he should do a ceremony of some kind? Ill-humoured egg-yolk taxis struggled by, jostling shoulders, headlights frowning at the constant stop and start.

When he got home tonight, minus his creaking burden, first he'd tidy up and then he'd get right down to finishing page twelve of *Union*'s premier issue, the wide bottom panel where the artist, Byron James, had pencilled the first group shot of the Union of Super Americans, these being the original United Supermen back in the 1940s. When American revived the title in the 1960s, nobody was comfortable with the word union, so they'd changed it to united. What it was, you'd got old characters like the first Streak, the Aeon, Doctor Coffin and the first Gold

Eagle, plus King Bee and Thunderman when they were skinnier and didn't have so many powers or gadgets, and a cuter Moon Queen who took minutes at the meetings. Milton Finefinger and Byron James were giving this a hard-boiled noir twist, like the panel Arvo would be inking later where the first Blue Beam and 1940s Thunderman were smoking. It was almost sacrilegious and the fans would all go apeshit.

Nearby, like a street away, was the asthmatic wheeze of garbage trucks engaged in picking up, and the reverberant clamour of their putting down. Ahead of him were liquor stores, unduly optimistic furniture boutiques, holes in the wall where you got vapes and newspapers, these kids crossing the street, and a patrolman. Grunting with exertion, Arvo put his head down and continued in his Herculean labour, his unwavering trajectory towards a river that was largely notional.

Feeling a need to rise above his body and his situation, he attempted to access his happy place by concentrating on the good things that were going to come out of this *Union* project. Worsley Porlock was their editor, and Worsley was a real sweet guy who didn't interfere and just let everyone get on with making a great book. He was about the most well-known editor working under legendary Brandon Chuff, and was swell company around the bar at a convention. Like, in San Diego last year, Arvo had got to hang out with Porlock, Dan Wheems, and Dick Duckley, who was managing the line of porno comics that *Bordello* magazine was gifting to the world. They'd had the greatest time, and Porlock told this story about walking in on David Moskowitz, the publisher and top guy at American, to find him – get this – sitting in a baby stroller! Moskowitz looks up at Porlock, and without cracking a smile, he says, 'Ain't it a hot night to be dragging that?' Wasn't that just insane? This was the fricking publisher, and he—

'I said, ain't it a hot night to be dragging that?'

It was the cop. A frozen nothingness announced itself in Arvo's stomach, and he didn't want to be there any more. He wanted the whole thing to be a dream, a hoax, or an Unlikely Story.

'Oh! Oh, you were talking to me. Sorry. Miles away. Yeah. Yeah. Yeah, it's a hot night, sure enough. Wouldn't you know it? Right when you've got stuff you're taking to the dump, and it's this, like you're saying, it's a hot night. Boy, tell me about it.' Oh fuck. Fuck, shut up. Shut up.

'So, what you got there?'

Simplest just to tell the truth. In his peripheral vision the word SONY flashed repeatedly.

'Aw, look, I know you're going to think I'm a real doofus, but, see, it's my girlfriend. She said how I'd gotta get rid of my comic books, or she was leaving me.'

The cop did something sympathetic with his forehead.

'Comics, huh? Yeah, I hear what you're saying. When I was a kid, I was a Massive head, with Beetle Boy, the Brute, Ormazda and all those guys. My mom made me burn the lot in our back yard, and after that, I guess I sort of hated her. That's some tough breaks you got, pal.'

To the contrary, this was a better break than Arvo could have hoped. The cop had been a fan. He understood about the kind of night Arvo was having. It was like a miracle.

'Um, actually, I sort of work in comics? I'm an artist, well, an inker. And I've never drawn Ormazda or the Brute, but what I'm working on right now, it's got King Bee and Thunderman in, if you've heard of them?'

Arvo was being disingenuous. He knew full well that everybody had heard of King Bee and Thunderman. The cop beamed like an eight-year-old.

'You're kidding! King Bee, are you serious?' The cop began to sing, in a surprisingly sweet baritone. 'King Bee! King Bee! Watch out criminality, here comes King Bee! He's a prince amongst protectors, and of bees he is the king, and with his partner Buzz, the crooks are sure to feel— ah, God!'

The very little breeze there was had evidently changed directions and it was, as mentioned earlier, the hottest night of a hot summer. So, the cop was retching, and the subject of their conversation changed rather abruptly from a spirited rendition of the *King Bee and Buzz* TV theme tune to stuff more along the lines of, 'Sir, you – Jesus Christ – you need to get down on the sidewalk with your hands behind – hhuch – hands behind your back.' And then, well, a whole lot of things.

This could have been a crisis for American, but by an almost unbelievable stroke of good luck, Todd Permian, who was the colourist on Massive's *Freak Force*, got picked up that same week taking underage boys back to his apartment so that they could see his 'sketches of the Rottweiler', by which it turned out that he meant his penis. While in normal circumstances either company would gleefully have used this ammunition to besmirch their rivals, in this case there was a tacit understanding that it was in everybody's interests to pretend that June had never happened. Officer Barnard received a commendation and a modest pay raise, which at least financed his boxset purchase of *King Bee and Buzz*, with all five seasons finally available on DVD.

4. (January, 1952)

CAESAR ON THE COUCH

(A transcribed session of psychoanalysis with Julius Metzenberger, as recorded 2 January 1952; reprinted in *The Comics Contemplator* #339, October, 2013, with permission from the Metzenberger family.)

(. . .)

JM: Yeah. Yeah, I see what you're saying. No, I guess that's fair. I guess that most of my, my, my acquaintanceships, let's call 'em that, that's going to be the people that I know outside of work, outside the industry. I keep those areas apart, if you know what I mean. I don't got friends inside the business, that's for sure. I know that. I know that I got a reputation, but a lot of that, I think that it's resentment, what you're seeing.

What I've done with Thunderman, they couldn't do that, what I've done since I took over. Thirteen years that fucking thing has lasted, and with this TV show that we got on the horizon, it can last another thirteen, too. You think that little Sammy Blatz at Punctual could do that? The fuck he could. Or that son of a bitch Jim Laws at Scientific? Sorry, at Sensational, they call it now. You think that he—

(...)

JM: Who, Jim Laws? He's the guy puts out those SP books that they got everywhere. Scientific Publications, as it was when James Laws Senior was running things, before that awful business with the, you know. With the piss. God rest his soul. He was an OK guy, you know? He was OK. But sonny boy, Jim Junior, he always was a deadbeat, my opinion. Now he's publisher, they dropped all the worthwhile and wholesome stuff, *The Life of Thomas Edison* and books like that, and now it's all things that are aimed at beatniks, at neurotics. It's unmanly, how I see it. I mean, just the titles that they got, *Sarcophagus of Murder*, *Cemetery of Death*, and then there's *Nutcase* ...

(...)

JM: *Nutcase*, that's their so-called humour title. It's unhealthy shit, is what it is. See, what they do – this is what makes my blood boil – what they do is, they make fun of things. Things everybody knows and likes, things they respect, like TV, movies, strips from out the newspapers such as your *Bitsy* and your *Flatfoot Floyd*, and then there's comic books. Oh, boy, do they like making fun of comic books.

(...)

JM: Yeah! Yeah, that's exactly what I'm saying: they're a comic book, and yet they're making fun of comic books? Of ordinary, decent comic books that are for kids, for healthy boys, and not for juvenile delinquents. You know Blinky? The short-sighted high school kid who's always walking into things? Yeah, well, in *Nutcase* what they did was 'Blanky – America's most featureless teenager', where, like, they've drawn the kid so he's not got a face, like he's a nothing, you see what I'm saying? Like this ordinary kid is boring, then they show him hanging round with kids that Jim Laws and his hophead writers think are ordinary, so they're making out and smoking reefer and all that. And this they think is funny? And then finally – you're going to love this – finally they get around to Thunderman. They call it 'Blunderman'.

(…)

JM: Damn right, I do. Damn right I see it as a personal attack. It's an attack on me, and on American. What those pricks did … OK. OK. So, like in the real book there's Thunderland that gets blown up by spacemen, you know all this, right? So what they do is, they got Blunderland, this crazy-looking thing, they got it blowing up because it ran into a stop sign that's just floating there in space, like that could ever happen. Then they got this little Blunder-baby, coming down to Earth, it gets adopted by this pair of hicks, these sharecroppers, I guess, from Delaware. Now, Delaware, that's where Si Schuman and Dave Kessler come from, the two kids who … well, I should say, they first came up with the rough, unformed idea of Thunderman. Basically, just the name and a few drawings of the purple union suit, you know? So then, there in this *Nutcase* thing, they got these what you might call city slickers showing up, who get these country boys to sign away their rights to Blunderman, so that he can work and make money for these city guys. And these three guys, there's three of 'em, I swear that this is no word of a lie, one of them's meant to look like me, this angry guy, looks like an ape and spitting when he talks. One, he's like Solly Stickman, guy who edits all American's science fiction books, and one, he looks like poor old Hector Bass who does the war books, *Our Unshaven Army* and all those. You see? You see what Jim Laws and those bastards at SP are doing? What they're doing is, they're raking up that stuff where they, Schuman and Kessler, where they started talking about lawsuits. This is humour. This is how they get their laughs. So yeah, damn right I take it as a personal attack. Damn right.

(...)

JM: Well, it's because of jealousy, like I was saying. It's resentment. May they burn in hell. They couldn't do what I've done, at American. You name one other publisher still putting out these long-underwear characters, still making money on 'em. Just ten years ago it was like you could hardly move for all these costume guys. There was the National Guard, Fishman, Silly-Putty Pete and Mr Wonderful – all big names, and where are they now? The Thunderman books that I do, the King Bee books, these are the only masked-man titles anybody reads. Yeah, yeah, there's *Moon Queen* that Sol Stickman handles, but I'm editor-in-chief so I see all the figures and – between us? *Moon Queen* sells a quarter of the copies that I do on *Thunderman* or on *Exciting*. Nobody knows how I do it. Nobody.

(...)

JM: My secret is, I can think like a child. I know the way they think. What I do is, when I'm not in the office, I hang out at schoolyards, soda fountains, any place like that. And if I spot a bunch of, you know, healthy young kids who are out there having fun, fooling around, maybe I'll start a conversation, let it slip that I'm the big boss at the company does *Thunderman*. The way their eyes light up, you ought to see it. Then I'll ask 'em about what they'd like to happen in the book, and maybe they'll say Thunderboy should have a dog like they got, so I give that to my writers, and next thing, we got Zando the Thunderdog. Or maybe they'll say – and these are good-looking, normal, healthy kids is what I'm saying – maybe they'll say how they'd like if Thunderman got in a fight with somebody the same as him but opposite. That's how I came up with Demento-Thunderman, and Thunderman's time-bottle, and all kinds of stuff. I think it's that I kind of have a little boy inside me, in my heart. That's what I think.

(…)

JM: Well, yeah. It's my job. It's what I'm doing all day. What else should I talk about?

(…)

JM: Thunderman? You're saying all I talk about is Thunderman? No, no, see, I don't think that's true. I talk about all kinds of stuff. Is that true, that I always bring it back to Thunderman?

(…)

JM: Huh. Well, put it like that, I guess … yeah. Yeah, that's an interesting point. Maybe I do.

(…)

JM: Hold on … do I identify? With Thunderman? No. No, of course not. Thunderman's for little kids, and I'm a grown man. Why the hell would I identify with …

(…)

JM: Yeah. Yeah, I did say that just now, didn't I? About the little boy thing, but … I don't know. You threw me a curveball here. I got to think about this. Thunderman, do I identify …

(…)

JM: Yeah, yeah, I'm thinking. I guess … one thing that I always liked with Thunderman was how he came from someplace else that got destroyed, and landed in America. So, he's an immigrant. Right there you got a thing where I identify. I never thought of that.

(…)

JM: My family? We came here from the Ukraine, it was more than fifty years ago now. Fifty years, can you believe that? I was just a small child, three or maybe four years old. I don't remember much about it, just what I got told. We had this little shtetl, little village, we were a respected family, by all accounts. My grandfather, he was the rabbi. Everybody, everybody came to him. Not that it made a difference. When the time came, we left just like everyone.

(...)

JM: That was the fucking Cossacks, the White Russians. Personally, I got no memories, but what I heard, those bastards were just raping, killing, burned the whole place down so that we had to ... hey. Hey, I just thought of something: that's my Thunderland, the shtetl. That's, like, that's the place I came from to America, the place that got destroyed by ... Holy crap! The Cossacks, that's the super-criminals, the pirate space-nation that blows up Thunderland. I never realised. I edited the book for all these years, I never realised. How about that? This is really something. This is something right here.

(...)

JM: No, no, I think that this is real important. I'm just trying to think if there was anything ... I guess there's Thunderman's time-bottle. You don't know that? What it is, is Thunderman's got this thing that he keeps at Thunder Mountain – that's his secret headquarters out in the desert. What it is, it looks like it's this big glass bottle, but inside it, Thunderman's got all of the collected light and sound from Thunderland on just one single day back in the past, before it got wiped out. It's just this one day that replays over and over, every time the same in every detail. And Thunderman ... excuse me. This is quite emotional. This ain't like me. His folks, Thunderman's folks, are there in the time-bottle, still alive, and Thunderman himself when he was just a little baby. They're still there, you know? All of his … all his memories he can't let go, I guess. That's like me. I do that. I think about the shtetl, just the little things that I remember, and the memories that I got of my grandfather, just one or two, you know, like little photographs. You'd see the guys out in the grain fields, working up a sweat when it was harvest time. I think about that stuff a lot. My memories, you see, because that place has gone, they're very precious to me. I feel like … I guess I feel that while I keep my memories safe, not everything's destroyed. So, that's it. That's my time-bottle, like Thunderman's.

(…)

JM: Anything else? I'm … I don't know, I'm trying to think. This stuff is very new to me, you know? I'm right now making these connections. I mean, this makes sense, these similarities, my life and Thunderman. It's got to be that way, because … see, all these things that make up Thunderman, the stuff that kids can know about him, these are my ideas! Well, what I mean is, I'm the guy who chooses which ideas get into *Thunderman*. They're my ideas in that sense. How it works, I'll get some writer coming up to me, let's say it's Artie Leibowitz, and he says, 'Mr Metzenberger, I got this idea: Thunderman goes back in time and fights the dinosaurs.' So, I say, 'That's a bum idea. I got a better one. How about Thunderman, he builds himself a base inside a hollow mountain in the desert? Write that story for me.' Then, day or so later, there's somebody else, let's say Heinz Messner, he says, 'I got this idea where these chunks from Thunderland when it blew up have turned into these things called Thunderstones that can be dangerous for Thunderman.' And I'll say, 'That's a bum idea. I got a better one. How about Thunderman goes back in time and fights the dinosaurs? You go away and write that story for me.' See? It's me, the guy who's choosing the ideas. That's why you're going to get these similarities. I just thought of another one. Thunderman can summon up a thunderstorm, right? That's like me, I got this reputation, with my temper. Boy, you get me mad, watch out! There's one writer so scared of me, I won't say who, I hear he keeps a pair of clean pants folded, hanging on a chair for when I call. Because right when the phone rings, every time, he's going to make a shit there in his underwear. Ha. You believe that? There's the power to summon thunderstorms, right there. (LAUGHTER)

(...)

JM: No, no, see, that's just the rough and tumble of the business. Everybody knows that. Everybody knows that, coming in the door. They know what to expect. It's a tough industry, what can I say? You got to toughen up, you're going to make it. And these writers, they think I'm bad, they should see the guys running American when I came in, around ten years back. Some of those guys, even me, they nearly made me shit my pants. Now, these were serious guys. Rat-a-tat-tat, know what I'm saying? I mean, these days they ain't quite so prominent, but back then? Oh, yeah. Yeah, sure. I met Hymie Weiss one time; Legs Diamond ... he was a smart guy, an interesting guy. Had this big picture in his bathroom, it's that pyramid that's got the eye in, off the dollar bill, seal of the Treasury. Strange guy. If you went out to take a pee it felt uncomfortable, like it was watching you, the pyramid thing. Maybe looking at your Johnson. (INAUDIBLE) Anyway, kind of a tangent there. What were we saying?

(...)

JM: Oh, yeah. Yeah, the similarities, do I identify, etcetera. Well, let me think. Hmm. There's – and I ain't sure about this one, it's just now coming to me as I speak – there's the Demento-Thunderman I mentioned earlier, who's like this monster who's the opposite of Thunderman. That's sometimes ... it's like, if something is going well, maybe a, a, a friendship, something like that, something that makes me happy, then, I don't know why I do it, I start acting crazy, like deliberately I'm trying to screw things up, does that make sense? It happens every time, like Felix Firestone turns his ray gun on me and I'm suddenly Demento-Metzenberger. 'What are beautiful, us make to ugly', the whole shtick. And there's another thing …

(…)

JM: No, this is not connected with Demento-Thunderman, this is a separate thing. This is what I was talking about just a minute back, about how I had the idea for the Thunderstones. Now, Thunderstones, what they are, they're these chunks, like I was saying. They're these fragments come from Thunderland when it exploded, when it got hit by the super-pirates' nuclear-ray thing, in the origin. Now, turns out that the nuclear ray, what's based on elements unknown to science, what it's done, it's made these fragments – what they look like is red, glowing crystals, like giant rubies, bigger than your head – it's made them radioactive, but only to people come from Thunderland. Thunderman, Thunderboy, Thunderdog – if they're from Thunderland, it poisons 'em and makes 'em weak, and then it kills them, right? It puts out this pink light what slowly turns 'em pink, and when they turn that real bright pink, they're dead. These fragments rained down on the Earth like meteorites, all burning hot and red, and every month or so, some crook or other – usually it's Felix Firestone – digs one of these glowing crystals up, and uses it to damage Thunderman. So much of that stuff's been dug up by now, you could build Thunderland again out of it, ten times over.

(…)

JM: Well, how this is relevant is what I was just getting to. See, with me, how it is, it's like the time-bottle, what I was saying about memories. Some of the memories I got, I'm what, I'm fifty-six? I done a lot of things. A lot of things. Some of my memories, the ones in the time-bottle, they're real precious to me. Other ones … well, other ones, they're private, you know what I mean? And if some enemy of mine – and trust me, I got lots of enemies – if somebody like that, some Felix Firestone, if they dig these poison memories up, then that could really hurt me, in all sorts of ways. Professionally, personally … it could maybe kill me. These bad memories, these things I don't want digging up, they're like my Thunderstones, you understand? Like they're my secret weakness, how they are with Thunderman.

(…)

JM: What?

(…)

JM: Well, that's just their colour.

(…)

JM: Why was …? I don't know. It's just the colour looked best printed up, is all. It could be any colour, I don't know; it could be blue, it could be green. I don't see why …

(…)

JM: It don't mean nothing. Why does every damn thing have to mean something? I'm wearing brown pants, what does that mean? You got a blue tie on, so, what, I should ask what that means? I don't buy it. What, is everything significant? That clock up there, what does—

(…)

JM: The hell I am! The hell am I defensive! You know what? This is all baloney. Turn that off.

(…)

JM: You heard. This is all so much bullshit. Turn that thing off now, before—(INAUDIBLE)

SESSION CONCLUDES

5. (August, 2015)

The six or seven weeks after the situation at Carl's Diner would have surely been the most eventful ones of Brandon Chuff's life, had he lived. Firstly, there was the incident itself, and then the shocking vagueness of the autopsy, as if the coroner had just said the first thing that came into his head. Next, Chuff's apartment burned down, and then came the shitshow that was Brandon's funeral, where a son nobody knew that Brandon had produced showed up, and Dan Wheems seemed so inexplicably distressed that he gnawed accidentally through the stitches that they'd put into his lip after the Carl's occasion, so they had the whole blood everywhere/kids screaming/Jerry Binkle fainting thing over again. This would, in any normal year, have been as dreadful as it got in the post-mortem Brandon Chuff experience but, as we all now know, that was before what happened halfway through the special tribute honouring Chuff and his efforts, at SATYRICON 2015 in late September.

Anyway, it was the Saturday, right after that upsetting Tuesday evening at the diner, when a still stitched-up Dan Wheems and a still reeling Worsley Porlock went around to Brandon's place to see if there was anything that they could do. Wheems only lived a street or two away, and the late editor-in-chief had given him a key to the apartment, to be used in the event of an emergency. Admittedly, the real emergency had been unhappily concluded four days previously, and so Dan and Worsley were aware of shutting stable doors after the horse had fallen face down in its spicy wings. But, as they saw it, somebody had to check that the premises were still secure, and pick up any mail that had accumulated, things like that. It was the normal, decent thing to do for somebody who'd been a buddy, a more well-known and well-paid professional competitor, and an immediate superior at one's place of employment. In addition, they each privately supposed that Chuff might, just conceivably, have a collection of considerable interest to comics scholars like themselves, albeit just to look at, obviously. And if not comics, maybe there'd be touching personal effects, just some memento of the guy: that pendant that he always wore back in the seventies, or his old Massive Militant Marauder Corps pin with its little pictures of the Brute, the Unrealistic Five and Beetle Boy – items of that variety.

Between them, they'd agreed to make this trip when everyone was sitting stunned and silent in the offices up at American, during the aftermath of Brandon's very public passing. Everybody thought their visit was a good idea, and even David Moskowitz, one of the upstairs people at the company, had said that he might drop by later on the designated Saturday, to pay respects and no doubt to check out Chuff's hypothetical collection. Dan and Worsley didn't talk much as they made their way along the sweltering early August streets to the bereaved apartment, Dan because the stitches in his lower lip made talking difficult, and Worsley because he was trying to process being editor-in-chief, which still felt like a marvellous and only moderately tragic dream. He'd naturally been devastated by Chuff's death, of course he had. Brandon had been both colleague and incessantly demanding boss, almost a bullying step-brother to Worsley, and he would be missed, no doubt about it. But, then, editor-in-chief. But, Brandon. But, then, editor-in-fricking-chief. You can imagine.

Wheems was of a more unsettled disposition. Frankly, after the grotesque display at Carl's the other night, Dan had begun to question many pillars of his previous existence. For example, comics continuity. Was it at all important, in the larger scheme of human life and death? And what about him and his friends, his industry associates? What in God's name had they become? What had this business done to them? How had it happened, and how could Dan Wheems get out of it? Behind all this was the persistent thought that Brandon Chuff's last moments on this Earth had been spent listening to a Jerry Binkle Mr Ocean monologue. Brandon had hated Mr Ocean. For that matter, he had also hated Jerry Binkle. Don't let me go out like that, thought Dan. Please. Anything but that.

His thoughts in turmoil, hardly any of them were to do with Brandon's orphaned comics.

Continuing along the boulevard into the messy afternoon, they were a poorly thought-through paradox; two tortoises without an Achilles in sight. The nothing that they had to say was deafening. Part of the problem was that the two men's relationship, a tenuous one at best and wholly comics-based, was not designed to handle real events like sudden death. In comics, dying was always conditional – there'd been so many tragic ends for Thunderman in the last nearly eighty years, American had brought out two successful *Greatest Deaths* collections.

And another thing with Dan and Worsley was the power gradient, shifting uneasily between the two of them over the Mylar-bagged years that the pair had known each other. They'd first met as teenagers at Jimjon Jackson's BeeCon1 in Albany, NY, although the 1 in BeeCon1 turned out to be superfluous as there weren't any more conventions called that, ever. They wrote letters to each other and met up from time to time for some years after that, attending so many conventions as a team that other fans referred to them as Blinky and his best pal Bottleneck, after the famous high-school duo. Dan, who had back then worn heavy-rimmed corrective lenses, had of course been Blinky. Worsley had been Bottleneck because he was, at that time, taking his first steps towards becoming a recovering alcoholic, which were basically those necessary to become an alcoholic in the first place.

Soon thereafter, Porlock had been given money by his stepdad and had published the fondly remembered, offset-printed fanzine *Comiclasm*, in which Dan had been invited to contribute an opinion column, 'Wheems Screams'. It was the first time he'd seen his work in print; his dry wit got him noticed by the younger freelancers at Massive and American, which ultimately led to Dan getting some script jobs on

American's poor-selling mystery titles, *Tower of Frightening* and *Chamber of Dreadful*. So, this was the first time that their status balance wobbled, with Dan now a pro and Worsley still a fan, but it was not the last time such reversals would occur. To start with, Worsley gave up *Comiclasm* and became a sometime dealer trading in original art, comics pages purchased from hard-up professionals who often did not fully understand their own work's value. Worsley's list of artist contacts soon became immense and his address book legendary, so sought after that when American appointed Worsley as assistant editor on *Exploit* and *Exciting,* nobody was the least bit surprised. This was around the time that Dan had got in that ungodly row with Hector Bass and had to quit American for Massive on war titles that nobody read, even their authors, such as *Captain Tantrum and his Subdued Seadogs*, or the uneventful *Sergeant Distant*. Then, with time and Jerry Binkle's Massive problems, Wheems found himself writing *The Vindictives* and became an overnight fan favourite, although these days maybe not so much. And now, with Brandon Chuff dead in a so-so diner, Worsley Porlock was American's new editor-in-chief. Between them, as they trundled listlessly towards Chuff's residence, they had a lot to think about.

When both feared that their teeming inner monologues might reach some threshold where they became audible, Dan Wheems ventured a conversational opener with, 'Fo, fum orpopfy,' and Worsley turned to look at him in startled silence for a second, then said, 'What?' Raising his voice while still maintaining his unintelligibility, Wheems near shouted, 'I fed, fum orpopfy. For pippy fake, I meme, "fpopped"? Ferioufly?' To which Porlock thought the best response was to nod gravely and say, 'Yeah, ain't that the truth,' hoping that this was in the ballpark.

What it was, at Chuff's autopsy, the coroner returned a verdict that the cause of death was Brandon having 'stopped'. The sum force of the eyebrows raised by this would have lifted a single eyebrow to the moon. When David Moskowitz had hesitantly brought the matter up and listed his concerns, the silver-haired and winningly paternal medical official – who was, by some three years, Moskowitz's junior – had smiled and rested one hand on the publisher's coat-hanger shoulder.

'Well, son, let me put it like this. Was there ever something that you kept around the house and never paid much mind to? Could be it was an appliance, or maybe a pet?'

Moskowitz had just nodded, marvelling at the immediate rapport established by the twinkling and genial mortal adjudicator. Why, he *had* owned an appliance once. The coroner continued.

'Now, I'm guessing that pet or appliance, time to time, you're gonna get some manner of malfunction, like smoke coming out, or it chews up your VHS tapes, or keeps bringing in dead birds from out the garden. Something where you know that it ain't working right, see what I'm saying?'

Moskowitz was mesmerised. He'd never met a New York coroner who talked like this before.

'When you got something like that happening, it's only natural you're gonna want to take the item into a repair shop – or a veterinarian, as it may be – and get it fixed, ain't that the way it is? Now, you can do that once, or maybe twice, but son, there comes a day when it don't matter what you do, you know that it's not gonna toast your muffins or chase after a delivery truck ever again. It's stopped. Maybe you don't know why it's stopped, but then after a while, you get to thinking that knowing the reason why it stopped ain't gonna get it started up again, looks like it's going to the dump one way or other, and it ain't like you can't get another one, most likely off the internet. I guess that what I'm trying to say is, it can sometimes be like that with people, too. We gave your friend a full examination, and in our opinion, there were no two ways about it. He'd just stopped.'

It all sounded convincing, although there were those who couldn't help but feel that Brandon Chuff's was still some way short of the gold standard in death certificates.

Despite their barely incremental progress, Dan and Worsley had reluctantly arrived, by this point, at the place where Chuff had lived, back when he was still doing that. It was a plain, two-storey building that had the apartment on its upper floor, above a recently closed outlet selling diving gear and trading under the name 'Scuba-Do'. Through the dust-cataracted windows downstairs they could see the laminated wraps still covering the walls of the stripped-bare interior, high-resolution seabed vistas where Paul Klee fish mobbed the intricately pitted Max Ernst corals, against peacock tones of perfect blue and green. Wheems briefly wondered if such close proximity to Scuba-Do had fuelled Chuff's scorn for Mr Ocean, then decided that he didn't have sufficient interest in either party to pursue the thought. He gazed into the photographic fathoms wherein gorgeous jellyfish and gum-pink octopi cavorted diffidently, sighed, and fumbled in his jacket pocket for the keys.

He'd never been allowed inside before. Back when Dan had been writing for American before his final interchange with Hector Bass, he'd sometimes walk from his place round to Brandon's in the morning so that he could get a ride to work. On these occasions, he'd seen the exterior – the place downstairs was then a Navy Surplus store; another maritime establishment, Wheems thought inconsequentially – but he had never been invited in. Harbouring now a sense of trespass, both excited and faintly disturbed, he twisted open the stiff lock to find the street door led on to a narrow stairway that ascended to Brandon's apartment proper. Even when Dan had located the switch just inside the door, the flight was only dimly lit and had a yellowing flypaper ambience. Turning from the twilight portal to his waiting colleague, he said, 'Fal we?' Porlock gave this his consideration for a moment, then said, 'What?'

With Wheems in front and Porlock bringing up the rear, the pair laboriously mounted creaking wooden steps into a xanthic gloaming. Halfway up, face down with cover splayed like some crashed bird, a pornographic magazine called *Indistinct Teen Facials* hung half off the seventh stair and flapped dispiritedly, near to death. Beneath a title font that had the children's-menu look of Comic Sans, a half-dressed cheerleader in possibly her fourth or fifth decade lowered her eyes in an attempt to see the matt black rectangle dependant from her philtrum. Dan stared numbly at the fallen masturbation prompt. He thought to venture an urbane remark to Worsley, but decided that it had too many sibilants and pressed on up the stairs instead.

They reached a temporary impasse at the top when they found that the door to Chuff's apartment was almost impossible to open. First assuming that it must be locked, Wheems tried the other spare keys that his dead acquaintance had bequeathed to him, before discovering that the door was merely jammed shut by some unknown object that had evidently toppled over on its further side. With difficulty in the slim-fit stairway, both comics professionals applied their weight and struggled until the unseen obstruction grudgingly began to move, crinkling and rustling as it did so.

Worsley Porlock was the first one in.

Chuff's hallway, in those first disorienting instants, was as Worsley had imagined the experience of either death or ayahuasca. All the laws of common sense and visual perspective from which human beings construe their reality were dashed aside like straws, revealing in a stark, apocalyptic moment the unnerving alien principles on which their universe was truly predicated.

There was no floor. Porlock waded crotch-deep in a static sea, choppy and rough but weirdly motionless, a riptide stricken by paralysis. Freeze-frame wavelets and whitecaps everywhere, and curling breakers poised as if to fall. There were abysmal troughs, and rising slopes that made one doubt the verticals and horizontals of the walls and ceiling, so that Worsley lost his balance for a second, staggering and startled in an endless maelstrom made of only paper, swirling and bone-dry. With none of the anticipated difficulty, he'd found Brandon Chuff's collection, and it wasn't comics.

It was forty years as measured out in bothersome erections, practically a lifetime of erogenous compulsion. Towering cliff-faces of pictorial erotica reared all about, landslides of smut in raucous colour or in sentimental monochrome, a rusty-stapled archive cataloguing masculine desire in the last days of an industrial era. Cleavage engineering. Garter belts that echoed the suspension bridge. Sculpted pudenda, waxed and polished like the hood of a Volkswagen. There, also, was a history of improvement in photography and printing, along with a lesson in the evolution of sensationalist calligraphy, titles that stirred three lonely generations: *Saucy*. *Frill*. *Bordello*. *Fisting Manicurists*. *Vaginado*. *Lesbian Insolvency?* – with an incorporated question mark, as if astonished by its own existence. Worsley realised he was hyperventilating as Dan Wheems bulged through the crack of open door behind him and said, 'Vefuff!' To which Worsley could not shape an adequate reply.

Bulky as astronauts, the two men gaped in silent awe at the subsiding porn-dunes of their new, predominantly pinkish planet, with its atmosphere all but unbreathable. Because of this, wisely inhaling via the mouth and not the nostrils, the pair's respiration had a pausing and metallic quality, as through a space helmet or iron lung. Despite remaindered daylight filtering through distant windows, a prevailing source for the pearl radiance that flooded this extraterrestrial expanse was the reflected glow of several thousand pallid moons, some cleft and some with nipples. Everywhere, embarrassed-looking women, dot-screen grey or colourised, contorted seemingly disjointed limbs into new constellations strewn across the crumpled firmament, the Rowing Machine, the Obliging Starfish.

Any task of caretaking the pair may have intended was transparently a hopeless one. All that was possible was a horrific trawl for souvenirs; reminders of the normal life that Brandon must have somehow had between the bouts of jerking off. Shivering, Porlock summoned his inch-deep reserves of willpower and attempted to get this deranging expedition under some sort of control.

'OK. OK, we got this. Let's just keep calm. We can cover more ground if you take the front of the apartment while I take the back.'

'Furely, Worfely, fplipping up if a mifpake. Im fcary mooveef fumfing allwaif happenf poo vuh perfon ferfing im vuh fellar …'

'DAN, SHUT UP! SHUT UP, DAN! I CAN'T UNDERSTAND YOU! I CAN'T UNDERSTAND A WORD YOU'RE SAYING! JUST … I'm sorry. Sorry, man. We're both under a lot of strain. Look, let's get this thing done, OK? OK, Dan?'

Always shocked by confrontation, Dan Wheems managed a tight nod and some staccato blinks before he turned away from Worsley to regard his designated end of their demoralising mutual problem. To be fair, Wheems was encountering a lot more strain from this absurd predicament than Worsley Porlock could have easily imagined. The new editor-in-chief, in common with his predecessor, was not unfamiliar with the wide and diverse pastures of contemporary stroke-material. Dan, on the other hand, had been caught by his mother in possession of a ballpoint pen whereon the lady's swimsuit vanished if you held it upside down, and ever since had left hardcore pornography alone. With first wife Susan, in the eighteen months that they were married, he had enjoyed intermittent but unfailingly polite carnal activity when this was what the situation seemed to call for. Otherwise, Dan's intimate imaginings for purposes of hand relief would typically involve two or more female members of the Unrealistic Five, Tomorrow Friends, Vindictives, Freak Force or United Supermen, and once or twice Esme Martinez. These internal vignettes were entirely voyeuristic, as Dan Wheems was too self-conscious to show up in his own sexual fantasies. Surrounded now by a Niagara, a Zambesi, of inverted women with their bathing costumes disappeared, he felt lost and obscurely threatened to his fragile core. What if, in some SP *Sarcophagus of Murder* twist, his fifteen-years-dead mother were to burst in now and catch him? Stifling an interior shriek, Wheems plunged into the glistening torrent and made for what he believed to be Brandon's front room, with girls working their way through college and moonlighting typists slopping cold against his leaden thighs.

Porlock, meanwhile, struggled through a salacious quicksand, striking out for the apartment's rear. Although more … hardened wasn't quite the word; perhaps resilient? … in his attitude towards spank literature than Wheems, Worsley was by no means unmoved to find himself aboard a fishnet ghost train. Just the stupefying quantities involved in Brandon's hobby made him dizzy, the immense expenditure in human time, the man hours or, more likely, man years that would be required to even briefly skim these avalanching genitalia, this mammary inundation. Chuff's enthusiasm and its decades-spanning sweep, as represented by the differing vintages of filth discernible in the surrounding foam of periodicals, was haunting. Launching himself on the literal bosoms of the flood, fighting against the shiny paper current to move slowly forward, Worsley couldn't help but notice titles he remembered from his boyhood, interspersed with more recent examples of the genre. He saw *Cad*, *Lothario*, *Rotter* and *Sex Pest*, and felt briefly sad and elderly to think that he'd forgotten the winking philanderer on *Rotter*'s masthead. Labouring through an opposing tide of slippery centrefolds, he thought, as if for the first time, about the nymphs and matrons, of the 2D wantons currently tangling or torn around his ankles. Many of them would be old by now, he thought, and many of them would be dead. Why did that trouble him? He thought about the countless lives consumed, one way or other, by this knowingly addictive global industry, but stopped short of direct comparisons with Worsley's own field of endeavour. He pushed on into the shaven undergrowth, teeth gritted, hopefully in the direction of Chuff's bedroom.

The exclamatory logos bobbing past, going the other way, were at that moment a gymnasium of verbs: *Suck*, *Screw*, *Lick*, *Fondle*, *Grope* and *Punch*, although this last turned out to be a soporific satire magazine from England. Worsley found his plight ironic, if he'd understood that word correctly. As a thirteen-year-old boy, to drown in scud had been his fondest hope, his unattainable ambition. Faced now with the almost unimaginable actuality, he saw, as with so many other things, the dangerous naivety of his youthful assumptions. To be physically interred in adult content like a fruit fly in licentious amber was, he now saw, not an unalloyed treat, as had also been the case with reaching legal drinking age or one day working in the comics industry.

Proceeding in the manner of a glacier, the terminal moraine of phalluses and lipstick crumpling volubly before him, Worsley took some several minutes passing a jammed-open doorway on his right, which gave him more than enough time to thoroughly inspect the room beyond. This, it transpired, had been Brandon's bathroom, and it was as deep in fuck books as the rest of the apartment – which implied that with sufficient volume, visual pornography behaved less like a solid than a liquid, finding its own level. Inching past the sex-crammed opening, he could at leisure study the deluge of technicolour lapping at the bathtub's rim, broaching the toilet bowl. *Fap. Squirt. Sophisticate. Incontinent Ballerina.* Desperately clinging to the idea of a world with normal physics, Porlock nervously considered the unsettling question of how Chuff had ever moved about in his own living space, or had transacted the most basic human functions without help.

It came to him, perhaps at the halfway point in his traverse of the bathroom door, that Brandon, of necessity, must have propelled himself on all fours over the uneven, listing surface of the swollen XXXX river, like a burly, quadrupedal water boatman. Too late to arrest the image or prevent it being etched with acid on his forebrain, Worsley realised that on at least some of these occasions, Chuff would have been naked. Conjured up unbidden, he recalled the classic scene from Ralph Roth and Paul Deeming's *Dracula*, where the count scuttles head first down a castle wall as if he were a great, black lizard. Choking back bile, he pressed forward on his Krafft-Ebing safari. He felt like a frightened choirboy in the abattoir of love.

After perhaps another quarter-hour, Porlock stood wheezing on the overflowing threshold of what was, from all appearances, his late superior's bedchamber. Like – well, it seemed – pretty much everything in Brandon's private life, it was submerged in a lake of high-definition squalor and greased Scandinavians. Incongruously, at the centre of the room, as visible to Worsley, was a beautifully worked four-poster bed like something from Hans Christian Anderson, if carpets of professionally lecherous ex-raincoat models had featured more prominently in his work. It even had an emerald counterpane, fresh-made and neatly smoothed, on which machine-embroidered floral silhouettes stood out, now black, now silver. From his previous envisioning of Brandon as undead Carpathian aristocrat, Worsley was wrenched abruptly to the folklore spectrum's other end, where Chuff became a princess – albeit one who'd rather let herself go – sleeping innocent amidst a swamp of gruesome copulatory dreams. He couldn't make his mind up as to which interpretation was the most upsetting.

Other than the oddly picturesque sleep-howdah, the one other furnishing that looked even conceivably accessible was an old-fashioned dressing table, standing not too far from the four-poster's footboard. Of the kind with four drawers and a threefold mirror, its three lower drawers were long since lost below the rising Plimsoll line of bi-curious acrobats, and thus not openable. If there was anything of Brandon's that might justify this nightmare trek into a dead chief editor's libido, it could only be in that top drawer, six feet across the buried room and maybe half an hour away.

He nearly turned back. There was almost certainly nothing of interest tucked away there, and from what he'd learned of Brandon thus far, there might well be something scarring and traumatic. Worsley didn't want to slog through what was, when you thought about it, thin-sliced timber, just to learn Chuff's favourite flavour when it came to lubricant, or to find photographs of barnyard creatures in bikinis. Even so, to have come all this way, to have endured all this unpleasantness; he didn't like the thought of making the demanding return journey without even checking. Maybe if he tried to look at this the way that Brandon would have done, to move the way that Brandon must have moved …

Feeling a touch ridiculous, Porlock got down on hands and knees atop two or three feet of juddering shame. He thought he probably looked like some cute but pitiable creature in a wildly inappropriate petting zoo. Not only was this crawling posture terribly infantilising, but it also didn't work nearly as well as he'd imagined. It was quicker than just wading through the mass of self-pollution pamphlets, to be sure, though much more nerve-wracking than he'd anticipated when he'd still been vertical. For one thing, the piled publications constituting his new terra weren't particularly firma, lurching with his every movement like a plain of sphagnum moss, or Jell-O, or perhaps a funhouse floor. His palms, already hot and damp with August, clung repulsively to the expanse of glossy stock on which he grovelled, further limiting his progress and his self-esteem.

He kneeled there, trying to figure out what he should do, his pose echoing that of at least two-thirds of the women he was kneeling on. This could not, after all, have been Chuff's method of mobility. He must have had some other strategy; something that Worsley wasn't seeing. Suddenly, his earlier observation – that pornography which had attained critical mass took on characteristics of a liquid – chimed again in his fevered awareness, as if offering a vital clue.

Intuitively, hesitantly, Worsley lowered himself belly down on to the lustquake filling Brandon's room, transitioning from doggy to a missionary style, and tried to swim.

It worked astonishingly well. Adopting a beginner's breaststroke, Porlock essayed a frog kick against the buckling, ripping pages he could feel behind, mangled against his intricately contoured trainer soles. At the same time, his hands plunged jointly forward before sweeping back to either side in scything, cover-rippling arcs that, unbelievably, drove his substantial body forward at considerable speed, his torso sliding easily over the slipping and subsiding gloss. Worsley was simultaneously startled and euphoric: when he'd been a little boy, this was the way he used to fly in dreams, wallowing in the air just a few feet above the dream-lit sidewalk. It was like he'd found his natural element at last, and as he swam across the crinkling, crackling reservoir of stale impulse, his were the graceful and enchanting motions of a lazing manatee.

In only a few strokes, he'd reached the dressing table, one hand clutching at the nearest hardwood corner in the way someone would grab the tiled end of a swimming pool in between laps. Levering himself up on his elbows, Brandon Chuff's successor tugged with one hand at the fancy metal handle of the topmost drawer, and with minimal effort, slid it open. Bracing against disappointment, Worsley slithered a few inches closer to the table, and peered in.

Oh His God. Was all of this a fricking dream? This surely could not be, and yet … no. No, this wasn't happening. This was incredible, like a religious miracle, a rush of transcendental fire.

Inside the drawer were comics, maybe twenty, twenty-five, sensibly bagged, not even what you'd dignify by calling a collection. Neither were there genuine antiquities, or at least relatively speaking – nothing from the forties or the fifties, no *Exciting* #1 or *Manhunt* #22. In fact, somewhat disloyally, considering that Chuff had worked predominantly for American, these were all books from Massive or Goliath, Massive's predecessor. What had made the supine Porlock gasp, however, was that these were all the number ones and first appearances. This was the origin of Massive, the nativity, front covers made as archetypal and familiar as the three kings or the baby in the manger. OHG.

Before Worsley's dilating pupils were near-mint first issues of *The Unrealistic Five*, *Freak Force* and *The Vindictives*, all with covers and interiors by the legendary Joe Gold. During 'Joltin'' Joe Gold's staggering conceptual eruption of the early 1960s, he'd created almost all of Massive's vast franchise portfolio single-handed, aided only by the fluttering, trilling byline of Satanic Sammy Blatz. *The Unrealistic Five*'s iconic frontage was exactly as the new chief editor remembered from his eighth year, when he'd passed on the now priceless *UF* #1 in favour of a mediocre Felix Firestone tiff in *Thunderman*. There was the wobbly, anxious-looking logo lettering in an anaemic blue, the ten-cent bullet, giant Comics Code seal of approval, number, month and mystifying lack of a publisher's imprint. There was Gold's perfectly weighted, shadow-friendly Unrealistic Five advancing apprehensively along a cracked and blasted urban avenue, herds of distraught New Yorkers scattering in the skyscrapered backdrop, and, up in the foreground on the right, the brutal armoured glove of the first issue's villain hanging into view. Surging towards the reader genie-like, his lower half a rumpling column of grey smoke, Fogmaster had a black-trimmed speech balloon proclaiming, 'Holy Scott! The **Creature Curator** plans to overrun the city with his creations!' His teammate, Dr Unrealistic, closer to the reader and transforming his right arm into a corkscrew, issued a responding bubble that read, 'Then he's reckoned without **Dr Unrealistic** and the **Unrealistic Five**!' Elsewhere, the avuncular John Monster lifted a cement mixer to use as a projectile, Insubstantial Girl walked through an upturned bus, and team mascot Electrikid sputtered and sparked with adolescent indignation.

Under that, *Vindictives* #1; the three brief issues of *The Brute*'s mistimed initial run; *Alarming Adult Reverie* #19, with the first glimpse of Robert Novak's Beetle Boy; *Tales of Astonishing* #37 and the debut of Ormazda; #1 of *The Alarming Beetle Boy*; the Human Tank in *Journey into Strange* #73; *Vindictives* #9 where Joe Gold's National Guard is back in action after dreaming in a nutrient bath since World War II … everything. Everything was there. Worsley had found his inner child, albeit face down in a dead man's porno horde. When he failed to ascend to heaven on the spot, Porlock was then left in a state of paralysing indecision. What to do? Should he tell Dan? Yes. Morally, of course he should. Of course he should tell Dan. Dan was the one who Chuff had trusted with the keys. Although. Although, just playing devil's advocate, was there a way that Porlock could … no. Best not even think about it. But, then, there were only, what, two dozen comics at the most? You'd think you could – he didn't know – just stick them down your pants or hide them in your jacket, something like that, but that really wouldn't work in Worsley's less than ideal current circumstances. Why hadn't he brought his shoulder bag? Why hadn't he just broken in the night before, with flashlight, mask and this year's price guide? Why hadn't he bought that issue of *The Unrealistic Five* in 1961, when it was right there on the rack at Mr Salter's? Why—

Off in the distance, in another world, Dan Wheems was screaming.

Porlock pushed the drawer shut with a guilty start. Flailing intuitively, he contrived to pivot, swivelling on his ball-bearing stomach until he was pointing at the bedroom door. Wheems was still shrieking, way off down the landing, sounding like a thing in danger of its very soul being extinguished. With three by-now-expert kicks, Worsley was through the door and striking back down the fuck-flooded passageway towards his caterwauling colleague, shifting to a butterfly stroke for expediency's sake. Both arms were flung in front like windmill blades, their backswing churning up a spindrift spray of scopophilia to either side, the shredded double penetrations, money shots and reverse cowgirls hanging beaded in the air. Each forward stroke pushed Porlock's face into the peppery must of wrinkled relaxation literature that he was swimming through, so that each time he broke the nipple-studded surface, he was forced to take great gulping breaths before the next submersion. Like a flying fish that bounced on the Pacific's peaks, or horny salmon flapping upstream, Worsley's progress down the landing had its own magnificence, and its own bow wave of mangled erotica in a big, spreading V behind him.

Wheems, apparently screamed out, was sitting on the partly submerged sofa in Brandon's front room with shoulders shaking and one hand up covering his face. When Worsley had dismounted from his flume of rut and pushed his rustling way into the parlour, Dan was in a place beyond words. The *Vindictives* scriptwriter could only point across the rippling surface of the lewd lagoon, gesturing at a bulging-open doorway that led off to an adjacent space. Bewildered and increasingly afraid, Porlock followed the ragged trench his weeping buddy had already dug, towards the murky opening and whatever lay beyond.

It was a largish room, and Worsley speculated that it may have once been the apartment's living room, though it had evidently been long since repurposed. Now it seemed to be some sort of storage area, containing only numerous cardboard boxes of a size approximate to an old, three-dimensional TV. They were all open-topped, each with a different year's date written on the front in thick, black marker pen. The dates appeared to reach at least as far back as the early 1990s. Back in the front room, Dan Wheems was sobbing audibly as Worsley shuffled further in amongst the ominous beige cubes. The nearer cartons, seemingly all from the current century, were full of packaging material, marshmallow-white in the subdued light. What might be concealed beneath the pallid nuggets, Porlock wondered? Bestial inflatables, or body parts with evidence of cannibal activity? In cautious half steps, he inched closer, to see better. When he was right next to the containers, he revised his earlier opinion with regard to what they held. It wasn't packaging material. For one thing, there were threads, and tags, and … what was it, exactly? Worsley leaned in, frowning.

It was two or three hours later, when the summer sun was low, that David Moskowitz dropped by. The publisher, diminutive but looking taller in a long black coat, jabbed at the buzzer by the street door, then stared blankly at the sea life on the walls of Scuba-Do until an ashen Worsley Porlock lumbered down the narrow stairs to let him in.

Porlock looked ill and was incapable of speech, even when in the presence of the ultimate upstairs man at American. (Subordinate to the corporate owners, obviously, but still.) When Moskowitz asked what was wrong, his new chief editor could only mutely shake his head and indicate that his superior should follow him to Chuff's apartment, up the worn, complaining steps. In Brandon's hallway, with his first appraisal of the pornographic inundation, the intensely nervous little man – Moskowitz seemed shorter every time his underlings encountered him – was dumbfounded. Even more unaccustomed to the monodextrous genre than Dan Wheems, the publisher could only blink through his designer spectacles and struggle for some utterance that was remotely adequate.

'Oh my gosh. I guess this explains why Brandon stopped.'

Moskowitz, largely unfamiliar with the adult world, supposed that this vast plethora of spicy entertainment, previously unimaginable, was the source of Worsley Porlock's haunted manner, but, of course, it wasn't. The new editor-in-chief, still silent, led Moskowitz through into a front room where Dan Wheems was curled into a whimpering foetal ball on the tit-littered sofa, which rose like an atoll from its lecherous Sargasso. As the chief executive absorbed this abject spectacle, too far out of his depth to comment, Porlock merely gestured to the anteroom's wedged-open entrance. He then sat down on the couch by the withdrawn and twitching Wheems, not meeting Moskowitz's eye and making it apparent that if the unsettled publisher wished to investigate the proffered cubbyhole, he'd have to do so unaccompanied. The writer and the editor were broken, Moskowitz concluded. This, whatever it was, was a job for management.

The boxes stood in failing light and mausoleum silence. David didn't like it, not one bit. All of those dirty magazines filling the front room and the hallway, spilling everywhere like psychic sewage from a ruptured main, they made him feel as if he'd never really known his former editor-in-chief. It wasn't the erotic content of the publications that disturbed him – sex was just another genre that he had no interest in, like funny animals or cowboys – but their terrible condition. How could anybody sane, whatever their enthusiasm, live with their collection in a state like that?

At least these enigmatic cardboard crates suggested an attempt at order, in amongst the carnal chaos. Cautiously, as one would expect from a comics publisher in those challenging times,

Moskowitz approached the marker-dated cartons, peering into each one as he passed.

Like Porlock, Moskowitz at first mistook the wadded balls of tissue for some kind of packaging material, then noticed that each crumpled paper clump had its own label tag, affixed with cotton thread and, possibly, a glue stick. What was that about? Pausing before a box with 2001 in black and hasty numerals on the front, he reached in and took one of the compacted plugs of Kleenex for a more thorough examination. Stiff and brittle like a dried white rose, on its appended label the date 'August 12' was inscribed in what David recognised as Chuff's distinctive, spidery hand. Throwing it back, he chose another, this one reading 'July 9'. The next had 'Sunday, May 13', and after that, a brief addendum that said 'Mother's Day'. Then March 18, November 2, February 14 – 'a romantic evening in', October 8, May 23 … by Moskowitz's estimate, there looked to be three or four hundred tissue parcels in each of a good two dozen boxes. He continued to sort through the crispy pillows, utterly bewildered but determined he should understand. At last his trapped and darting eyes alighted on a lone anomaly, a small black label tethered to its rosette with black thread and written on in fine-point silver Sharpie. His manicured fingers trembling, he fished it out.

'September 11 – today, a new Pearl Harbor.'

David stared at this, and blinked some more, and thought about it.

Worsley Porlock looked up, unsurprised, as Moskowitz's miniature hobgoblin form came backwards at high speed out of the storage space, a movie character on rewind with his frantic dialogue squeaky and reversed. He suddenly stopped dead, turned in a semicircle and threw up on Brandon Chuff's flat-screen TV, where it poked out from the front room's licentious topsoil. Moskowitz's violent heaving, hoarse and with a canine quality, caused even Wheems to open one despairing eye and contemplate the wretched vista for some fifteen seconds before closing it again, seeking escape in an attempt at self-inflicted catatonia. The day outside went on with its decline.

Over an hour passed with the three men crouching there amongst the hills of dream and quaquaversal strumpet-cascades; crouching, staring, no one saying anything, nothing to say. Night had begun to filter into the apartment, falling in a sooty, fine precipitate. Away in the ongoing movie of New York, sirens were stitched across the distant dark in threads of shimmering blue.

Eventually, Porlock broke the silence with a lame suggestion.

'We could, you know, we could leave it all here, maybe. We could just, you know, go home.'

Through the corrective lenses, David Moskowitz's eyes were feverish and intense.

'No. No, no, no. We can't just leave it. There'll be people coming here, the landlord, perhaps relatives. Did Brandon Chuff have relatives? He didn't look the type who had a family, but you can never tell. We can't take any chances. If there's people coming here, all this could wind up in *The National Enquirer*. It might end up doing damage to the company, and that can't happen.'

This last point was no remote consideration. With the comics industry having for some years been in a condition of collapse, rumours of buyout were forever in the air, so any minor scandal had potential to screw up a deal and greatly inconvenience the parent company, which, in this instance, was the all-powerful Brothers Brothers corporation. No one wanted Brothers Brothers mad at them, particularly David Moskowitz.

Dusk settled like obscuring ash, and electronic wristwatches continued with their fake, unnecessary tick so as not to confound the elderly. Wheems and the abyss carried out a mutual inspection. Flies buzzed listlessly, so, after a few minutes, Worsley tried again.

'Couldn't we, I don't know, couldn't we get it to the dump or somewhere?'

Both of Worsley's ideas were, of course, put forward in the hope they might allow some covert opportunity to salvage those first issues hidden in Chuff's dressing table. As it was, Worsley would end the night screaming inside and feeling a bereavement he knew he must never share with any other living soul. Now, though, sitting in Brandon's darkening jerk-silo, David Moskowitz's adenoidal snarl was shot through with contempt.

'Are you insane? That's probably what Arvo Cake was planning, with his girlfriend. No. There has to be some way that we can fix this. Shut up, both of you, so I can think.'

Wheems hadn't said a word for several hours.

After a simmering hush, the publisher appeared to reach, internally, some calm and windswept summit of decision. Lifting up his small, sharp-featured head, he gazed with action-hero gravity through the descending gloom at his unravelling associates. Outside, a passing car sent lazy orange rays across the ceiling of this room drowning in prurience.

'I know,' Moskowitz said, the highlights dancing in his spectacles. 'I know what we can do.'

6. (May, 2016)

A lovely day on the periphery of Gary, Indiana, and up in the glassy azure was a single mashed-potato serving of white cloud, as clean as anything Charlie Morelli ever saw. It wasn't just the white of folded laundry in a washing-powder ad, or of unbroken Alpine snow, or perfect teeth. A galleon carved from vapour, it was white as God, a pinnacle of pristine all those other whites could only dream about. It glowed with purity and hygiene to a point that almost made Morelli want to cry.

He was a wiry little guy, this Charles Morelli. In his middle seventies, he still had a good crop of dust-grey hair and a great tan, although he guessed it made his face look kind of leathery. Blue pants, cream shirt, same every day. He'd sometimes get a little crazy with the socks, just for variety. He moved around the square green baize of his front garden, tending to his flowers with an unhurried gait suggestive of tremendous patience, sunlight golden on his weathered cheek.

Ask him about himself, he'd give it to you straight: born Providence, Rhode Island, 1929, his parents Joseph and Irene Morelli. Flunking out of high school, he'd worked at his father's bakery then moved to New York with the family in 1951, explaining where he'd got that accent. Married to Joan Summers, 1963, a pizza business in Connecticut that didn't work, divorced in 1970, no children. Since then, managing a vacuum-cleaner dealership in Cleveland until his retirement in 2005, when Charlie had moved here to this place, just outside of Gary. Huge Sinatra fan, having a lifelong interest in horticulture. That was the whole story, every time, practically word for word.

His house, the pastel pink and well-appointed property behind him as he pruned and weeded by the picket fence, was just about the only place out that way that had anybody living in it, which was good. Morelli looked up from his gloves and shears to cast a wary eye at the For Sale sign in next door's front yard. He'd been here for, what, ten years now? The next-door house had been stood vacant all that time, and Charlie liked it that way. It would probably all come to nothing, he consoled himself, returning to his pruning. Who the hell would want to live here anyway, with nothing much outside a general store for miles? No, it was all OK. He was OK.

He was attending to his roses. Roses were the ones that smelled nice, something like Turkish Delight, but better. In Charlie's experience, you tended to get quite a lot of them on greetings cards. The ones that he was fussing with at present were a sort of violet colour, and were called something. Those bugs like fat and furry hornets drifted amiably from flower to flower as Morelli clipped and trimmed, and he'd admit, if pressed, that he felt pretty good. This was a good life. Charlie didn't get as stressed or angry as he used to do, nor did he face all the same problems and anxieties.

Unconsciously, he registered the faraway buzz of an engine, quieter to start with than the furry hornets but then rapidly becoming louder, nearer. Probably it wasn't anything. You didn't get a lot of vehicles out Charlie's way, but six or seven times a week there'd be a car, a truck, a deafening biker, things like that. He'd long since stopped reacting every time he heard a motor, but he'd not stopped noticing them. This one was an SUV with tinted windows, roaring down the otherwise deserted road towards Morelli's house. The old man's scrutiny of his rose bushes seemed to become more intense and focussed, his face buried in the large and fragrant blooms. He licked his lips, which suddenly were dry, and thought how much he'd like a beer right now.

The car swept past, not even slowing down, and in a moment it was gone from sight. Morelli straightened up, and breathed. This gardening business, if you overdid it, could raise quite a sweat. He peeled the gloves off, dropped them on the lawn beside his shears, and went inside to get that beer. The magic cloud of cleanliness was still above his house, which he found strangely comforting.

Charlie Morelli had, conspicuously, no connection whatsoever to the world of comics.

7. (July, 1969)

That summer's theme, in retrospect, was probably 'Americans approaching new and unknown worlds'. In the hot months of 1969, beyond Earth's atmosphere, Buzz Aldrin, Michael Collins and Neil Armstrong watched the solar system's most gigantic lunar body, technically a minor planet, swelling in their viewport. In Los Angeles, yet equally beyond Earth's atmosphere, Tex Watson, Susan Atkins and Patricia Krenwinkel wriggled like caterpillars through the dark towards a bright house on Cielo Drive. And fifteen-year-old Worsley Porlock, with a catastrophic haircut, almost skipped along the sparkling mica streets of Albany, NY, on the way to his first comics convention.

Worsley had been living in New Jersey for around four years now, since his mother had remarried and they'd moved there from Milwaukee, with his former sometimes-uncle Paul, now made permanent-stepdad Paul. He didn't really keep in touch with his dad Ray, who he'd heard had some kind of problem with his liver, and was still at his old job back in Wisconsin. They'd talk once a year by phone, at Christmas maybe, although now that Worsley thought about it, not last year. Perhaps the year before that, but he wasn't sure. He guessed he sort of missed his old man, probably.

Anyway, this was his first time in Albany, the sun was shining, and Worsley was more excited than he could remember being since his relatively recent childhood. He was headed for the Billingham Hotel, declining and yet still respectable, which served as venue for the long-awaited (at least six weeks) BeeCon1.

He'd learned of the convention's almost inconceivable existence just a month or two ago, there in the usually dull letters page of *Manhunt* #316, which in itself had been a usually dull publication ever since they camped everything up in imitation of the recent *King Bee and Buzz* television show, or at least in Worsley's opinion. He'd only picked up the issue out of habit, hadn't cared for either the lead story or the backup Rocket Ranger nonsense, and was glumly skimming through the letters of complaint in Manhunt Mailbag, when he came across a missive from ubiquitous King Bee enthusiast and letters-column stalwart, Jimjon Jackson.

Formerly James Jonathan Jackson the Third, Jimjon had adopted his new name for the first issue of *Bee Attitude*, his boyishly exuberant King Bee fanzine. Now, presumably with *Manhunt* and American's approval, he was plugging the world's first King Bee convention, to be held in Albany that coming July. Worsley had been both incredulous and thrilled. It wasn't that he was that interested in King Bee, but that this was a comics thing – a thing from Worsley's private universe – yet manifested, shockingly, in the real world, where other people could experience it too.

As was the custom those days, Jimjon's mail address was right below his letter. Worsley had sent off the requisite five-dollar registration fee that had been mentioned, and within a week was in possession of the first convention newsletter: four pages in two folded sheets, with violet mimeograph printing and a smell like methylated spirits. On the cover was an OK cartoon by Jackson himself, with King Bee posed like Atlas holding up a globe made out of characters from other comic books or from newspaper strips, like *Flatfoot Floyd* and *Squinty*. Inside there were updates on the con itself – former *King Bee* delineator Davis Burke was going to be there, and Sebastian Squires who'd played Carruthers in the TV show – and also ads for five or six amateur comics fanzines, a phenomenon that Worsley hadn't previously been aware of. These included Jackson's own *Bee Attitude*, along with *Comics Addict* from Snit Whitley in Ohio, the distinguished *Hooded Vigilante* from fan-turned-pro Jerry Binkle, *The Massive Collector* out of Washington, and a peculiar item called *What The – ?* made by a Milton Finefinger in Boston. Consumed by a burning need that wasn't there before, Worsley had sent away for all of these, with *The Massive Collector* and *Bee Attitude* already gratefully received.

Some of the articles and the fan illustrations were terrific, others maybe not so much, but that wasn't the point. The point, for Worsley, was that these were artefacts that testified to the existence of a different country, where they knew about Joe Gold, and understood the difference between the two Moon Queens, and would not see Worsley Porlock as some manner of subnormal introvert. It was a realm that he felt he'd been seeking all his life, like when Kid Unicorn from Freak Force found the Mutant Motherland concealed there in the icy Himalayas. Best of all, though, this uncharted planet turned out to be just a bus ride across town from where Worsley was living with his mom and Paul. In fact, its blazing portals were now just a little further down the street, where he could see the Billingham Hotel's sweetly old-fashioned sign hanging above the stream of 1969 pedestrians.

This had to be the place. As Worsley neared the hotel entrance, he spotted two teenagers on their way in, the taller boy in a

Vindictives T-shirt. On the sidewalk right outside there was some little kid, maybe eleven, twelve, wearing enormous spectacles and getting lectured by a worried-looking pair who had to be his parents, looking like he wished the earth would open up and swallow him. Poor bastard. His heart soaring, Worsley bounded up the white stone steps, through the revolving door, into the lobby. He then followed a hand-lettered arrow sign and the two laughing teenage boys down a brief flight of stairs, towards a hotel basement with BeeCon1 posters everywhere.

It was a wonderland, assuming wonderland was half a dozen young guys in a conference venue, talking, reading comic books and having a good time. This, evidently, was the BeeCon1 reception area, and at the centre was a trestle table with convention booklets piled on top of it, along with plastic name tags and what seemed to be the con's attendance register. Seated behind this was a beaming man in his mid-twenties with a shock of ginger hair who turned out to be Jimjon Jackson. Worsley, momentarily surprised, had been expecting someone younger.

Stepping up, he introduced himself and thanked Jackson for sending him *Bee Attitude*. His startled eyes alighting only briefly on the fifteen-year-old's hair, as if it were a missing limb, Jimjon shook Worsley's hand enthusiastically. He gave Worsley a plastic tag, a booklet, and loaned him a pen so he could fill his name in on the tag. He said he hoped that Worsley would enjoy himself, and seemed about to offer him advice about the hair, but then thought better of it. Jackson put a tick where it said 'Porlock' in his register, and Worsley walked distractedly away, already leafing avidly through the convention booklet with its schedule of events and its donated sketches from a range of pestered comic artists: King Bee as imagined by John Capellini, Robert Novak, Preston Williams, Davis Burke and, unbelievably, Joe Gold! Moving like a somnambulist or someone underwater, Worsley drifted haltingly in what the arrows said was the direction of the dealers' room.

This had the size, the intimacy and the atmospherics of a church bazaar, except that nobody was old. Tables around the outsides of the room, and then a square of tables in the middle there, like circled wagons. This left a rectangular path for convention attendees to bob around, like plastic waterfowl in an old fairground Hook-a-Duck attraction. Just the hotel-carpet smell and murmuring sound of it were thrilling, and the visuals were a fireworks display realised in card and paper. There were comic books of every vintage, covers glowing with forgotten 1940s colour, and fantastic paperbacks whose jackets dripped with warriors, abominations, nude princesses, violet alien skies.

Dumbstruck and numb with wonder, Worsley circumnavigated his daydream emporium. There was the sweet smell of cheap incense issuing from somewhere, and a gentle undertow of music that meandered from The Ventures, of whom Worsley was aware, to shimmering and mystic-sounding things by San Francisco bands he didn't know so well. Wrapped in a daze of perfect satisfaction, he paused at each stall and felt obscurely sleazy, like a voyeur, ogling goods for free while knowing he could not afford to buy them. There were books like *Massive Men's Adventures* from the 1940s, back when Massive were still Punctual, its cover rich with violent detail that depicted Fishman, the original Fogmaster and the National Guard, all grinning while they slaughtered buck-toothed and banana-coloured Japanese infantrymen in inch-thick pebble glasses. He was rendered near immobile by the sighting of an early *Thunderman*, like, #87, somewhere around there, when Felix Firestone had a beard, moustache and different-coloured hair while pesky Thundermite looked like a leprechaun. He briefly fantasised about possessing it, this thing from before Worsley had even been born, but it had a white sticker on its plastic wrapping that said twenty dollars, which was almost all the money that his guilty stepdad Paul had given him for the entire weekend.

The table next to this turned out to be the one harbouring both the smouldering joss stick and the tape recorder with a psychedelic playlist. Representing either a mail-order business or a shop called Seventh Heaven, the compact but fascinating stall was managed by a young man with long chestnut hair who wore a stars-and-stripes bandana, and a very pretty blonde girl who was probably his girlfriend. Up until he saw her, Worsley wasn't consciously aware that BeeCon1 was otherwise a wholly masculine environment, and her appearance was as unexpected as it would have been in a guy's washroom. While she bagged customers' purchases behind the table, she maintained a smile of quiet amusement, for which Worsley was unduly grateful. Since, in his experience, female expressions varied from disinterest to dislike to disbelief, he'd settle readily for quiet amusement. And the stall itself was laden with intriguing, captivating things he'd never seen before. While the long-haired proprietor was talking animatedly with a tall youngster who laughed down his nose a lot, and the amused blonde girl made change out of a cardboard box, Worsley investigated.

There were science fiction paperbacks and magazines from England that had covers without swirling galaxies and, frankly, looked a bit upsetting. Up the back, there were a couple of American or Massive's more progressive, trippy comics such as *Professor Abnormal*, *Solar Sailor* or *The Aeon*, but these were outnumbered by far more exotic items. At the front were copies of *Disturbing* and its sister title *Inappropriate*, two classy comic mags in black and white with gorgeous painted covers, put out by Shaw Magazines, who usually did periodicals for horror-movie fans. By being magazines rather than comic books, Shaw's publications dodged the Comics Code Authority and could hire all the legendary artists, like Jeff Pleasant and Slim Whittaker, who'd worked for SP comics in the fifties. Worsley had his eye on an edition of *Disturbing* where the cover image showed a frightened hunter running at the viewer through a winter forest, with a pack of shadowy but hot-eyed wolfmen in pursuit, chasing him through the snow between the black and frozen midnight trees.

Elsewhere were what seemed to be fanzines, but with standards of production and design that put professional material to shame. There was the scholarly but energetic *Graphomania*, and something else called *margins* that was an experimental magazine of comic strips edited by Slim Whittaker, with artwork by his many famous colleagues. Worsley's pulse was racing, and this was before he noticed the assortment of underground comics in the table's middle reaches.

He'd heard about these, but had thought they were illegal. *Squack*, *Findmuck Funnies*, *Drugless Douglas*, and a tabloid offering called *Yellow Zeppelin*. His hand quivering slightly, hoping that the blonde girl wasn't watching, Worsley casually picked up *Squack* #3 and started flipping through it with what he hoped was an unimpressed look.

Jesus Christ. The cover was a beautifully drawn and coloured cartoon version of the Whore and seven-headed Beast as featured in the Book of Revelation. Worsley could have looked at it all day, but then the opening story had some average guy trying to suck himself off with a vacuum cleaner, getting pulled inside and finding a libidinous nirvana. The piece following, by yet another radically distinctive artist, wasn't even a real story – more of a delirious progression of transmuting shapes which, at one point, included the newspaper-strip delinquents Kurt and Karl both having penetrative sex with that stout, bowling-pin-shaped mother/aunt/cook/governess or whatever the hell she was. Worsley, unable to believe his eyes, decided there and then to buy *Squack* #3, although this meant he'd also have to buy *Disturbing*, *Graphomania* and *margins* to disguise the squalid intent of the purchase. Trying to look serious and scholarly, he interrupted the stall owner's conversation with the gangly teenager to ask if he could pay for his selection. While the amiable hippy and his clearly entertained assistant dealt with this, Worsley was left to stand in awkward silence with the older, taller kid, who looked to be around eighteen. He offered Worsley an appraising grin.

'Nice hair, hnohh-hnohh-hnohh-hnohh.'

Worsley, who had no idea what he looked like – one attendee at the con shaved off his own hair and applied to join the military after seeing Worsley – was about to thank the stringy adolescent for the compliment, when the boy startled him by adding, 'Hey! You're Worsley Porlock!'

This, as it transpired, was Milton Finefinger of Boston, and he fumbled in his holdall before handing Worsley a Manila envelope containing the new issue of *What The – ?* that Worsley had sent him a dollar for. Apparently a special BeeCon1 edition, on its cover was a crude but funny cartoon of King Bee and Buzz, which showed the apian avenger standing in a puddle of his own intestines while remarking to his horrified young chum, 'See, this is why I'm not supposed to use my stinger.' Finefinger was likeable enough, and he and Worsley talked while the blonde Mona Lisa bagged the latter's underground sex-comic and its camouflage. The stallholder, whose name was Sean, rejoined the conversation so that Worsley noticed the American publisher's logo on the comic book that he was holding. It appeared to be an issue of *Thunderman's Girlfriend Peggy Parks* – a title that no serious comic reader had looked at in years – but what he could see of the cover art looked wrong. Not bad – incredible, in fact – just … wrong.

'Excuse me, what is that? It looks like *Peggy Parks*, but …'

The proprietor smiled genially.

'Oh, you haven't seen this one? This is what me and Milton were just chewing over. It's not in the stores until next week, but I know someone who works at American. Here, take a look.'

Sure enough, it was *Peggy Parks*, but it was drawn and written by Joe Gold. Worsley experienced extreme cognitive dissonance. This was exactly like those dreams he had of being in some corner store he didn't know, where there were comics that could not conceivably exist, like *Beetle Boy and Blinky's Christmas Stocking* or *Thunderman Gone*. He gaped at the impossibility, there in his hands, as the bandana-wrapped stall owner helpfully explained.

'Yeah, it seems like Massive jerked Joe Gold's chain once too often. Way I heard it, he told Sam Blatz to stick *The Unrealistic Five,* Ormazda and the National Guard up his ass, then took off for American, where he's planning a whole raft of new titles. At American, when they asked him if there were any of their publications that he'd like to try his hand at, he apparently said, 'What's your poorest-selling book?' And then when they said,

'*Peggy Parks*,' Gold said, 'Give it to me. I'll fix it.' That's how come you're holding it right now. Try not to dribble on it, OK?'

Worsley couldn't understand how he had never realised previously that Peggy Parks was such a fascinating character. Here she was, racing at the reader down the bore of what looked like a Joe Gold version of a cyclotron, wearing a silver and black jumpsuit that had straps and valves and tubes all over it, the tar-pool of her shadow keeping pace and slithering beneath her as she ran. She'd even got a trademark Joe Gold ink-curl on her chin, as if to signify her substance and determination. Following her down the barrel of the atom smasher was what looked like the Caretaker, an old Joe Gold hero from the 1940s, and then one of Gold's beloved kid gangs, the Boy Desperadoes, also from the war years. An overexcited blurb promised the reader they would fathom the 'Mind-bending Mystery of the **Alternity Complex!!**' And meanwhile, Thunderman was nowhere to be seen.

Still basking in the comic's aura, equally electrifying and disorienting, Worsley gave it back to Sean the young entrepreneur, and then told him and Milton Finefinger he hoped he'd see them later. With his bag of treasures and the copy of *What The – ?* beneath his arm, the fifteen-year-old Porlock floated off into the thickening crowd, concussed with marvels.

At the far end of the dealers' room, set on a solitary table, was what had been advertised as BeeCon1's art exhibition. In reality, this was less than a dozen smallish pieces, most of them by fan artists and all of them in black and white, but it was his first glimpse of comic-art originals and Worsley was entranced. There were two pages by convention guest and former *King Bee* illustrator Davis Burke, who'd worked on *Manhunt* and *King Bee* throughout the 1950s. This was when the character was simultaneously at his best and at his most ridiculous, battling goofy-looking aliens, and every other issue getting turned into 'The Polka-Dot King Bee' or something equally inane and charming. Up close, Burke's art was a revelation. There were arrows and instructions in blue crayon, fragile pencil lines that hadn't been erased, and in the areas of solid black were smeary traces of the artist's brushstrokes. Worsley had a sudden overwhelming realisation of the artwork's physicality; of how the printed pages he could skim in seconds had been laboured over, patiently, for hours or days by real people, bent over real drawing boards and making marks on paper, one line at a time. Thousands of pages, days and people poured into the service of imaginary super-guys. It made him briefly dizzy.

The next table over was a stall devoted to King Bee exclusively, with current issues, pricey older books, posters and lobby cards from the two King Bee movie serials and, obviously, merchandise related to the TV show. Standing beside this, studying a die-cast miniature of the Bee Buggy with disdain, was the same little kid with outsized spectacles that Worsley had seen in the street outside the Billingham when he arrived. His name, according to the hastily scrawled name tag, was Dave Wheels. Having himself just been included in his first fan conversation with Bandana Sean and Milton Finefinger, and knowing how much that had meant, Worsley felt an enormous pang of sympathy for lonely-looking Dave Wheels, and so asked the boy if he was a King Bee fan.

'Not especially. I mean, you want the truth, I thought the TV series was for idiots. It sure didn't do comics any favours. No, King Bee's OK, but I'm more of a Massive guy.'

This so closely articulated Worsley's own position that he straight away accredited the twelve-year-old with a near-supernatural level of intelligence. They seemed to hit it off right from the start, and Worsley felt a glow of warm benevolence for how he'd taken pity on the friendless younger boy. Meanwhile, the younger boy was feeling pretty good about himself for how he'd not been mean to the rejected social outcast with the terrifying hair. The pair got on so well and didn't really know anyone else, so that when lunchtime came, they went together to the diner down the street from the hotel and had fries, burgers and a Coke each, while excitedly reviewing their new acquisitions. Wheels was most impressed by Worsley's copy of *Disturbing* – Worsley didn't show him *Squack* – and said he'd wanted to buy *Inappropriate*, but didn't think that he could smuggle it home past his parents. It seemed that the youngster was an undercover lover of Shaw Magazines, about which he was very well informed considering he said he'd never owned a single issue. He told Worsley that the lead writer on *Inappropriate* and *Disturbing*, Denny Wellworth, would be showing up at BeeCon1 the next day, but that Wheels wouldn't get to see him because his overprotective parents would be turning up tonight at six to take him home. Worsley, who'd heard that fans unable to afford a hotel room could sleep at the convention's all-night film show, made a note to attend Wellworth's talk tomorrow but felt it would be insensitive to mention this to the forlorn Dave Wheels.

After their meal they went back to the Billingham, where they hung out together for what was left of the afternoon. Despite their mutual antipathy towards King Bee, they both went to hear Davis Burke talk in the hotel basement's other big room, and were glad they had. In his mid-sixties and now doing highly paid commercial work for grown-up magazines, Burke was a self-effacing little guy who seemed pleased and surprised that there was anybody interested in the comic books that he'd done ten or twenty years ago. He talked about his influences, mostly Lester Gentle's Flatfoot Floyd, with what Burke called 'its stylish and dramatic balance between black and white', which left most of the teenage audience not even puzzled. He secured his biggest laughs with candid anecdotes – Burke was a naturally funny storyteller – about his time on King Bee for American. When asked about King Bee's 'creator' Richard Manning, Burke was smiling, twinkly-eyed and devastating.

'Richard Manning was a guy who liked to wear cravats and smoking jackets. He had this idea about a character called Ladybug Man, in a red suit with black spots. He couldn't write or draw to save his life, so he calls up Ron Blackwell, a great comics writer that I worked with on King Bee for many years, a real nice feller. Blackwell tells him Ladybug Man is the worst idea he's ever heard, and that he ought to change it to King Bee. Then Manning hires the artist Edward Hannigan to draw the character, and Hannigan and Blackwell come up with the Droll, and Buzz, and everybody else. They write and draw the whole thing, but the only credit on the book is Richard Manning's. Last I heard, he was in California turning out these dreadful, dreadful paintings. And apparently, even his crappy paintings, he hires someone else to do them. Big pal of Sam Blatz, as I remember.'

After that it was around five-thirty. Worsley sat with Dave Wheels while they waited for the latter's folks to come and pick him up. They swapped addresses so that they could correspond, and Worsley called it a historic moment in the partnership of Worsley Porlock and Dave Wheels, to which the younger boy responded, 'Who's Dave Wheels?'

Worsley was thus still cringing slightly when he stood outside the Billingham some minutes later, being introduced to the distrustful-looking parents of Dan Wheems, the fan formerly known as Dave Wheels. Mrs Wheems thanked Worsley, dutifully, for looking after her young son, but in a way that made it clear she thought he was most probably a trainee child molester, with a child molester's haircut. The Wheems family then went back to her sister's place, who they were visiting from Indiana, and Worsley went back inside the hotel where he tried to find somebody else to talk to.

He was partially successful, hanging out with Milton Finefinger discussing *What The – ?* and, incredibly, trading a 'hi' with the blonde girl from Seventh Heaven on his way back from the men's room. Finally, fortified by another diner trip, he settled in a corner of the room where he'd seen Davis Burke and readied himself for the all-night film show.

It was an unusual experience. It started with a haunted run of animated cartoons from the 1930s, black, white and a pearly grey like X-ray plates, contemporary tunes like 'Viper Rag' spooky and crackling on the soundtrack. Titled *Tadpole Tex* and featuring an immature amphibian in a Stetson, the creation of forgotten animation-wizard Ole Knutson, these were short, surreal, and filled with surely accidental metaphysics, like when Tadpole Tex encounters what seems to be God imagined as a giant white frog, who sends the hapless pollywog to a strange pond-life purgatory full of microorganisms with demonic faces. Feeling tired already, Worsley thought they might be the cartoons that people see behind their eyelids just before they die.

Next up were all the episodes – eight? Ten? Fifteen? A hundred? – of *The New Adventures of King Bee and Buzz*, the second movie serial from RKO to feature the two characters, made in the 1940s. In its own way, it was as unsettling as *Tadpole Tex*. For one thing, the costumes were slightly wrong, with the antennae on King Bee's mask looking droopy, as if they were made of felt. The outfits also drew attention to the fact that, in real life, made from real fabrics, superhero suits were sort of wrinkly and preposterous. And there were other things. The actor playing Buzz seemed to be in his early twenties; the Bee Buggy was an ordinary car, looked like a beat-up Oldsmobile; and worst of all, King Bee's hideout, the Hive, was now a kitchen table and a microscope. In one scene, leaning out of the Bee-Oldsmobile and talking to King Bee in a street full of people, Buzz pushed his domino mask up to his forehead like the whole secret-identity thing didn't matter. You could hear those members of the audience who weren't talking about the imminent moon landing gasp in disbelief. The villain, rather than the Droll or someone else out of the comic, was a standard Oriental fiend called Dr Dragon, who had some kind of special-effect death ray. Worsley found it hard to keep his eyes open, and by the sixth or seventh chapter, he was sound asleep.

When he woke very briefly some time later, it was during Fritz Lang's five-hour-long masterpiece *Siegfried*, although being only half awake, Worsley assumed it was still part of the interminable serial. From the brief sequence Worsley remained conscious for, it seemed that Dr Dragon turned out to have been an actual dragon all along. King Bee had evidently killed the villain, then had taken off his wrinkly costume so that he could bathe in Dr Dragon's blood, observed by twittering birds in the surrounding treetops. As his mind began to slide once more into a warm and comfortable oblivion, Worsley construed this as a cinematic pun about the birds and bees which, in his last scant moments of awareness, he thought very clever and sophisticated.

A few hours after that, he had another short stretch of lucidity. Unfortunately, this was halfway through a showing of bizarre, low-budget exploitation flick *Bee Kong a Buzz-Buzz*, made three years before by maverick director Dexter Fairfield Harris for about four hundred bucks, and borrowing satirically from the King Bee TV show. Worsley, dreaming with his eyes open, was not aware of this, and took Harris's plotless spoof as a continuation of the movie serial he thought that he was watching: it appeared that bathing naked in the lifeblood of his enemy had taken a huge psychological toll on King Bee. He now had noticeable stubble and a paunch, spoke with a different accent, and his costume had devolved into an utter travesty. The hero was depicted in a sleazy nightclub, giggling and sipping on what might have been a marijuana cigarette, dancing the Hully Gully while surrounded by at least a dozen topless women. The disjointed narrative of the RKO serial had unexpectedly veered into tragedy, with noble King Bee made into a leering barfly as a punishment for killing Dr Dragon and then using the dead villain as a shower accessory. The stripy sentinel was doing shots and dry-humping a stripper as Worsley passed out again. He hadn't even noticed that the tawdry final episode had been in near-fluorescent colour.

He woke properly around nine in the morning, when the hotel staff came in to clean up the convention room in preparation for Sunday's activities. He splashed water on his face out in the washroom, and then made another visit to the diner for a hearty breakfast. While there, he ran into someone else from the convention who was even younger than Dave Wheels/Dan Wheems, a happy, cheerful boy called Arvo Cake. Worsley, making conversation, commented on just how strange that King Bee serial had been, to which Cake, thinking of the scene where Buzz had pushed his mask up, readily agreed. He really was the sweetest kid.

The rest of that day, after Worsley's interrupted sleep, was something of a blur, best reconstructed later. In the morning was a hastily convened fan-artist's panel, where the most arresting element for Worsley was that one of the assembled fanzine illustrators – a nice, talkative guy who went by the name or nickname Christmas Day – was black. Like with the blonde girl helping out at Seventh Heaven, the guy being black was what made Worsley realise that the rest of the convention definitely wasn't. He decided that if he ran into Day he'd praise his art, which Worsley hadn't seen, so nobody would think him racist. Also in the morning was the panel with Sebastian Squires, TV's Carruthers, being interviewed by an excited Jimjon Jackson. Having had enough of King Bee after the upsetting avant-garde experience of the movie serial, Worsley elected to sit that one out and went instead to read *margins* and *Graphomania* in the almost deserted BeeCon1 reception area. Later he saw Arvo Cake again, who'd heard the Squires interview and said the English actor had talked mostly about how he liked living in cottages with people the eleven-year-old hadn't heard of, like 'dear Johnny Gielgud'. Both thought that this might have been the actor in the TV series who played King Bee's foe the Tickler, but weren't really sure. In any case, it didn't sound like Worsley had missed anything.

He skipped lunch after his heroic breakfast and, that afternoon, witnessed his first comics convention fancy-dress event. No more than eight or nine attendees had been bothered to make costumes, but the competition still managed to be hilarious. Joint winners were two kids who dressed as the Shaw Magazines mascots, Uncle Inappropriate and Cousin Disturbing. The joint runners-up were Sean from Seventh Heaven and his girlfriend, in beekeeper outfits that had dozens of toy bees attached to them by thin pieces of wire. Claiming to be the apiarists Dr James Reed and his wife Susannah, King Bee's parents, they ran round in circles screaming then dropped dead, thus recreating the iconic origin scene as portrayed in *Manhunt* #22.

The con's last scheduled panel was a sort of amiable debate between some of the younger writers in the industry, most of them former comics fans, and followed on almost immediately from the fancy-dress contest. The biggest name amongst the panellists was that of Jerry Binkle, currently a hit with fans for his exciting and enthusiastic work on Massive's *The Unrealistic Five*. Beside him were two younger writers from American – Ralph Roth, who'd done some stories for the mystery title *Tower of Frightening*, and Brandon Chuff, who'd been writing King Bee in *Manhunt* and was rumoured to be taking on the script duties of *United Supermen*. Binkle seemed irritated by his fellow panel members, Roth looked terrified and hardly said a word, while Chuff, hugely self-satisfied, said nasty things about the other guests and then pretended he was only kidding. But it was the last of the four writers, sitting at the table's other end from Binkle, that Worsley was really there to see, and who he was the most impressed by.

Denny Wellworth, in black turtleneck and jeans, elastic-sided boots and a thin leather coat, was the best dressed amongst the four, and also seemed to be the funniest and most intelligent. He was distinctly different to the others in that he appeared to have a life outside the comics industry, and didn't seem to care much about superheroes. His main interest, he said, was not so much in characters as in what could be done with visual storytelling, with the medium itself. When Brandon Chuff said, 'Denny here's a real know-nothing when it comes to superheroes. No, I'm only kidding,' Wellworth smilingly replied, 'I'm sorry, Brandon, but when I'm off work, home with my wife, the subject of your scripts for *King Bee* doesn't really come up very often.' Everybody laughed but Chuff and possibly Ralph Roth, who still looked trapped and frightened. Wellworth talked engagingly and modestly about working for Shaw, with all the SP artists who had been his heroes as a teenager, and how much he enjoyed writing without the limitations imposed by the Comics Code Authority. He told a fascinating anecdote about Jim Laws, the SP publisher and writer, who'd apparently been coming down from pep pills when he gave his testimony to the Senate subcommittee looking into juvenile delinquency, the thing that more or less brought the Code into being.

After the discussion broke up in appreciative applause, Worsley saw Denny Wellworth standing on his own, smoking a Marlborough in the reception area. Summoning up his courage, he approached the writer, told Wellworth how much he'd liked the talk, and asked if he'd mind signing Worsley's copy of *Disturbing*. Wellworth not only obliged – 'To Worsley Porlock, with regards from your Disturbing buddy, Denny Wellworth' – but he stood and chatted to the awestruck teen for some ten minutes, just as if they weren't admirer and admired. Learning that Wellworth had occasionally worked on the Human Tank for Massive, Worsley asked him what he thought about Sam Blatz, who Worsley had heard several critical remarks about over the BeeCon1 weekend. The writer laughed.

'Satanic Sam? Oh, everything they say is true. He cheated Joe Gold, Robert Novak, all those guys, and I doubt that he's ever written anything that's more demanding than a shopping list. But … well, I don't know. I don't think Blatz is evil so much as I think the guy's maybe got something wrong with him. Before I got into the business – this is 1960 when I was a teenage nobody – I can remember seeing Sam Blatz sitting having breakfast in a booth at the same deli I was in. And he was talking to his food. He sat there staring at his plate, like he was listening to what it had to say, and then he'd answer it, and it went back and forth like that for the whole meal. Whether he ever ate it, I don't know. It can't be easy eating something when you've had a heart-to-heart like that.'

All things considered, it had been the most amazing and transformative weekend of Worsley's life. He said goodbye to Denny Wellworth, then did a last circuit of the hotel basement shaking hands with Jimjon Jackson, Arvo Cake, Milton Finefinger and finally Sean from Seventh Heaven, although sadly not Sean's girlfriend, who had gone home early. Striding down the front steps of the Billingham into the dazzling July sunshine, purchases beneath his arm, Worsley felt filled with purpose and ambition for the first time ever. He'd been reading comics since he was a child, but this had been his first experience of the comics world, a world he realised that he wanted to be part of all his life. He couldn't draw or write, but then, by all accounts, Sam Blatz and Richard Manning were both in the same position. Standing waiting for the bus – that he still had the money for – to take him back to Jersey, sunlight pouring on his earnest features, Worsley carelessly made the career decision that would seal his fate, then watched some ants for the next fifteen minutes.

Meanwhile, on or near the moon, the three Apollo astronauts were dealing with an unanticipated side effect of their historic mission. With no atmosphere to shelter them from the torrential radiation pouring from the sun, all three were inadvertently exposed to an amount that changed their body chemistry. Neil Armstrong found he now had the ability to turn himself into a sentient liquid, while Buzz Aldrin could control and generate magnetic fields. The least irradiated of the three men, Michael Collins, paradoxically was the most drastically affected and became a hideous magma-monster, with tremendous strength and a big heart. Laying one bulky glove atop another, the three swore a solemn oath and, as the Ultranauts, returned to Earth and solved all of the planet's problems. Thwarted in their evil plans for an apocalyptic race-war, Charlie Manson and his Family were locked up in energy-prisons on the moon's dark side forever. War, disease, hatred and hunger were abolished, so that 1969 became known as the year when everything just kept on getting better. Worsley Porlock married the blonde girl from Seventh Heaven, and everyone on the Earth thereafter led fantastic lives, at least until Cosmax arrived from space in 2025 and ate the world.

8. (June, 1954)

Jim Laws in the hot seat and he's sweating not with June but with amphetamines he takes them for the long late deadline nights and hopes they'll get him through this bullshit but but but it's going on so long and these four guys these senators look like they think Jim's the most entertaining thing they've seen all day well no surprises there when Jim's the only one the single solitary soul who's proud of what he publishes the only one prepared to stand up and defend it when all these flag-waving Bible-thumping sons of bitches are just coming at the Constitution in wave after wave and if the industry just takes this sitting down they're going to end up with this Comics Code thing this white flag that Stickman and those other assholes at American or Blinky are attempting to run up the masthead at this very moment making like they're being morally responsible when it's just thinning out the competition what Jim has to do is focus and try not to lick his lips so much or do that thing where he rotates his jaw because there's plenty riding on this not just SP and the chair's hard and that Morton guy who's the chief counsel looks as if he's winding up to take another pitch—

MORTON: Mr Laws, you mentioned earlier that you'd inherited your business, Scientific Publications, from your father. Could you tell us more about that?

LAWS: My father, James Laws Senior, published America's first comic book collection, *Funnies on Parade*, back nearly twenty years ago. He saw the comic book as an important tool that could help educate America and do a lot of good. He founded Scientific Publications to inform the country's children about great Americans like Thomas Edison and about new scientific theories or inventions. When my father died in an unpleasant accident, the business came to me and I renamed the company Sensational, so as to more honestly represent the new direction that the line would take under my leadership, although I still consider our books educational.

Jim pours himself more water takes a sip tries not to lick his lips and can't help thinking of his father that was one hell of a way to die the best that could be said was that Jim Senior wouldn't have known anything about it just one moment he's there teeing up for the eighth hole he's happy he's relaxed and the next instant he gets pulverised literally pulverised by thirty pounds of frozen urine let go by a jet plane that was right then passing overhead like the old man was struck down with a bolt of piss not lightning by a God Jim's dad knew wasn't there maybe that's how it goes with atheists and God thinks fuck why waste a thunderbolt but but but Jim is getting off the point here and he'd better concentrate because one of the senators is frowning and now the chief counsel guy is—

MORTON: 'Sensational' would seem to indicate a very different policy from 'Scientific'.

SEN. FRASER: Mr Laws, you say your father's publications had a beneficial influence upon the children reading them. If comic books are capable of altering young people's minds to this degree, how can you then be sure that your books have no deleterious effect upon their readership?

LAWS: Senator, with great respect, I think that that's a matter of intention. Our writers and illustrators are amongst the finest in the field, and can make sure a story will have the effect that was intended. In the instance of my father, it was his intention to produce books that would educate the public scientifically, while in my own case, the intention is to educate our audience morally, so that they might be better people and better Americans. Were you to read our letter pages, I think that you'd be surprised by the intelligence and the maturity with which the social issues we raise in our stories are debated. Please remember that a story dealing with the terrible effects of juvenile delinquency is hardly an encouragement to that behaviour.

– *no more than the Bible is encouraging its readership to massacre the innocents or have sex with their daughters or go crucifying people although in his current circumstances Jim is having doubts about that last one can these people genuinely not see all the moralising him and Feinman put into those stories all the skill and care guys like Slim Whittaker Jeff Pleasant Arnie Eckstein all those guys put into making sure they got their point across and it was only SP had the balls to talk about this stuff about the bomb the Klan the brutal cops the ordinary*

Americans all gone privately crazy in the suburbs can they not see all of that or is this something else that's going on here where the outcome was agreed before the hearings even got announced but but but maybe that's the pills the paranoia making Jim suspect that this is all a set-up and why would the powers that be waste all that effort on a bunch of unimportant comics anyway sure Jim knows all about the uproar with the Wertham thing Seduction of the Innocent *but seriously one book with a few bits in* Ladies' Home Journal *and that's all it takes to bring this bullshit down on Jim and everybody else no no no paranoid or not there has to be a bigger picture Jim's not seeing and there isn't time to think about it now because Senator Fraser's saying something to the other Democrat Senator Henning now they're both looking at Jim he hopes the pills are going to last this out it's just they're keeping him up here so long much longer than the others and they've got so many questions that he's—*

SEN. FRASER: Mr Laws, I've read a number of the stories in your titles represented here as exhibits, and a majority appear to end in murder and dismemberment without any suggestion of moral instruction. If you are so confident in the redeeming social value of your publications, you would surely have no hesitation in submitting your books to a regulatory authority of the kind that was suggested earlier today, to ensure that they have the salutary effect that you intend?

LAWS: No, sir, I would not.

SEN. FRASER: And yet I understand that you do not support the version of these regulations we have seen this morning?

LAWS: There's a difference between accepting a regulatory authority in principle, and agreeing with the document that was presented in draft earlier. Some of those proposed regulations I agree with, whereas other ones, I don't.

– like like like for example that part where it says that it's forbidden to have the words Death or Murder as part of a comic's title and why didn't these cocksuckers just go all the way and outlaw the word Nutcase too that way they could put all of SP's biggest sellers out of

business in one fell swoop without even working up a sweat but no no they don't mention Nutcase *even though Jim knows that that's the book that really burns the asses of those bastards at American and Blinky who it just so happens are the major parties when it comes to drawing up this Comics Code thing and so this is their revenge those petty little shits this is the way they get their own back over fucking Blunderman and fucking Blanky that Jim ran in* Nutcase *and does he regret that now yeah sure he does sure he regrets it he regrets not letting Lenny Berman show the business types cornholing Blunderman's creators or show Blanky joining the John Birch society that's Jim's regrets but but but maybe now is not the time it feels as if they're starting to go harder on him now these senators like this is when they start to show their teeth or maybe Jim's just getting tired it's hard to tell he's been up here so long—*

SEN. FRASER: I'd like to move on to this text piece in *Sarcophagus of Murder* #17 as represented by Exhibit no. 10. Its title reads 'Don't be a Commie Stooge', and it makes reference to Dr Wertham and his book while claiming that the people most in favour of suppressing comic books are communists. Are you the author of this article?

LAWS: Yes, sir, I am. The piece makes reference to the fact that communist groups from around the world – including England, I believe – have launched attacks on comic books so they can indirectly criticise the US and its values.

SEN. FRASER: You are surely not suggesting that those people who do not approve of comic books are communists?

LAWS: No, sir, simply that the Communist Party is at the forefront, globally, of the attempt to stifle comics, and the group whose disapproval is the most vociferous. I certainly was not implying that persons connected to these subcommittee hearings might be communists, and I am confident our readers would have understood that.

– yeah but Jim could say more on that subject about what he'd heard and his you know his speculations when the rumour is that

Wertham either is or could be made to look like he's a communist and in the current climate that's the end of him the end of his career so when the FBI drop by and spell this out and tell him they can make it go away if he cooperates then he's all ears and what they want this is according to the story what they want is Wertham should work on this book links comics with delinquency because because because yeah actually why would they do that it's like Jim was thinking earlier about why go to all this effort for something as trivial as comic books and sure he'd like to think that SP's books were that important and that influential but he knows that that's not it and there's no reason for this persecution for this bullying unless unless unless what if it isn't comic books they're after here what if it's the pulp magazines that some comics financially support like say the science fiction mag Galactic Stories *that its publishers couldn't keep bringing out without the money they get from Galactic Comics and the science fiction magazines the science fiction magazines have been about the only platform in America that's been unanimous in putting down that prick McCarthy and maybe that's it maybe this is all fallout come from the House Un-American Activities Commission where they want to silence the science fiction field without it looking like that's what they're doing so they set the dogs on comics first knowing the pulps will all come tumbling after but but but this isn't helping with Jim's current circumstances his predicament and he's starting to feel as if they've got him on the ropes these senators and Jim had better have his mind set on the job in hand and not keep hopping on these trains of thought that take him out into the wilderness that take him nowhere—*

SEN. DERNE: I'd like to ask a question. Mr Laws, are you not being disingenuous in your replies to this committee? Are you serious in your contention that your publications are meant to be morally instructive to their readers? I draw your attention to Exhibit no. 7, *Cemetery of Death* #14, and to that issue's second comic story, 'Playground Games'. To summarise, it is the story of a Mr Johnson, a corrupt civic official who announces plans to close a much-loved children's playground so that he can profit from a big hotel development planned for the site. The children of the neighbourhood are shown reacting tearfully to the announcement, asking if there isn't anything that can prevent the closure. Finally, in the last panel, we learn that these children have killed and dismembered the official, and have then somehow augmented their play area with his body parts. The seats of swings are the man's severed forearms, while the ropes supporting them are his intestines. His plump torso is pressed into service as a trampoline, and the man's head adorns the centre of the merry-go-round. His legs have become the two ends of a grisly see-saw, with the children all depicted playing happily amongst his customised remains. The story's moral, if there is one, is delivered by a leering character known as 'the Necro-Filing Clerk' who says, if I may quote, 'Heh heh heh! Well, Death-Devotees! So Mr Johnson finally got kids to like him – and it wasn't just the weeping children who went all to pieces!' Mr Laws, how can you possibly suggest that such a story is intended to improve its audience morally?

LAWS: I think, I think you should remember that this is, you know, it's *Cemetery of Death*, which, clearly, it's a horror publication. And our readers, they expect this – I guess – ghoulish humour from us. What it does, I think, it makes light of the situation and it tells the reader they should take the story as a kind of joke or, or, or like a folk tale where there's something violent at the end, like, yeah, say, when the woodsman bursts in and chops up the wolf and rescues Goldilocks's grandma from inside him. It's like that. Only it's not a wolf, it's a civic official. We've updated things.

– shut up shut up shut up what now he's trying to tell them that SP's books are like Goldilocks and that civic officials are like wolves just what the fuck exactly is Jim doing here but but but that guy Derne he's one of the Republicans he'd come at Jim full on he came out swinging and it took Jim by surprise and when they take a story out of context like that they can make it sound like like Jim didn't

know like it was meant for kids as young as the ones in the story like the story's trying to get these little kids to dismember officials and it's oh no what it is he realises is he's crashing crashing on the pills running on empty and he volunteered to come here and to testify and speak up for his books he was so proud of and now this and everything's collapsing he's collapsing and it's all because they kept him talking here so long and now and now he feels like he's some kid who's up before the principal except that there's four principals and they're not principals they're fucking senators why did Jim ever put himself through this what did he think he would achieve and so he's crashing and he can't think straight and here comes Fraser now the Democrat he's shuffling through the exhibits he's got a face like somebody just farted and Jim has to admit that this don't look like what you'd call good—

SEN. FRASER: If I may, I'd like to redirect you from the content of your publications to their cover illustrations. If we could look at Exhibit no. 12, *Sarcophagus of Murder* #22, and in particular at its front cover. Mr Laws, at any time in my description, if you think I am misrepresenting what I see, I'd be obliged if you'd correct me. Down the illustration's left side are three cameo caricatures contained in circles, these being your trio of so-called 'Ghastly Greeters' – the Corpse-Clutcher, the Necro-Filing Clerk, and the Morgue-Minder – who introduce the various tales within. The cover's greater part, to which these portraits are appended, shows us the interior of a large department store, perhaps not unlike Macy's, in what is apparently the Christmas period. Over towards the picture's left is a large, decorated indoor Christmas tree that has its upper boughs obscured in shadows cast by the department store's high ceiling. Around the tree's base, on the shop floor, we see customers and store staff looking up in horror at the tree's top, where we see, in silhouette against blue shadow, that a seated female figure, hopefully a dead one, seems to be impaled. Down in the store below, children are crying, mothers are fainting, sturdy

American fathers are biting their knuckles, and a security guard appears to be vomiting in a cash register. I put it to you, Mr Laws, that this is a scene wholly without redeeming social merit, that has furthermore been both conceived and drawn with no consideration of its moral impact, nor of the most rudimentary standards of good taste.

LAWS: I, I, I, I disagree. I think, I think that how it's drawn, how it's designed, it's in good taste. You can't, you know, the way it's drawn, you can't see anything, the way we've got the shadows there. The horror aspect, see, it's all in how we've got the looks on people's faces, how we've got the horrified expressions. So, the horror's not direct and, and, and actually I think it's kind of subtle, what we're doing there, so, no. I don't agree. I think it's in, I think the cover's in good taste.

SEN. FRASER: I see. And what, if I may ask, would be your definition of a cover that is in bad taste?

LAWS: Well, you know, that's very difficult … it's very hard to say, I mean, it's all subjective, but I guess that if we'd had the artist, if instead of how we've got it in a long shot, if we'd done a close-up so that you could see the treetop going into her vagina, that would have been in bad taste.

– *and straight away Jim knows he could have handled that a fuck of a lot better because now the whole world seems to have just stopped and all the sound and movement have gone out of everything so all four senators are sitting frozen looking at him with the same expression on their faces like their noses are attempting to retract into their skulls their gaping lips are curled back almost inside out eyes shrivelling in the sockets into hard glass marbles of contempt disgust consuming hatred while all colour has drained from the face of the stenographer and the chief counsel claps one hand over his mouth and stares as if at an appalling train wreck with a hundred dead and all this in a silence so complete that Jim can't even hear the hum of traffic in the street outside now one by one the senators are standing up they're gathering their papers and exhibits all without a word without removing the unblinking glares of utter loathing from him for an instant now they're all leaving the chamber even Jim's attorney Marv who came along to show support and be a friendly face can only shake his head eyes full of tragedy and follow them out of the room so Jim's left there alone and doesn't know what he should do and though time doesn't seem to pass he notices the shadows of the microphones are getting longer on the tables then eventually the cleaners come in Puerto Rican women who don't look at him but trade meaningful glances with each other as they clean around him and then even they are gone so Jim sits motionless in the committee room as daylight gradually subsides and knows that it's all finished sure he can continue* Nutcase *as a magazine and get around the code thing that way but the vision that he had for comics that's all over and the lights are going down the lights are going down and Jim knows this is it this is his thirty pounds of frozen piss the lights are going down and even when they hit pitch-black it feels like they've still got a way to go—*

9. (November, 2015)

PAGE 1.

Panel 1.
OK, this is a one-page strip that has nine panels, all the same size, arranged in a three-by-three grid with a banner heading at the top that reads: **The Origin of THUNDERMAN – *Who he is and how he came to be!*** Maybe over to the far right of this banner, contained in a circle, we could have a head-and-shoulders shot of Thunderman just smiling at the reader, probably in a late thirties/early forties art style where his eyes are sooty wrinkles. Moving on to the strip itself, in this first panel we are in a teenage boy's room in a working-class house in Delaware, in 1937, and it is night-time. Up in the left foreground, looking into the panel away from us in an approximately head-and-shoulders close-up, we see seventeen-year-old science fiction fan and

amateur fanzine artist David Kessler, who has his sketchbook open and visible as he works on a rough illustration, holding the open pad in his left hand while drawing with his right. Kessler has fair hair and wears round, wire-rimmed spectacles. He is smiling with teenage enthusiasm as he sketches, his expression earnest and open: a Depression-era American kid having fun. He is drawing a line illustration of Thunderman, but this is not the Thunderman with which we're familiar. Instead, this is a bald, villainous science fiction tyrant, wearing a typical 1930s science fiction outfit – all tunics and high boots as I remember – and striking a megalomaniacal pose, hands raised and clawing at the air. The only similarity with the present-day character is the Thunderman chest emblem, the letter T with a thin black cloud forming its crossbar and a white lightning bolt as its riser, which the bald character that Kessler is depicting has on the front of his tunic. Looking past Kessler and his sketchbook into the room, over in the right near background, we can see Kessler's best friend Simon Schuman, also seventeen. Schuman, slightly shorter and more compressed than Kessler, with dark curly hair but the same eager and enthusiastic teenage grin, is seated full-figure just off-panel right, but is leaning into the right near background, facing left as he types on a battered old Underwood that stands on a small wooden table positioned in the centre near background directly beneath the room's window. As he types, Schuman looks across the room and grins at Kessler. I really want to get across the thrill, the fun, the genuine teenage excitement that these kids are getting from creating something together. As for the room they're in, it's cosy, shabby and lamplit. Perhaps we can find one of those oppressive wallpaper designs of the era, with the outsized floral motifs, and paper the room with it here? See what you think, and then do what looks best to you, as ever. If there's room, we might see a couple of pulp science fiction magazines lying around the room, with titles like *Unbelievable Stories* or *Spicy Astronaut*. Out through the window that is positioned directly above the typewriter, to subtly underline the science fiction nature of what is being worked on, we are looking out into the black Delaware night, with perhaps a couple of distant and lonely stars, burning low on the dark horizon. The caption might sit best down towards the panel's bottom right corner.

CAPTION: DELAWARE, 1937: TEENAGERS **DAVE KESSLER** AND **SI SCHUMAN** CRAFTED FANZINE TALES OF ALIEN TYRANT **THUNDERMAN**, INSPIRED BY PULP SCIENCE FICTION MAGAZINES.

Panel 2.
In this second panel, we cut to a different American night; a different American year. We are now outdoors, in a dark and secluded unloading area somewhere in New York, and it is maybe 1926, at the height of Prohibition. The scene is possibly lit by an isolated street light somewhere in the panel's right background, if that gives us the noir atmospherics and shadows that I think this shot would benefit from. Down in the bottom foreground, we can see at least part of two or three stacked bundles of pulp magazines, cross-tied with string, which have been piled on the ground, up close to us. If we can make out the covers, they are all for the same issue of something called ***SPICY TORTURE Stories***, and they have covers showing a near-naked 1920s blonde, manacled to a dungeon wall and being menaced by a leering hunchback with a branding iron. These magazines stand forgotten in the bottom foreground, while the panel's real business is transacted in the near background beyond that: over to the far left of the near midground we can just see the rear of a 1920s delivery truck protruding into the panel from off, its rear doors open. Unloading crates of what is clearly illicit booze from the back of the truck, we see two fairly stereotypical hired goons of that 1920s vintage, thuggish and brutal faces, maybe one of them smoking, one of them in a peaked cap. Both are full-figure. As they unload the booze, we see a well-dressed racketeer standing watching them, full-figure in the right far midground,

his hands perhaps sunk in the pockets of his expensive mohair coat and a thick cigar jutting from his self-satisfied smile, a wisp of grey smoke escaping up into the starless night above. This is bootlegger and publisher Albert Kaufman, overseeing his latest shipment of alcohol, with his pulp magazines stacked at the rear of the trucks to conceal the real contents from Feds or border officials. Kaufman is maybe in his forties here, a well-fed man who wears his short black hair slicked back, his dark eyes twinkling and gloating. He probably wears a broad-brimmed hat, a pricey suit and well-polished shoes. Again, perhaps the caption is down in the panel's lower right.

CAPTION: PRINTED IN CANADA FOR PUBLISHERS LIKE MOB ASSOCIATE **ALBERT KAUFMAN**, PULPS EXISTED AS COVER FOR TRUCKING CANADIAN BOOZE INTO PROHIBITION AMERICA.

Panel 3.

Now, in this final panel on the top tier, we jump to the relatively small main office of American Comics in New York, on an optimistic spring afternoon in 1938. Up in the right foreground, leaning back in his creaking thirties office chair and looking into the panel away from us, we see Albert Kaufman, now in his fifties and probably still with a smouldering cigar wedged into his faintly predatory smile. Here, he is wearing an ordinary 1930s business suit and looks slightly less obviously gangster-like, although he maybe still wears a diamond pinkie ring. Looking across Kaufman's desk – which has a couple of finished pages of David Kessler's Thunderman art resting on it, this time in panels, and showing a character that looks much more like a simplified early version of the present Thunderman than the bald megalomaniac we saw being sketched in panel one – we are looking at David Kessler, left, and Si Schuman, right, as they sit facing us and the smiling Kaufman across the art-littered desk. Both of the eighteen-year-old boys are slightly better dressed here than in panel one, since they're in the big city and are hoping to make a good impression, and both of them look happy and excited to be received so warmly by these nice New York publishers. Kessler, over on our left of the midground, perhaps has a scuffed portfolio in his lap, from which he is enthusiastically extracting yet another page of comic-strip artwork. Schuman, on the right, is holding one of his typed scripts and is perhaps pointing to it as he jabbers away enthusiastically. Standing behind the two seated boys, with one of his hands resting on each of their chair backs, leaning in with a smile to match Kaufman's, we see American Comics' lawyer, Sidney Rosenfeld. Rosenfeld is taller and leaner than Kaufman, balding but still with dark hair at the back and sides, clean-shaven and with a decent-looking face for a man in his fifties. He sports spectacles with heavy black rims and probably wears a black suit, white shirt and a black tie. If there's any room in the background, there could be framed copies of *SPICY TORTURE* or the poorly drawn front cover of the first issue of *MANHUNT Comics* hanging up on the wall. The caption here should perhaps be down towards the panel's lower left.

CAPTION: REDESIGNING THUNDERMAN AS A HERO, IN NEW YORK THE WORKING-CLASS BOYS ATTRACTED THE ATTENTION OF KAUFMAN, AND COMPANY LAWYER **SIDNEY ROSENFELD**.

Panel 4.
In this first panel on the second tier, we have an abrupt shift of visual register as we switch from a documentary style to an early forties comic-cover style. We are apparently in the offices of the German high command sometime between 1942 and 1945, at least to judge from the swastika flag hanging on a wall in the near background. A 1940s-style Thunderman, his eyes slits of righteousness, is springing into the panel's midground from

the left, in a suitably dynamic pose, and delivering a thunder-powered punch to the jaw of a cartoonish and flailing Adolf Hitler. From the right bottom foreground, a stereotypically square-headed Nazi storm trooper – no, I don't know what he's doing in Hitler's office either – is perspiring and looking comically frightened, in roughly a head-and-shoulders close-up, as he discharges his machine gun at Thunderman, only to have his bullets bounce off the character's chest. The caption would probably fit best down to the bottom left of the panel.

CAPTION: WHEN KESSLER AND SCHUMAN ENLISTED IN 1942, FORMER UNION LAWYER ROSENFELD HAD THEM SIGN THUNDERMAN'S OWNERSHIP TO AMERICAN FOR THE WAR'S DURATION.

Panel 5.

In this panel, we intermingle the documentary and the comic book aspects for symbolic effect: it is a sunny day in New York, and we are up on the roof of the American Comics building, although it doesn't have to be identified as such; it's just a flat roof. Up to either side of the foreground, we see partial rear views of both Albert Kaufman, left, and Sidney Rosenfeld, right, as they both stand facing away from us into the background, both around half-figure and both with their hands knitted complacently behind their backs. Perhaps in Rosenfeld's hand we can see a rolled-up contract, presumably Kessler and Schuman's. Looking between and beyond them into the panel's midground, we can see a full-figure image of Thunderman – maybe a tidier, 1960s version here, avuncular and smiling – about to touch down on the rooftop as he descends from the clear New York sky with one leg already extended beneath him. He faces directly towards us and the two men as he lands, smiling, and slung over each of his muscular shoulders is a gigantic sack with a large **$** symbol printed on the side of each bag. If we can see Kaufman and

Rosenfeld's faces, they are smiling quietly and confidently. Of the two captions in this panel, how about we put the first one at the top, while the second caption we place in the bottom centre of the frame?

CAPTION: THEY NEVER GOT IT BACK.
CAPTION: IN ANIMATED CARTOONS, MOVIE SERIALS, SYNDICATED STRIPS AND TV SHOWS, THUNDERMAN MADE AMERICAN A VERY WEALTHY COMPANY.

Panel 6.
In this final panel on the second tier, we cut to a morgue in New York, sometime in the later 1960s. The morgue, by its nature, is cold, austere and white. Naked on a marble slab in the bottom foreground we see the supine head and shoulders of the dead and now much older David Kessler, although we can only see a little of the back of Kessler's balding head, because the white-sleeved arms and hands of a mortuary assistant are reaching into view from off-panel left and pulling up a cloth to cover the dead artist's face. Rather than being a white mortuary sheet, the cloth in question is actually Thunderman's cloak, with the thundercloud-and-lightning-bolt letter T in the centre of it, being raised to cover the dead face of Thunderman's co-creator. For compositional reasons as well as light-source reasons, I think we should have a single small window set high on the wall in the centre near background. The two captions here should perhaps both go in whatever space is available up towards the top of the panel.

CAPTION: WHEN **BROTHERS BROTHERS** PURCHASED AMERICAN, SIDNEY ROSENFELD BECAME THE CORPORATION'S CHIEF LAWYER.
CAPTION: MEANWHILE, ARTIST DAVID KESSLER DIED, BLIND, IN AN UPSTATE INSTITUTION.

Panel 7.

This first panel on the bottom tier shows a scene in a twenty-first-century city by night, probably New York circa 2012. We are positioned directly across the street from a modern movie theatre that has big and enthusiastic lines of people filing into it, past its box office. According to the cinema's illuminated hoarding, it is showing that year's Thunderman reboot, *MAN of STORMS*. Up in the foreground, over on our side of the street, we have an anonymous Brothers Bros executive standing just off-panel left and reaching into view as we see him holding out, in one well-tailored hand, a rather small bag of cash with a rather small **$** sign printed on its side. Reaching into view over on the right, from where she stands just off-panel right, we see the arms and hands of a young-to-middle-aged woman: in her left hand, nearest us, she holds a contract, and in her right, she holds a pen with which she is signing it. Looking between the arms of these off-panel people, we are gazing across the street to where the latest Thunderman seems to be doing big business, judging from the queuing crowds. Perhaps both captions could go at the bottom here, beneath the arms extending in from off-panel either side.

CAPTION: BROTHERS BROTHERS PROSPERED WITH SUCCESSFUL THUNDERMAN MOVIES. THUNDERMAN'S CREATORS DIDN'T.

CAPTION: YEARS LATER, THEIR FAMILIES SETTLED, FOR A FRACTION OF THE CHARACTER'S VALUE.

Panel 8.

The penultimate panel is a sort of documentary shot that reuses compositional elements from a couple of our preceding panels. In it we are in the nice New Jersey home of mob boss John Gotti's aunt. Up in the foreground, standing mostly off-panel to either side and facing away from us, as with Kaufman and

Rosenfeld in panel five, we have two mobster goons in bad-fitting suits, with their hands behind their backs. The one on the right is maybe holding a cosh. Looking between them into the chintzy domestic midground, we see a floral-print sofa arranged facing us with a coffee table set in front of it. Sitting on the sofa facing us, looking nervous and out of their depths, we have an executive from Brothers Bros on the left, looking up worriedly at the foreground mobsters, while seated to our right of him, we have an executive from *DISTANCE* magazine, bent over the table as he hurriedly and tremulously signs his part of the contract. Standing behind the sofa and leaning forward with both hands on the sofa's back to either side, reprising his pose in panel three, is a now older Sidney Rosenfeld. Rosenfeld is in his seventies here, the hair around the back and sides of his head white instead of black, but he still possesses the same malefic coiled-spring energy as when he was younger, and as he leans in over the men signing the contract, he still has the same vulpine smile. Perhaps in the background, as a homely touch, there might be a framed photograph of a smiling John Gotti hanging on the room's rear wall. The two captions here should perhaps go bottom centre.

CAPTION: BROTHERS' MERGER WITH **DISTANCE** PUBLISHING, ARRANGED BY SID ROSENFELD, ANNOUNCED THE CORPORATE ERA.

CAPTION: THE DEAL WAS SIGNED AT JOHN GOTTI'S AUNT'S PLACE.

Panel 9.

In this final panel, we are looking at a traditional shot across the waters at Manhattan Island and its business district, with the twin towers of the World Trade Center rising up over to the left, towards the clear skies of a sunny day. The island should be positioned relatively low in the panel here, to leave plenty of room for the sky. In the heavens over Manhattan we can see a gigantic, spectral half-figure shot of Thunderman; an outline without colour amongst the drifting clouds, as if this were Thunderman's benign ghost or his immortal spirit or something like that. He has his left fist resting on his ghostly hip, in his traditional power stance, while his right hand is raised to his brow in a kind of informal salute, waving goodbye to the reader and smiling good-naturedly and paternally as he does so – the big, friendly Thunderman in the sky who watches over us all. Of the two captions here, the first floats somewhere in the panel's middle reaches, while the second goes down at the bottom, towards the left. Over in the bottom right corner of this last panel, where it might traditionally have a small box that reads 'The End', I propose we have a miniature Thunderman 'T' emblem instead, with the cumulonimbus crossbar and the thunderbolt upright.

CAPTION: THAT'S WHO THUNDERMAN IS. THAT'S HOW HE AND CORPORATE AMERICA CAME TO BE …

CAPTION: … AND THE WORLD WOULD NEVER BE THE SAME AGAIN!

10. (March, 1987)

Eighteen months dry, so the light still jangled and the overwhelming detail of each moment was like ground glass, sometimes, in his eyes. Porlock walked down Fifth Avenue towards his introductory meeting with the people at American, towards his lifelong goal of being a professional of some kind in the comics industry, his gait robotic and his feet leaded with destiny.

He'd started drinking in his teens, and in his early twenties with determination. At the time he'd sold and traded comic artwork as a demi-living, pages picked up off acquaintances from Worsley's fanzine days. The fledgling business had involved a lot of time spent at convention bars, and sometime in amongst all that, Worsley was married to Ramona, only something must have happened because then he wasn't. It was devastating, probably. He couldn't actually recall enough of their relationship to say for sure. Renata! Renata, not Ramona. Why did he keep doing that?

It hadn't been long after Ra … after Renata left that Worsley's low points slid into debasement's infrared extremities. At ChiCon '84, he'd woken in a dumpster with shit in his hair. Then, at ChiCon '85, when the exact same thing had happened, it had come to him that this could be some sort of warning sign. He wasn't superstitious, but the dumpster had been up in the same corner, the same parking lot, behind the same hotel on both occasions. How could that …? Anyway, it was around then Milton Finefinger had pointed out that Worsley – with his contacts in the industry, with his address book – would be the front runner for an editorial post at American, if not for all the dumpster/shit-in-hair type incidents.

Worsley had protested, being drunk, at this characterisation. He'd pointed out to Milton and Milton's transparent conjoined brother that the industry's finest creators – many of them – had been alcoholics, like SP's Slim Whittaker, *King Bee* writer Ron Blackwell, Sam Earl who'd created the immortal Silly-Putty Pete, Bert McIntyre of Fishman fame, and on and on, until Finefinger noted that approximately half the names on Porlock's list had perished of cirrhosis and the rest had shot themselves. Besides, American's head honcho David Moskowitz, as a teetotaller, would be unlikely to find Worsley's argument convincing. Whereas if he were to dry out, they were always looking for assistant editors and suchlike at American, particularly on the slumping Thunderman books. That, right there, had given Worsley Porlock the incentive to turn things around. Why not trade his reliance on booze for his original addiction to the surely harmless comic book? He'd joined a twelve-step program, and the part requiring him to have faith in a higher power, he'd thought of Thunderman.

In many ways, he mused as he proceeded down Fifth Avenue, his childhood hero was the one who'd saved him. Worsley had been falling into someplace black and bottomless where excrement was hair gel, and then, in mid-air, somebody had caught him and had borne him up into the light and breeze, like he was an out-of-condition Peggy Parks on one of her bimonthly plunges from an office window. Glancing up at the belittling towers to either side, it struck him that there were a lot of office windows around here for a vivacious and inquisitive young girl to fall from.

Looming now before him was the Brothers building where American had offices at 777, with a dazzling white neon sign to that effect up on the roof, so that the numerals were visible from right across the city. He remembered Denny Wellworth, maybe joking, telling him that this was a deliberate reference to a book about kabbalah by notorious English black-magic guy, Aleister Crowley. Denny had a marijuana-generated theory that the ancient Hebrew magic system had been employed by the Brothers Brothers corporation to cement their power, or summon Elder Gods, or some business like that. It had been pretty funny, the way Denny told it.

Like a bank, the building's lobby was all marble, with the churchlike hush fringed at its edge by echoed whisper. Well-presented men and women came and went in demure quiet, lugging their briefcases through the great columns of sunlight propped against the front glass. The prevailing mood was of immediate and natural respect for power, and Worsley found he was OK with that. American, he knew, was on the twenty-eighth floor. Almost tiptoeing, he made his way to a side concourse where two banks of elevators faced each other across tiles that were marmoreal and sibilant. Locating one that had floors twenty-five to forty as its promised destinations, Worsley congregated with a random half a dozen staring strangers, silent as a baby funeral, watching the bright ruby numbers counting down towards them. Nine eight seven six five four three two Ground Floor. Bing.

The doors slid back with a self-satisfied intake of breath, and in the elevator was a monster. Eight-limbed, a bespoke arachnid but demonstrably bipedal, it stood quivering grotesquely at the centre of the otherwise deserted carriage. Readjusting the parameters of the word 'alien', the mind reeled, failing to provide a category for what it was looking at: the creature, or perhaps the object, seemed to face towards the elevator's rear, at least from the alignment of its handmade oxblood brogues. All six of the thing's upper limbs were folded in defensively around the polyester thorax, four of them emerging from the horror's back, the upper pair in navy with pink spots that folded down like wings across the shoulder blades, the lower white and hairless and tensed like a backward cricket's. As it shook and trembled, it made sounds that were uncanny, oscillating between different growling registers, one deep, one deeper still, as in the strange throat-singing of the Tuvan people. Growling, shivering, the otherworldly dignitary made its debut to the small, stunned crowd stood on the far side of the gaping doors, where no one moved save for their pupils dwindling to pinpricks, atoms, quarks and then gone altogether. An unfathomable, hideous angel, it spoke only to apocalypse.

Then the eruptive boiler shuddering ceased, the rasping and inhuman dual voice fell silent, and the rear limbs gradually unpeeled themselves. Part arthropod and part amoeba, the reality-defying entity next fissured into two discrete and separate life forms. Suddenly, the carpeted and spacious box contained a stony-faced executive in his late fifties and a short, blonde businesswoman in designer clothes and possibly her early forties. Neither of the pair looked at the still frozen spectators, not as if they were avoiding eye contact, but more as though the dumbstruck onlookers outside simply did not exist on their attenuated plateau of awareness. Smoothing down her dotted navy skirt, the woman said, in a surprisingly deep voice, 'So, you can get those contracts to me by next week?', and there was the brief buzz of a drawn zipper before her associate replied, 'I'll see what I can do.' Then they both turned towards an audience that were apparently invisible to them and exited the elevator, moving independently away across the shining, shushing lobby murmuring beyond.

Without acknowledging what they'd just witnessed, Worsley and his fellow trauma victims entered the vacated space and jabbed requisite buttons. It had been a drive-by haunting. They ascended in a redolence of fornication, wildly different individuals united by their desperate longing not to be there; by the certainty that on their separate and distant deathbeds, they and all these other people that they didn't know would whimper at the same appalling memory, made family by monstrosity. There was an old guy at the rear that Worsley thought was maybe crying.

When the doors sighed open at floor twenty-eight, he disembarked and was immediately transfixed by shock at where he found himself. In panic, he turned back towards the elevator but it was already gone, whisking its sex-bombed passengers towards the building's unknown upper reaches.

Porlock stood in an unpopulated corridor that had the look of an unwelcome acid flashback. Walls of citric yellow had been overprinted in electric turquoise with a pattern as if two or more sheets of concentric-circle halftone had been overlaid, so the resultant moiré flickered into butterfly ellipses as Lorenz attractors or berserk magnetic fields, an aura of anxiety and stress made visible. Extraterrestrial, the décor made it just about impossible for him to get his bearings, and he bitterly reflected that addressing his drink problem had been meant to rule out episodes like this.

Down at the corridor's far end, like some mirage viewed through a heat haze of pulsating colour, a tall man was standing by a watercooler with his back to Worsley, too far off to call to. His spatial awareness floundering in weaponised interior design, like that of a CIA mind-control experiment, Porlock progressed between the spiralling and spinning walls with the exaggerated stagger of a furloughed sailor yet to find his land legs. Eighteen months' hard-won sobriety and here he was, stuck in a Hitchcock titles sequence, stumbling like a baby. The distant figure further down the psychedelic tunnel did not move, nor, for a scary thirty seconds, seem like it was getting any closer.

Then, in a confused perceptual rush exacerbated by the wallpaper, Worsley was in a small reception area with an abandoned desk and just the one guy at the water cooler, maybe a receptionist taking a break or something. 'Boy, am I glad to see you,' gushed Worsley in relief after the corridor.

The life-size resin replica of Ambrose Bell, secret identity of Thunderman, made no reply.

Porlock was frightened now, and in that elongated moment felt as if he hung above a garish abyss where he had no way of knowing what was real. Then Brandon Chuff rounded a corner into the untenanted space and said, 'Worsley Porlock! Jesus Christ, you look like shit, man. No, I'm kidding.'

Worsley was just pleased to spot a friendly – or at least, passive-aggressive – face. He babbled a hello to the *United Supermen* writer and editor, then let Chuff lead him down the swirling migraine passages for a full tour of the American experience. They first called at the office of Pete Mastroserio, wherein the company's executive director was involved in a robust exchange of views with writer Jerry Binkle over – it goes without saying – Mr Ocean. Mastroserio, a rumpled figure made of duvet meant to trick the guards, was saying that the last time anybody on the planet had been interested in the subaquatic sentinel was in the 1970s, when a fired colourist had crudely drawn an erect penis jutting from Kid Ocean's swimming trunks that nobody had spotted before it was on the newsstands. Jerry Binkle, who had longed to see an eighty-page giant Mr Ocean annual since the age of twelve, was differently persuaded. Blond hair thinning, pink with indignation, Binkle was a strawberry ice cream dessert confronting Mastroserio's more substantial smoked-fish entrée, when they never should have been on the same menu. Both men cordially greeted Worsley for about five seconds, then resumed their bellowed threats and imprecations as if Chuff and Porlock were no longer in the room. 'Look, Jerry, no offence, but seriously? I wouldn't wipe my ass on Mr Ocean.' 'Pete, you know that I respect you, both professionally and personally, but I am going to hunt you and your family down and kill you all for this.' Picking up signals that their visit was inopportune, Worsley and his snickering Virgil backed out of the office and resumed their jaunt through the eye-rupturing Inferno.

Wandering in the mechanically tinted labyrinth, it came to Worsley that these halftone halls and life-size comic characters were, in some strange way, flattening him, turning him to something two dimensional, as if his entry to the industry were also entry to a new life as cartoon, conducted in the depthless confines of a coloured page, forever slightly out of register. He wondered distantly if a prolonged exposure to this wilfully unreal atmosphere, month after month, year after year, explained the mangled personality that typified a long-term comic book professional. Deciding that most probably it did, he nonetheless continued blithely with his own adventure into that career.

With Chuff, he next called at the office of the venerable *Thunderman* line editor, Sol Stickman, who had seemingly been born a septuagenarian at some remote point in America's eventful past. After the deafening crossfire of Pete Mastroserio's hostile environment, Stickman's more orderly enclosure was a polished-wood oasis of congeniality and calm, though not without its own extra dimensions of unease. Foremost as a disquieting element was Stickman's practised and mesmeric patter, honed across a hundred thousand bagels-and-lox breakfasts into something in between off-Broadway shtick and the Egyptian *Book of Coming Forth by Day*:

'Trust me, you're gonna go far. Like I always say, if it was up to me, further the better. Ever hear o' Hugo Gernsback? Used to shine my shoes. He had this nutty idea for what he called "Fictional Science", like how gravity's a kind of glue that things secrete, but it's invisible, and stuff like that. I told him, "Kid, change those two words around, you could be on to something. Otherwise, don't waste my time." These guys, what do they know? It's like Herb Wells, this Brit who wanted me to agent for him one time. He'd show me his novels that he couldn't sell, like *The Moving Through Physical Space Machine*, which was about a wheelchair, or *The Man That Everybody Could See*. *War of the*

Adjacent Parishes, that was another. I said, "Herb, look, you're an OK writer. What you don't got is pizazz," and I suggest he make these little changes, nothing major. Next thing, the guy's telling me that I'm the greatest editor or literary agent that the world has ever known, so I say, "Yeah, sure. That and five cents will buy me a cup o' coffee. Now get outta here, ya bum." It's like I said at Julie Metzenberger's funeral when all his relatives were trying to drag him from the coffin so that they could kick him, "I've met more shmucks in this business than I would have as a shmuck collector, out collecting shmucks in Shmuckburgh, Pennsylvania." Anyway, so, Worsley Porlock. You look like the kind of half-developed guy who probably grew up in awe of me. I'm guessing that you're gonna wanna see the scrapbook. All you late-stage foetuses are basically the same.'

Without waiting for Worsley's answer, Stickman rustled in an office cupboard and produced the promised scrapbook, tombstone in the form of document, before trapping his speechless guest beneath its aeon-spanning weight. Numb and uncomprehending, Porlock turned the matt black pages that were badged with clippings from archaic newspapers, letters and postcards signed to the science fiction agent from dead literary giants, or photographs of Stickman, always seventy, in a variety of different cities, towns and decades, generally in winter, with his breath a white silk hanky draped upon the air. 'See that eight-month-old baby in the pushchair? Stephen King.' Fighting a mounting sense of obscure panic, Worsley flipped through the funereal pages of this dreadful ledger until coming to a tipped-in photographic print, spectral and bleached where too much light had been allowed in, that he thought he recognised as a daguerreotype. It showed Sol Stickman, in his sempiternal dotage, standing grinning with one hand clasped round the shoulder of a smaller, frailer man who peered mistrustfully into the lens, confused and squinting. Porlock slammed the scrapbook shut before his lurching psyche could confirm that it was definitely Edgar Allan Poe.

Later, and with hindsight, he considered that most probably he'd been in shock, because he had no memory of exiting Sol

Stickman's room, and only seemed to fully regain consciousness when he and Brandon Chuff were once more in the whirling technicolour of the corridor, en route for David Moskowitz's office. It was here, Worsley was certain, that the publisher would put him through the formal interview that would decide his future in the comics industry, or lack of one. It was here, also, that Chuff grimaced apologetically and said, 'Worsley, I'm afraid I'm going to have to ditch you here. There's work that I need to get back to, so I'll leave it up to David to tell you that you're a worthless putz, and that American is never going to be dumb enough to hire you. I'm just joking.'

Chuff then disappeared into the bilious vortex. Porlock knuckled hesitantly at the varnished oak and realised that his palms were sweating. Long, excruciating moments passed without the knock being acknowledged, and he was about to leave the building and his dream job there and then, when, on the far side of the door, a nasal yet imperious voice enunciated the word, 'Come.' Uncertainly, he waited, but the message didn't seem to have a second syllable. Swallowing hard, oiling the cool brass doorknob with his copious perspiration, Worsley went.

Within the softly lighted crepuscule of Moskowitz's workplace, the unnerved interviewee came finally to notice that none of the rooms he'd visited thus far had windows. Disconnected from the passage of the day and human time, the hours at American were small hours nested in continuous night. The publisher's huge desk was at the chamber's centre, soaking in a pool of strong light from above that only served to reinforce the sense that this was a place of interrogation. Moskowitz did not look up from the small print that he was studying as Porlock entered, leaving Worsley to assume that he should find his own seat and wait quietly for the other man to notice him. Other than Moskowitz's swivel chair, however, there weren't any other places in the spacious office to sit down, except for a three-legged wooden milking stool, positioned on the carpet opposite the engrossed publisher. Worsley stood blinking at this for some time – was it a joke; a test; an infantilisation technique; a cost-cutting measure; all of the above? – then sat down anyway.

Even without this child's-eye viewpoint, Moskowitz was an imposing man, three or four inches taller than the crouched job applicant. Behind his light-framed spectacles, the unquiet eyes were watchful, while his neat moustache gave the impression of a mind as trimmed, as orderly. After a small eternity, he shuffled pages, tapped them on his desk edge to align them, put the stack to one side and, at long length, lifted his incurious gaze to meet the frightened stare of Worsley Porlock.

'Worsley. So. At last we meet.'

They'd met already at a number of conventions, although Worsley didn't feel it was his place to mention this. He gave a strangled chirp, and nodded.

'Well, I've heard a lot about you, Worsley. Not to beat about the bush, the things I've heard have mostly been disturbing. Not least the insanitary incidents at ChiCons '83 through '85 – three times in the same dumpster, for God's sake. How could that possibly have happened? Never mind. I take it that you've put your drinking days behind you, is that right?'

Three times? Skateboarding Jesus, how could Worsley have forgotten ChiCon '83? Admittedly, alcoholism wasn't a great aid to memory, but still the revelation shook him badly. Nodding vigorously in response to the last question, his head a struck punchbag, Porlock made another inarticulate noise, like an injured squirrel, that he hoped sounded affirmative. Moskowitz studied him in silence for a while, probably still trying to figure out the shit-in-hair thing, and then, after a long stretch of mute deliberation, ventured his next question.

'What is the civilian name of Clock Kid?'

What occurred next was as startling for Worsley as the news of his disgrace at ChiCon '83. A district of his mind he didn't know existed, a closed-down and shuttered place he hadn't visited in years, chugged, on the instant, into full industrial life, as if remembering its vanished purpose.

'Gorlo Vamm.'

How had he known that? The publisher's sharp-featured face remained impassive.

'What about his world of origin, his birthplace?'

'Haxor.'

Porlock, to his own astonishment, had suddenly become a factory of unimportant information that was eager to burst out. Across the tidy desktop, Moskowitz allowed himself the faintest apparition of a smile and went on with his questioning. Expanding Lad? Distorted Boy? What about Indescribable Lass? With his string of correct answers unbroken, Worsley started to feel as if he was acing this, and all without a word of spoken English. Bixil Preen, Zaloora. Lom Tertarvis, Margalanth, and Drilpa Nool, Wulpezer. Now that Worsley thought about it, David Moskowitz had always had a reputation as a fan of the Tomorrow Friends, but who knew that he'd integrated it into his interview technique so thoroughly? It was at this point that American's beloved leader asked what turned out to be his last question. Fingers steepled. Leaning forward.

'Have you ever in your life considered making a time capsule with your chronological and spatial whereabouts inside, a note intended for the fiftieth century and the Tomorrow Friends, instructing them to travel back through three millennia and accept you as a member?'

Worsley gasped and drew back physically, recoiling from the question and forgetting he was on a milking stool. He was, then, belly-up and kicking on the deep-piled carpet as he answered. Everything had just collapsed, and he no longer knew exactly where he was or what was happening.

'Yes! Yes, when I was five years old! How did you …?'

Moskowitz's tight smile broadened now, revealing the incisors. As the interviewee floundered, struggling to roll on to his front, the publisher stood up and walked around the desk with one manicured hand extended, bright eyes glittering.

'Congratulations, Worsley. Welcome to American. I'm going to make you an assistant editor, and put you with Sol Stickman. He could use some help on *Exploit* and *Exciting*.'

The apparently successful applicant was by now on both knees, as though at prayer. His new boss stood before him, grinning with unknown delight, an open palm now reaching down that didn't seem intended as a hand-up. Feeling more obliged, tiny, and vulnerable than he'd been since infancy, Porlock felt that he had no option save to formally shake Moskowitz's hand while in a kneeling posture, like a freed slave. He was mumbling his bewildered gratitude and wondering how this whole business could have possibly been more undignified, when he found out: in through the office door, without so much as a preliminary tap, swept the diminutive blonde woman in designer clothes that Worsley had, only an hour ago, encountered copulating in an elevator. Moskowitz, without relinquishing his new employee's hand, said, 'Mimi! Come on in, meet Worsley,' and the full awkwardness of the situation became glaringly apparent.

Mimi Drucker was American's vice president, seemingly parachuted in from nowhere as a personable figurehead when Brothers Brothers bought the business and decided it should look like a legitimate concern, as opposed to the Mafia-front operation it had been at its inception in the days of Albert Kaufman and Sid Rosenfeld. Her perfectly applied vermillion lipstick crinkling in amusement, looking every bit as pleased as David Moskowitz, she briskly crossed the room and made the publisher release the kneeling man's hand so that she could commence shaking it. Her voice, though feminine, was at a deep, subsonic frequency that riot policemen were forbidden to deploy.

'Worsley, I've heard so much about you. Good things, and not just your ChiCon accidents.'

His line of sight approximately level with the VP's pink-and-navy bosom, Porlock found that he was mesmerised by the huge 1950s plastic bangle – a Carmen Miranda circlet of grapes, pineapples, bananas – rattling up and down around the wrist of the hand shaking his. She kept this up far longer than was necessary, her and Moskowitz both smiling down at him with horrid satisfaction, like they were replacement parents he was being introduced to. There was something about Worsley's supplicatory position and the rhythmic motion of their clasped hands, something about Drucker's eyes, which made him think he was unwittingly participating in a non-consensual sex act of some indeterminate variety. What made it worse was Porlock's lack of certainty about whether she'd noticed him when making her post-coital exit from the elevator. He was fairly sure she hadn't, fairly sure she and her brief but intimate acquaintance hadn't noticed anybody, but what if she had? His mind raced and the fruit-bowl bracelet clattered back and forth, making the noise of ceremonial bones. At last, after she'd had sufficient non-specific fun, she let him go, and she and Moskowitz allowed him to stand up. Both decorously averted their executive attention while he did this, like they would have done if Worsley had been pulling up his pants, so as not to embarrass him.

Neither seemed so interested in him after he was upright. There was a reiteration of his duties, starting from that coming Monday, under Sol Stickman on *Exploit* and *Exciting*. Mimi Drucker, with a note of mild concern in her basso profundo, warned him that she'd seen 'poor Hector Bass' on her way in. Instructing Worsley not to worry if the Metzenberger-era senior editor attempted to strike up a conversation, she assured him Bass was harmless, when until that moment he'd had no cause to think otherwise. Then she and Moskowitz turned to each other and began discussing schedules on the summer crossover event, this being *Difficulty on About Nine Earths*. Worsley stood listening with interest for a while to a proposed cull of alternate-timeline Thundermen, including the cartoonish Thunderbunny from World Gimel, and the villainous, masked Plunderman from morally reversed World Daleth, before realising he had been non-verbally dismissed some minutes earlier. As unobtrusively as possible, he conscientiously righted the milking stool and made his silent way back to the office door, while Moskowitz and Drucker weighed the fate of the alternate-nineteenth-century Native American variant Thunderchief (World Tzaddi).

His heart thudding hollow in his heaving chest, he slipped out into the lagoon-and-lemon of his new workplace's labyrinth.

Without Chuff, Porlock found himself in a new category of lost. Electing to make only left turns, on the basis that this would eventually take him somewhere else, he bobbed on seas of quease and skirted optic whirlpools, drifting miserably along identical, scream-coloured corridors. His second such bend sinister delivered him into exactly the same place, save for the added detail of a gnarled old figure that seemed mostly made of eyebrows, standing frozen at a doorway halfway down the hall, forever reaching for the doorknob. Worsley realised that this was another Ambrose Bell, a life-size replica of someone from American's dishevelled continuity, possibly King Bee's dad. He was thus cautiously manoeuvring around it when, without the slightest motion and without removing its brow-shadowed raptor eyes from the unreachable door handle, the shop-window dummy spoke to him.

'Huh. I guess you must be this Worsley Porlock guy I heard so much about. Three times in the same dumpster, is that right?'

As rooted to the spot as his interrogator, Worsley was unable to do anything but wince affirmatively, which the testifying piece of hallway furniture seemed to accept as a response.

'Well, I've heard worse. Heinz Messner had that happen to him eight years in a row, and this was back before they had conventions. "Don't go to Chicago" is the truth I extricate from this. It was the dumpster in the corner of the lot, right, out behind that hotel, the Imperial? Yeah, that was how it was with Messner. Could be it's a mathematically unlikely fluke of probability, or could be it's a highly localised Egyptian curse, just on that dumpster. My name's Hector Bass.'

When Worsley had been working at American for a few weeks, he would have had some several encounters with the famous *Our Unshaven Army* writer-editor, usually at around this time of day, and would have come to understand at least a little of the man's predicament: two years before, Bass had apparently been visited by an unspecified mental collapse, perhaps as a delayed result of his proximity to the intimidating Julius Metzenberger. Since then, Bass had turned up at his office every day, but had proved psychologically incapable of opening or passing through its door. The moment his hand moved towards the handle, all the unresolved things, all of the remembered painful moments on the portal's other side, commenced their whispering, telling him he should come on in, reminding him that they were all still there, right where he'd left them. Bass would stand transfixed for getting on an hour each morning, his exerted will in fierce competition with that of the doorknob, then, with a heart-wrenching sigh, acknowledge his defeat and turn around to go back home until the next foredoomed tomorrow. But, as pointed out above, it would be a few weeks before Worsley became conversant with the paralysing agonies of Hector Bass, so for the moment he was stuck down a shock corridor in conversation with an inexplicably immobilised industry legend and his eyebrows.

Gaze still fastened to the unrelenting entrance, Bass seemed glad of even fleeting company and treated the fledgling assistant editor to a variety of crazy comics-business anecdotes, the vast majority of them unhappily concluded. 'I remember Daisy Brenen, used to do the colouring on all the war books, when they let her go. She'd got no pension, got no medical insurance. She was asking me what was the surest means of suicide. I told her twenty storeys on to concrete ought to do it. Listen. Listen to me. There's something that's at the very top, at the top of this company, and what it is …'

The sentence, like the transit of that liver-spotted hand towards the handle, remained incomplete. Bass had reverted to his resin statue form. After he'd waited a full minute for a punchline that was evidently never going to come, Worsley squeezed past the door-arrested veteran and his antlered eyes, continuing along the visually confounding passage in search of an exit other than the one involving twenty storeys on to concrete.

At long last, Porlock was once again in the unoccupied reception area, where Ambrose (Thunderman) Bell waited for him, leaning on the watercooler and a great deal livelier than Hector Bass. The mannequin's faint smile now seemed to say, 'I know about the dumpster.' From reception, Worsley could locate the elevator where, he was relieved to learn, frenetic coupling on the downward journey was not mandatory Brothers Brothers policy, although a woman who had iron-grey hair and horn-rimmed spectacles still chose to glare at him prohibitively all the way down to the lobby.

Outside on Fifth Avenue, he was astonished to discover that there was still sunlight, and that it was still the same day as when he'd walked in. He thought his interview went pretty good, considering. He was now, for the first time, a professional in the same field that had already cast its spell on Brandon Chuff, Sol Stickman, Mimi Drucker, David Moskowitz and Hector Bass. He was a citizen of Thunderland, and, at the age of thirty-three, had realised the one ambition that he'd ever bothered formulating. After this, he was quite sure, the rest of Worsley Porlock's life would be plain sailing. As he sauntered back along the windswept boulevard towards his subway stop, thousands of snoopy redheads plummeted attractively from countless dazzling windows, careful bobs and knee skirts unperturbed by the velocity of their descent, a shower of fated loveliness. And all that time, malingering in his civilian guise by a fake watercooler, Thunderman did not catch any of them.

11. (March, 2021)

[–] ClockworkLemon 58 points 8 days ago

Couldn't agree less. How does an industry that's sitting in a mess of its prolapsed intestines rate as 'more fun than it's ever been'???

<#>

[–] Tomdabomb 16 points 8 days ago

TBF, I think that maybe it was meant sarcastically.

<#>

[–] Screamingontheoutside 52 points 8 days ago

Prolapsed intestines is about right. Massive are in limbo because The Vindictives: Stalemate keeps not coming out, meanwhile American seems to be doing everything it can to dismantle itself with blunt scissors. I'm so depressed about the state of things, I didn't even bother checking out that COMI-COnLine thing they did about a week ago. I haven't even got the strength to laugh any more.

<#>

[–] tuvoti_322 12 points 8 days ago

So, staking an entire art form on a bunch of transient movie franchises turned out to be a bad idea. Who knew?

<#>

[–] IdleHans 45 points 8 days ago

I'm currently going crazy under lockdown and at such a low point that I actually took a look at COMICOnLine. IMHO, it was what you might call unintentionally interesting.

<#>

[–] maryquitecontrary 19 points 8 days ago

Somebody should have told American not to run a company with scissors.

<#>

[–] ClockworkLemon 42 points 8 days ago

Yeah, just read @fashionablebob_878's post again and I hear it now. My bad. My SOH has been bled from me by a million painful cuts.

<#>

[–] splatterpuss 27 points 8 days ago

Right on the nail about American. Have those people done anything right this century? First Union gets cancelled when its first inker chops up his girlfriend, and its second goes to jail for organising illegal dog fights, then there was the Monkey Christ Thunderman business in the United Supermen movie, and now they're down to a dozen books and a skeleton staff and they're calling it a great opportunity, FFS.

<#>

[–] ShootMoreMessengers 36 points 8 days ago

Isn't the whole Monkey Christ comparison being sort of unkind about that cleaning lady who messed up the restoration job on that picture? She was just a devout old lady doing her best.

<#>

[–] The … Ridiculator 14 points 8 days ago

Good point. It's definitely an insult to that talentless and misguided cleaning lady to compare her honest endeavour with the corporate clusterfuck they made of Stephen Beacher's head. It's the movie that American's whole cinematic universe is resting on, and they give the retouching to somebody's nephew who's got Photoshop. The Monkey Christ woman would have done a far better job.

<#>

[–] Screamingontheoutside 37 points 8 days ago

My worst thing about Covid is there aren't any school buses for me to walk in front of. If this is what my options are down to, I guess maybe I should go total nihilist and visit COMI-COnLine after all. @IdleHans, you terse tease, WTF do you mean by 'unintentionally interesting'?

<#>

[–] wherehavealltheglowersgone 61 points 8 days ago

TBH, it's unfair to just dump on the comics business when the whole world is dysfunctional right now. Could be society going nuts is why comics are like they are.

<#>

[–] tuvoti_322 9 points 8 days ago

Or vice versa. Comics have been dysfunctional for the last thirty years. When I see QAnon Jamiroquai parading his dazzle camouflage through the Senate, I'm seeing the bastard offspring of Sam Blatz, possibly literally. These people are all self-identified cartoons, and I don't think comics are completely blameless on that score.

<#>

[–] Lord_Stranglebang 48 points 8 days ago

Preach! And has anybody noticed how the whole QAnon 'children caged under a pizza restaurant to feed subterranean paedo-demons' idea is the exact same story as 'Don't Fondle Your Food' from Tower of Frightening #19? Just saying.

<#>

[–] GreatWhiteSnark 16 points 8 days ago

Heavens! Are we suggesting that the comics industry is, in some way, a metaphorical microcosm for the whole of society? Man, that's deep.

<#>

[–] IdleHans 34 points 8 days ago

@Screamingontheoutside, you are practically like a brother or, conceivably, sister to me, but I think you've really got to see this one for yourself. Just look at the 'What's Coming up from American' panel discussion, and keep an eye out for the new-look Worsley Porlock. I promise you, it will be like an icicle nailed through your soul.

<#>

[–] GiveMeLibertyOrGiveMeCheese 27 points 8 days ago

I don't think I'm technically even waiting for The Vindictives: Stalemate any more. I can't properly remember how Foolsmate ended, except half the characters turned out to be Krugg shapeshifters or something. Dan Wheems wasn't the greatest writer in the world, or even necessarily on his sofa, but at least he gave the National Guard and Human Tank noticeably different personalities. Whatever happened to him?

<#>

[–] lulucthulhu 19 points 8 days ago

IDK. He seems to have dropped out of comics around five years ago and nobody's heard from him since. Apparently his goodbye letter/suicide note was partly in the form of a comic strip where he talks about Kessler and Schuman, like that was the industry's founding crime. But you're right, he was a better writer than most of the people at Massive except Denny Wellworth. When I was still in school, back in the noughties, that Brute Force series he did was something of a guilty pleasure.

<#>

[–] The … Ridiculator 8 points 8 days ago

Now, see, for me, that would have been strangling domestic pets and starting fires.

<#>

[–] eliot_evans 33 points 8 days ago

I started fires with copies of Brute Force. So, doubly guilty, but doubly pleasured ☺ ☺

<#>

[–] Triumph_Of_The_Ill 12 points 8 days ago

@tuvoti_322 definitely on to something, and the end of Vindictives: Foolsmate a perfect example, with half of the last administration's appointees turning out to be Krugg shapeshifters. Or something.

<#>

[–] splatterpuss 19 points 8 days ago

The Thundermonkey-Christ fiasco is just so emblematic of American right now. It's not like I was asking a lot of United Supermen, but when the guy who's arguably the main character ends up looking like that, you have to wonder. They'd tried to take out Stephen Beacher's beard and dreadlocks with the fucking blend tool, so Thunderman's head in half the scenes is a smeary mess, except the ones where it looks like a screaming armpit. TBH, it was so hard to look at that I never got round to being outraged by the movie's many other problems. Maybe that's why they did it?

<#>

[–] SweetWeaselJackson 47 points 8 days ago

I heard that the movie planned for after Stalemate is called Vindictives: Kicking the Board Over and Claiming You Would Have Won.

<#>

[–] Screamingontheoutside 25 points 8 days ago

OMFG!! THE FUCK WAS THAT? Seriously, everybody has to take a look at this. Jesus.

<#>

[–] IdleHans 28 points 8 days ago

I rest my case.

<#>

[–] Tomdabomb 12 points 8 days ago

Is this the COMICOnLine thing you were talking about, with Worsley Porlock on a Zoom panel?

<#>

[–] Screamingontheoutside 18 points 8 days ago

What's happened to him? That spinning thing one of his eyes is doing, and the way his movements look like he's barely even a solid. My dad has grand mal, and I've never seen anything like that!

<#>

[–] RudysMisplacedMicrophone 34 points 8 days ago

I read that Stephen Beacher is suing Brothers, because since the Monkey Christ footage, he's not been getting romantic leads like he used to.

<#>

[–] maryquitecontrary 11 points 8 days ago

Checking out COMICOnLine right now.

<#>

[–] eliot_evans 30 points 8 days ago

Moi aussi.

<#>

[–] Screamingontheoutside 16 points 8 days ago

@IdleHans, that will stay with me forever. Happy now?

<#>

[–] Tomdabomb 9 points 8 days ago

Holy shit! And what is the stuff he's saying about Thunderman over and over? Is that his sales pitch?

<#>

[–] IdleHans 24 points 8 days ago

Seems to be. As far as I could make out through the frothing, he was talking about some stuff they've got coming up in the Thunderman titles. It sounded like, 'I wish I could tell you what Thunderman has in store for you,' only like about eighty times with a voice like a falsetto bat. I was shaken.

<#>

[–] Screamingontheoutside 12 points 8 days ago

@IdleHans, you are truly the devil's workshop, like everybody says ☹ ☹ ☹ ☹

<#>

[–] maryquitecontrary 9 points 8 days ago

Oh Jesus. I am so sorry I ever said anything bad about anybody in comics. Those poor guys ☹ ☹ ☹

<#>

[–] lulucthulhu 13 points 8 days ago

AAAAAAAAAAGH!

<#>

[–] eliot_evans 23 points 8 days ago

#CANCELHUMANITY ☹ ☹ ☹ ☹ ☹ ☹ ☹

<#>

[–] Triumph_Of_The_Ill 7 points 8 days ago

Merciful God! We need the Didn't Happener

☹ ☹ ☹ ☹ ☹ ☹ ☹ ☹ ☹ ☹ ☹

[–] GiveMeLibertyOrGiveMeCheese 23 points 8 days ago

☹ ☹ ☹ ☹ ☹ ☹ ☹ ☹ ☹ ☹ ☹ ☹ ☹ ☹ ☹ ☹

<#>

[–] splatterpuss 15 points 8 days ago

☹ ☹

<#>

[–] SweetWeaselJackson 41 points 8 days ago

☹ ☹
☹ ☹

<#>

[–] RudysMisplacedMicrophone 26 points 8 days ago

So, no take-up on the Stephen Beacher lawsuit, then?

<#>

[–] RudysMisplacedMicrophone 24 points 8 days ago

hello?

12. (September 2018)

'IS IT A CLOUD? IS IT A METEOR?' – *Finefinger's Brief History of Thunderman On-Screen (Published in Collectors' Fugue #330)*

1: The Essler Studios' Animated Thunderman Shorts (1941–1943) *****

Let me say right from the get-go that this list is chronological rather than in order of merit, although, as it turns out, the first listing is the best, the last is the worst, and the ones in the middle are kind of middling. Thunderman's screen exploits, a little like the progress of the Egyptian dynasties or the career of Orson Wells, start out wonderful, end up in advertisements for cheap sherry, and may well perfectly demonstrate the concept of entropy.

Although there could be cine-antiquarians out there who will disagree, while Thunderman is arguably the first superhero in print, he is certainly the first to make it to the screen. So, a study of Thunderman's screen history is as good a way as any of understanding superhero movies as a whole, before they either wink suddenly from existence, or else continue to submerge the medium of cinema in bilge until the end of time, the way they've done for comics. That's what I'm telling myself is the reason I'm wading through this junk, anyway: that there may yet be some glimmer of social significance amongst the spandex, after all. Let's see, shall we?

It should first be pointed out that in 1941, both cartoon animation and Thunderman were relatively new ideas. Having unburdened David Kessler and Si Schuman of their most important intellectual property in 1942, the people at my former employers American Comics must have been delighted by Thunderman's perfect suitability for a comic book business that was then in its birth throes: a strikingly colourful figure in that grey Depression landscape, that could go anywhere, do anything, and, in a visual medium, could generate unprecedented visual spectacle of a kind that the despairing and marvel-starved audience clearly couldn't get enough of. It would hardly take a genius to realise that an endlessly kinetic character who could fly, bench-press the moon and outrun lightning might be even more successful if presented as stop-motion animation.

And so it proved to be. When American approached the Essler brothers, already making a mark with their *Belinda Beep* and *Out of the Pencil-Sharpener* animated shorts, and suggested that they make an animated Thunderman, the business-minded Bernard Essler was reluctant to take on the project. In what may have been an effort to discourage his prospective clients, Essler told them that for Thunderman to be done properly, each short would cost them $90,000, to which they immediately agreed. And so, perhaps with mixed feelings, Bernard and his brother Abe embarked upon what were to be some of the most beautiful and sumptuous works that Essler Studios ever had a hand in.

The cost and care lavished on the project is visible in almost every frame of the fifteen theatrical shorts completed between

1941 and 1943. Much of the main action is rotoscoped, and the figures have been carefully shaded to provide modelling and a near-3D sense of solidity. This illusion of mass and weight is particularly impressive when combined with the Essler brothers' impeccable feel for visual dramatics: the scenes with a tiny Thunderman pitted against something of much greater size – like the comet he catches and then throws into the sun in *Peril of the Planetary Pool-Shark*, or the amok giant construction-robot in *War of the World's Fair* – are perhaps the best realisations of the character's appeal, in any medium, ever.

If you're interested in my bullshit theory as to why this should be, then for my money it probably has something to do with the character's ontology, ontology being the study of what can be said to exist, as opposed to epistemology, which is the study of what we can know. The only Thunderman that can be said to exist is the perfect and ideal one, who is made of nothing more than lines on paper or acetate, and the Essler shorts are the purest and most glorious expressions of this: the true imaginal essence of this fictional character in a moving, speaking, unbounded form. It's when you materialise Thunderman as a flesh-and-blood human being with pubic hair and a rental agreement that you start to run into trouble. Maybe it's like how ancient cultures may have told stories about superbeings like Zeus or Jehovah, or depicted them in statues or paintings, but anybody dressing up and pretending to actually *be* them would have probably been in for all kinds of divine retribution.

So, yeah, the Essler animated shorts are all well worth looking at, and some of them are little masterpieces. *Empire of Worms* is especially rewarding for its climactic battle between Thunderman and the colossal Worm-Emperor that has kidnapped Peggy Parks, when the hero cuts the writhing monster in half with his Thundervision, only to find himself battling two thrashing, segmented horrors. If the saga of Thunderman on-screen could have been left to rest there, then I feel we would all be in a much happier world, if only because I wouldn't be writing this. But it was not to be …

2: Pacific movie serials, *Thunderman* (1948) and *Thunderman vs. the Riot Ray* (1950) ★★★★

When Pacific Pictures released these fifteen-part serials, it was hardly as if they were entering uncharted territory or making any kind of risky moves. Since the success of newspaper-strip science fiction hero Zoom Wilson as a motion-picture serial only ten years before, it had been evident that modern special effects were capable of sustaining a moderately fantastic narrative for the required number of episodes. Meanwhile, the popularity of Essler Studios' animated shorts made Thunderman an ideal candidate for the same treatment. There were even plans to cast *Zoom Wilson*'s bleached-blond leading actor Flip Fraser as Thunderman, but happily the part went to experienced serial-hero Donald Adams, whose dark, steely gaze was perfect for the role.

Although by any reasonable cinematic standard they are no doubt terrible, I found both of these serials hard to dislike. The performers are all doing their absolute best with the material, and both Donald Adams as Thunderman and Josephine Derwent as Peggy Parks are particularly winning. The wrinkly costume, creaking special effects and ludicrous cliff-hanger cheats (Peggy had bailed out of the plane we saw her crash and die in last episode; the high window she fell from was on the second floor above a shop awning; the coroner who pronounced her dead was just joking to lighten the mood) somehow serve to cocoon the enterprise in a fuzzy grey blanket of affection, which the grainy black and white action only enforces. Concurrently, there is something haunting about these exact same qualities. In 1943, we had been given the Esslers' full-colour, unrestrained vision of the real Thunderman. Now, five years and one Hiroshima later, it was as if this comparatively prosaic, dish-water Thunderman was the only version that we could allow ourselves. The comet-tossing champion of the animated shorts was now more relatable, more drab, more vulnerable-looking – a more managed expectation of American godhood. The earnestness of Adams's performance and the whole venture's utter lack of cynicism may also, to modern eyes, add a rather melancholy aspect to this generally haunted atmosphere.

Both serials are adequately plotted, with the first featuring heavily accented foreign spies who seem themselves unclear whether they're resurgent Nazis or infiltrating Reds, while the second features an entertaining turn from veteran screen heavy Laurence Bays as Felix Firestone. The effects of Firestone's 'Riot Ray' in the 1950 serial are ingeniously (and cheaply) augmented with real footage of riots or public unrest, and both productions have an air of being reasonably innovative for their times. That said, I still find their most interesting aspect to be in the unlikely area of the credits. This feeds into what I was saying above about the character's ontology: in the first of the two serials, a decision was taken, probably by Julius Metzenberger at American Comics, that Donald Adams should not be given a screen credit for his portrayal of the cumulonimbus crusader. Instead, the initial publicity and the movie posters claimed that since no human being could ever play Thunderman – an unusually frank admission of the point I was making earlier – the superhero had kindly stepped in and offered to portray himself.

We need to take a closer look at what is happening here. A comic company, that knows a significant number of its readers are technically adults, is attempting to convince this audience that Thunderman is actually a living, breathing entity who exists in the same reality as it does. While some have maintained that this was American's attempt at a cute publicity stunt, I'd have to say that doing anything cute has always been completely out of character for this famously rapacious outfit. Furthermore, trying to persuade the public that an omnipotent being from another world is watching over it seems less like establishing a publicity campaign than it does an attempt at some kind of commercial religion.

Perhaps this echoes an American desire or need to feel that even the most exceptional individuals are no different to ordinary citizens, and that the altitudes they inhabit are somehow still within the reach of the average working stiff. Whether it's a pro-fascist president and quintuple bankrupt who was born a billionaire, or an extraterrestrial who can see through walls and withstand a direct hit from an atomic bomb, it's apparently necessary to our self-esteem to insist that this is a regular Joe who we could see ourselves having a couple of beers with, or maybe organising a panty raid. We are, it seems, more comfortable with our American gods if they are tawdry ones whose costumes tend to bag at the knees.

With all of the above taken into account, we are left with two movie serials that are like silvery postcards from a lost or abandoned American dreamtime, a place where nobody swore and our deities wore crumpled clothing just like we did. Whatever their merits, these generally well-done and well-acted pieces would arouse public interest in Thunderman to the point where an orchestrated campaign to embed the character in the national group-mind could begin in earnest.

3: Bugle Pictures, *Thunderman in the Underworld* (1951) ★★★

Piggybacking on the moderate success of the previous year's *Thunderman vs. the Riot Ray* serial, Bugle Pictures' *Thunderman in the Underworld* had a slightly plumper Thunderman and a markedly more slender budget. Yet, despite its sometimes comical special effects, this is still an interesting movie for a number of reasons.

For a start, this is the first Thunderman feature film and also the first superhero movie, and here we can see the establishment of a template for much of what would follow. Secondly, this is the movie that provided a foundation for the subsequent TV series, situating the character in a medium that was even more culturally permeative and, in the 1950s, was dealing massive blows to what had once been Hollywood's entertainment monopoly. And thirdly, there is the strange aura of the film itself – in the peculiar impact of the role upon the movie's leading man, we start to see the impersonation of superhumans looking less like a career choice and more like a syndrome.

Victor Richards, star of *Thunderman in the Underworld*, had experienced a difficult upbringing, and it would clearly be unfair to claim that playing Thunderman was the beginning of his many problems. All the same, it doesn't look as if it helped. Reportedly, right from the outset, Richards hated the idea of playing Thunderman and only took the role because his agent had assured him that the movie would only be seen by little kids, that no one in the grown-up film field would remember it, and that it would consequently have no impact on Richards' serious acting career. Which, as far as prophecies go, could have been easily outperformed by Richards' daily horoscope. Or a stale fortune cookie.

The gathering miasma of depression that Richards seemed to bring to the character is perhaps best exemplified by Richards' greeting on first meeting co-star Vera Marshall: 'Welcome to the toilet, sweetheart.' Marshall's presence as Peggy Parks does much to lift the film's spirits, but cannot dispel the sense that Thunderman isn't really enjoying being Thunderman.

The fact that much of the movie's action takes place in a sewer may have inspired Richard's initial greeting to Vera Marshall, and certainly doesn't seem inappropriate. That said, the underground setting jibes nicely with our developing idea of Thunderman as an attempted American god, in that a trip to the underworld seems prerequisite for many gods, heroes and mythical figures such as Orpheus, Persephone, Gilgamesh or Jesus. This, however, does nothing to raise the movie or Thunderman into the realm of the mythical, when Victor Richards' aggrieved presence is doing so much to pull the film in the opposite direction.

Richards was roughly the same age as his predecessor, Donald Adams, and in his early thirties when he took the role. He was a different physical type to Adams, however, lacking the latter's lithe physique and dark-eyed good looks. If Adams brought the character a touch of silver, Richards brought a touch of lead. Somehow, Victor Richards realised Thunderman as a bulkier, older-looking man, with the forced bonhomie that comes with a drink problem and a generally depressed, defeated manner. In short, Thunderman had become a perfect American dad, like mine and everybody's that I knew, who didn't look like he was even getting any from Peggy Parks.

Ironically, this metamorphosis into Thunderdad seems to have completed the character's descent into the sorry material world, and to have ensured his acceptance at the heart of the national psyche. This, at the time, seemed to be the rumpled, careworn and increasingly tipsy Thunderman that America felt comfortable with, that America wanted.

4: WBC television series, *The Adventures of Thunderman* (1952–1959) ★★★

The budget for *Thunderman in the Underworld* had been, appropriately, somewhere below floor level, and this may have contributed to the film being enough of a financial success to make an ongoing TV series based around the same formula seem economically viable. The movie was re-edited into two halves, with these becoming the opening pilot episodes of the new series. It became clear early on that not only would the show retain many of the same cast as its big-screen forebear, it would also inherit its predecessor's frugal production values: a recreation of the famous origin scene, with the elders of Thunderland debating their artificial world's imminent destruction at the hands of interdimensional super-pirates, will reward sharp-eyed viewers when they notice that the elders' costumes are the repurposed outfits of numerous 1940s movie-serial heroes. I personally spotted elders in hand-me-downs donated by Zoom Wilson, Devil of Dawn Island and the National Guard, but you younger people with better memories and better eyesight may well detect more.

The series, for the most part, progresses competently enough, and there are likeable performances from Vera Marshall and new addition Jeff Trench, as rookie photographer Teddy Baxter. Acromegaly-afflicted actor Rondo Hatton, on the other hand, is wildly miscast as Felix Firestone, an avoidable error when the second movie serial's perfectly adequate Firestone, Laurence Bays, must surely have been available. Predictably, though, the show's biggest casting problem resides in Victor Richards himself.

The show's success must have seemed like a two-edged sword to the increasingly troubled actor. On the one hand, Richards was more wealthy and more famous than he'd ever been or could ever have expected to be. On the other, he was becoming permanently cemented into the identity of Thunderman in the nation's eyes, and, under the strain of this, his alcoholism and his chaotic personal circumstances were beginning to spiral out of control. And just as the burdens of the Thunderman persona would become Richards' own, so too did the melancholy actor's flattened spirit come to be inextricably entangled with the perceived nature of Thunderman.

For one thing, as with the omission of Donald Adams's name from the early movie-serial publicity, there was a similar case of ontological creep going on with Victor Richards. With his increasingly sozzled avuncular appearance and manner boosting his appeal as an average American who could exhale hurricanes and travel in time, and with televised appeals such as 'Thunderman endorses National Flashlight Battery Inspection Day' becoming more frequent, it was clear that to a large section of the public, 'Victor Richards' was just an alter ego like Ambrose Bell – an irrelevance, when they knew they were looking at the one and only real-life Thunderman.

This slippage of identification was starkly underlined by an incident in 1956 when Thunderman – not Victor Richards – was advertised as presiding over the opening of a department store. Amongst the attendees was an eight-year-old boy who turned out to be carrying a loaded gun. Levelling the weapon at the costumed Richards, he announced his intention to possess a bullet that had been flattened against Thunderman's invulnerable chest home as a souvenir. I find it telling that Richards' enviably calm response was not to explain that he was just a human actor who was playing Thunderman, but, astonishingly, to remain in character and point out to the child that a bullet bouncing off his steely hide might well kill an innocent bystander. Admittedly, this was just one little kid, but when we recall all the letters sent to soap opera characters by their adult fans, informing them that their on-screen spouse is having an affair, we start to realise how blurred the line separating fact from fiction is for many people, even without deliberate attempts to persuade them, for commercial purposes, that an impossible superbeing is as real as they are. Victor Richards, in the minds of a few million people, was inescapably America's own endearingly paunchy Thunderman.

The profound national shock when his suicide – or very possibly murder – was announced in 1959, then, cannot be overestimated. I was around eight years old myself at the time, and I can recall a stunned and appalled disbelief that in some ways was a precursor to what the country would experience four years later with John Kennedy's assassination: in both cases, a human being was made an embodiment of America's imagined spirit, essence and soul. And in both cases, when America's soul was in such a position that it perished of a gunshot wound in wretched and suspicious circumstances, the emotional impact on America's still living heart and body was devastating.

And that was just the effect that Victor Richards and his death at the age of forty had on the nation, when the effect upon the character of Thunderman was every bit as severe. The tragedy and sadness of Richards' life and relatively sordid demise had seeped into the fabric of Thunderman himself, and the character would subsequently not appear on-screen for almost twenty years.

5: Brothers Bros, *Thunderman* (1978) ***

I can already hear groans and curses over my three-star rating for what many consider the greatest Thunderman movie of all time, but I can only remind you that this is just my personal and highly biased opinion, which you are free to ignore and almost certainly will. I should also advise you to buckle up, because this commentary only becomes more mean-spirited and perfunctory from here on in, as the illusion of Thunderman's physical existence is ever more perfectly and expensively realised, while the character's mythic essence, and whatever meaning he may have had, become things that we apparently no longer possess the art to capture, and fade from view altogether.

By 1978, the Brothers Brothers corporation were the long-time owners of American Comics and had evidently decided that after twenty years, with the Victor Richards story largely forgotten, it might be possible to relaunch their potentially valuable property to a new audience. Determined to dispel the unhappy spectres of the character's past, the company were prepared to spend enormous amounts of money to achieve their ends. Sir Laurence Olivier was cast as Thunderman's father, Zoron, rumoured to have been paid a thousand dollars per *syllable* for his few impeccably delivered lines before he and his flying city are destroyed by super-pirates. Equally surprising, but presumably less costly, was the choice of Dirk Bogarde to play arch-enemy Felix Firestone, a genuinely menacing performance that was all but lost in the directing. The sole casting difficulty came in finding a big-name actor willing to play the main character, perhaps because the role still had a lingering odour of bad luck amongst the acting community. Both Robert De Niro and Harrison Ford had apparently declined the part, which eventually went to relative newcomer Saul Richard. Although I'm sure there were superstitious misgivings regarding the actor's surname being so close to that of his fated predecessor, Richard brought a genuine commitment to the role, and had something of Donald Adams's dark-eyed good looks. Equally spirited in her performance was Elaine Merchant, as the first Peggy Parks to even suggest that there may be an element of sexual attraction in her relationship with the purple paragon.

So, with a strong cast, big budget, and special effects that were, for their time, pretty much state of the art, what, you may ask, is my problem? Well, I have a couple. First, there is the matter of tone: why employ Sir Laurence Olivier to lend such gravitas to the movie's opening scenes, only to undermine Dirk Bogarde's attempts at a truly sinister Felix Firestone by making him into a high-camp character worthy of the King Bee TV series? Who was this film aimed at, exactly?

This is my second problem – despite the clowning around of the Firestone scenes, this appears to be a movie that is chiefly concerned with establishing an adult audience for 1930s children's comic book hero Thunderman. The relationship between Thunderman and Peggy Parks is foregrounded to the point where it seems that this romance narrative is the film's central story, perhaps in an attempt to give the hoped-for adult audience a conventional formula they could relate to. And the presentation of the film in general seems geared to this same end, slick and colourful with a late 1970s airbrushed quality to its glamour. It is, deliberately, a million miles from the hokey, threadbare, black and white charm that had been more than adequate for a forgiving audience of children. With its big-budget aura of importance, it is attempting to persuade people that a man from another dimension in a purple and gold opera costume is a serious dramatic proposition for grown-ups.

It is as if Thunderman's corporate owners had perhaps come to realise that a divine, imaginal entity cannot be conjured into ordinary, physical, American reality without becoming ruinously degraded in the process, and had instead elected to create a smooth and gorgeous artificial American reality where such a being could comfortably exist. Looking back from today's perspective, the seamless, moneyed and good-looking vision of America conjured by the film looks very similar to the yuppie dreamland that, with Ronald Reagan, would arrive within a year or two. For all the film's proficiency, there remains something about it that is only bland and reassuring – yet in spite of, or perhaps because of this, the movie was enthusiastically received, making a sequel inevitable.

6: Brothers Bros, *Thunderman II* (1980) ***

This, essentially, is more of the above, and is only enlivened by a marvellously deranged and power-crazed turn from Malcolm

McDowell as exiled Thunderland despot, Lord Varex. Richard and Merchant's relationship continues to take centre stage, although, as in almost eighty years of Peggy Parks continuity, nobody has the faintest idea where to go with it without irreversibly ruining the whole supposed dynamic.

7: Brothers Bros, *Thunderman III* (1983) **

By this point, after five years of diminishing returns and dwindling budgets, it had become clear that the franchise had lost not only its lustre, but also its wheels. Vincent Price does his best as comedy villain the Toymaster, while an older Mickey Rooney is acceptably bizarre as otherworldly prankster Thundermite, but neither can rescue the movie from a sense of impending doom.

8: Brothers Bros, *Thunderman IV: The Search for Love* (1987) **

With the release of *Thunderman IV*, that doom had arrived in full force. There's no denying that the movie's intentions were good: leading man Sam Richard wanted a story where Thunderman brings enduring love, tolerance and harmony to mankind, but what became of those intentions would be nightmarish if it weren't also kind of funny. Problems with the budget – there wasn't one – meant that instead of being shot in New York, Thunderman's home city of Macropolis was relocated to Birmingham in the English Midlands, with the city's famed Bullring shopping centre visible in many of the backgrounds. Another, possibly greater difficulty was that wanting a popular British director who was within budget, the film's producers had chosen Val Guest, perhaps without realising that his biggest semi-recent commercial success had been with 1974's softcore sex comedy, *Confessions of a Window Cleaner*. When Saul Richard quit the movie in protest at Guest's proposed changes to the initial utopian concept, *Confessions* star Robin Askwith became the next incarnation of Thunderman. *The Search for Love* was reimagined as Thunderman's personal search for erotic satisfaction, and most of the supposed humour lies in the mullet-styled hero using his Thundervision to see through the walls of ladies' changing rooms, complete with BOI-OI-OING sound effects. Having failed to gain the unembarrassed adult audience it was hoping for, the franchise was now apparently seeking a viewing public of sniggering schoolboys, and the disaster that was *Thunderman IV* (I've given it two stars because it's hilariously watchable) would ensure that it was the last big-screen outing for the character for the remainder of the twentieth century. Thunderman had ended once in tragedy and once in farce. Perhaps a wiser culture would have learned from this.

9: Brothers Bros television series, *When Ambrose Met Peggy* (1993–1997) ★★★

Starring Brian Ball and Kate Porter, this was a perfectly serviceable light romantic comedy, if one of the participants being omnipotent and from a different species fits your criteria for 'light'.

10: Brothers Bros television series, *Littleburg* (2001–2011) ★★★

With Asher Tarrant as young Ambrose, Cherish Montcourt as teen sweetheart Pauline Price, and Derek Danner as youthful frenemy 'Flick' Firestone, this was a perfectly serviceable high school mystery-adventure, if one of the participants being etc. etc. fits your criteria for 'serviceable'. And if you don't mind that the series' only compelling mystery is 'Why haven't they called this thing *Thunderboy*?' (Spoiler alert: whenever a superhero changes a successful name or basic costume, or drops out of the continuity altogether, it's always because they were dying sales-wise or, as in this instance, because there was talk of legal action from the character's plundered creators, Thunderboy's being the estate of Simon Schuman and David Kessler.) The take-home message from this period of the character's screen career would seem to be, 'it's OK to do something with the superhero Thunderman, as long as it isn't really a superhero story, and as long as you don't really mention Thunderman'. However, these shows would seem to have once more raised the tantalising possibility of Thunderman as a viable on-screen property, as the following entries surely attest.

11: Brothers Bros, *Thunderman Comes Back Again* (2006) **

Just as 1978's *Thunderman* came nearly twenty years after Victor Richards' shocking death had sent the original screen franchise down in flames, so too does this offering from director Dennis Midler arrive almost two decades after Robin Askwith's pumping buttocks had horribly concluded the character's second lease of life. It's well enough done, and with the then current beginnings of the CGI superhero movie boom in the air, it must have seemed like a sensible idea, yet the only vision the movie offers is a yearning nostalgia for the Saul Richard days – leading man Christopher Gent is Richard's near doppelganger – and it does nothing to demonstrate why the twenty-first century would need a Thunderman. But, with Massive's properties like Freak Force heralding the start of the Massive Cinematic Universe, Brothers and American must have felt an urgent need to get their most famous character up there on the cinema hoardings again. It would take them around seven years.

12: Brothers Bros, *Man of Storms* (2013) **

Since the late 1980s, the comic book industry has been suffering from the self-inflicted malaise of having to realise its originally delightful children's characters as 'dark', grim, and, if possible, psychopathic versions of their former selves, to service the needs of a dwindling crowd of habituated superhero fans, whose physical age has long since outstripped its emotional equivalent. Well, in *Man of Storms*, that malady/fashion finally catches up with Thunderman. As for the film's eye-boggling special effects, I should confess that I would rather see an enormous fake rat-tail dragged across a studio floor while Vera Marshall acts her horrified response than witness the gleeful citywide carnage depicted here; the knowledge that whatever spectacle we are seeing is achievable given enough money robs it of any genuine wonder or awe. When most of our contemporary superhero movies are showcases for their escalating special effects, then the question of which film has the greater cinematic or artistic value becomes a matter of competing CGI workshops, and goes better unasked.

13: Brothers Bros, *King Bee vs. Thunderman: Supermen United* (2016) **

I saw an online review of this movie that said, 'It has all the drama one would expect from a story that exploits the legendary, age-old enmity between pollinating insects and meteorological phenomena', and I can't think of anything I can usefully add to that.

14: Brothers Bros, *United Supermen* (2017) *

And here we are, at the end of the line. The reasons this long-anticipated American Comics game changer in the box-office wars with Massive is such an unqualified disaster are manifold, but somewhere underneath them all is the sorry fact that neither of the major comic book companies have even a pretence at continuity any more. None of the characters seem to be sure which version of themselves they are at any given time, and might anyway suffer a visit from the Didn't Happener and end up as someone else entirely at the next semi-annual reboot. The United Supermen of America are now a couple of different squadrons with a galaxy of rotating members, and don't really constitute enough of a definitive entity to make a film about. Especially not one as mangled as this.

The basic incoherence of the comic book business is perfectly represented in the making of this movie. As is apparently standard practice in today's film industry, rather than have a coherent and well-conceived script from the start, the current preference is to assemble an expensive cast and then shoot a lot of scenes that the producers or director thought would be 'cool'. Then, at the editing stage, when it's realised that there is nothing remotely resembling a story, the actors are called back in to shoot the additional footage necessary to make any kind of sense of the existing travesty.

All this happened to *United Supermen*, with one added complication being an abrupt change of directors halfway through the process, and another being the ridiculous tale of what has been called either 'Monkey Christ Thunderman' or 'Thunderasta'. What had happened was that after finishing the initial shoot on *United Supermen*, actor Stephen Beacher – who had played Thunderman since *Man of Storms* – had moved on to his next role, this being marooned hermit Ben Gunn in a new adaptation of *Treasure Island*. The method-school actor had already grown dreadlocks and a lengthy beard in preparation for the part, and when he was recalled as Thunderman for the reshooting of *United Supermen*, his pirate-movie's producers insisted that he be neither shaven nor shorn. This might have still been somehow salvageable had a thrift-conscious and priority-blind Brothers Bros not entrusted the necessary digital retouching to someone who was plainly barely competent, and who left both Stephen Beacher and Thunderman looking, indeed, like the notoriously botched 'Monkey Christ'.

At least here, at the bitter end of the character's trajectory into physical being, Thunderman has finally gained some kind of resemblance to a religious figure. Can we stop now?

13. (May, 2014)

'No, I'm good with my Pepsi, but you go ahead and get another. I stopped drinking getting on thirty years ago, '85, before they took me on at American. It was kind of a condition of employment, I guess. Dave Moskowitz, he's, like, teetotal? So, no. No drink. But if you're making any more trips to the powder room, then count me in. And you get as wasted as you want. It's what conventions are for.

'So what was I saying? I was telling you about Milt Finefinger and Byron James's new forties project, and then I said how Byron was doing *Anal Robot* for Bordello Comics and … right! Dick Duckley. You were asking who he was. I can't believe you never heard of Dick Duckley.

'Duckley, he's the editor on the Bordello porno-comics line. Me who got him the job, in a lot of ways. But what's really funny is, I mean, you've seen Bordello's stuff, right? Superheroines giving blow jobs and taking it up the ass and whatever. What's really funny is that Duckley, who's editing this smut, he's this super-straight religious guy, or anyway he used to be.

'First time I met him would be '98, '99, something like that. I started out dealing in comic art before they hired me at American, and I still do a little now and then. Anyway, back in the late nineties, I get this handwritten letter – and the guy's handwriting is just beautiful – asking if I can find pages of Lou Shapiro's work on the old *Peggy Parks* comic and, get this, he's signed it, "I remain, sir, your obedient servant, Richard S. Duckley".

'So I'm expecting he's this old geezer, but he sounds like he's got plenty of money, so I write him back, tell him I'll see what I can do. How it works – and don't tell anyone I said this – but up at American they got these vaults where the originals are kept, going back fifty, sixty years. Most of the artists are dead by now anyway, and I have kind of an arrangement, yeah? I pick up these absolutely terrific Shapiro pages from *Peggy Parks* #14, and say I'll deliver them by hand.

'Yeah, I know. He's out in Connecticut and it's quite a haul, but I'm intrigued, you know? I drive up there and it's this big old house right out in the middle of nowhere. I ring the doorbell and this young guy answers – younger than me, anyway. Maybe his mid-thirties? I ask if I can speak to Richard Duckley, figuring it's this guy's dad or something. He says, "I'm Richard Duckley."

'He invites me in and we talk, and I get the whole story. His mom and dad were these strict religious conservatives who thought the sixties and the seventies – all the sex and the drugs – they thought it was just all the work of Satan, literally. They inherited a lot of money, so they hire tutors – all guys – and they raise Duckley in this, like, indestructible bubble of Jesus, right from when he's a baby.

'He never goes to school; he never plays with other kids. Never even gets to see a photograph of a young woman until he's in his late teens. By the time he got to read a daily paper, it would have these square holes in, where they'd cut out pictures and articles they didn't want him to look at.

'What cracks me up, he told me that the first pretty girl he ever saw was Peggy Parks. No, I'm serious. Turns out Duckley's dad got it into his head there was some kind of religious message in *Thunderman*, how "Thunderman" is just a primitive name for God and like that, so those are the only comic books his folks let him read: *Thunderman*, *Exciting*, *Teddy Baxter*, *Peggy Parks*, and so on.

'You should have seen him looking over those Lou Shapiro pages, where Peggy Parks is at some interplanetary beauty contest in a fifties one-piece swimsuit, like I was showing him hardcore animal porn or something. He bought all the artwork – no, I don't want to think about what happened to it, either – and asked if I could get him any more. I don't know. I guess I took pity on the guy. I mean, his parents sheltered him from the world all those years.

'There was no TV in the place, no radio, no phone. He was this big, shy, overgrown Christian kid who didn't know how to talk to people or how to act, not with guys and certainly not with women. He's living like this until '96, so he's around thirty-three, when Mom and Dad get totalled in a car wreck and, bang, he's on his own.

'Sure, his folks left him the house, lot of cash in trust funds, and he's got people who call by to clean and stuff, but when you think about it, it's like the guy's totally alone on an alien planet he don't know the first thing about. You can see, somebody like that, how he'd identify with Thunderman.

'Next couple of years, I'd travel up to see him once in a while, if any new artwork had turned up. One time, I found this nude *Peggy Parks* cover that Lou Shapiro had done as a joke for Sol Stickman, and Duckley just about went crazy. He told me he was starting to worry about how long Mom and Dad's money was going to last, and thinking that maybe he should get some sort of job.

'It's like, this is someone who knows nothing of the world or adult life, who's never even attended kindergarten. OK, in all that tutoring, it turns out he's picked up a great command of formal English, he's a whiz at math – and of course he knows absolutely everything about Thunderman – but other than that, he's like a giant newborn baby with a jerk-off fixation on Peggy Parks. The only job I could think of that he'd be qualified for was maybe something in comics.

'See, I think I was like a mentor figure for him, and – hey, watch out! Nearly spilled that. You're going to be pretty tanked by the time you meet your buddies at that bar later. Where did you say it was again? Really? So, the Burgess, that's the old Imperial? Ha. No. No, it's nothing. I was just thinking of something funny, that's all. What was I … oh, right. Getting Duckley a job in comics.

'We talked a lot about what his options were, now he didn't have his parents watching his every move. I told him he could get a TV, watch movies – hell, he didn't even have to live in Connecticut if he didn't want to. He could sell up the house, rent an apartment in New York, maybe get work in the industry. His mouth was open like none of this had ever occurred to him.

'Over the next few months, I helped him get the logistics figured out. I mean, I liked the guy, you know? Still do. Duckley is like the funniest guy. Not intentionally, but he's completely hilarious. And I knew the industry people would think so too, Brandon and those guys. Dick Duckley was just, like, one hundred per cent made for comics. So, he sold the house and he got a place in Manhattan.

'He was like Alice in Wonderland, or maybe the kid in *Home Alone*. He got a widescreen TV, and I'll never forget his face when I told him he could watch porn on it, like he didn't know that was possible or legal. I mean, he barely knew that television was possible or legal.

'It was hard getting him out of his apartment for a while. He was just shy, kind of awkward. He knew he didn't really fit in anywhere, so he wasn't socialising and didn't know anybody except me. And he was much too scared and self-conscious to try out at any of the comic companies. Then one day, I was at his place. I was chopping out a couple of lines, he asked what I was doing.

'No. No, no drink, no drugs, nothing like that. He'd got no experience of anything. But once I'd introduced him to the Peruvian manoeuvre, it was like he finally found what he needed, you know? It gave him, like, confidence, so he could do all these things he'd never done before. He could have a drink; he could talk to women. He even managed to land a job at American for a while.

'No, he did OK. He was enthusiastic about everything, he talked about Thunderman all the time, and he didn't fuck up more than anybody else. And Brandon, Ralph Roth, those guys, well, we all thought Duckley was pretty entertaining. When he discovered conventions, it went off the scale.

'Like, I remember this one time at San Diego, where we talked him into taking a trip down to Tijuana, see the sights, you know? We got the guy completely destroyed on tequila, then we took him to a show where this woman's fucking a donkey. I mean, the look on Duckley's face. It was priceless. Thinking about it, actually, that might have been his first con, that year's San Diego.

'What, this is your first con? Seriously? And your first time in Chicago? Boy, how about that! Here, this calls for another drink. Let me get you one. No, no, it's good. I'm on expenses. Hey! Hey, over here? Get this guy another of what he's having,

OK? And another Pepsi for me. Thanks. Your first con. That is so great. No, no, I'm just laughing. I'm laughing because I'm happy for you.

'Yeah, Duckley. So, like I say, being cooped up with his parents all those years, when he finally gets a taste of modern life, it's like the guy goes completely berserk. He's drinking, he's doing a whole ton of coke – and porn! I never knew a guy watched so much porn. Funny thing – rather than all this getting him fired from American, like I thought, it's what gets him an offer somewhere else.

'Well, you know, he'd got this big reputation back then as the Thunderman-and-porn guy. He's at one of these conventions, he gets talking to somebody who it turns out is Sylvester Lewis. He's the number one guy at Mike De Matteo's *Bordello* magazine, OK? He talks to Duckley for a while, he gets the idea for superhero porn, Bordello Comics, and making Duckley senior editor.

'Yeah, I know, it's crazy, right? This is a guy who, twelve months before, he doesn't know what porn is. And it's only through porn he finds out what pussy is. I'm not kidding. When Duckley tried dating, believe me, it was a fricking disaster. I mean, now he's OK. We got him some numbers, these real nice girls, good postings on Craigslist, so now he's OK. Back then, though …

'What, the Duckley dating stories? Well, the best one – and this is ironic, because this is the one I end up getting the blame over, can you believe – the funniest one is Joanne Jackson. You heard of her, right? She handles foreign rights for City Comics. Anyway, she was dating Duckley, and he's freaking out; he doesn't know what to do. So, he knows I'm experienced, he comes to me for advice.

'He says, "Worsley, you've done it with girls. What do they like? What am I supposed to do?" So I tell him – and this is a joke, right? I'm joking – I tell him that girls talk in a sort of code when they want sex, OK? You know, when they're really turned on they tell you "stop", or that they're calling the police, but that's when they really want you to give it to them. I mean, it's obvious I'm joking, right?

'But what happens, next convention, I got Joanne Jackson yelling in front of everybody, telling me I'm a pervert. Boy, she was so mad, and I'm saying, "Joanne, I was joking." It was hilarious. It was obvious he'd told her, "But that's what Worsley Porlock said I should do," so right away I'm the bad guy. She still won't speak to me, but, you know, it's a funny story all the same.

'So, that was the end of Duckley's dating career. Like I said, we explained to him what prostitutes are – yeah, I know. Can you believe this guy? – and now he's got that situation kind of under control. And he's doing good at Bordello. I mean, he was saying money was getting tight a month or two back, but he must have figured that out, I guess. He seems OK for cash now, anyway.

'Hey, look at the time. It's only a quarter off eleven. Yeah, I know, I just didn't want you to miss out on meeting your buddies is all. It's OK, you still got time. The old Imperial – the Burgess now, you said – you go left out the front doors and it's just a couple of blocks. Ten minutes, tops.

'Anyway, it's been real good talking to you. No, no, I probably won't see you tomorrow morning. I'm leaving kind of early, and you'll probably be up in your room, washing your hair or something. Huh? No, no reason. You just got good hair, you know? Nice, clean hair. Looks like you take care of it, is all I meant. No. No, you go on. You have a great night with your buddies.

'And enjoy the rest of ChiCon, OK? I'm guessing, from the look of you, I'm probably going to be meeting up with you here next time, am I right? Maybe the next several times, who knows? Maybe I'll even get to introduce you to Dick Duckley someday. Ha. Yeah. Yeah, you take care, pal. Left out the door, you can't miss it. So long! Yeah. Yeah, see you next year. Bye. Bye …

'Hahaha. Shithead.'

14. (July, 1960)

One blue morning, in the days prior to becoming publicly Satanic, Sam needed a hearty meal before he could face work up at the offices on Lexington. Under a china sky without a crack, he danced, almost, on sparkling sidewalk in his tilted hat, his jacket slung over one shoulder like Sinatra; in his snazzy sunglasses the very spirit of Manhattan, that was how he felt.

Like everybody there on the new decade's doorstep, he was sure, Sam's head was full of monsters. Monsters seemed like all he got to think about in those days, but at least Sam's monsters looked great, drawn by Gold or Novak, so that all he had to do was dream up wacky names. Sometimes he'd change a word or two in the suggested dialogue that the artist pencilled in beside the panels, sure, but mostly it was names – Klorg, Vuxor, Zim Zam Zub, etcetera. Occasionally he'd need to come up with an adjective – say, 'Vuxor the Unnameable' – but, then, that was what writers did.

The names were an internal jazz to which Sam shuffled, tapped and skipped over the crossing: Baragam, Vavu, Zar, Goragoom, Dadeet the Inconvenient. The bell he triggered going through the door was like a little cymbal tap or triangle, right at the end. The day was bebop.

Just the air inside the deli, how it smelled and tasted, was a non-refundable advance on eating. Stepping sideways, awkwardly, into his favourite booth next to the entrance, Sam took off the hat and sunglasses to put them with his jacket on the plump sage vinyl of the empty seat beside him. Loosening his tie for looks rather than comfort, he lifted a finger to attract the waitress's attention, then ordered pastrami, rye, eggs sunny side up and a pot of coffee, same way that he always did.

Sam dug the reassuring atmosphere the place had, as if nothing much had changed since 1930. Rich brown wood stain, ivory tiles and dark green paintwork, with the coffee maker venting drawn-out sighs of hot exasperation somewhere in a busy kitchen. It was classical, the colour scheme, like an old-fashioned pharmacist's, and for some reason always put him distantly in mind of his late mother. Casually, he cast an eye over the other customers, but it was just the same as ever at this hour of the morning. There were lots of guys his age or older, more than half of them in publishing or some related business, and no broads except the waitresses. Some kid around nineteen who'd got kind of a hipster look was perching near the counter. He glanced up at Sam expressionlessly and then went back to the paper he was reading. Probably he was a playwright, author, journalist, something like that, hanging around the big boys, hoping to overhear about some work, some other writer guy who's just dropped dead, so he can pay his rent. Good luck to him, thought Sam. Good luck to all those struggling bastards who weren't smart enough to be related to a publisher.

His food arrived while he was inwardly debating whether Torgam was a better name than Targom. He thanked Hi I'm Judy, and had just lifted his cutlery in preparation for the coming battle when, like in the Bible, Sam Blatz heard a voice from nowhere. In that suddenly refrigerated instant, it seemed possible it was the voice of God, Sam's conscience, telepathic aliens, or something else most people doubted the existence of. The tone was fatherly, concerned, and yet obscurely terrifying.

'So, Sammy. How are things? Don't look around. Just keep on with your breakfast.'

It was someone in the booth behind him, and Sam wasn't hungry any more. He waited a few seconds for his brains to end up topping his pastrami, then, voice trembling, ventured a question.

'Say, am I OK?'

The background conversation bubbled in its uneventful cauldron, and the remote coffee maker voiced again its scalding, damp frustration. The voice from behind was chuckling now.

'Don't be a fucking idiot. What, like someone who wanted to do that would do it in a crowded deli? Real-life situations, Sam, you have to think them through realistically, the way that things work in the normal world. It's a good job you're not a writer, that's all I can say.'

Sam's mind was racing, trying to remember if there'd been anyone in the booth behind when he came in, or, if not, somebody who'd entered while he sat there, but this got him nowhere. Untouched, his fried eggs regarded him, their custard gaze slowly opaqued as if by death.

'So this is not a mob thing?'

His invisible interlocutor sighed, coincidental with the distant coffee maker.

'No, Sam. No, it's not. But since you raise the subject, how's Frank Giardino working out, up at Goliath? Maybe you should have his Uncle Sal in, posing for one of those creature books you do.'

He swallowed, and became aware of sweating palms gripping his cutlery, unnaturally tight, his knife and fork unmoving and bolt upright, like somebody waiting for their dinner in the Sunday funnies. It got worse, this conversation, by the moment.

'You know about Giardino?'

He put down his knife with a slight clatter, picking up his cup to gulp the just-boiled blackness back like lemonade. The voice was disappointed now, that of somebody talking to a child.

'Oh, Sam, come on. Do you know about Klorg, the Mushroom that Walked like a Man? We know Frank Giardino, and his Uncle Sally, and all kinds of things. Of course we do. It's like I said just now: we're not the mob. We're not the family, Sam. We're the company. Ted says hello.'

And just like that, Sam's cranial floor gave way, and right there, in the summer deli, he plunged eighteen years into the cold splash of the 1940s. He'd joined up in '42, but Sam had never been a Brooklyn tough guy like Joe Gold; never been someone you could imagine ducking bullets in the trenches. What Sam Blatz had been was smart, with a keen instinct for self-preservation, which made him a shoo-in at Signals Intelligence, where he sat listening in on everyone's transmissions, sharing his discoveries with the Office of Strategic Services, as it was known in those days. Ted had been the name – or very likely not – of Sam's phone contact at the OSS. In any other circumstances, it would be heart-warming, the way Ted had kept in touch from time to time since the cessation of hostilities, though at that moment, warmth was not amongst the many things that Sam's heart was experiencing.

'Oh. Right. So, uh, how are you guys doing?'

Over by the counter, glancing up occasionally from his paper, the young Denny Wellworth overheard this, but assumed the question was addressed to Sam's fried eggs. Oblivious to scrutiny, Sam stared out through the glass door, at the back and forth of ordinary schmucks along the sunlit street outside, and briefly wished that he was them. Licking his lips and sounding dumb in his own ears, like someone talking to a Ouija board, he sat and waited for the spirits to reply.

'Us guys? Well, thanks for asking. I guess we've been doing pretty good, us guys, over these last ten years. We've worked as management consultants all around the world, places like Guatemala and Iran, the Philippines, providing them with more effective leadership because, well, that's what us guys do, and all of it legitimate, above board. Other people's countries, that's within our remit. So, it's just the idea that we might be doing stuff here in America makes people nervous, although, the way us guys see it, whether things are happening here or overseas is a grey area, a matter of interpretation.'

Right outside, the sun squandered its golden bounty on a mongrel pissing up against a hydrant. People spilled like sauce over the street at a green light, and Sam could hear the power, blood and foreign war, its measured breathing in the booth across his shoulder. He desperately wanted to get back to christening monsters, but the man who wasn't there had just stopped talking, and Sam felt the onus was on him to fill the silence, as the wheezing coffee maker couldn't do the job all by itself.

'I, I don't know what you mean. How does—'

The cask-aged voice cut in at once.

'I'll give you an example. Art, Sam. Let's talk about art. I don't mean the stuff you publish, where you pay those suckers twenty bucks a page. I'm talking real art, stuff gets sold for one, two hundred thousand dollars. Now, this might surprise you, Sam, but us guys, we're not philistines. We keep up, Sam. We keep up with the arts world. You could say we're patrons. Naturally, we don't like everything we see. With art, you've got to show discernment, that's my feeling. But to get back to what I was saying, what's the nationality of art? Is it the place where it was painted, or the place that it's a picture of? Is it the place that bought the painting, or the world that it will influence? See what I mean? We interfere with art, it's a grey area. Like art, it's open to interpretation, right?'

Sam didn't know where this was going, and he wasn't sure he'd like it when it got there. Eyes fixed bleakly on his cooling breakfast, he concluded that the safest course of action was to only speak when it seemed absolutely necessary. So he swallowed some more coffee and said, 'Right.'

'Right. So, amongst the art we don't like, there's this Soviet stuff, constructivism. You'll have seen it: three or four big Russian guys in undershirts, seen from below. Muscles all over, and all of them looking in the same direction, gulls sat on a fence, with stern expressions like they just saw someone wipe their ass on Stalin's photograph. One of these big-chinned bastards will be holding up a sickle, and up in the sky there'll be these jets on fly-past. "Dignity of Labour", as they call it, and the art collectors, they're all going wild about this stuff that's basically an ad for communism. You can see, I think, how us guys might see art like that as lacking aesthetic value.

'What we're thinking is, how come there's no art movement based on our ideas, on life here in America, do you see what I'm saying? How come capitalism doesn't have its own art, as an ad campaign, when it invented ad campaigns? OK, it's hard to make the people in line at a bank heroic, or the deadbeats on a Ford assembly line, but what about our product? What about our junk, Sam? Tins of beans and boxes of detergent, even shitty comic books. The stuff we sell, why don't we turn that into modern art? So, what we do, we find guys making stuff we like – there's Robert Rauschenberg, Claes Oldenburg, a couple guys like that – we spend a little money helping their careers and suddenly they're big sensations. Pop art, Sam. Popular art. Remember where you heard it first.'

Beyond the glass, big clouds had temporarily obscured the sun. Unhurriedly they dragged their bigger shadows down the street, wiping their grey on everybody's eyes, so that life wasn't quite as great as it had been a minute earlier. Trapped in a conversation that he didn't understand, Sam edited his troubling reality to something that would work for *Journey into Strange*, where Agent Steel, let's say, tells Sam that Spaktoom the Impossible is on his way to fry the world, and that Sam, with his special knowledge of these ludicrously named monstrosities, is the one guy America can turn to.

'Now, at this point, Sam, I'm guessing that you're thinking, "Yeah, but what has all this got to do with me?" Is that about right?'

Sam, who had, in fact, been wondering how he was going to handle the whole Spaktoom situation with just guile and lying, merely said, 'You know it.' Agent Steel, let's say, continued.

'Well, Sam, it occurred to us, through dealing with the upper reaches of the art world, that we might be missing something. I mean, real art, sure, it has its influence, but only on a tiny and well-off minority. You want to reach the average shit-heel on the street, high art's no good for that, the galleries and salons. For that, what you want, it's not the upper reaches. It's the gutter. It's the dregs of culture, stuff that no one in a million years is ever going to say is art. It's you, Sam.'

A large fly, its swollen abdomen in brilliant iridescent blue, alighted on Sam's cold pastrami. Certainly, he could have waved it off, but by then he was in a funny mood. He'd gone already through the five stages of grief about his breakfast, and had reached acceptance that he wouldn't get to eat it. That being the case, he figured that the blue-tail fly would at least see the most important meal was not completely wasted. Unaware of Sam's unusually altruistic deed, the disembodied voice went on.

'And what we're seeing when we look at comic books – not just yours, everybody's – what catches our eye is all the super-guys. Granted, there's not so many of them as there were ten, fifteen years ago, but, all the same, it looks to us like they've still got potential. Think about it. Super-guys, we only make them in this country. Christ knows why, but there it is. As symbols go, they're uniquely American. They're like our musclemen with sickles, only ours got better undershirts. We're thinking that, these saps in the long underwear, could be they'd make great propaganda vehicles.'

The fly, using its built-in straw, was sipping Sam's pastrami like a soda. Having, as he thought, a relatively firm grasp on at least this passage of the creepy dialogue, Sam felt that he might confidently raise a trenchant matter.

'Yeah, but, see, except American, nobody's doing costume characters no more. It's like nobody wants them since the war. Besides, you're talking to the wrong guy here. Up at Goliath, what we do, it's monsters, western books, a thing or two for teen-age girls – *Ellie the Escort* and like that – but we've not handled costume heroes since we gave up on the National Guard, four or five years ago. Other than Moon Queen, Thunderman and King Bee at American, the super-characters are finished.'

In the following pause before reply, Sam heard the whisper of newspaper pages being turned behind him. He considered that the voice from off might be so bored with this meandering discourse that it was furtively reading *Flatfoot Floyd*, but then thought differently. More likely the newspaper was a screen held up in front of the guy's face, so nobody could see that he was talking. Turning pages every now and then would make it all look natural. Sam wished he had a newspaper, or even a brown paper bag with eyeholes. Cloak-and-dagger stuff was tense, but, more than that, it was embarrassing.

'Not finished, Sam. We beg to disagree. I don't know if you've seen the figures that Sol Stickman's pulling in with his new *Streak* book at American, but I have, and believe me, they're impressive. Maybe three, four times the money that you're getting from your swishy cowboys and your gibberish monsters. And while you make a compelling argument about your company not doing costume characters, I couldn't give two fucks because the point of our refined discussion here today is that it *will* be doing them.

Although, I don't know, we were thinking that you're going to need a good company name. I mean, Goliath, he was maybe seven, eight feet tall? Sam, we got bigger Harlem Globetrotters than that. And he gets wiped out by some little Jew kid with a slingshot? That ain't quite the image we were hoping to project. It ought to be a name that's bigger than Goliath, that sounds unassailable, invulnerable to harm. We'll leave it up to you, Sam. You're the wordsmith.'

Wait a minute. What was that, did he just say – ? No. No, no, no. This wasn't happening. Change what they published? Change the company name? Sam felt the air go out of him like he'd been gut-punched, like there in the deli he'd had a piano dropped on him and nobody had noticed. And the tone the phantom voice had – it was clear this wasn't a suggestion, a polite request. It was more like his life had just been requisitioned, and he didn't know if he was going to throw up, have a heart attack or else burst into flames. When words came, they were in a squeaky, pleading babble.

'Hey, hold on, I mean, I can't, it's, it's, it's not my company, it's my wife's father's, Jackie Berman. He's the guy who owns Goliath. I can't just … look, please, it's not that I don't want to help you, but you've got to think of the position that you're putting me in here. Couldn't you – I don't know – couldn't you take this to American? The costume-hero thing, they're more experienced than us. Plus, they got all the big names that people already know about, like Thunderman. Couldn't you—'

'Sam?'

The word, quietly delivered, was a stopper in Sam's gushing, spraying bottle. The blue-bellied fly, perched motionless now on the glistening petticoats of Sam's pastrami, seemed to stare directly at him with its compound gaze impassive, like a traffic cop. It rubbed its hands together in anticipation. When the voice spoke next, Sam found it hard not to imagine it was coming from the fly.

'Sam, we're not interested in American. A company like that, they've got a lot of money and aren't so susceptible to our inducements. What we're looking for, what suits us, is a needy, third-string little operator like yourself,' the fly said. 'And besides, the costume heroes at American, they're playboy millionaires, or they're from space, or there's some magic bullshit. How does that reflect our country's values, Sam? Why can't good, ordinary Americans, like nuclear scientists, cyberneticists, arms manufacturers, why can't people like that be super-guys? See what I'm saying?'

The fly broke off briefly, so that it could take a shit, then resumed its intimidating lecture.

'Anyway, you're somebody we know, who we've worked with before. Remember? Ten years back, we asked if you could turn the National Guard to a red-beater – all those bad guys like Ratski Fatski, Dirty Marx, Ivan Agenda – and back then, Sam, you were real obliging. Think of this as like that, only bigger. Play it right, and this is a much larger opportunity for you, for us, for everyone.'

The talk of opportunity led Sam to think that maybe, after all, the fly was somebody he could do business with. He narrowed his eyes slightly, so it knew to take him seriously.

'So, what, you're saying these super-guys, you want them fighting commies?'

The fly nodded.

'Well, that never hurts, Sam. Never hurts. And that's another area where you score higher than American. When did you ever see King Bee or Thunderman tackle a communist? So, sure, lots of red bad guys, that's always a good thing, although this time, reds aren't going to be our first priority. This time around, tell you the truth, we're more concerned with atom bombs.'

The fly had lifted off and buzzed away halfway through that last sentence, and so Sam was left to have a conversation about nuclear bombs with the real person in the booth behind him, rather than a magic talking bug. He made the high-pitched, querying noise that people make when told that what they're being asked to do is in some way associated with atomic weapons.

'Well, I'm glad you asked. You know what keeps America on top, Sam, ultimately? You know what America's position in the world is resting on? It's missiles, Sam. ICBMs with big atomic payloads, and on us having more missiles than the other guy. For that, you need a good supply of weapons-grade material – uranium, plutonium – which in turn will require a whole mess of atomic power plants to produce the stuff. So what you're going to see through this next decade is a lot of places like that being built, commissioned or whatever. This is a good thing. Atomic power, it's a good thing, but every now and then you're going to get a little this, a little that, explosions, leaks, that kind of thing. And all the peaceniks and the liberals will say, "Oh, goodness! This atomic energy is simply too bad," or, "I lived ten miles from a power plant, and now I got a two-headed baby," or some shit like that. You see, Sam, what this all comes down to, it's an image problem.'

Sam was staring hollow-eyed out through the glass of the front window. Customers were entering or leaving through the heavy swing door, shuffling back and forth in front of him, but Sam Blatz wasn't seeing any of them. In his feverish imagination, he was seeing the white nuclear fireball, its dilation down the thronging avenues, with skyscrapers and cops and dogs and hydrants melted into vapour and sucked up the mile-wide trunk of a great smoke sequoia that blots out the July sky, with shadows of executives and hookers flash-exposed and printed on the brute emulsions of a library wall, with cars and comic books all bursting into flames, and then the flames themselves bursting into flames, and in his thudding heart, he prayed Spaktoom was going to get here first. The best response that he could manage was a tremulous, 'How do you mean?'

'It's all the movies, Sam. All the TV shows and the science fiction stories, where you get a little radiation and it straight away turns everything into a giant monster. Giant people, giant lizards, giant ants. I mean, a giant ant, that's a Chihuahua with more legs, right? Or some nonsense where there's been a nuclear war and everyone's a mutant with their faces falling off.

Mutation's good, Sam. It's mutation that makes evolution work, but all these negative depictions, what they're doing is, they're making people think that radiation's dangerous, that it's going to turn them into something ugly and enormous. So, then, we were thinking, what if there were stories where the people get irradiated, but instead of ending up with, like, leukaemia or something, they turn into super-guys? I guess it's what you'd call a metaphor: atomic energy has made America into a superpower, so maybe it could do the same for individual citizens – that's basically the point we're hoping you can get across for us. And don't you worry about Jackie Berman. Once you tell him how much dough he's going to make, he'll come around. You're a persuasive guy, Sam. That's one of the reasons why we like you.'

Out beyond the glass, New York was absented in flat ash, right to the horizon. There were no giant ants, no mutants, nothing any more to look at. It was sort of sad, but then Sam shrugged and thought, well, if not him, then someone else would do it anyway, and then the sun came out again and there were still people and automobiles, and he felt OK. He had some questions, sure, but they were more pecuniary than moral.

'Yeah, but, like, even if I can dream up all these radioactive super-characters, how do I know they're going to sell? Next to American, we only got a small share of the market. Then there's the time factor to consider. These new books; changing the company name; it's going to take a while.'

Through all this, customers, unnoticed, came and went between the green-and-ivory deli interior and the ice-cream-cone day outside, and whenever the door was opened, then the bell would sound its tiny chime, ring-a-ding-ding.

'You've got until next year. That's non-negotiable. As for the characters, all that you've got to do is what you always do: you give our brief to one of the real talents that you got in harness – a Joe Gold, a Robert Novak, anyone except Frank Giardino – and then you sit back and take the credit. And please, Sam, don't worry your nightmarish little head about whether these books will sell or not. They'll sell. They'll sell with such profusion that it will attract attention, and you'll be a big phenomenon, just like we did with Rauschenberg. That's why they call it pop art, Sam. It's popular. Two or three years, the way we figure, you could even beat American. You leave all that to us.

'Now, Sam, I've got to say, you've been a real sport about all this. This can't have been an easy chat we've just been having, not from your perspective. I mean, who am I? I come in here, I interrupt your breakfast, how I talk to you could be interpreted as, I don't know, contemptuous, and I don't even introduce myself. Crazy coincidence, I know, but my name's Ted as well. I'm your new Ted. So anyway, we figured it was only fair you got to have a say in this, so that you knew how much us guys appreciate your input. Go ahead, Sam. Tell me how you feel, about me and this whole proposal. Don't pull any punches. I'm all ears.'

Well, now. This was more like it, treating Sam more like an equal than some little hustler who was so scared of them, he'd do anything they asked and they just had to snap their fingers. This was more like the scenario with Spaktoom. Putting down what had become a purely ornamental knife and fork, he pulled himself more upright in his seat and retightened his necktie. Straight away, he found that he felt more professional and more on top of things, like if a feller could control his neckwear then he could control his circumstances, that sort of a deal. The deli's customers were entering and exiting, same as before – Sam saw the blue-assed fly depart, out through the door and straight up to the fiftieth floor, it looked like – but he paid all of this no attention as he readied himself to state his position, with the eloquence that only he could muster. He could almost sense that Agent Ted, let's say, was leaning forward, maybe taking out a notebook bound in human skin so he could jot down Sam's opinions and ideas. Filled with new confidence, Sam cleared his throat and drew a breath.

'First of all, oh surreptitious seeker of security, let me say that in Snappy Sam you've secured someone suitably sufficient to your subterfuge, so seek no substitutes, señor! You've got a platinum-plated promise from a pillar of the publishing protectorate who pledges to provide a plethora of post-atomic paragons to puzzle, please and push pernicious pro-bomb propaganda at pre-adolescents with perhaps presumptuous impunity! Blatz is your boy, so brace yourself to be bedazzled by a bountiful bouquet of brilliance from the boss of badinage! The iteration of ideas and images intended to initiate and influence, insidiously, immature and introspective innocents' imaginations into interest in intercontinental instruments of infamy is my immediate intention!'

This was going good, he thought. It sounded like Agent Ted Steel, let's say, was hanging on Sam's every word, attention rapt like he was in some cockamamie trance, enchanted by a master hypnotist. You could have heard a pin drop. Thus encouraged, Sam continued with his pitch.

'Mark ye my musings manfully, oh mentor to Machiavelli! Meditate most meaningfully, maestro, on the masterpieces of mentation minted monthly by my mainly molten mind! Sample the startling – some would say spectacular – spontaneous suggestions spouting like spermatozoa, squirting from Sam's supercharged subconscious, swami! Mutant Mike, a guy you'll like! X-ray Pedestal Man and Glowy the Boy Nightlight! Extra-Fingers Harpsichord Kid! This stuff writes itself! Real Smart Six-Headed Woman! Damaged Chromosome Crusader! The Untreatables! Suffer me not to stay suspended, shipmate! Simply state your singular selection from my smorgasbord of strontium sentinels, so sooner we can stammer our soft sayonaras. Which is it to be, my taciturn tormentor?'

Evidently, it was a tough choice. Sam almost heard the flywheels of deliberation whirring in the agent's mind behind him. He knew he could be impressive when he had to be, and so allowed himself a smile of satisfaction in the general direction of his ruined breakfast as he added, 'Well? I'm waiting for an answer. It's time you made up your mind, muchacho!' Denny Wellworth was just going out the deli door, and heard this last part. Shaking his young head, appalled, he hoped to Christ that wasn't how all writers ended up, where their one friend was a dead sandwich.

As the deli emptied out, Sam sat with his eyes fixed on the now cataracted eggs, and started to feel slightly put out by the agent's indecisiveness. Suddenly, a disturbing thought occurred to him. Slowly and imperceptibly, he started to rotate his head, one degree at a time, and then, when he heard no command to stop, he turned his upper body so that he could see the booth behind. And then he said, 'Son of a bitch.' The asshole had most likely left around the same time as the fly.

Muttering angrily, he gathered up his sunglasses, his rakish hat and shoulder-decorating jacket before striding petulantly out into the morning air. Wouldn't you know it, as he made his hungry and humiliated trudge across the street, who should be lumbering across the other way but Spaktoom the Impossible. Oh, finally! Spaktoom was about ninety feet tall and a dirty pink, like he was made of melted birthday candles. His tremendous weight left truck-sized, three-toed imprints of compressed concrete and black macadam everywhere he trod, and when he spoke, the interstellar tyrant's words had got a thick black edge around them to convey their guttural, inhuman timbre.

'Where is the human known as Blatz the Unbelievable? Spaktoom is told that Blatz is the one earthling who might possibly dissuade him from his frying of your puny globe!'

Sam chewed his options over. He could get another sandwich somewhere else, then take it up to Lexington and eat it in his office. 'Sorry, pal,' he said as he walked past the towering abomination and went on along the street, 'I never heard of him.'

Behind him, he could hear the deli sizzling up as the extraterrestrial enormity commenced its disappointed rampage. It was a pity, but Sam Blatz had bigger things to think about.

15. (September, 2015)

He knew he couldn't take it any more. He knew that if he didn't get out of the industry, a step unthinkable only a month before, then, one way or another, it would finish him. It would reduce him to a glyph, a quickly understood cartoon, the way it did with everything and everybody. He would be emotionally compressed, all his development abruptly capped at twelve years old, so that the only way that anyone could grow was laterally. He would come to have the look of someone spiritually taller who'd been stepped on, his complexities boiled down to an alliterative one-word summary, and he'd be Doleful Dan until the day he died. He'd be a giggling porno dwarf, a Brandon Chuff, a Worsley Porlock, or a catastrophic Mr Ocean casualty like Jerry Binkle. One way or the other, an inane grotesque, a sideshow shocker, and he knew, he knew, he knew he couldn't take it any more.

It had been coming for some time, years probably, but ever since that horrifying evening at Carl's Diner, it had been too close, too finely detailed to ignore. It was the sheer stupidity of everything – him chewing through his lip, Chuff having died and no one noticing, then Binkle fainting and Finefinger getting punched out by the waitress on account of his unfortunate Bell's palsy sneer. In fairness, this last incident had a redeeming upside: Jo, the waitress, had been mortified to learn of Finefinger's affliction, so had sent him flowers as an apology, and since then they'd been dating. This was nice, but measured up against the horrors of the comics business, it was coughing at Katrina.

Then, only a few days after he'd been bleeding, panicking, and trying to push his colleague's lifeless body out on to the gleaming diner floor, there had been … Dan still couldn't bring himself to think about that awful night at Brandon's place, with Moskowitz and Porlock. What they saw, and what they did, and all those breasts and assholes and vaginas burning. Theoretically, that was still something Dan could go to actual fucking prison for if anyone found out, the next cell down from Arvo Cake. While this was an unbearable source of anxiety for somebody like Dan, who'd never had a library fine, it paled to insignificance beside the rustling, soul-flensing dread he'd known in Chuff's apartment. Just the fact of its unbearable existence and the way it made him picture Brandon's inner world. Those little labels with the dates in tiny writing, the balled-up commemorations of what Chuff had evidently thought to be his finest moments, masturbating through a stupefying shift between millennia. That sudden re-evaluation of a human life, surrounded by ten thousand watchful orifices – that, and not the arson, had been what had broken something crucial in Dan Wheems.

He hadn't really been right since. This was his sole excuse, his only explanation for the ghastly exhibition he'd made of himself at Brandon's funeral, an eerie replay of the fatal diner incident that was, if anything, more terrible than the original. The problem was, no one had been expecting Crosby Bunsen. Nobody had known that Crosby Bunsen was a thing.

The funeral had been two weeks back, at the end of August. Dan's nerves had been in a state of near collapse since he'd been a participant at the bonfire of the obscenities. He hadn't been in any fit condition to attend, he saw that now, but in the end had made himself, convinced his absence would somehow expose him as the firebug. This, in retrospect, had been a hideous miscalculation.

Given that there didn't seem to be any of Brandon's family in attendance, it was thought appropriate his colleagues take up the front row of seats. There had been Ralph Roth, Worsley Porlock, Jerry Binkle, Milton Finefinger and David Moskowitz – who, weirdly, looked a little shorter than he had only a week or so before, and must have just been wearing lower heels. This line-up had left room for Dan Wheems at the end, with a sole empty space between him and the aisle. Right from the start, when they'd been sitting waiting for the service to begin, there'd been an atmosphere of violin-shrill tension, or at least that's how it had appeared to Dan. Him, Moskowitz and Porlock were apparently unable to prevent themselves from constantly exchanging guilty glances, and Dan caught himself nervously nibbling at the stitches they'd put in his lip after the travesty at Carl's. So, he was obviously in a delicate condition before Brandon Chuff walked in and took the end seat next to him.

Although he'd read and written scores of horror stories, Dan had always taken the position that the characters' reactions to the supernatural were too stagey and melodramatic – all the sudden drops in temperature, the paralysing fear and so on. Now, though, with his inner narrative swerved disconcertingly from Philip Roth to M. R. James, he'd felt as if reality were caving in, as if his bones were made from smouldering dry ice, absolute zero, so cold that the atoms would cease their vibration and then he, the bench that he was sitting on, and all New York would be collapsed into a dense, translucent nuclear jelly known as a Bose-Einstein condensate. It's fair to say that Dan had hastily revised his previous opinions on how it might feel to have a dead man sitting next to him, then.

Because it was definitely Brandon Chuff. It just was. Brandon Chuff when he'd been in his early twenties, which implied an afterlife where people were forever at their prime. The apparition had the curly, mousy hair; the minimalist fringe of beard; the wire-rimmed spectacles. Unlike the other mourners, Brandon's spectre wore blue ectoplasmic denim and a pair of ghostly sneakers. When Dan had gambled his sanity upon a sideways glance, the sight of Brandon's trademark pendant dangling around the spirit's neck – the one Brandon had worn at all those early seventies conventions – had spiked Dan from bowel to brain like an annihilating icicle. The revenant was even smiling enigmatically at a fixed point in the mid-distance, just as Brandon had done on that fatal evening.

Nailed down to his seat with dread, Dan's fraying mind had sorted frantically through ghost-Chuff's various potential motives for this visitation. Could it be benevolent, intended to grant Dan some closure after all that porn at the apartment, to remind him of the vital human being Brandon had once been, before the comic books and self-pollution ruined him? A final nod from the departing editor-in-chief, so that Dan could at last forget the tags, the boxes, the rosettes of tissue, forget everything? That this communication was meant for Dan Wheems alone was clear from the stark fact that Brandon was apparently invisible to everybody else. (Although he'd realise some days later that this was because he'd blocked the view of everyone in the front row, and no one else attending had the first idea what Brandon Chuff had looked like in his early twenties.)

After a full minute had elapsed without the wraith evaporating into mist, Dan's sanity was near its breaking point, and he was gnawing on those stitches now. If this had been a fond farewell, a reassurance from beyond, then Chuff would have already faded to a twinkle, leaving nothing but that irritating smile. It had occurred to Dan around then that the only other likely reason for this posthumous appearance was infernal retribution, like something from *Tower of Frightening*. The glaring truth unveiled itself, hitting him like a ton of frozen bricks: this was about the fire.

Oh God. Of course. It had been Dan that Brandon had entrusted with the key, Dan who had blundered in on the dried sperm necropolis, Dan who had panicked and manhandled Brandon's still warm corpse back in the diner. It was all a classic SP comics set-up, that would surely end with Wheems cremated in Chuff's place, while at the final panel's bottom right, the Necro-Filing Clerk would cackle and say, 'Heh, heh, heh! Looks like Dan's working up a SWEAT over those HOT books that SPARKED poor Brandon's BURNING DESIRE! I guess it's STREW you later, CONFLAGRATOR! Heh, heh, heh!' Sitting beside the deceased writer-editor and shuddering like a washer-dryer on its spin cycle, he registered the thrilling taste of copper in his mouth before Dan realised what he must have done.

What had next happened had seemed quite without volition, as if some neurological imperative had suddenly remembered what it had done last time Dan was in this kind of situation, unable to speak and spraying blood, penned in his seat by the unbudging bulk of Brandon Chuff. Acting according to some fear-imprinted muscle memory, he'd voiced an inarticulate squeal in a gout of crimson and initiated an attempt to push Chuff from his seat, thereby effecting his escape. Which, since this occasion was without a diner manager applying equal force from Brandon's other side, was more of a success, if you could call it that: the startled young man had said, 'What the fuck?', and tumbled noisily into the aisle. Somebody who turned out to be Ralph Roth had grabbed Dan from behind and shouted, 'Dan! That isn't Brandon!', but by then the whole place was in uproar, so that Jerry Binkle fainted, Milton Finefinger stood up and shouted, 'I'm not laughing! It's Bell's palsy,' and blah blah attending officers blah blah official caution blah blah blah.

Actually, when the cops showed up, Dan had been so unhinged that he'd confessed to burning down Brandon's apartment, although, luckily, no one had understood his blood-flecked gibberish. When Ralph Roth volunteered to drive Dan to the hospital, the police had just seemed relieved, like everybody else, and most especially like Crosby Bunsen, who'd been as relieved as hell.

Ralph had given him the Bunsen story over coffee up at Dan's place, after they were back from getting his lip restitched at the hospital. Roth had expressed his gratitude to Dan for giving him an excuse to leave Brandon's funeral, and had been sympathetic about his hysterical and bloody-mouthed attack on the young man who'd looked so much like Brandon Chuff. The only reason Roth had realised who the guy must be, he had explained, had been Chuff's drunk confession a few years before, up one night after a convention.

Linda Bunsen had been an aspiring colourist back in the early 1990s who'd made the acquaintanceship of Brandon Chuff. As she would later tell her offspring, he, her son, was how she'd got her shitty colourist's job on *Omnipotent Pre-Teen Militia* at American. And lost it, pretty much as soon as she'd begun to show. Chuff, raised on superheroes with unflagging moral standards, had, characteristically, denied paternity despite the almost comically exact resemblance between him and Crosby Bunsen, as the curly-haired child had been named. Of course, it had eventually all been sorted out with blood tests, but by then, Brandon's initial failure to acknowledge Crosby as his son had made its mark on the resentful youth's developing psychology. Already near identical to his dissembling progenitor, the boy had gone out of his way to underline and strengthen the disputed similarity. He'd dressed and worn his hair the way that Chuff had in old photographs the kid had seen, and had been ghoulishly delighted when he'd found the pendant that his mom had, for some reason, kept, forgotten in a drawer for more than twenty years. According to the guys who'd stayed on at the funeral after Ralph and Dan had gone, when Crosby had recovered from Dan's bloody, unintelligible onslaught, he'd stood up to read a eulogy that had begun, 'Dad was a selfish prick who never did a fucking thing for me or for my mother. No, I'm kidding.' Everybody had agreed that he was very like his father.

Roth had stayed at Dan's place for an hour or two, just to make sure he was OK. With Dan's mouth how it was, they didn't really have a conversation, although the intelligence that passed between them had proved something of a turning point for Wheems, in terms of subsequent career decisions. Ralph had asked him what his underlying problem was, and after he'd repeated 'If buff comiff' several times and they'd finally established he was saying, 'It's just comics,' Ralph had gone on to commiserate at length regarding the deficiencies of their profession:

'Huh! Tell me about it. It's like every story, every anecdote somebody starts to tell you in this industry, you know it's going to end up somewhere horrible. It's always "Zoom Wilson's creator drove his car into a wall but wanted to take someone with him", or else, "Sam Blatz used to sit up on a filing cabinet and drop the artists' pay cheques on the floor so that they had to bow before him when they stooped to pick them up". Or it's "And then he killed himself"; "And then he had to sleep up at the company offices to meet his deadline and he had a heart attack"; "And then he chopped his girlfriend up". It's either tragic, or it's dreadful, or it's both.

'I mean, OK, I've worked in other industries and, yeah, I know that they're all pretty much like this. I know shit like this happens everywhere, but with the comics business it seems fifty times worse, and do you know why? It's the absurdity. I worked it out. It's the huge disconnect between these dopey fucking children's characters and the appalling lives of the guys writing them and drawing them. And publishing them. It's like, on the one hand, you've got Silly-Putty Pete transforming himself into a hot-air balloon so he can fly to Mars, and on other, you've got Sam Earl blowing out his brains after an indiscretion at the Playhorse Mansion, where they'd got him drunk, he'd fucked one of the Fillies, and felt he'd betrayed the wife he loved. It's the absurdity, the bathos, which is right next door to the grotesque and the unspeakably horrendous. That's the comics business.

'Or at least, that's what I used to think was the whole explanation, but the longer I work at American, the more I think that something else is going on as well. Some of the things I've heard about the upstairs people at American, some of the things I've seen …'

At this point, Dan Wheems had said, 'Futchuff?', and then had to say it eight or nine more times before Roth understood that he meant 'Such as?'

'Well, such as Sol Stickman. Back a year or two ago, I saw a feature in one of the Sunday magazines about an archaeological discovery near the Black Sea, in what were once the eastern reaches of the Roman Empire. They'd unearthed this old mosaic from the first century that they believed was a depiction of the writer Lucian, who'd written the first journey to the moon. They showed a photograph of this thing, and there standing next to Lucian in the mosaic there's this old bald guy in a business suit and glasses; he's got one hand on Lucian's shoulder and the other hand is giving a thumbs up. I'm telling you, Dan, it was really fucking eerie. Or what about David Moskowitz? Has nobody but me noticed he's getting smaller? When I met him in the seventies, he had to have been six foot, six foot one. See, you weren't working at American for very long before you had your falling-out with Hector Bass and went to write for Massive, so you haven't seen the worst of it. I mean, there was the stuff with

Mimi Drucker after her big therapeutic breakthrough, as they called it.'

Here, Dan made the interjection, 'Wobabowber?', and it was thus a minute or two before Ralph Roth had been able to continue with his monologue.

'Dan, seriously, you can't say anything about this, right? But, look, when you were at American, before the thing with Bass, you must have got called into Mimi's office at least once, right? There's no need to speak, OK? Just nod or shake your head.'

Briefly closing his eyes, he'd nodded. Yes, Dan Wheems had been in Mimi Drucker's office.

'Yeah. So you recall its centrepiece, the thing she couldn't help but talk about?'

Once again, Wheems had nodded, swallowing warm spit and cringing from the memory.

'Buh pip-puh.'

Roth, becoming gradually accustomed to his fellow writer's bubbling diction, nodded grimly.

'Right. The picture. The big-ass framed photograph up on the wall, taken by Avedon or somebody, with Mimi's dad, the senator, out playing golf with General Pinochet. Good, then. You've seen it. And when you were in there, did she do the thing she always did?'

Dan's nod this time was fast, mechanical and difficult to stop. Yes, Mimi had done the thing. The thing was a compulsive indecent exposure, where it almost – almost – seemed like the vice president was unaware that she was doing it. And she was always doing it, knees opening and closing, opening and closing, back and forth, hypnotic like a set of windscreen wipers. Or she'd sometimes sit with one leg over each arm of her swivel chair, depending on her mood. She'd do this anywhere. She'd done it to her editors, her writers, and her artists, irrespective of their gender or their age. She'd done it for a hall of slack-jawed thirteen-year-old boy scouts at a Thunderman-themed presentation, and she'd once come very close to doing it on air with David Letterman. It wasn't even sexual. In fact, the obsessive, broken-clockwork quality was genuinely frightening. Roth sighed.

'OK. You know all that as well. Mimi's behaviour back then – the basketball team, and the screwing talent on her desk below the ventilator so that everyone could hear her, or the story Porlock always tells about the elevator on his first day at American – well, who knows what was up with her? My best guess at the time was that having a little power in the comics industry made people crazy, so they thought they could do anything they wanted to, like it was all a dream. But Mimi Drucker, after she'd had her supposed breakthrough, it made all that other stuff look normal, healthy even.

'What it was – and this is, like, five years ago, in 2010, sometime around then – I'm up at American and Mimi Drucker suddenly emerges from the moiré, does a double air-kiss and says she's got something that she wants to show me in her office. Straight away I'm thinking, "Please don't let it be her cervix," but there's something in the way she's acting that seems different. Even her subsonic growl has got a kind of girlish and excited lilt. So, then we're in her office, and she's sitting on her desk, and she holds out her hand to ask me what I think. There, on her finger, she's wearing a diamond wedding ring that must have cost more than my house and is about the size of Mimi's head. I look surprised and ask when she got married, and she sort of smiles and gestures to this little picture that she's got framed on her desk. I have to lean in closer so that I can make it out.

'It's … it's a wedding photograph. There's Mimi on the right in this incredible white wedding dress, and how she's smiling in the shot, she's happier than I've ever seen her, like she's just lit up with joy. Then, over on the left, you've got the groom.'

Here, Ralph had broken off. His hands, Dan had observed, were shaking.

'Dan, I'm not making this up. The groom, there in this picture she's got on her desk, Dan, it's the photograph. The other photograph, the one from off her office wall, her dad and Pinochet. It's standing there beside her in its gilt surround, about as tall as she is, and up at the frame's top centre someone's sticky-taped a yarmulke. I'm staring at it for maybe a minute and a half before I even start to figure what it means, before I understand that Mimi Drucker is now married, legally, to an inanimate black and white photograph of her own dad, the senator, and a notoriously evil Chilean dictator, playing golf. And worse, she's showing me this picture of her special day, expecting me to come up with some celebratory compliment. All I can manage is, "Gee, Mimi, I'm so happy for you. You both look so … glossy." And she gives a little rumble of delight and tells me that she knows.

'It's around then I notice that the bigger photograph, the one that's now her husband, it's no longer on her office wall. There's just one of those faintly darker rectangles you get. I ask about it, and she tells me "Daddy-and-Augusto" is at home, and that she's promised that she'll take him back a DVD that they can watch together. It turns out the marriage was suggested by this therapy the company's providing for her, to alleviate the problem with her sex drive. Something about making a commitment to the thing that means the most to her, the thing that truly makes her happiest, and that, apparently, was Daddy-and-Augusto. I'm just sitting there and trying to take all this in, when she adopts a confidential tone. She tells me she knows what I must be thinking, which is a lot more than I do, and says that she wouldn't want me thinking her married relationship with Daddy-and-Augusto was anything other than platonic, or that there was something, I don't know, incestuous about it.

'Then she … Dan, this was the worst. The worst thing that I've ever seen. She sat there on her desk, and then she did her thing. Still with that same fulfilled and dreamy smile, she started opening her knees. And, you know, normally it would be sudden, halfway through a conversation and they'd just flip open like the pages of a heavy book, but this time it was different. It was slower and, I don't know, it was more theatrical, like she was drawing back the curtain on some great dramatic statement of our times. She moved her knees apart, a centimetre at a time, and I … I couldn't look away, like it would seem discourteous or something. She … she wasn't wearing any underwear, and when her legs were open all the way, there was …'

Roth's eyes, ringed with charcoal, stared maniacally at the admittedly unsightly carpet, but were evidently seeing something infinitely worse. At last, when Dan Wheems had exhausted all the feverishly imagined possibilities for what there might have been up Mimi Drucker's skirt, Ralph had looked up at his unfathomable, Frankenstein-lipped host with an expression like King Lear might have if he'd just learned that he was being audited.

'Dan, there was nothing there. No hair, no genitals, just … nothing. Or, I don't remember, maybe there were pores. I don't know. It was like a G.I. Joe, without the ball-and-socket joints. And there were no, there were no scars, like there'd be if she'd had cosmetic surgery. You have to understand this, Dan: everything had just gone, without a trace. When Mimi sees I've got the idea, she demurely shuts her knees and smooths her skirt down, then she looks at me with this real serious expression and she says, "It's just, my thing with Daddy-and-Augusto. I don't want you thinking something weird is going on." Me, basically, I'm still in shock, so I'm just going, "No, no, Mimi, haha, not at all." And then it's like the exhibition's over, but just as she's showing me the door, she gets all whispery and conspiratorial. She says, "Ralph, I want you to remember that this company can give you anything. The company wants what we want, Ralph. It wants that we should have our heart's desire. I promise you, there's someone watching over us, here at American." And then I'm off and running down the eye-strain corridors and trying to remember which way daylight is.'

Roth had looked broken. He was sitting there, just shaking his head silently over the heat death of his coffee, like the interlude with Mimi had been a last straw, the one outrageous comics-business anecdote too many that had snapped his back. Dan had been overwhelmed with empathy, and felt the story about Drucker – surely metaphorical – had perfectly encapsulated everything that he himself had started feeling about comics since the death of Brandon Chuff: the way the business unsexed and dehumanised the people working in it, and the way it sucked them into an insane alternative reality, where there weren't walls or limits, nothing but a kind of endless psychiatric freefall which, right at the start perhaps, might feel like flying.

It was probably right there that Dan Wheems had decided that he absolutely must get out of the demented industry, while he still had a nervous system capable of doing so. The fellow feeling between him and Ralph, two brothers in adversity, was like a great and sombre current in the room. He clapped one hand supportively upon Roth's shoulder, and he talked his heart out in a way that he had never done before. With rhetoric like flaming, beaten gold, he'd spoken of four-colour comic books as a false flag of innocence, flown from a cesspit of depravities and racketeers. In burnished syllables, he'd catalogued the startling details of his epic contretemps with Hector Bass, and settled all those rumours that abounded with a lyric flight of argument more like a song. He'd cursed the comics field resoundingly as a half-witted abattoir of children's dreams, and sworn that sooner would he pluck out his own eyes than toil another moment in this vineyard of life-eating trivia and emotional arrest. He railed against his own Sammy Awards, now badges of a terrible infirmity, an illness of unowned adulthood. Using finer language than at any other point in his career, Dan spoke his human truth, a torrent of volcanic phrase and fulmination that might set the night afire. Unfortunately, all that Ralph Roth could make out was 'Ubuffuff wuffuffabuff' for around twenty minutes, after which he'd given Wheems a weary smile and said, 'I hear you, pal. I hear you,' this being at least technically true.

Roth had departed shortly after that, so Dan had ordered Chinese takeout and then sat up late with his mind racing, wondering if he was really going to have the nerve to go through with this. Did he have the stones to walk out on a job he'd wanted since he'd been a twelve-year-old, effectively walk out of his whole life and not come back? He didn't know if he, or anyone, could truly do that; didn't know if it was even possible. But then he had to, if he didn't want to end up turning into Worsley Porlock, Mimi Drucker, Brandon Chuff, or something worse that was beyond imagining. After his meal arrived, he'd pulled the four trade-paperbacks of his *Vindictives* run down from the shelf and thought he'd read them through again, perhaps to rediscover his lost fondness for the field in the groundbreaking series that had earned Dan both his Sammies.

He found that he still enjoyed them, couldn't put them down, so it was nearly three o'clock before he got to bed. He remained proud of all his work, which in the early nineties had been so innovative. That scene where he'd had the original Vindictives meeting up again after some years, as older individuals. The atmosphere and the comparative realism of his dialogue, like the famous interchange between Ormazda and the Brute – nobody else had been attempting stuff like that back then. He could be justly satisfied with what he'd done, and yet …

And yet, the work, it wasn't really his. He'd not created the beloved characters that everybody bought the book for, the established icons that lent all Dan's knowing modern riffs their resonance. He hadn't come up with the National Guard, the Brute, the Human Tank, Ormazda, Miniman and Minimaid, or the idea of sticking them together in one book called *The Vindictives*. That was all Sam Blatz and Joe Gold, which was just the same as saying it was all Joe Gold. A tough kid from the tenements, blessed with a comic book imagination more fertile than anyone had ever seen, who'd had everything taken from him by Sam Blatz and Massive Comics, and who, if you added up the billions that the Massive superhero films had made already out of his creations, was a victim of the single biggest theft from any individual in human history. Was this, then, all that Dan was proud of, his complicity in robbing someone genuinely talented of what was theirs? Was this the best that today's industry professionals could say about themselves, about their work? He took these thoughts to bed with him, and, in the morning, saw he had no choice: he knew he couldn't take it any more.

In consequence, he'd gone up to the Massive offices with all of the determination he could handle, and the complete absence of a plan. Originally, he'd intended to explode in on Gene Pullman, Massive's current, overbearing prick-in-chief, and make some sort of heartfelt condemnation of the industry while handing in his resignation. Then he thought about it some more and decided that this was way too much trouble. Pullman would most probably be out somewhere, pulling a bullion robbery or something, and even if he happened to be in, wouldn't have given two shits about whether Dan Wheems quit, or got run over, or became a member of the Man-Boy Love Association. It would just be one more story about Doleful Dan and his unending barrage of dissatisfactions. No, what Dan would do is just go in, clean out his desk and write the company a letter, handing in his notice and explaining his decision. He was looking forward to it, getting all that poison off his chest.

His visit to the offices on Lexington provided none of the catharsis he'd been hoping for. He'd gone up in the elevator to the fifth floor where the legendary Massive 'Pigsty' was, and lingered wistfully a while outside the separate office that had once been occupied by Denny Wellworth. Denny had checked out with prostate cancer getting on for three years earlier, but before that, and before departing for American, his office had been an oasis of calm rationality amidst the brutalising tension-factory that was Massive Entertainment. Denny had been the best writer in the business, and perhaps the only grown-up. Possibly through the self-confidence that came with knowing that, he'd never become the infantilised, embittered sphincter that a large majority of his contemporaries ended up as. Dan had almost worshipped Denny and his wife Diane, both gone now, and when Denny had been dying at the hospital, Dan had been in to visit him near every day. Denny had even shown enthusiasm when Dan had suggested he record an interview, some final thoughts about the comics business, on Dan's phone. Although the piece was never published, Dan still had the transcript somewhere and had thought, as he stood gazing mournfully at what had once been Denny's door, that he should dig it out.

To reach Dan's little side room – too small to be thought of as a proper office – had entailed the usual dispiriting forced march through the Pigsty itself. He'd paused there at its entrance to collect himself and draw a fortifying breath, before abandoning all hope and flinging wide the gates of hell.

When he'd been ten and had first read about the Monstrous Massive Pigsty, on the 'Pigsty Postings' page they'd had in all the monthly books, Dan had imagined it as an exciting adult romper room where everybody was exempted from the burdens of maturity, and could remain enthusiastic schoolboys pretty much forever. In his prepubertal mind's eye, he had pictured Joltin' Joe Gold trading funny stories and cigars with Rabid Robert Novak, Jittery Jeff Stevenson or Frisky Frankie Giardino, while Satanic Sam himself sat crouched over his typewriter, inventing all the characters. Could be that Winsome Wendy Dietrich would be fixing everybody coffee, but because she genuinely wanted to, and not because they made her. He'd thought it an Eden that had superheroes.

The collective workspace that he now stood at the portal of was, say, the size of four average living rooms. There at the centre was a five-by-six grid of open-topped boxes that resembled indiscreet lavatory cubicles, and almost every one contained a worried-looking penciller or inker digging graves for their own talent. Windowless, with less than ideal artificial light, the fog of desperation and anxiety that hung immediately over these creative cattle pens was almost visible, a stale cigarette smoke of the psyche. Like battery hens whose once sharp sensibilities had all been clipped for their own good, men with the eyes of massacre survivors hastily sketched interlinking ovals, convulsed balloon animals Dan recognised as larval forms of Beetle Boy, the Brute, or Dr Unrealistic. Here and there, the pittering rain of fingertips on keyboard marked a writer's oubliette, and somewhere somebody was muttering, 'I *think* I have a plot. I *think* I have a plot,' over and over, in a flat tone which to Dan suggested that most probably they hadn't. It smelled neither quite as bad, nor quite as fresh and natural, as an actual pigsty, although both felt, undeniably, like places of confinement for unhappy animals. He knew a couple of the inmates, and they caught his eye but quickly looked away, not through dislike, but through a fear of fraternising when they should be toiling, every lapse easily spotted in their open-plan panopticon.

The oblong path bordering the perimeter of the industrious and fraught central enclosure had some six doors leading off from it, into the individual side rooms where the editors and writer-editors like Dan were stationed. From the varying degrees of wear apparent on the carpet, itself an upsetting pickle-green, one could deduce which routes were the most popular and which were most often avoided, like the near-untrodden stretch outside Gene Pullman's office, which Dan happened to be then approaching. He had heard somewhere that when top predators – like wolves – were introduced into a population of their primary prey – like caribou – they would unfailingly establish something called a fear map. This contained once popular zones, such as grazing areas, that had since been abandoned through the increased likelihood of being chewed to death, in favour of less nourishing but safer destinations. The deep carpet pile outside Gene Pullman's office hadn't looked like it had seen a lot of grazing lately, put it that way.

Walking past the shunned door, which was open, Dan had been relieved to learn that Pullman wasn't in that day, although the ambience was still thick with his presence: what had been an ordinary comics-business office unit now existed in a state of superimposition with a well-equipped, high-tech gymnasium, part of Pullman's shot at physically transforming himself to a superman. His office chair had been displaced in favour of an exercycle flanked by weight machines, while near one wall, the photocopier had been designed to function as a vaulting horse. Miniature treadmills were strewn casually around like throw cushions, for moments when the occupant might find themselves just staring blankly at a wall, and didn't want to waste the workout opportunity. Surmounting all of this, hung from the ceiling by a length of chain, was Pullman's flying harness. This had been installed so he could personally model as his self-resembling creation Best Guy, for the frightened artists sitting with their sketchbooks in the punchbag-crowded room below.

One of the many reasons Best Guy hadn't really worked, then, was contingent on Gene Pullman's own atypical anatomy. The thing was, Pullman was unusually wide. Not fat, by any means, just … wide. He looked like he'd been drawn in ballpoint on the skin of a balloon then laterally stretched, or as if he were showing in the wrong screen ratio compared with everybody else. Frankly, it made Dan's eyes ache looking at him sometimes, as if he were a particularly fiendish optical illusion. And on top of his unfortunate appearance, personality and reputation, Pullman was just plain unfortunate. When one considered all the awful things that had chanced to occur on Pullman's watch – employees dead from overwork, or the few thousand pages of Joe Gold's originals that had been stolen just before the company had been legally required to give them back to him – then it was difficult not to conclude that the poor guy was simply monumentally unlucky. Rumour had it that he'd been the young writer referred to in the Julius Metzenberger psychiatric session they'd reprinted in *The Comics Contemplator* back in 2013, the young man who'd kept clean pants beside the telephone for those bowel-emptying emergencies whenever Metzenberger called. Dan thought he understood how a career trajectory that started out like that could end up with somebody dangling from an office ceiling, dressed up in a special extra-wide costume, pretending to be Best Guy.

Dan continued past Gene Pullman's office to the more well-trodden reaches of the gherkin-coloured carpet further on, around a sharp right turn, where his own side room was located. Opening its door for what he realised with mixed feelings might be the last time, Dan stepped into the tiny Skinner box that for the last five years he'd forced himself to see as 'cosy'. To be fair, Dan hadn't needed anywhere near the amount of space that

Pullman obviously did, not having to accommodate as many barbells, hanging ropes or wall bars.

All his room had was a desk, a chair, and a free-standing bookcase where Dan's reference material was stacked untidily, this being the 'Heirloom Editions' that reprinted all the earliest canonical adventures of the individual characters comprising the Vindictives. Perched atop the bookcase was Dan's brace of Sammy Awards, one to either side, for symmetry. Each was a nine-inch figurine caricaturing Massive's founding father Sam Blatz, supplemented by cartoonish horns, barbed tail and pitchfork, but wearing a Luciferian smirk that was unquestionably Blatz's own. The walls were papered with dynamic posters and promotional material, most of them hyping Dan's own books, a décor he'd thought casual and modern when he'd at last been awarded his own office back in 2010, but which now seemed self-congratulatory and teenage. Dan had sighed, as had his worn-out swivel chair when he'd lowered his worn-out body into it.

Part of the reason that Dan found his work environment so thoroughly depressing, he was sure, was the persisting ghost, or at least aura, of Frank Giardino. Giardino was the glaringly talent-free inking veteran who'd occupied this so-called office several people before Dan, and it had taken Dan a while to figure out how come an inker – especially one as incapable as Frisky Frankie Giardino – had his own room, while guys like Joe Gold and Robert Novak were out slaving on the Pigsty's sweatshop floor. Dan had joined Massive some years after Giardino left, and had thus never met the man in person, but he could remember a blurred photograph he'd once seen. It had been in the filler pages of a twenty-five-cent reprint book called *Massive Milestones* in the early sixties, a cheap bonus feature where they'd thrown together snapshots of 'the Pigsty Posse'. There'd been stocky little Joe Gold, his arms folded proudly and a cigar stub protruding from his grin; there'd been myopic and retiring Robert Novak, half turning away as he flinched from the camera; and there'd been Frank Giardino. In the picture Giardino had been grinning, like Joe Gold, but whereas Gold was grinning with the viewer, Frisky Frank was grinning at them, because they were all just marks and didn't know the real deal like he did, squinting on a sunny afternoon approximately half a century ago.

The story with Frank Giardino, as Dan had eventually learned, was one almost entirely situated in the true crime section of the bookracks. It had seemingly been common in the forties and the fifties for the smaller comic companies to get a visit from their local Mafia franchise, offering advice on how the publishers could keep their offices from burning down. Goliath Comics had been no exception, but Sam Blatz had managed to put his unique Mephistophelean stamp on the deal, by offering to hire the unemployable young nephew of respected capo Salvatore Giardino, rather than just paying the protection money. Nominally, little Frankie was an inker, if you defined 'inker' as somebody who went over pencil lines in ink, rather than as an artist in their own right who would lend the pencilled page all of its volume, weight and texture. Frisky Frank's only distinction, everyone agreed, was that it took a very special talent to make Joe Gold's art look merely adequate.

One of the ways in which Frank Giardino had accomplished this unprecedented feat was through his need for rigorously scheduled oral sex. Perhaps by some arrangement with Frank's Uncle Sally, there'd be a professional fellatrix booked to show up here at Frisky Frankie's office every weekday afternoon at five o'clock, with punctuality a paramount consideration. So, if it was getting to around four-thirty and he'd still got one of Joe Gold's gorgeous pages for *The Unrealistic Five* to ink before he got his daily blow job, Giardino would take an eraser and remove a number of the background skyscrapers, or rub out what he thought to be extraneous figures from the artist's detailed crowd scenes. Some months it had almost been *The Unrealistic Three*.

Dan had always assumed that having Giardino at the company, an authentic minor Mafia associate, must have in some way tickled the unbounded ego of Satanic Sam. Blatz had enjoyed hanging around with Giardino, perhaps hoping that some of the organised-crime glamour would rub off, and there had been the much-repeated story of when Frisky Frank had taken Blatz out to a gentlemen's drinking establishment owned by his uncle Sal. Unfortunately, Sam Blatz only had a tenuous grasp on ordinary reality, and none at all on the Five Families reality that Giardino's uncle represented. When confronted by a room heaving with Mafiosi – that included, possibly, Frank Giacomo – Blatz had impishly elected to denounce them all as 'dirty rats' in a poor imitation of James Cagney, and then mimed mowing them down with an imaginary tommy gun. As fifty men wearing identical expressions of murderous incredulity reached as if for an inside pocket, Frank had Frisked for his employer's life: 'No, please, this guy's an idiot. I'll get him outta here.'

Sat there in Giardino's former workspace, haunted by the residue of his many unlikeable transactions, it struck Dan that the non-inker's death in 2005 had been as suspect as his life. The first that anyone had heard of Giardino's unforeseen demise had been with the announcement of his imminent closed-casket funeral. Chins had been stroked and brows creased, particularly when somebody said they'd seen Frank looking frisky just the week before. Best guesses were witness protection, or, more probably, something to do with piscine dormitory arrangements.

It was all just as Ralph Roth had said the night before, how every comics-business anecdote was guaranteed to end up with a suicide, a liver failure, mental breakdown or some other kind of a closed casket. On Dan's desk was an unopened envelope emblazoned with the logo of Satyricon 2015, no doubt fresh imprecations for Dan to confirm his presence at the usually febrile gathering in late September, only a few weeks away, which, in his current doldrums, Dan felt disinclined to do. Satyricon had, for some years, been more of a bizarrely costumed interspecies orgy than a celebration of the comics medium. The event's sole function, almost certainly, would be the generation of brand new repellent narratives and freshly minted legends of degeneration. Something absolutely horrible might happen, anything at all, and all that would come out of it would be another utterly hilarious yarn in Worsley Porlock's morbid repertoire. Wearily, Dan had shoved the envelope aside and gone back to considering the reason he'd returned there, to the erstwhile gangster love nest that he'd tried to think of as his office. His intention had been to reclaim some fond mementos of his funny-book existence before he abandoned it, but by then he'd been feeling nauseous and having second thoughts.

From their lofty positions on the bookcase high above him, his Sammy Awards had leered down at Dan knowingly, one to each side. It had been something like the way that animated cartoon characters made ethical decisions, with a vice or virtue perched on either shoulder, except that this was a comics-business version and it had no virtues. Thus, with only devils offering advice, the choice was not between the good and bad halves of an individual, but between the evil and the genocidally monstrous. The Satanic Sammy on the left might lead with, 'Salutations, Seeker! Why not do something disastrous that you'll regret forever?', while the Sammy on the right might come back with, 'Eyes right, Explorer of Eternity! Don't listen to that faggot! Cook and eat your way through a whole orphanage! Do something everybody will regret forever!'

Dan had been slumped in his seat and thinking hard about all this – Sam Blatz, the industry, Joe Gold, Mimi Drucker, Frank Giardino, Brandon Chuff dead in a diner, Chuff's apartment burning and his funeral, Gene Pullman, Denny Wellworth, everything – when he had noticed that the constant inner voice of his frustrations and anxieties, which he'd lived with his whole adult life, had fallen silent and was gone. He wasn't sweating, wasn't tapping his foot uncontrollably or chewing his replacement stitches. With a dawning sense of wonderment, he'd realised that he was at peace, and, in the perfect clarity of that enchanted, unexpected state, he'd known for sure what he must do.

He hadn't taken any of the promo posters or Heirloom Editions, and had left the ring binder with his reviews and clippings where it was. He hadn't glanced at his unopened mail, especially the invite from Satyricon; had not retrieved his Sammies from their vantage point up on the bookcase; hadn't taken anything. He'd simply stood up and, after a last look round, had left the room. He had retraced his steps along the sour green carpet, passing the averted gazes of the labourers in the outside cubicles, passing Gene Pullman's office with its gaping door. Taking a last peek at the Best Guy flying harness, he'd allowed himself a faint half-smile. No heirlooms, no conventions, no awards and no reviews. If anybody at that company had seriously wanted to cheat gravity, then they had only to put down the Massive burden they were shouldering. Then they'd have known what flying was.

Dan Wheems had floated through the Pigsty door and, with a fond, respectful nod, past Denny Wellworth's former base of operations. It had been like waking from a lengthy dream of dull, conveyor-belt employment, with the dawning understanding that it wasn't real, and that he didn't need to do it any more, and that he never had. Dan hadn't thought that it could be as easy as deciding 'no more' halfway through imaginary dialogue between contending Sammy statuettes. Industry terminology and complex protocols of office politics flaked from him now like sloughed-off snakeskin, to reveal the new, pink individual underneath. Why, he'd not even reached the street doors yet, was still descending in the elevator, but already he'd forgotten the gradations of enhancement for the variant covers. His heart soaring, giddy with his sudden weightlessness and full of new ideas for how he wanted to approach that resignation letter, he'd taken a cab to his apartment.

This was where he was now, his mind brimming with exciting plans and fresh conceptions which, for the first time in years, did not involve the National Guard or Human Tank. He'd run through all the practicalities of his forthcoming leap to nowhere, and it all looked doable. He'd had a stroke of luck some years before, when *Vindictives: Choosing Pawns*, the first film in the franchise, had just been released. The second volume in Dan's run, with sombre flashback references to the team's origin, was in the stores around then and it sold in quantities not seen before nor, as it turned out, since. In short, not being burdened by a family, by a cocaine-and-hooker habit, or by both, Dan had a healthy sum in his account. He could afford to move out of Manhattan altogether, maybe find a place in the Midwest, where he'd grown up. He had enough to get by comfortably for a few years, buy him some time while he commenced the Great American non-graphic Novel that he'd always meant to write. Without employment or a monthly vehicle to transport his ideas away, Dan found that he was having new ones every other moment, a rush of invention that he hadn't felt in ages, and that he would have to find something to do with. Something literary, without pictures.

To that end, he'd had some thoughts about the manner of his quitting: stopping work for Massive Comics would require no more than a brief letter, or perhaps just a text message. Saying goodbye to the entire comics field, however, seemed to call for something more creative, something that encompassed all Dan's thoughts and feelings in some kind of artful closing statement.

It occurred to him that opening this statement with a page of comic strip would be both novel and appropriate, provided it addressed the issues that were central to the cloudy argument that he was forming. As he thought about it, sitting at a kitchen table in the blue-white underlighting of his open laptop, he began to see that the comic book industry's most emblematic story was also its first. It was the narrative of David Kessler and Si Schuman, sitting up together on those starry science fiction nights in Delaware, building with ink and paper a new kind of creature, powerful enough to bend their lives and warp the culture that surrounded them with its tremendous gravity, the force of its attraction. Dan could even see a way to link the theft of Thunderman from his creators with the birth of corporate America, the whole idea expanding into larger territories the more he thought about it. A spontaneous image out of nowhere came to him, a panel with Dave Kessler supine on his mortuary slab, while, reaching into view from off, an orderly draws up Thunderman's golden cape to cover Kessler's face. That sold Dan on the concept. That's what he was going to do, whatever it turned out to be.

The venture's possibilities were opening like a flower. In Thunderman, he had a microcosm of the comics industry, while in the industry he had a microcosm of America. His farewell address could be a thing of several parts, to include all the disparate affairs that needed to be talked about, like a collage or a mosaic. He could investigate the whole notion of Thunderman from a variety of angles, until all that it was possible to know or say about the character and his effect on culture had been captured. He'd include that Denny Wellworth interview, and a few other things that were announcing themselves to him as he typed out his preliminary notes. He didn't have a title, but was confident that one would show up in its own good time. This was all going to be so great.

What he would do, he'd send his multipart farewell note in to one of the more serious and dignified trade magazines, and then he'd vanish. He'd just disappear. His contact with his fellow industry professionals was largely non-existent as it was, and if it should cease altogether then most probably no one would notice. Dan felt limitless, euphoric, wondered why he hadn't done this sooner. All the stress that had evaporated once he'd stepped out through the Pigsty doors, God only knew what all that had been doing to him. He felt sure that his decision to leave comics would make an enormous difference to his life expectancy, amongst so many other things.

His fingers were on fire. He opened a new document in order to commence work on the Kessler and Schuman comic strip, put page one, panel one, up at the top, the same as always, and got down to work, immediately so immersed that his apartment faded from awareness.

Sitting there ignored and silent on Dan's sofa watching this, the Human Tank's sigh echoed in his silver helmet. Disappointed human eyes slid sideways in their metal slots, to gaze enquiringly in the direction of the Brute, seated there next to him. The blue behemoth shook his huge head in disgust and expressed his opinions that this shit was cold, and that he wasn't going to sit around for any more of it. Beside him, at the sofa's other end, the National Guard could only nod in sad concurrence. Dan Wheems, bent over his laptop, wouldn't even look at them. Resignedly, they stood up, one by one. The Guard picked up his stylised-eagle shield from where it leaned against the coffee table, and they filed past the oblivious writer as they headed for the door. Clearly annoyed, the Brute kicked over Dan's wastepaper basket on the way, because they, after all, were the Vindictives.

They let themselves out, and didn't really come around to his apartment after that.

16. (January, 2021)

And with a thousand heads, it poured as Sunday sunlight on the famous avenue, behaving like a varicoloured gas or like an organism, speckled and gelatinous. Tossing and stamping, making ritual presentations, undulating in a mile-long New Year's dragon that had flags for streamers, it advanced on its desired catastrophe.

Against an appalled hush, it whistled, barked and chanted. It laughed, and called out the names of people that it wanted killed. Ahead, a white rotunda lifted into blue noon on the marbleised exhaust jets of its columns, while the writhing, composite immensity flowed in to flood its foreground with a fractious ocean of resent that spilled on to the alabaster portico. It dashed its swarming head upon the stately frontage and exploded into radicalised butterflies, their flapping banner wings painted with bars and stars and swastikas; with Gadsden snakes and letters of the alphabet and Jesus Christ.

It grew a myriad of hands that bristled with professionally printed slogans, two-way radios, Tasers, ziplock handcuffs, pepper sprays and pipe bombs, and it wore a T-shirt promising that work would make us free. Borne on its shoulders were the makings of a gallows, and it came to celebrate the violent passing of coherence, history and fact. From in its multiplying pipe organ of throats, the compound voice declared a catalogue of pulp hallucination, and within its aggregated mind, it felt itself becoming the forge-lit impasto of a future patriotic painting. Its blood singing with rich pigments, heart engorged with hot impossibilities, a beast of people howled at inconvenient reality.

His consciousness partly dissolved by working from home during the pandemic, Worsley Porlock blinked at the TV screen and had no idea what was going on.

About him stretched the merchandising showroom that was his home office, dining room, and, sometimes, when he didn't have sufficient motivation to move from the sofa, bedroom. Every horizontal surface had become a balcony from which his favourite characters – as costly cold-cast figurines, poseable action figures, neotenic plushies, cubist Lego-people, plump inflatables – gazed down on Worsley in his King Bee boxer shorts as he attempted to both watch TV and read a magazine at the same time, and was equally unsuccessful in either endeavour.

He'd been sent the magazine, which was called *Kulchur* and was evidently a revival of some fifties thing, by Milton Finefinger. Milton had left the industry four years ago, partly in sympathy with Dan Wheems, partly in disgust over the ongoing non-publication of his *Union* book, and had been doing well with film reviews, opinion pieces, things like that. He'd married Jo, who was now managing Carl's Diner, and seemed happy. He'd sent Worsley *Kulchur* magazine because the current issue had the only article on comic books that Finefinger had written lately, and the first such that the magazine had published. It was called 'A Spandex Wrapper for the Naked Lunch' and seemed to be about neurology, though Worsley wasn't concentrating hard enough to make much sense of it. This was in part because of all the crazy stuff on his muted TV, but mostly it was Worsley's invitation upstairs at American, in five or six weeks' time, that was the source of his distraction.

Was this a promotion, or some prelude to promotion? He'd been editor-in-chief more than five years now, and a couple of vice presidents had come and gone since then. The post was vacant at the moment, and he couldn't help but speculate. Alternatively, this might be connected to the fact that, as chief editor, he had presided over the most crippling decline American had ever seen. And although none of this was Worsley's fault, he couldn't think of any way in which he'd helped the situation. Maybe he was being taken upstairs to be vanished, as was rumoured to have been the case with Mimi Drucker. This exhausting oscillation between apprehension and anticipation clearly wasn't doing Worsley any good, and so he tried once more to focus on Finefinger's article.

'If you've spent time, as I have, in the company of junkies, you'll have noticed that while many can avoid the clichéd image of the drug addict, a number of the stereotype's trademark aspects will still be broadly applicable – a certain pallor, itchy arms, a startlingly efficient diet plan, and money going missing. Basically, there are sufficient symptomatic similarities, across this diverse group of citizens, for us to state with some degree of confidence that we are looking at a bunch of people needing urgent treatment for their intravenous drug dependence. It is the intention of this article to argue that the same thing can be said of some contemporary comic fans: as with the drug-habituated, any social growth is terminated and the superhero addict is admitted to a subculture with people whom they may dislike, but who share their affliction. One might also note that whether they crave heroin or hero, a distinctive tenor of complaint, consuming need, and victimhood seems to be common to both these communities.'

Which seemed, to Worsley, more than a touch harsh, and there was nothing in his own real-life experience to justify such an invidious comparison. He'd never been sucked off by somebody who needed money for their next issue of *The Alarming Beetle Boy*. He put the magazine down on the sofa next to him, amongst the company of empty pizza boxes and a scattering of this month's complimentary copies from American. These, in the industry's currently straitened circumstances, totalled just over a dozen titles, all featuring characters attached to currently stalled movie franchises. So there was *Moon Queen*, *Thunderman*, *King Bee*, *United Supermen,* and a few others, like the smash-hit super-villain team *Americans for Evil.* This was, like, a fifth of the amount of books the company had been putting out this time last year. He knew the industry would pull out of its nosedive because, well, it always had before, and because a world without monthly comic books was unimaginable, but if he hadn't possessed the confidence that came with being an insider, he guessed that the current situation would look like garishly coloured death throes; a super-extinction of some kind.

Yeah, there'd been the pandemic, and then the whole comics distribution system had collapsed, with panicked publishers suggesting they could maybe set up lemonade stands on street corners and sell all their titles that way. It was like the crisis management ideas that twelve-year-olds might have. Then, as the dominoes kept falling, all the movies that the industry had let itself become dependent on stopped coming out, and even the top company no longer looked as Massive as it had before. A lot of things had happened that were beyond anyone's control, but if the comics field was honest with itself, it had commenced its swansong some years prior to the conspiracy of bats and pangolins that gifted Covid-19 to the world.

One major problem seemed to be that nearly everybody working in the business – artists, writers, editors and publishers – was a promoted comic fan who, though they might know everything about King Bee, had no original or viable ideas of their own that might conceivably alleviate the comic world's near-terminal condition. Yet another difficulty was the readership, presently atrophied to something like a hundred thousand devotees, most of them middle-aged or older, a core audience that wasn't merely shrinking, but was literally dying off. And which – since everybody had decided that comics weren't just for kids, then that they weren't for kids at all – meant that the industry had no way to replace those vanished readers, having confidently sawn away the branch it had been sitting on. The fans were drying up, blowing away, while the immortal, ageless beings – whom they had grown old and lonely in the service of – could only stand on Worsley Porlock's stereo or coffee table, looking down on all this anxiously and wondering if they were next.

Restless with several months of more-than-usual inactivity, and agitating uselessly about what might be waiting for him upstairs at American in six weeks' time, he once more picked up *Kulchur*, but had only read a line or two before his eyes were drawn away to the impossible carnival imagery that washed across his silent TV screen.

Black-jacket myrmidons with glassy shields and faces seemed to melt away on contact with a mega-hydra that was made untouchable by its prevailing whiteness. Revolution as rock festival or sports event, attempted coup as a reality-show entertainment, playing out with Constitution on the one side, Independence on the other, Legion in the yawning gap between. Colony organism, Man o' War, a millipedal mass now bounded half the whited sepulchre. It pressed from west and east, constricting, and its spangled pseudopodia cried out in rage or prayer or nervous jocularity as tear-gas puffballs blossomed here and there on the perimeter, to no appreciable effect. Windows announced their final music, and the secret dread of all authority poured in to flood authority's inviolable palace, sent by an authoritarian. With a vestigial ideology of black and white hats, although largely carpeted in red ones, it extruded tendrils on the Senate floor and, suddenly, important people were escorted by trained killers, somewhere far from the influx of amateurs. Confronted by a wave of frightful jubilation, knowing military backup – a bad visual – would be unforthcoming, the blue line inside the Capitol had never felt so thin, so vulnerable. But, by then, the cataclysmic pageant was begun in earnest.

Worsley's eyes weren't that great, so he couldn't read the ticker tape of on-screen captions from this distance, but he thought that the whole thing might be to do with Trump.

He shook his head and blew air down his nose ambiguously. Worsley had conflicted feelings about the whole Trump thing, but foremost amongst them were a feeling of exhaustion and a feeling of deferred guilt that he hoped to put off for as long as possible. Of course, he'd not actually voted for the horribly tenacious nearly former president, but then he'd not voted against him, either time. Embarrassingly, back in 2016, he'd been loud in his support of the reality TV star, telling anyone who'd listen that Trump's great appeal was that he 'wasn't part of the political establishment', to which some had responded that he needed the word 'even' in there somewhere, maybe after 'wasn't'. Porlock didn't really have an explanation for why he had thought the way he had, although in his defence, a lot of other comics guys had been of the same mind.

Possibly it had to do with the exaggerated cartoon aura that the guy had, or at least as Worsley saw him. Back in 2016, everything had got a kind of superhero atmosphere about it, not least Donald Trump, or, as supporters still referred to him, the Donald, like the Streak or the King Bee, as if it were his superhero name. That year, six of the dozen biggest-grossing movies had been superhero films, and he supposed that there had been a feeling as if people wanted this to be a simpler world, that they could understand. They wanted big dramatic threats and enemies, no matter that they strained all credibility, and also wanted some improbable and memorable character to offer them solutions that were simple, and as unbelievable as the imagined menaces they pledged to combat. Just how the electorate had come to be in such a malleable state, Worsley had no idea.

Taking a further glance towards the televised melee occurring on the room's far side, he found himself less able to relate to what was going on than to, say, an inadequately plotted boxset season closer. Scratching unselfconsciously inside his King Bee boxers, decorated with explosive onomatopoeia, he reluctantly retrieved Finefinger's *Kulchur* essay from amidst the comics and cardboard containers on his sofa, and attempted to pick up where he'd left off.

'One might ask, even if this fan attention could be justifiably described as some far-fetched addiction, how can anyone be sure that superheroes are its focus, rather than some other aspect of the medium or industry? In answer, I'd suggest the questioner peruse contemporary comics threads, and find out for themselves: the structures and the storytelling possibilities of comics aren't discussed at all, implying little or no interest in the comics medium. As for the industry, creators would seem largely to be mentioned in relation to some character or storyline, while even companies are only talked about in terms of just how badly they are serving both their readers and the properties they own. Fan loyalty is not, then, to the artists and the writers who create the figures that they so admire, but to the characters themselves.

'Even a craftsman as revered as Joe Gold could have his creations stolen without any protest from the readership, but if some aspect of the Human Tank or National Guard's by-now-mangled continuity is treated with the slightest disrespect, they feel entitled to protest in droves. Their attitude is perhaps best explained with recourse to our central metaphor of drug addiction, in that those habituated to cocaine don't care about the work conditions of the peasants who pick all the coca leaves. Their loyalties can only lie with those who furnish them directly with the thing that they depend upon. Their loyalties can only lie with the cartel.'

Returning *Kulchur* to the fellowship of fast-food and fast-fantasy containers littering the couch, Worsley was saddened to see someone else who'd retired from the industry running it down the way Dan Wheems had done. He also felt demoralised by the whole air of breakdown and bitter recrimination that had settled on the comics field over the last four or five years, coincidental with the present outgoing administration ... and his own tenure as editor-in-chief, now that he thought about it. His assembled figurines and painted idols, on their various domestic perches, seemed to share with Worsley this forlorn assessment.

While he knew that he was just imposing patterns on a random sequence of events, he couldn't help but feel that

Brandon Chuff's untimely stoppage at Carl's Diner had precipitated an abysmal chain reaction of immense complexity and woe. When he had burned down Brandon's awful mausoleum of lust with Wheems and Moskowitz, all the time knowing that those priceless first appearances and origins were going up in pornographic smoke, he'd somehow understood that he was damned. Then fellow arsonist Dan Wheems had gone spectacularly nuts at Brandon's funeral, attacking Brandon's son and disappearing from the industry immediately after. He'd left nothing but an incoherent rant against the comics business, which was probably where Milton Finefinger got the idea. At least Wheems wasn't present for the Brandon Chuff memorial and tribute at Satyricon, that year in late September, so had not included the horrific incident that happened there amongst his catalogue of disenchantment. Even if he had, Worsley supposed, it surely couldn't have made comic books look any worse. Their terminal decline, by 2015, was becoming glaringly apparent.

One huge problem was that almost everyone in editorial, throughout the business, was a comic fan like Worsley, who sometimes appreciated good ideas but never had them. Thus, when sales had gone into a tailspin, everyone had panicked and had pounced on half-baked notions as potential salvation, without having any way of telling whether the ideas were good ones, bad ones, or even ideas at all. At Massive, for a while, it seemed as if they figured a new colour was as good as a new concept, so there was the Yellow Brute, the frankly hideous Mauve Brute and a full spectrum of Beetle Boys that ranged from Chartreuse to Magnolia. American, meanwhile, had locked itself into a cycle of unending reboots, overhauling their whole continuity every few years, until nobody had a clue which Earth was which, or what the hell was going on. In recent years, the company's most talked about achievement was a 2018 issue of *King Bee* in which the apian avenger's pollinating apparatus was made briefly visible. Worsley glanced at his cabinets where different versions of the character were incarnated, posturing in resin or in plastic, and was quietly relieved to find that the balls-out King Bee was not amongst them, although such a thing most probably existed.

Anyway, so, Trump had happened, Covid happened, the replacement inker on Finefinger's *Union* went to prison for arranging dog fights so Milton had quit the business, and nobody ever got a goodbye phone call from Dan Wheems, which Worsley found a little hurtful. OK, he could see that Wheems had needed to get out of comics, but the two of them had been through so much, just in those few hours they'd spent in Brandon Chuff's apartment, and a postcard would have been nice. Instead, not a word in over five years; silence that outlasted the whole Trump administration. Although, had it, really? Just how serious was this armed Mardi Gras descending on the Senate going to prove? Despite his efforts, Worsley's eyes were drawn, wet compass needles, to the TV's irresistible magnetic north.

Bypassing a stone epidermis and the slippery glass mucous membranes, now inside the body politic itself, clumps separated from the central mass as it metastasised throughout the building. Some cells drifted past historic canvasses and disapproving busts as though on an unguided tour, gait and expression those of mesmerism volunteers. The great transgression, the impossibility, had been enacted. Now the disappointing Real was broken, and inside it was a grand and rapturous dream where there weren't consequences, there weren't laws, and nobody would go to jail. Pink men in grey fatigues heaved giant Confederate banners back and forth, painting the air, eyes full of burning resolution and a paralysed bewilderment. The creature swirled through hallways with crisp echoes and through booming chambers where the national past was sleeping. Jeering polyphonic and unstoppable, it scissored officers between bulletproof doors, or posed for selfies with their less obstructive colleagues. It demanded hangings, and it suffered cardiac emergency. Where it had been, footprints in shit, and blood on the marmoreal bosom of Zachary Taylor. Portraits were exfoliated, statues blinded by corrosive residues. Horned and incredulous, a possibly ironic Medicine Man rolled back the gleaming floor tiles of the world and stepped, wide-eyed, into a paranoiac dreamtime.

Sitting alienated on his sofa, Worsley felt the emptied canyons of New York extending eerily about him. If he looked at what was happening on TV from any sort of editorial perspective, this was well beyond the point where he'd have called the writer in to have a serious discussion: this was irredeemable and utter narrative collapse. This was American reality become a crappy superhero comic book, in the last senseless issue before abrupt cancellation. He supposed he should have seen it coming when Kellyanne Conway dressed as Thundergirl for Trump's victory ball, or when Anthony Scaramucci posed during his ten-day reign in classic Thunderman flight posture, with Thunderman treasuries and posters and *Exciting* #1 facsimiles behind him. What he saw on TV was the slapstick end of a cartoon administration, with a floundering plot much like what he expected from the next Vindictives movie, if they ever brought it out.

In an attempt to rouse his flagging spirits, he allowed himself to daydream over that forthcoming upstairs visit, and his future prospects as, perhaps, the new American vice president. His TV at that moment was reporting calls to lynch the old one, but Worsley remained oblivious to the material world's intrusions. He was somewhere else, imagining how it was going to be when he was, like, practically running the whole company. All those ideas he'd had, over the years, for how he'd do things better if he got the chance – now was his opportunity to put them into practice, if he could remember them. There was his great idea to have the Streak change back to his original costume, and his idea to have King Bee die but then, after a few issues, it turns out to be a hoax. And there'd been others where those came from. What about if all the characters wore hats? Or what if Thunderman did something, and then something happened? Worsley was on fire.

But then, maybe the upstairs world might have its problems, too. He thought about the last time he'd seen David Moskowitz, outside of a Zoom conference. It must have been in late 2019, when he'd called in up at the offices, and had been told that Moskowitz was, for some reason, in the building's basement. Worsley had dutifully gone down in the elevator, and, as he'd been promised, there he'd found the publisher. Since, with Dan Wheems, the two of them had burned down Chuff's apartment, they had rather tended to avoid each other out of mutual embarrassment. Having thus not set eyes on Moskowitz for some considerable time, Worsley was startled to discover that the publisher now looked to be a fraction under five feet tall, and more astonished still to learn that Moskowitz had found a broom from somewhere and was sweeping up the basement area obsessively. He'd answered Worsley's work-related queries but had made no reference to his janitorial activities, save to remark that he liked making sure 'that everything was shipshape down here'. He seemed unaware of any psychiatric symbolism in his actions, which made Worsley think that nobody at Brandon's place that night had managed to get out wholly unscathed. Dan Wheems was ghosting everybody, Moskowitz was lost in Jungian spring-cleaning, and Worsley was sitting in his King Bee boxers, watching the world fall apart without a fundamental understanding of, well, anything.

Still, even if the higher echelons of comics management were fraught with difficulty, should the point of next month's visit be to offer Worsley a promotion, then he'd take it. The alternative was to remain at the same career level, decade after decade, until you went mad and ended up like Jerry Binkle. Worsley had been in the audience at the cinema with Binkle and his wife Elaine to see *United Supermen*, and the appalling film had been the least of his ordeal. The movie's languid gesture at a plot, presumably to placate older comics fans, centred on the iconic villain from the superhero combo's first appearance back in *Comic Clarion Presents*, an interplanetary comb jelly known as Coelentero the Controller. At the movie's climax, when United Supermen inductee Mr Ocean employs his control of marine organisms and makes Coelentero hang itself with its own tendrils, it had been too much for Jerry. While the other audience members were convulsing in hysterics at what would come to be called 'Monkey Christ Thunderman', Binkle had stood up in his seat and started yelling at the screen: 'He'd never do that! Mr Ocean wouldn't do that! Don't you morons understand? His best friend was a jellyfish! Fufu meant everything to Mr Ocean! Everything!' It had been mortifying. Everyone was telling Binkle to sit down, and in the end his wife Elaine had Tasered him.

Thinking of Binkle's seemingly lifelong fixation on the watery wonder prodded Worsley's free-floating awareness in the general direction of Finefinger's article. He wasn't sure he got its drift, but if he did, it was a drift he didn't care for. Still, he ought to finish it, so the next time Finefinger said that Worsley couldn't read things without pictures, he could cite 'A Spandex Wrapper for the Naked Lunch' in his admittedly threadbare defence. Grunting dismissively before he'd even started reading, Worsley picked up *Kulchur* gingerly, like he suspected it however it was spelled.

'Nevertheless, how can I justify comparing costumed characters with an addictive substance like cocaine or heroin? I think the answer lies in the word "costumed".

'I was reading recently of the important role that colour serves in those time-wasting games, like Krystal Krunch, that you find yourself playing on your phone, obsessively, until the small hours of the morning. It appears that certain hues and certain colour combinations are addictive, triggering our reward chemicals. If you should doubt this, simply alter your device to greyscale and see how long Krystal Krunch retains your interest.

'From an unrelated feature in a science magazine, on recent findings from the field of neurological research, I learned the startling fact that a child's mind can be rewired by exposure to a logo or an emblem, much as hatchlings will emotionally imprint on the first object that they notice. On reflection, neither of these notions should have been a big surprise. I can remember playing with those big, old-fashioned marbles as a little kid, and how I'd make up names and even personalities for special favourites, based on nothing more than the mystique that different colours held for me at that age.

'Also, I recall the reassuring, almost sacred aura that surrounded product names in their distinctive, emblematic fonts. The Coca-Cola logo, for example, with its curls and swoops, spoke to both classicism and refinement, and would not have looked incongruous above the radiator grill of a prestigious European car. Combine that with a bottle shape almost identical to stone-age sexual fetish figures that I've seen, and what you have is an assault upon the individual by semiotic means and with commercial purpose; an intrusion with immense subliminal persuasive power, on many unsuspected levels. When we speak of brand names, we should ask ourselves just what the substance is that's being branded, that's to have the sizzling, red-hot logo stamped upon it, if not our own forebrains.

'Finally, it came to me that the heroic costumed characters that had so captivated me when I was small could be effectively reduced, within my infant consciousness, to a chest emblem and a colour combination. Long before I knew Thunderman's name, I knew the T-shaped cloud and thunderbolt, and would speak of him as "the gold and purple one". Now, if commercial packaging is styled intentionally to attract and to habituate an adult audience, how much more potent might it be with products that, for forty or so years, were aimed exclusively at young, impressionable children? Might that not be enough to shape and to enslave a generation, keeping them, like junkies, in a needy and infantilised condition where they cannot individuate successfully, or become genuine adults?

'And could that not explain the dwindling colony of people who've been harmed by this innocuous comic book conditioning? To judge from the depressive tone apparent in most mainstream comics threads, the audience is no longer enjoying the material that it is nonetheless addicted to. The hardcore comic book habitué appears to have been placed in the predicament reported frequently amongst long-time users of crack cocaine: the strong sense of diminishing returns, with every pipe attempting to get back to the angelic purity of that first hit, with each attempt more disappointing than the last – but simply stopping is, of course, out of the question. What makes the comics fan's dilemma worse, if anything, is that the "first hit" that they hope to recreate with each month's issue is the irretrievable, lost rush of their own childhoods.'

There was more, a page or two, but Worsley figured that he'd read enough. He looked up at the silent phalanx of United Supermen, Vindictives, Freak Forcers, Omnipotent Pre-Teen Militiamen and Unrealistic Fivers crowding on his windowsills or bookshelves, but not one of them saw fit to dignify Finefinger's diatribe with comment. He knew how they felt. If Finefinger's hare-brained hypothesis was right, then every fan's collection – which included Worsley's own – would be like hoarding hypodermics, blackened spoons and bootlaces; or like those cardboard boxes in that room in Brandon Chuff's long-gone apartment. Worse, if what Finefinger said was true, it might prove actionable. Irritably, he mulled all this over as he let his barely focussed gaze slide back towards the muted flat-screen television on the room's far side.

Antibodies, armoured T-cells, were by now deployed and had reclaimed the glorious debris, with the viral invader forced out into January's early dusk, and skirmishes all through the violet hour into the black ones after. Scores arrested, scores more injured and five dead, not counting the attending officers who'd take their own lives in despair over the next few days. Fragments of the conglomerated thing were left behind, having in death reclaimed their names and individuality, along with shouting placards and adhesive loud assertions, hallways ankle-deep in slogan and the tatter-litter of flags from both sides in various nineteeth- and twentieth-century conflicts seemingly still unresolved, all of it destined for future musea of American convulsion. The great effort to expose troublesome fact as fiction, while establishing pulp picture-story narrative as universal fact, slowly evaporated over Washington. Into the chill pandemic night, electoral processes resumed their clockwork action, and fatal upheaval gradually subsided to become a hoax, a dream, or an Unlikely Story. Everything would be rewritten, reimagined, retrofitted. There would be no damage to the continuity.

Examining the cerise tyre tread left across a white paunch by the waistband of his boxers, Worsley Porlock took in none of this. He was still thinking about Milton Finefinger's contention that fun-loving hobbyists at a convention, of whatever age, could be equivalent to toothless maniacs talking nonsense in a crack den. Worsley threw down the unfinished magazine on to his coffee table, where its impact sent a seismic ripple through the less stable collectibles that were assembled there.

Finefinger, he told himself, was just another bitter and resentful guy, exactly like Dan Wheems, who couldn't take the pace of today's comics industry, and who now seemed intent on spoiling it for everybody else. Well, Worsley didn't – couldn't – buy it. The idea that superheroes were like some insidious substance that would stunt their followers' emotional development was so much horseshit.

On the table, Worsley's bobble-headed Rottweiler nodded in uncontrollable agreement.

17. (December, 2012)

Some Last Thoughts: The Denny Wellworth Interview

WHEEMS: Denny. How's it going, man?

WELLWORTH: Ah, you know. I have bad days, I have worse days. Good to see you, Dan. Thanks for coming in. Is this that interview thing that we talked about?

WHEEMS: Yeah, if that's still OK. You've got to let me know, though, if you're getting tired. Don't want to wear you out.

WELLWORTH: Don't worry, Dan. It's not the interview that's going to kill me. What was your first question?

WHEEMS: Yeah, right, sorry. I suppose I'd like to get some background. What was the scene like, when you were first in comics?

WELLWORTH: The comics scene? There wasn't one. Oh, there were comics, just like there was bubblegum, but, then, we didn't have a bubblegum scene either. How things were back then, it's probably hard to imagine from today's perspective. I was born in 1940, so I was a teenager in the late fifties when I started trying to find work as a writer. And it was a very working-class environment at that time – not just comic books, but paperbacks and magazines. They had an audience of mostly working people, and it was a field where a wise-ass kid from a working family could maybe find some paying work. I'd hang out in the diners where I knew that writers went to get their lunch, so I met Sherman Glad, Heinz Messner, Artie Leibowitz, all those guys. They did comics, sure, but what I'm trying to get at is, back then, to make a living, we'd do anything that looked borderline legal. Other than inventing all those costumed heroes for American, Sherman turned out pulp paperbacks under around a dozen pen names. He did science fiction, westerns, fantasy, historical adventure, hard-boiled crime, pornography ...

WHEEMS: What, Sherman Glad? You're serious?

WELLWORTH: (LAUGHS) Dan, you're a youngster, so I don't expect you to appreciate the vast importance of pornography to young, aspiring writers in the 1950s. There must have been two, three dozen publishers who specialised in literary stroke-material back then, before home video or the internet. And then there was Olympia Press, Maurice Girodias! What bliss it was to be young in those golden days! (LAUGHS) No, seriously, you were a struggling writer and you couldn't sell the Kerouac-copy masterpiece that you were working on, then you could always turn out *Teenage Nympho Nurses* in a weekend and make maybe fifty bucks. In fact, I'd wager *Teenage Nympho Nurses* and the like have saved more cherished literary careers than anyone could comfortably admit to. (LAUGHS) So, how it was in those days, you'd take work where you could find it. I'd done comics scripting work for the newspaper strips, and figured I could scale the process up to handle six- or eight-page stories in a comic book.

WHEEMS: I didn't know you'd done newspaper strips back then. Which ones?

WELLWORTH: Oh, well, you know, I wrote eighteen months of Operative Z.

WHEEMS: I thought that that was what's his name, who did Zoom Wilson? Andrew Donald?

WELLWORTH: Yeah. I'd thought the same myself. So had Bill Terensen, the penciller, and Harvey Norse, who inked the thing. We all thought we were Donald's only help on Operative Z, and it turns out the bastard wasn't doing any of it! In my life, I never met a sneakier son of a bitch. Even his fatal auto accident, it was a suicide attempt. His second, as it turns out, and both times he'd tried to take somebody with him. No, don't get me started on the guy. I only mention him to illustrate that back then you could find yourself doing all kinds of work. The time I most enjoyed, working in comics, that was working for Roy Shaw on *Inappropriate* and *Disturbing*. I'm not saying Shaw was any better than the others – like, the pay was nothing special – but he always treated me OK. He trusted you enough to let you follow up on your ideas, you know? It was a lot of fun, working with people like Slim Whittaker and Robert Novak and the rest, trying out new things and improving myself as a writer. Sure, I made a lot more money later on, but later on was when the comics industry had turned to something different, and the work got less and less enjoyable, until we reach the present situation where the superhero movies rake in more and more, while all the superhero comic books are haemorrhaging readers by the month. No one knows what to do. Nobody ever thinks, 'Hey, maybe if we did, like, better comic books, then things don't have to end in smoking ruin!'

WHEEMS: I know what you mean. Where did the comics business go wrong, do you think?

WELLWORTH: I think it's more it never went right in the first place. I mean, when comics started, they were seen as throwaway junk meant to keep the lower classes happy. I guess the idea was that poor people are stupid, childish and won't understand a narrative unless there's pictures with it. And I'm talking here about newspaper strips, before the comic book was a larcenous gleam in Albert Kaufman's eye. So when the comic book appears, it's aimed at the same class, and most of its top talent comes from that class, too. With Kaufman, when him and Sid Rosenfeld stole Thunderman from Kessler and Schuman, what they did was found the comics industry using bootlegging as a business model, one that's largely unchanged to the present day: find someone talented – Kessler and Schuman, Robert Novak, Sherman Glad, Joe Gold, Slim Whittaker, and on and on – then cheat them out of their creations and discard them. If they're working-class creators like, well, all the guys I just mentioned, then it's easier to swindle them because they weren't brought up by families that spent a lot of time discussing lawyers, contracts or percentages. You cheat them, you discard them, you get other guys to write and draw their characters, then you strip-mine the property for all it's worth until the end of time. That's how it works, right?

WHEEMS: If 'works' is the word. It's not working so good at present, from the look of things.

WELLWORTH: Yeah, well, that's because the comics business made the same dumbass mistake that all industry made, which was assuming the resource they were exploiting to be infinite and inexhaustible. They figured that they could beat up and rob a Joe Gold with impunity, because there'd be another talent just as good and just as robbable along within a year or two. Now, you and I both know the sun will have grown old and dim and there still won't have been another Gold, but management are not creative individuals and they have never understood the first thing about how creators work. So, when a new Joe Gold fails to show up, you give his books to artists who can do lame versions of Gold's style, but can't invent a single thing that's new. And when there's no replacement Sherman Glad, because he tried to form a union so they fired him, then they're just left with the eager-beaver fans they hired to take the place of Sherman and Heinz Messner and the rest, people like Brandon Chuff. These people, they're not artists, they're not writers, they're just fans of artists and of writers, and the generation that comes after them will be the fans of fans, and so on, to the directionless mess we're in at present.

WHEEMS: What you were saying about Sherman Glad trying to start a union, it's funny – my friend Milton Finefinger has this proposal in up at American, it's for a series about the old 1940s super-team, the Union of Super Americans, a lot of whom were Sherman Glad's creations. Milton's idea was to depict the team like it was really an attempt to unionise the superheroes, with characters from working backgrounds such as Thunderman on one side, and aristocrats and millionaires like Moon Queen and King Bee making the argument against. Milton's calling it *Union*.

WELLWORTH: Yeah, I know Finefinger. That laugh he has, it makes me want to kill him, but he's a nice guy, and of the current crop, he's a good writer. And this *Union* thing sounds like a good idea, almost like it's referring to the thing with Glad and Messner and the other guys, by making it about their characters. That's clever, but I'll tell you what, it's never going to come out, not in a million years. There'll be some perfectly good reason why it can't be published, that's entirely unconnected with the fact that it's about forming a union, but you're never going to see that book. Not from American. If

Dave Kessler and Si Schuman had had access to a union, then the entire comics business as we know it never would have happened.

WHEEMS: Well, I guess we'll see. You don't see the industry changing any time soon, then?

WELLWORTH: No, I don't. I don't see where the impetus or energy would come from to do that. It's like I said, that comics was a medium created for – and largely by – the lower class, but those creators are all dead or have retired, embittered, from the field. So, what you've got is comics that are by, for, and about the middle class, exclusively. And as for how well they compare with comics as they used to be, I think that if you look at all the superhero movies that do well, you're going to find they're adaptations of things that Joe Gold or Sherman Glad created fifty, sixty years ago. When they run out of old material, what are they going to do? Start making movies out of seventies and eighties junk like *Best Guy*? (LAUGHS)

WHEEMS: So you're not a big Gene Pullman fan, I take it? (LAUGHS)

WELLWORTH: Gee, Dan, that's remarkably perceptive. What gave me away? Was it how I left Massive for American when I got ill, because at Massive under Pullman they refused to let me have medical cover? Or I have I got some other subtle little 'tell' that I'm not consciously aware of, like the way I automatically mime strangling or stabbing someone if his name is mentioned? (LAUGHS) Did I ever tell you my Gene Pullman story, of why I should probably be the most hated man in comics? No? This was the seventies, when I was editor-in-chief at Massive, right before I got promoted sideways to direct their more creator-friendly Legend line. So anyway, I was there in my office up on Lexington, having a script conference with Mark Shane, and we're going over stuff, and suddenly Gene Pullman marches in, flings the door open, real dramatic, and tells me he's angry, like I couldn't have deduced that by myself. Now, bear in mind that Pullman's just a junior writer at this point, OK? So, he starts yelling how one of the characters in some book, maybe it was *Freak Force*, has done something that Pullman thinks is immoral, something he would never do. I think they'd, like, annihilated an entire parallel universe or something, which, to be totally fair, is something I would never do myself. But that's beside the point. Pullman demands that I pull publication on the book, or else he's going to quit there and then. I tell him I'm not going to do that, but that I accept his resignation. Pullman looks stunned, as if he'd not imagined in a million years that his dramatic gesture could work out like that. He turns, completely speechless, and he staggers from my office like he's going to the gallows. Me and Mark get back to what we were discussing, and then, like five minutes later, Pullman literally crawls back in to beg me for his job back. When I say he crawls, it isn't even on his hands and knees. He's prostrate, flat down on the floor, and the guy's weeping. What was worst, you know how Pullman's sort of … wide? Like from the front he's in CinemaScope, but side-on he looks kind of flat? Well, you've got no idea just how disturbing Pullman looks until you've had him crawling at you, sobbing and face down. Honestly, Dan, it was like an unusually wide and lumpy rug was halfway through developing a nervous system. Frankly, it was hard to look at. In the end, I told Pullman to get back to whatever he was working on and we'd forget the incident had ever happened. Naturally, years later, I'm at a convention with Mark Shane and he says, 'Denny, you do realise that if you'd not cancelled Pullman's resignation all those years ago, you'd have spared everyone at Massive from the hell they're going through? You're like one of those bastards who passed up the chance to stab Hitler to death when he was eight years old.' (LAUGHS) What could I say? The truth was, I felt sorry for the guy. Also, I couldn't bear to see him undulating on my floor a second longer. He looked like a mollusc that worked out.

WHEEMS: You know, when I first started reading comics, when I was, like, twelve or something, I liked Massive, sure, but what I liked best were the ones my parents wouldn't let me read, like *Inappropriate* or *Disturbing*.

WELLWORTH: Dan, I'm blushing. I feel like we ought to get a room or something.

WHEEMS: No, I mean it. Back then, if you mentioned comics to someone, they wouldn't automatically assume that you were talking about just one genre, about superheroes. There were horror stories, war stories, science fiction and a dozen other kinds of story. How come it was superheroes came to dominate the industry?

WELLWORTH: Beats me. I've always done my best to dodge the fucking things. What is it about superheroes? Let me see. Well, they're a home-grown American phenomenon that never really seemed to take ahold anywhere else. It's like they're something that emerges naturally out of our culture. Partly I think that they're from our constitutionally guaranteed entitlement to American sneakiness. Like, if you're going to do a thing that might conceivably land you in trouble, then it's best to do it with a mask on, or dressed up like something else, or both. If it's the Boston Tea Party, we dress up as cartoon Red Indians. If it's a torchlight rally with the Klan, then we dress up as ghosts. So if we're self-appointed vigilantes with a taste for beating up the underclass, it's only natural that we should dress as foxes, beetles, bees, attack dogs, or, I don't know, platypuses or whatever. Also, there's our attitude to violence. It's a country where, since the frontier days, nobody trusts anybody else, and so we sleep with guns under our pillows, and our ideal way of settling a situation is to shoot someone from ambush. We're not fond of conflicts where we haven't got some kind of tactical advantage, so the superhero fantasy of being indestructible or having huge, retractable steel teeth is kind of reassuring. They're our dream life. They have morals, they help the oppressed, and, with their special powers, are outstandingly good at something – all the things we haven't, don't, or aren't. They are our negative space, ethically, and simultaneously they are the American Dream's most apparent white supremacist embodiment. No, no, please don't protest. I'm on a roll. As for what the superhero means to its contemporary audience of largely adult hobbyists, I'm not so sure. I think for some of them, they took it up around thirteen as an alternative to normal puberty, a way they could duck out on all the trials – and also on the personal development – by relocating to United Supermen headquarters for the next ten, thirty, fifty years, until all of the social responsibility was over. They're a way to maintain emotional stasis, and to stay connected to a relatively carefree childhood in the face of a progressively more complex and more alienating world. I think that's why they're so important to the readers, but I think there's something else as well. I think that characters like Thunderman are actually important to the fabric of America.

WHEEMS: How do you mean?

WELLWORTH: Well, you look back at what America was like for the first ten or twenty years of the twentieth century, you're looking at a country that could barely hold itself together. National identity had nothing that it could cohere around. Americans all came from different countries, they spoke different languages, had different politics, different religions, and they came from different races, different classes. It turned out that the one thing, the only thing, that they could all agree on was, they all liked the same vaudeville songs on the radio; they all liked reading *Flatfoot Floyd* and drinking Coca-Cola. They liked Dickey Dog cartoons, and they liked Thunderman. Popular culture is the only glue that holds America together, and I guess that's why it all needs stealing from the people who created it, and gifting to some big, trustworthy corporation with capitalism's best interests at heart, and who'll guard these valuable properties more closely than some writer or some artist with their crazy ideas and their crazy politics. You wouldn't want these national assets to be in the hands of radicals, or black people, or women – not unless they were already corporate mutants such as Mimi Drucker or whatever it is that Gene Pullman's meant to be, where the class and race and gender stuff is no big deal next to the tentacles and Cyclops eye. Or that's my theory, anyway.

WHEEMS: Denny, this stuff is great, better than anything I could have hoped for, but I'm getting conscious of how long I've kept you talking, and I'm thinking I should wrap this up. Is one more question OK?

WELLWORTH: Sure. And don't be so apologetic. I know I look dreadful so you can't tell, but I'm having fun with all these questions. Ask away.

WHEEMS: Well, as you were saying earlier, you've worked at both of the big companies. How do they compare with each other? Do you have any preferences?

WELLWORTH: No, no, I don't think so. I don't think I have a preference. I think they're both equally diabolical, but diabolical in different ways. With Massive, it's just no-nonsense industrial brutality, police-state atmospherics and the rule of fear – your basic 'Human Tank's boot stamping on a human face forever' deal. (LAUGHS) But at American, for my money, it's not so thuggish and authoritarian, but it's much creepier. If Massive is like a Victorian workhouse, then American is more like a late Roman mystery cult. You've seen the Ambrose Bell they've got in the reception there? It's like, in some Neoplatonic way, they honestly believe these characters are real, that they're alive on Sherman Glad's World Aleph or someplace like that. They know they can't come out and say that without sounding crazy, but deep in their hearts, I think they need to feel that it's all somehow true. I think that in a world where our traditional ideas of God have pretty much disintegrated, but where there's that fundamental human want for something sacred, maybe some kitsch monster such as Thunderman is all that we've got left that feels like a religion. There. So, have I satisfied your morbid curiosity?

WHEEMS: You've always done more than that. Denny Wellworth, thank you for your time.

WELLWORTH: Dan, I can't jerk off no more, so, seriously, it's my pleasure. (LAUGHS)

18. (September, 2015)

Though there will fortunately never be pornography that's comprehensible to three-year-olds, Satyricon went to considerable effort in imagining what such a thing might look like. **WELCOME TO SATYRICON!** Throughout the history of orgies, never had there previously existed opportunity for thousands of participants to publicly convene, provocatively costumed as high-booted power people or as cartoon animals in fishnets, have their gasping permutations advertised from coast to coast, and get a goody-bag to take home with them. **WELCOME TO SATYRICON!** Approximately thirty floors of inappropriate obsession, hotel corridors with Escher tessellations of ingeniously interlocking furries, and in one secluded nook, Ormazda's sunburst helmet with a pre-loved condom in it. **WELCOME TO SATYRICON!** It was a long, long way from Jesus and Connecticut.

Dick Duckley's tummy harboured a few caterpillars, not yet hatched to butterflies, when he arrived in the capacious lobby, making a far less arresting entrance than he would accomplish later. Some convention staff were hard at work assembling the Brandon Chuff memorial exhibit in the foyer, where serene glass elevators lifted silently into the atrium's cathedral heights, and the low murmur of incoming guests was like a wake or lullaby. He registered, then stood in the reception area with his head tipped back, drawing deep breaths to calm the caterpillars, trying to take everything in. This world was just so big, and for some time now, he'd suspected that it wasn't even the right world, as if he were the wrong alternate version of himself, stuck on the wrong alternate Earth.

He found the main hall, hardly the asylum circus that it would be later, but still jiggling with activity, still noisy, and looked in on the Bordello Comics stand. Tony and Steve were there, manning the booth and stacking up trade paperbacks for the *Orgasmics* signing in the afternoon. There was a washed-out-looking blonde girl in a long coat that he thought might be the model that they'd hired to dress as Oral Lass, but, obviously, there wasn't any easy way to ask her that. Then Steve said that Amanda in accounts had called him, saying she'd been trying to get ahold of Duckley, and did Duckley have his phone switched off? Dick Duckley giggled, said he'd see to it, and in his bowel, unfurling monarchs tested sticky wings.

Making excuses in a series of unfinished sentences, he told them that he needed to check out his room and drop his bags off, but that he'd call by to hang out later. Turning before they could see his churning face, he pushed his way back through the gathering crowd, towards the lobby and its crystal elevators. Out of all the people that he squeezed past, Duckley was the only one in disguise as a normal person. While he waited for his ride up to the twenty-seventh floor, a pair of demons sauntered past him, one male and one female, fire-engine red with horns and tails. Both looked at him with knowing little smiles, and Duckley was immediately certain that they weren't a couple playing dress-up; that they were aware of all the business with Amanda in accounts; and, worst of all, they weren't in any hurry. They could take their time. He wasn't going anywhere. When his glass box arrived, he flung himself inside and pressed the buttons for his floor, heart hammering. The door slid shut. Shaking their spiky heads and chuckling, the tag team devils walked by without looking at him, flicking barbed and crimson tails behind them.

The transparent car ascended, and his view of the transfigured lobby swelled beneath as in a bulbous lens. A hundred costumes swirled, become a marbling of delirious colour wherein pagan gods and storm troopers vaped genially, and different species traded contact details. Bilious hallucination, eddying about a central altarpiece commemorating the deceased *United Supermen* scribe and late editor-in-chief, its huge framed photograph of Brandon Chuff in flattering black and white receding underneath the elevator's see-through floor. Duckley exhaled.

Internally the Lepidoptera were thriving, rousing in a gorgeous murmuration, painted sails batting his lungs and fluttering in his throat. For all he knew of science, it might only be their flapping excitation that allowed the glazed cube to rise up, into the gaping atrium that rang with whispered sibilants. The herd phantasmagoria of the lobby was a drift of pointillism now. This whole crazed celebration, Duckley felt, it was like everybody knew that this was the apocalypse, and not just him. This was the time of Revelation, at least for Amanda in accounts. Everything hidden would be made clear as an elevator. Everyone would know what he had done, and not just Momma, Poppa and the other angels, who all knew already. Momma would be crying, and his father would be so, so mad that Duckley was almost relieved to know he wouldn't have to meet with them in heaven, not if the vermillion duo downstairs meant what he assumed they did.

For late September, Dallas seemed uncomfortably hot, an appetiser for inferno. Surmounting his background radiation of anxiety and fear were spikes of furious resentment at the person who'd initiated his hell-bound trajectory. He'd heard unsympathetic people say that this was Worsley Porlock, but that wasn't so. Porlock was Duckley's friend, almost an older brother, while the author of Dick Duckley's fall from grace – the succubus who'd dragged him by his penis from salvation – that was Peggy Parks. That was the flame-haired, winking Jezebel who his own poppa had delivered him into the lewd and practised hands of, when he'd been no more than a defenceless boy.

The outhouse made of windows chimed discreetly to announce that it had reached his floor, and he stepped out to fitted-carpet altitudes. Almost as soon as he'd emerged from its fishbowl interior, the elevator's door resealed itself with a pneumatic sigh and it commenced its downward journey back towards the lobby and its soup of cruising harlequins. Laying the damp palm of his bag-free hand against the smooth wood of the balustrade, he leaned his upper body over and peered down to watch the square-cut, hollow gem in its descent. Three or four hundred feet below, the lobby was no more, now, than a vividly infested Petri dish. Experiencing moral vertigo, he turned away from the colossal dried-up wishing well and set off through an arrowed labyrinth, seeking sanctuary without personality, but with a spyholed door that he could double-lock.

Once in his room, he sat there on the bed, heavy as Rodin marble, and fished out his mobile. Six missed calls, all from Amanda in accounts. He thought if he just listened to the first one, then perhaps it wouldn't be as bad as he'd imagined.

'Dick? This is Amanda in accounts. I need those cash receipts you promised me, like, straight away? I know you're off at the convention, but you need to sort this out right now. The people at head office are concerned, Dick, and this isn't going to wait till Monday. Call me when you get this.'

Oh, God. Oh, God, this was terrible. She sounded so steamed up, and that was just the first of her unanswered voicemails. He decided not to listen to the rest. He stood up. He sat down again. He stood up and paced like a stuck automaton along the strip of space between the bed and bathroom, making the high-pitched and frightened 'nnnnnnnnnn' sounds that he'd made since childhood when he didn't want his circumstances to be happening.

His life enclosed him like a band of hornets, vying for attention with the swarming butterflies inside. Raised in Connecticut, raised in seclusion, just his momma and his poppa and his tutors, and so Peggy Parks had been the first girl outside Momma that he'd ever seen, and how could they not know what that would do to him? And when they died, nnnnnnnnnn, he'd been all alone except the help and Thunderman, but his friend Worsley rescued him, and got him his dream job in comics, and explained about the powder that gives people confidence, and sold him a great page of art with Peggy naked so you could see everything. And it was all terrific, but he hadn't known that he'd need so much confidence, or that it cost so much, or that he'd get through it so quickly. Nnnnnnnnnn. Back at the start, when things were great, he thought he'd got it figured out: the world ordered by God that his momma and poppa had believed in wasn't this world. From his observations, Duckley had concluded that the world that he was in, with virtue ridiculed and with vice everywhere unpunished, was most probably the morally reversed World Daleth, where the Droll and Felix Firestone were the heroes who protected everyone from Killer Bee and Plunderman. So good was bad, and bad was good, and he'd had sex with women and got drunk, and all his friends thought that was funny, so he'd started stealing money from Bordello Comics, where he worked, to pay for all the powdered confidence, and now, nnnnnnnnnn, now Amanda in accounts was asking for receipts and, nnnnnnnnnn, and butterflies were coming down his nose, and, nnnnnnnnnn, what was he going to do?

Then all at once, amidst his pacing turmoil, Duckley knew. His problem was itself the answer to his problem. He retrieved the jar with his supplies in from his shoulder bag and took it through into the bathroom's bright electric hum, where he did three fat lines, which killed the butterflies like DDT, and straight away, this surely temporary snag looked nowhere near as bad. Promising, even.

He'd always been pretty certain that Amanda in accounts had got a thing for him. When Duckley made a dirty comment, she'd make this tight little smile to let him know she liked it when he talked like that. So if he told her that he'd put those receipts in the mail to her, like, weeks ago but, like a jerk, he didn't send them registered, then she'd most likely shake her head and smile indulgently and say she'd smooth the whole thing over with head office, and maybe they'd date.

It really did feel so much better now he had a plan. He exited the bathroom a new man and went to stand before the window, where he gazed out over Dallas with a roguish smile – a super-villain overseeing his domain. Only he didn't know what he was looking at, nor yet in which direction, so he fixed himself a Scotch out of the minibar to take the edge off, and went back to sitting on the bed. He guessed that he'd been getting pretty crazy there, before his confidence had been restored. He felt sort of ashamed now, and especially about his unfair thoughts concerning Peggy Parks. None of his problems – which were solved now – had been Peggy's fault, and even with her red hair, she was not the scarlet woman of apocalypse that he had thought her in his panic. Peggy was his muse, his girlfriend that he shared with Thunderman, and he was lucky that he had her in his life, because without her, her and Worsley, now his parents were no more, well, there'd be nobody.

He swirled the liquor in his glass and took a muddy aesthetic pleasure in the tilting of the surface's ellipse, half silvered, with Dick Duckley looking back at him. He thought of Poppa, all those years back, and what he now realised was his father's own unique theology, where any entertainment was a snare of Satan, except Thunderman. He remembered Poppa's voice when the old man explained it to him. 'God the Father has been worshipped under many names since history began, as Yahweh, Zeus or Jupiter, and all these names mean Thunderman.' Poppa's interpretation had gone kind of haywire after that, chiefly because he had mistakenly thought Thunderboy to be the son of Thunderman, rather than Thunderman himself when he was younger. In his father's even-newer testament, the teenage Thunderboy was Jesus, sent to our world by his father, Thunderman, from heaven, which was Thunderland, except that Poppa had got that mixed up with Thunder Mountain, and had probably conflated Thunder Mountain with Olympus. He could understand how Poppa got confused, when the one thing more complicated than the continuity in comics was the continuity that's in the Bible, and combining them, to say the least, was an ambitious crossover. His father hadn't done a bad job, all in all, on his Thunderman heresy. Abner and Eliza Bell became Joseph and Mary, Felix Firestone's name alone made him an obvious Satan, the Tomorrow Friends were the disciples, Peggy Parks was Mary Magdalene, and possibly Zando the Thunderdog was the dog in the manger, although Duckley felt that Poppa had been reaching with that last one.

Shafts of gold light fell into his room and striped the crisp white pillows. Everything was good again now. His convention head was on, and he was at a gathering famed for its fornicating franchises. What was he doing up here on his own? He put on a clean T-shirt from his bag, one with a winking Oral Lass that bore the legend 'Going Down', and just in time remembered his convention ID lanyard, worn albatross-style about his neck. One more line as a top-up and then, with his key card safe in a back pocket, he stepped out into the hyperreal fugue of Satyricon.

The dream-plague of the lobby had by now transmitted lurid masquerade infections to these upper reaches, so that corridors and landings thronged with creatures leaked from haunted television features a half-century old, from movies with special effects as leading men, comics creations from six months ago who had already been rebooted out of continuity. He saw a waist-high pack of Matrakoy Dust-Dwellers, robed and hooded, who were perhaps flirting enigmatically with a cohort of halfling warriors from Mittelgard, but it was hard to tell. Beneath grey cowls or dog-faced helmets, they were either persons of restricted growth or grade-school kids, and neither was a wholly nerving prospect. As he waited for the lucid elevator, he watched a prismatic paint-chip spread of Beetle Boys, some five or six of them, group-hugging into a configuration like an antique TV colour-test card. It looked like a single multiphasic personality attempting, strenuously, to reintegrate.

His first descent into the stylish abyss of the atrium was measured, then, and stately. Unlike his ascending journey, anxious and preoccupied, he had the time to notice things he hadn't seen on his way up. For instance, he had overlooked the numerous banners hanging from the landings of – it looked like – every third floor, that proclaimed their message in a bold, black font a yard high: **WELCOME TO SATYRICON!**, like in the entrance hall when he'd come in. Eight repetitions of this bellowing calligraphy scrolled up past Duckley's entranced gaze before he reached ground level, and emerged into the sexy nightmare of the lobby, feeling full of beans and over-welcomed.

Everything seemed more relaxed, seemed livelier, more jubilantly populous, though maybe some of that was just his improved mood. The Brandon Chuff memorial exhibit looked completed, with the central portrait flanked now by white roses in an ostentatious sprawl and, rising from this, enlarged reproductions of Chuff's best-remembered covers, on what looked like music stands. He was surprised and childishly delighted to see a small gathering of attendees dressed up as the United Supermen, all ten of them, presumably part of the tribute that was scheduled later. Moon Queen and Red Fox appeared to be a couple, which in terms of continuity was somewhat jarring, but apart from that, the detail work on all the costumes was superb. The way Duckley was feeling, it was all superb.

And then, to make it all superber, he saw Worsley Porlock supervising the memorial display and hitting on the woman dressed as Eagle Girl. When Porlock noticed Duckley, he excused himself expertly from the avian adventuress and walked across to greet his socially inept friend, who was also his continuing experiment in ethics. Porlock slapped him on his already damp back, called him the Dickster, and insisted that the two of them retire immediately to the convention bar so that they could catch up. This sounded like a good plan to the Dickster.

In the bar, as crowded as a Bosch or Breughel landscape, the two editors secured a relatively quiet corner, there amidst speed-dating aliens and endless carrier bags of merchandise. There were a lot of skin-tight women drifting back and forth, and Worsley Porlock's eyes went with them as, distractedly, he listed his concerns about the Chuff memorial presentation later.

'Man, I really hope that this goes well. The company could use a boost, you know, just for morale. Since Brandon died, I'll tell you, it's been one catastrophe after another. First, he drops dead in that half-baked diner incident, with Dan Wheems bleeding everywhere and Jerry Binkle fainting. Then, at Brandon's funeral, it happens all over again. Still, fingers crossed, nobody's heard from Wheems since then, and looks like he's a no-show here at the convention, so maybe we'll at least get through this memorial thing without a lot of screaming and blood everywhere. I wish I was in your shoes, over at Bordello, where you can fit all the editing around the jerking off, right?'

Duckley laughed and nodded, although until then he hadn't truly understood that editing and jerking off were separate things. He liked talking to Worsley, and he liked the bar with all its slutty monsters. The light fittings, bar top, bottles, cyborgs, broadswords, spectacles, battle bikinis – everything was twinkling and he was floating in a galaxy of constellated highlight. With a Diet Coke or two inside him, Porlock gradually became more upbeat, and enthused to Duckley about the new inker that they'd found to replace Arvo Cake on Milton Finefinger's book, *Union*. 'He's a great inker, and his style works really well with Byron James. And best of all, he's this real gentle guy who isn't going to massacre his girlfriend. I saw on his CV how in his spare time he's, like, a vet – or anyway, he's somebody who works with animals. I've got high hopes, the same as with this Chuff memorial. I really think it's going to end this run of bad luck that the company's been having.'

Later, in what little time he had to think about such things, Duckley decided that he maybe needn't have spent so long talking in the bar with Worsley Porlock, when he should have been at the Bordello stand for the *Orgasmics* signing, but, hey-ho, that was conventions. At last Worsley pointed out that it was nearly time for Brandon's tribute, and that he'd said he'd catch up with Eagle Girl to offer her support, possibly moral, in her role. They shared a culturally appropriative fist bump and said that they'd see each other later, probably at some post-human afterparty. Porlock hurried off, going where eagles dare, leaving Dick Duckley to find his way back to the Bordello table, through what had been formerly a fine mist of imaginary people, but was now a quivering solid of mismanaged colour and unorthodox protrusions. It took nearly half an hour for him to navigate the horns, fins, Vorg Assassin body armour, and somebody as a steampunk Flavor Flav who had watch parts all over, before Duckley hove in view of the Bordello booth.

The signing looked like it was over, and from the diminished stack of trades that he could see behind the stall, it had gone relatively smoothly. The book's artist, Chris Pulaski, was just finishing a sketch of Anal Robot for a couple of *Orgasmics* fans, while writer Terry North and the blonde woman who was maybe Oral Lass had left already, from the look of things. Tony and Steve were putting the unsold books back in boxes, and it seemed like everything was OK, but their faces when they saw him there was something wrong and in his stomach he felt bad and Steve was walking over to him what was what was going on and then the world around him speeded back up like a rewound phonograph, and there was sound again, and Steve looked near to tears and he was saying, 'Dick, you've got to call Amanda,' and something about how the company were sending people, no, that couldn't be right, sending people to the con to talk to him about, no, about thirty, no no no no, thirty thousand dollars and they'd be here soon and oh what was he going to do, but he knew there was nothing, nothing, there was nothing to hold on to.

He was terrified, the colour draining out of him like hourglass sand. Turning away from his distraught employee without speaking, Duckley did his best to run back through the paranormal push towards the lobby area, which is to say he barely strolled. With cartoon heads and helmets everywhere around him, he was like a child abandoned in a ball pit, making his 'nnnnnnnnnn' sound with every ragged breath. He didn't have a plan or a direction, except, maybe, if he got back to his room, picked up his stuff, he could get out before these people from head office got here, change his name, become a drifter, something, anything. Caught in the viscous crowd, he struggled past recesses where extragalactic Nazis shoved mail gauntlets down the laddered tights of elves, past threesomes that involved two breakfast-cereal mascots and a rabbit, past solitary objects where he didn't know what they were meant to be but they were weeping, and it all looked evil to him now. It all looked crazy.

In the lobby, it was even worse. The Brandon Chuff memorial presentation had begun, cramming the space with a perspiring press of inappropriately costumed mourners that he had to shoulder his way through to reach the elevators. Duckley's panicked, whining stumble was made more conspicuous by the crowd's silence, as they listened reverently to the United Supermen reading the dialogue balloons from Chuff's widely respected #121, 'The Call of Coelentero'. Somebody dressed as Rocket Ranger said, 'As one extraterrestrial to another, my Neptunian senses tell me you are troubled, old friend.' To which a tall, thin guy dressed as Thunderman replied, 'You're right as usual, Nark from Neptune. Coelentero can control us. He can make us into monsters.' Numerous members of the audience voiced their appreciation at this classic line, while many more called Dick Duckley an asshole, as he rampaged through their hushed assembly doing his weird squealing noise. He was just glad that Worsley Porlock didn't seem to be around to witness Duckley's interruption of the ceremony, after all that he'd said about wanting it to go well. If he hadn't had his mind on other things, he might have also registered that there were only nine United Supermen, with Eagle Girl not in attendance. As it stood, however, he could only think of doom and his remaining rations of cocaine.

Then he was in the elevator as it climbed clear of the ground floor and its night-sweat fauna, with his view of the event below occluded by his own scared breath that greyed the glass. Wiping an oval with his sportscoat sleeve, he thought he saw two men in suits and sunglasses, just coming in through the main entrance, but it couldn't be the company guys already, could it? Maybe it was just people in cosplay as the pair of CIA vampire-squad agents from that movie *Stakeholders*. He hoped that might be what it was, although hadn't one of the agents in the movie been a black guy? Duckley found he couldn't swallow, and the crawling glass-box elevator made him feel like he was being tried for war crimes in The Hague. That was always the problem with ascensions: they took far too long, compared with other directions of travel.

On floor twenty-seven, there were fewer free-range travesties of reason than there had been earlier, but Duckley still managed to spook three separate horror franchises as he ran past them, with his strangled whining ringing in the corridors behind him. Why had he stayed drinking for so long with Worsley Porlock? He could be halfway to somewhere else by now, but it was too late and the people from the company were probably already in the building, and he couldn't go back down without them seeing him. He could remember having dreams like this, and so he squeezed his eyes tight shut hoping this might be one of them, but when he opened them again, it wasn't.

Finally he reached his room, although it didn't feel like his room any more. It wasn't safe. The light was prickly and wrong, and Duckley realised he was crying as he stuffed his dirty T-shirt and some other oddments in his holdall, short of breath and panting like a locomotive having sex. It wasn't fair that this was happening to him. He was just someone who liked Thunderman. He knew he wasn't average, what with his background, but, as far as comics went, he felt that he was representative. He wasn't a bad guy. He'd seen how everybody else was acting, and assumed they were on morally reversed World Daleth, so that it was all OK. Except it turned out that it wasn't, and now he was in more trouble than he'd ever been in, and he felt he deserved more than this from Thunderman, for all those years of study, all that loyalty. Duckley knew all there was to know about the character, and this was the way Thunderman rewarded him. Then he remembered the cocaine.

What made most sense, he pseudo-reasoned, was to take it all at once so that he wasn't carrying it if he was caught. This time it didn't work the same. The increased dose made him feel like a superhero, but it was a frightened superhero, so he just felt super frightened. They were probably already in the building, and he'd got to get out, just get out, fast as he could. He grabbed his bag and, unaware that he was bleeding copiously from one nostril, burst out of his room into the silent corridor, like gibbering and gory refuse from a backed-up drain.

By this point his thought processes weren't even mammal. There was some vague notion of finding the service stairs and leaving through a hypothetical rear entrance, but this was shot through with thoughts of Thunderman, and Momma, and damnation. In a too tight skull, his brain was poached in simmering cerebrospinal fluid, and he felt the blanched words and ideas as they flaked away into the boil and seethe of his insoluble predicament. This was the end, he knew it. He was finished. He was crying again now, his nose still bleeding as he blundered down the narrow corridor, pinballing into walls and around corners, and all of a sudden there was someone walking down the carpet-quieted passageway towards him and, just like that, he was in another world.

He knew then that his desperate plea to Thunderman, to his heavenly Father, had gone neither unheard nor unanswered, and the proof approached him hesitantly down the green hush of the hallway, where her lovely face was shining with concern for him, and it was Peggy. It was Peggy Parks. Or it was someone kind and beautiful who was in cosplay as her, but that didn't mean a thing because symbolically, symbolically she represented Peggy Parks, and, like an angel, she had come to rescue him. Sobbing his gratitude, he staggered into her consoling arms and pressed his face with all its human juices in the molten copper tresses that cascaded to her shoulders. Then he put his hand between her legs and tried to kiss her.

Her name, on the badge he hadn't noticed, was Patricia Ross. She worked there in the hotel as a junior manager, and had red hair. Like many younger people, she had never heard of Peggy Parks. She bit Dick Duckley's cheek, called him a motherfucker and then started yelling for security.

Moaning with horror and incomprehension, Duckley ran on down the hall towards the landing he could see at the far end. Behind him, he heard Peggy talking on her phone, angry and crying from the way it sounded, telling somebody the floor number and that it was a big curly-haired guy with a bloody nose, who had a thirteen-year-old girl preparing to perform fellatio printed on his T-shirt. But he hadn't got a bloody nose, and Oral Lass was, well, was older than thirteen, and all of this was terrible and made no sense, and all he could do now was run, just run.

Out on the landing with its chrome-steel rails and wooden balustrade, there was a scattering of ostentatious vigilantes, goblins, hard-light holograms, and two big men in matching maroon jackets rushing at him from along the walkway, both with serious expressions, from a franchise that he didn't recognise. He turned and started pounding carpet in the opposite direction, around the stupendous atrium that echoed faintly with the dialogue of the late Brandon Chuff, from far below. 'Great Suns! Coelentero has his tendrils in the mind of Blue Beam! Anything could happen now!'

He wasn't thinking anything coherent, and the whimpering sound he made in flight was all his language. He could hear the maroon men not far behind him, shouting 'Sir', and all the lights and colours and reflections rippled past him in a rush of photon-vomit. Duckley's lungs and heart were hammering against his breastbone, frantic to break out and stage their own less cumbersome escape. 'Surrender to your destiny, United Supermen. The power of Blue Beam's azure amulet will have you as my slaves until your final breath!' Lifting his streaming eyes, he looked ahead of him, and …

Leaning languorously up against the balustrade a few yards away were the male and female devils that he'd spotted earlier, while he was waiting for the elevator. Both were drinking cocktails with umbrellas. The she-demon watched as Duckley thundered down the landing at the two of them, raising one painted eyebrow questioningly, and behind, the maroon voices were still Sirring him. There wasn't anywhere to go, so with a lurching sideways movement like a bucket slopping over he

spilled

past

the

railing

WELCOME TO SATYRICON!

into

a

spinning

abyss

WELCOME TO SATYRICON!

with

want

for

angels

WELCOME TO SATYRICON!

(no angels save for Eagle Girl, whose golden wings were spread on Worsley Porlock's hotel bed)

and

he

fell

keening

WELCOME TO SATYRICON!

through

tiers

of

mythos

WELCOME TO SATYRICON!

through

the

glass

elevator

WELCOME TO SATYRICON!

(more accurately, he went in the top, and something that had been him came out through the bottom)

meat

and

crystal

raining

WELCOME TO SATYRICON!

upon

bad

dialogue

rising

WELCOME TO SATYRICON!

up

from

the

lobby

—where he burst on impact. Rocket Ranger threw up on Gold Eagle, while the Streak, keeping in character, just ran as far as possible. The 'Going Down' shirt made it worse. A Grand Guignol precipitate, he spoiled the snowy roses, speckling the black and white framed portrait as an offering. And Brandon Chuff, with hair and beard like Faunus, smiled all saturnine upon his abattoir arcadia.

It was Worsley Porlock's best Dick Duckley story ever.

19. (May, 2016)

If it had been a film, then in this opening shot there would be a black freeway carpet rolled out to the flat horizon, as if for important visitors. Some lambswool snags of cloud hurry across Midwestern blue from left to right, and a strong breeze is evident in intermittent wuthering against the microphone and in the urgent signalling of wheatgrass stems, up close, down in a foreground corner of the frame. There is the angry insect wheedle of a distant engine, some moments before the vehicle makes itself visible as an expanding bead of silver grey, there in the visual centre of the careful composition.

Dan Wheems, six months out of comics, was discovering how it felt, being alive. Behind the wheel, his tinted windows wound down, dressed in adult clothing unadorned by licensed properties, he was as happy, in the wind and sunshine, as he'd ever been. He guessed that part of it was being back here in the state where he'd grown up, but mostly it was shedding the immense, unrealised weight of his career. He hadn't known what it was doing to him, not until he'd stopped and had been shocked by how immediately different his existence seemed to be. He felt as if he'd spent the last few decades on some hellish prison planet with tremendous gravity, that had an atmosphere of cyanide and methane. Finding out that he could breathe and wasn't made of lead had been an ecstasy.

He slowed to let a startled-looking rabbit get out of his way, supposing that the wildlife didn't have much traffic to become accustomed to out here, which he thought a good omen. If only he could locate the house with the For Sale sign that he'd half-wittedly driven by the week before, then this could be the first idyllic afternoon of many: living here in fine seclusion, working on the novel about childhood that he'd started, with just rabbits and this endless sky for company.

It wasn't only how much better life was without comics that had startled him, but also how the comics business looked, viewed from outside. How small it was; how cruel and how ridiculous.

All the warped personalities the industry either attracted, or else bent and fashioned for itself out of naïve enthusiasts who'd been expecting something else. He couldn't understand why he'd not bailed out of the business years ago, though in a way he could. Part of the answer was just plain human inertia, and part was the fact that, from the inside, comics people and their weird behaviour could seem almost normal. Insular in their relationships, they tended to surround themselves with others from the same field who'd reflect or possibly surpass their oddness, which allowed them to believe that they were in a regular, acceptable reality. Which often made them a lot odder.

Dan was grateful he'd escaped in time, though he'd admit that even that escape was qualified. Removing himself from the comics field was one thing, stopping thinking about comics was another. Constantly, he'd find his mind alighting on some decomposing gobbet from the mental garbage-tip of trivia that his career had left him with, when that was the last thing he wanted to be thinking of. If, on the news, they talked about the National Guard, then for a moment he would think they meant the character and not the military auxiliary. Somebody mentions gold, and he'd immediately assume that they were talking about Joe. He probably should have anticipated some sort of reaction – thirty-something years in any field would leave you with a lot of baggage, and especially an enterprise almost designed to be obsessional, like comics – but Dan wished he could stop doing it, or at least not in public, where it was embarrassing. For instance, when he'd visited his bank to tell them of his imminent change of address, the guy he'd spoken to had got a name badge on that said 'A. Bell'. Dan jokingly enquired whether he got a lot of people asking him if he was Thunderman, to which the guy had just looked puzzled and said, 'What?'

Noticing that the sky was now the precise shade that he privately thought of as 'Brute blue', he sighed and figured a complete recovery was no doubt going to take a while. He was reminded of a fact that he'd picked up from Milton Finefinger, whose younger days had been more countercultural than Dan's.

Milton had said that junkies, when they'd kicked their habit – for however long – would often volunteer to be drug counsellors, a socially applauded cover for their real objective, which was to continue their involvement with a drugs world that was all that they could think or talk about. If Dan found himself helping fifty-year-olds over a *Vindictives* binge, he'd know he was in trouble.

Judged by the faint migraine shimmer of the ruled horizon, it appeared the day was going to be a hot one. He just hoped he'd not imagined that For Sale board, or had not remembered it on the wrong stretch of road or something dumb like that. His fantasy that he could be a proper literary author, living miles from anywhere and shunning interviews like Salinger or Pynchon, had congealed over this last few months from idle dream to psychological necessity. After the awful spectacle he'd made of himself at Brandon Chuff's funeral, he'd been observing radio silence and had not contacted anybody in the industry. He'd put his farewell dossier together, with the Thunderman script, Wellworth interview and all the other stuff, and it was published in *Collectors' Fugue* without eliciting much in the way of a reaction or response, but the important thing for Dan was that he'd written it. His lip was better and he could speak normally again, since, for some reason, having quit the comics world, he was no longer trying to eat himself alive. He'd burned his bridges, settled his affairs and moved from his New York apartment to a rented room in South Bend while he scouted out a permanent address. Dan was committed, now, to his new life, and there could be no vacillating. Change or die, those were his options.

He'd forgotten how much he liked Indiana, especially up north here where Lake Michigan was spitting distance. He could see it now, a glittering beyond the far trees on his right, apparently immobile in the crawling parallax. Dan had grown up in South Bend, back before he'd stupidly attended BeeCon1 in 1969 and given his mom the ambition to move to New York after her sister, Dan's Aunt Brenda. In a gold glow of nostalgia, he'd originally thought that he might find a place in South Bend, so he could relive his childhood or some idiotic urge like that, but going back there had just demonstrated why that wouldn't work. South Bend was obviously different now, as was Dan Wheems, and if you added the velocity of change for each of them, that gave the force for the collision of estrangements. South Bend wasn't run-down, any more than everywhere was run-down, but it was no longer where he'd grown up, and he was no longer who'd grown up there. All the place could be for him was a progressively more disappointing reconstruction, where they were forever getting it all wrong. Much better finding someplace new that was nearby, so that he wouldn't have to overprint all of those precious memories.

That was if 'someplace new' really existed and was actually a property that was for sale, rather than an abandoned filling station that he'd misinterpreted as it blurred past. This last was the conclusion that he was reluctantly approaching, being fairly sure he should have come across the place by now. Hell, if he went much further, he'd be in Chicago. Before Dan could stop himself, a comic book brain that was in withdrawal had reminded him that Banner Comics had been published in Chicago, and begun to list the outfit's questionable highlights. He felt angry – at his inability to stop converting everything into a comics reference, at his driving all the way out here to find a dream home that he only thought he saw, at this whole 'new life' nonsense. He was just about to turn around and drive dejectedly back to South Bend when, right out of nowhere, there it was ahead of him.

OK, it was two houses side by side, one white, the other pink, a double cone of strawberry and vanilla for a sunny day, but it was definitely the right place. He saw now how it was the vanilla property that was for sale, while the pink house had some old guy in its front garden, watering the flowers, with his hose set to a fine spray that fanned pint-sized rainbows everywhere. Dan hadn't previously realised just how beautifully the residence was situated, at least when approached from this direction. It was practically right on the lakeside. As he neared the picture-perfect buildings, slowing down to pull in, the old man switched off his hose and killed the rainbows, turning to regard Dan with his face completely motionless, his eyes coloured the same as the May sky.

The gardener looked to be around five-six, five-seven, lean and sinewy with muscles of beef jerky, a good head of white hair, and skin like a weather-beaten satchel. Nothing in the man's appearance was remarkable except his socks, which had contrasting stripes of neon green and neon orange. Dan switched off the engine and the old guy was still staring at him, frozen in place and not even blinking. He had one of those old-fashioned Norman Rockwell faces, classically American, that automatically made you assume you knew it from TV or somewhere. In his stillness was a kind of tension and a barely noticeable apprehension, and Dan realised belatedly that he might well be the first visitor this place had seen in months or years. For all the man knew, Dan might have been sent here by the IRS, a debt-collection agency, or some scheme that locates birth parents using DNA. Anxious to reassure someone who might be a potential next-door neighbour, Dan got out of the car with his hands up, in apology, leaving the keys in the ignition.

'Sorry, man. I didn't mean to startle you or anything. I was just driving by and noticed what a beautiful environment you've got here. I grew up in Indiana, down in South Bend, and I guess I'd thought of maybe settling here again, now I'm retired. My name's Dan Wheems.'

Dan stuck his hand out. The old fellow stared at it as if it were an alien artefact for a few seconds, and then offered up his own in a surprisingly firm handshake. Raising his blue eyes, he gave Dan a wide grin that lit his fissured features like an ivory sun over a rusted desert.

'I'm Charlie Morelli. Yeah, I gotta say, I wondered who you was when you drove up like that. Didn't I see you go by here a week, ten days ago?'

The voice was unmistakably from Brooklyn, and the question served to underline how very sparse the traffic was in this neck of the woods, if his last drive past had been such a big event that the guy still remembered it. On Dan's way over – now he thought about it – he'd not passed another vehicle in getting on three quarters of an hour. You could get up to anything out here.

'Yeah. Yeah, you may have done. That's probably when I first saw this place, and since then I've been trying to remember where I saw it. Say, that's quite a New York accent you got there.'

Morelli nodded genially and chuckled.

'It's a funny story. I was born in Providence, Rhode Island, back in 1929. Irene and Joe, my mom and dad, they ran a bakery, and so when I flunked out of high school that was where I worked, you know? Dad moved the business to New York in 1951, and naturally I went along, which explains where I got the accent. Then, in 1963, I marry this cute girl, Joan Summers, and, I'll tell ya, that was the biggest mistake I ever made. I tried to run a pizza joint out in Connecticut, but then, in 1970, the bitch walked out on me. Thank God we'd not had any children, that's all I can say. I moved to Cleveland and worked at a vacuum-cleaner dealership until 2005, when I retired out here. I'm crazy about gardening, and I'm a big Sinatra fan.'

Dan smiled and nodded, but was privately bemused. The tale was nondescript and overdetailed, certainly, but for the life of him he couldn't see how it was funny. Drifting bees emitted sounds like distant aeroplanes and nosed amongst the roses, as Dan made an effort to restart the conversation with this friendly old guy and his probably generic aura of familiarity.

'That's one heck of a story. So, 2005, you've lived out here around ten years now? You must probably have known the people had the place next door.'

Charlie Morelli glanced up at the white house with the messy garden that adjoined his own.

'No, I don't know who lived there. Place was empty when I got here.' Turning, he subjected Dan to an appraising look, eyes narrowed so the wrinkles looked like woodgrain. 'You said you was thinking about settling here, where you grew up, right? So, I'm thinking it was that For Sale sign in the yard next door what made you stop. Is that about the size of it?'

Dan swallowed nervously. He'd not considered that Morelli might not want a neighbour, and he hoped there wouldn't be bad blood affecting his prospective tenancy.

'Um, yeah. I won't deny I'd thought about it. I appreciate that you must like it out here on your own, the privacy and everything. If I were to put in an offer, would that be a problem?'

Charlie looked down at the lawn and rubbed the back of his neck with the hand that wasn't still holding the switched-off hosepipe. He looked more like somebody that Dan had seen before than ever, maybe an exasperated senior doctor in an old TV show. He snighed wearily, somewhere between a snort and sigh, and raised his head to look at Dan with a conflicted frown.

'Look, I'll be honest with you, you'd have asked me that a week ago, when you drove past before, then I'd have probably said beat it, you know what I mean? You seem like a nice guy and everything, but I'd kind of got used to my own company. Since then, though, I been thinking. I'm not getting any younger, and what if I have an accident here, miles from anywhere? And it might be good for my nerves and my mental health, having somebody I could talk to just once in a while; that's what the doctors say. I guess a guy could go nuts living out here on his own. I sometimes worry on my own behalf. I mean, will you look at these fuckin' socks! What kind of normal adult guy wears shit like this? No, go ahead and call the people on the sign. It could be you'd be doing me a favour.'

Both men were laughing now, Dan Wheems with huge relief. He knew that he still had to go through all the complicated balls-ache that was part of buying property, but right there in that moment, he felt that he'd made it: he'd escaped the comics industry, if only by moving halfway across America so that it could no longer find him. Charlie and Dan started talking like old friends, both looking forward to each other's company when they were right next door. Morelli said how glad he was that Dan had shown up on his doorstep.

'Naturally, I'd have liked it better if you'd been some stacked broad but, hey, what's a heaven for, right?' The old man was smiling, and although Dan felt a bit uncomfortable about the sexual banter, he was more absorbed in Charlie's grin and in the look he had, squinting against the sunshine. With the light like that, he almost looked like … Dan's jaw dropped in sudden realisation, and he burst out laughing at his own childish thought processes, his own preposterous inanity.

Morelli was still grinning at him, but now with puzzled amusement.

'What's so funny?'

It took a few moments to get Dan's self-deprecating mirth under control, and then he wiped his eyes to offer explanations and apologies.

'I'm what's so funny. Honestly, if you knew what a jerk I was, you wouldn't want me moving in next door. See, what it is, the job that I was in, when I retired six months back, I found out that I still thought about it all the time. It was like everything I saw, I couldn't help but be reminded of some little detail out of my old life.'

Morelli nodded like he understood. 'Yeah, I'm like that with my old work. You know, the dealership in Cleveland? Some jobs, I guess they come back to haunt you, right enough.'

Dan started chuckling again.

'Boy, they sure do. When I was looking at you there, the thing that made me laugh is that I caught myself thinking you looked like someone from the dopey business that I used to be in, this guy called Frank Giardino. Seriously, I'm going to need some of that hypnotherapy, so that I can forget about all of this useless junk.'

Morelli was still grinning. Probably he'd met a few New York neurotics back when he was slinging baked goods for his dad.

'Huh. So, this guy, he was real handsome like me, is that what you're saying?'

Laughing, Dan was quick to reassure his new friend that Morelli was the better looking of the two men, by a mile. He really liked the sparky and plain-talking little guy, and thought it boded well that they could kid each other like this. Charlie wore a quiet and thoughtful smile, as if he was most probably considering the self-same thing, just gazing absently at Dan's car and then glancing up the road where it ran on beside the lake. The old man nodded like he was agreeing with himself on something, maybe that inviting Dan to live next door had been a good decision. He appeared to realise suddenly that he was still holding the hose, and dropped it on the lawn where it fell into lazy coils, a sunning viper. Turning to regard the younger man, Morelli gave Dan a conspiratorial wink.

'I'll tell you what. Two guys as civilised as us, we didn't ought to be out in this sun, sweating like animals. What say we go inside and grab a beer, so we can find stuff out about each other?'

So that's what they did. If it had been a film, then in this closing shot there'd be the house's faded pink exterior, seen from the sunlit garden. Yellow roses nod encouragingly in the lower foreground where a drone explores, efficient as an engineer. In the near background, we see Dan and Charlie go in through the door, laughing and chatting, hands on shoulders, closing it behind them. With bees humming and birds trilling intermittent arias on the soundtrack, we hold on the closed front door for maybe fifteen seconds, then somebody coughs, it sounds like.

Hold five seconds more. Cut to black screen.

20. (February, 2021)

Locked down by cold and Covid, much reduced in both people and purpose, New York had been turned into the set of an abandoned Cecil B. DeMille extravaganza, a gigantesque cheese-dream after the financiers had pulled all the money. Fifty-storey silence. Everywhere, haunted by absences. A post-disaster movie wanting for an evident disaster, *Nothingnado*. Even the obligatory newspaper moths that fluttered down the gutters with torn headlines to backstory the catastrophe were nowhere to be seen. It was the end of things with endings. It was the humanopause, or maybe the apocalapse.

For Worsley Porlock, heading to his invitation upstairs at American, it was his big day, and, as with most big things, trying to keep it heated seemed to be a major problem. Worsley had a mask on – giving him the Brute's nose, mouth and chin, which seemed disloyal for a visit to American but was the only one they'd had in stock – and therefore wasn't leaving smokestack plumes of condensation in his wake, like the few unmasked people he could see there on the all but empty avenue. He passed one unmasked man who appeared frightened and offended at the same time, and who had on a red baseball cap that bore the legend Make America There Again. Everything steamed and shivered, and the whole thing felt like entropy for commerce.

Or perhaps that was just Worsley, who had barely slept the night before and who was viewing the semi-deserted city through insomnia's fractured lens. With apprehension and anticipation staging simultaneous TED Talks in his head, slumber had managed to evade him, and he'd filled the pale hours streaming *Glenfield* season one, so then he'd been disturbed as well as wakeful. *Glenfield*, unbelievably, turned out to be a dark and gritty reimagining of Blinky, named after the astigmatic character's hometown. Now known as Bradley Brown so as not to offend the partly sighted, Blinky's optic defect had been retooled to allow him visions of a strange, Lovecraftian netherworld, and best friend Bottleneck was managing a meth lab from a back room of Pop's Soda Shop. In the first episode, the naked corpse of Blinky's high school teacher Mrs Grimsby was discovered, wrapped in tinfoil, in the trunk of Blinky's beat-up old jalopy, and things got more gritty from there on. If Worsley had remained in bed and suffered through a series of those micro-nightmares that attend the sleepless, then the residue of free-floating unease he felt now would be near identical to that which came with having watched six episodes of *Glenfield*. It had all just been so wrong, like having a beloved childhood teddy bear crawling towards you with a knife between its teeth. So, on this already unsettling morning, Worsley found himself further disquieted by Blinky, of all fucking things.

When at last he arrived at 777, its reverberant lobby was jam-packed with nobody, save himself and the Indian man at the reception counter who, with worried eyes above an ice-blue mask, tracked Worsley's progress through the ringing emptiness towards the elevators. It was as if the soap opera of the world was trying to ride out a writers' strike, with all the motivation, dialogue and narrative at a dead stop and Bobby Ewing frozen there forever, stepping from the shower.

To underline the Marie Celeste state of things, the elevators all stood open and available. On Worsley's solitary and unhurried journey to the twenty-eighth floor, he had time to be concerned about what he might find there. These last few months at American had been disastrous, with many of the experienced staffers having been let go, and all but a few books on permanent hiatus. Maybe that's what his trip to the building's higher reaches was about: to tell him comic books were over.

On floor twenty-eight, the door shrugged open in disinterest as to whether Worsley disembarked or not. As people lost the will to live, things lost even the will to be inanimate. He stepped out to the queasy moiré of a corridor that, after decades of familiarity, still had the forceful nausea of that first paralysing glimpse. He didn't know if it was those low-energy bulbs that they had or if his eyes were getting worse, but in the labyrinthine hallways of American there lay a pall as though the light itself were dusty and untended.

There was no one at the front desk when he came to it, but then, there never had been. More unusually, on the desk itself was a brown paper bag with a half-eaten sub protruding from it, over a week old to judge from the proliferating starbursts of near-turquoise mould. Behind him, there was a faint scrabbling, and when he looked he saw with fascinated horror that a colony of vermin – mice, he hoped – had somehow eaten through the front of Ambrose Bell, and were apparently inhabiting his stomach cavity. Although the hero-in-disguise still lounged insouciantly against his dried-up watercooler, he looked destitute and ill, with his good-natured smile now straining to a grimace.

Unnerved by both silence and the perfume of decay, Worsley strayed further down the throat of the distressing corridor. In some stretches, light fittings stuttered and recited insect poetry. For want of anybody to infect, and so as not to be mistaken for a Massive-loyalist jihadi, Worsley pulled his Brute mask down around his chin and went on through the carcass of a thirteen-year-old boy's imagination. He'd reluctantly accepted that this was to be no ordinary call-by at the stables of American before he turned a corner and encountered thirty-year-dead Hector Bass.

More accurately, Worsley was confronted by what seemed to be a newsreel of the deceased *Our Unshaven Army* chronicler. Bass was in crackly black and white, a film-loop of himself on damaged 1920s stock that stood before what had once been his office door, some distance down the hall, reaching one sparking silver hand towards the knob and then retracting it. As Worsley cautiously came nearer, the electric phantom glanced towards him and appeared to be aware that he was there, but was unable to communicate. The lips worked in the anguished face, but Bass was seemingly trapped in a bygone era before talking pictures, so whatever he was saying wasn't audible. Only the pleading eyes could express his impossible predicament, staring from under the St Elmo's fire that flickered in the hanging gardens of their brows. It was as if Bass had resolved he would reclaim his room or die, but was incapable of doing either. He was almost ready to come back to work, eternally.

Needing to get to David Moskowitz's office further down the optical-illusion hallway, Worsley edged around the silent movie ghost, and when Bass caught his gaze, he pulled a sympathetic mug and did a jazz-hands shrug in order to convey his helplessness. He pointed to his wristwatch and thumbed down the corridor behind him, indicating that he'd like to get involved in the dead man's unfathomable situation, but that he had an appointment. Grey tears trickled on the fragile celluloid of Bass's cheeks, but by then Worsley had gone hurrying down the ugly passage without looking back.

He'd seen the apparition of a man who'd died last century, and on the one hand, he supposed he should be screaming or reporting it to someone, possibly an exorcist, but, then, this invitation upstairs, in career terms, was just so important that he mustn't get distracted by psychic phenomena. He barged on down the hall, resolving that his mind would process the Bass incident when it had time, but that time clearly wasn't now. Besides, on rounding the next bend, all thoughts of Hector Bass were driven from his mind by the nine-year-old boy, pacing impatiently and scowling at his mobile phone to check the time, there in the pulsing thoroughfare.

Was he here with a parent, or was he maybe some kid who'd won a competition? The boy was approximately four foot six and, from the way he dressed, was probably the coolest nine-year-old at his expensive private school. He'd got an extra-small official football jacket on, and although Worsley didn't know much about current prepubertal footwear trends, he thought that the child's sneakers looked impeccably state of the art. He wished he'd had a mom and dad who could afford to spend that kind of dough on him when he'd been that age, although, now that he got nearer, Worsley saw the youngster didn't look particularly grateful or contented with his comfortable lot in life. His face was lined with stress, and hair that had looked blond from further off revealed itself as mousy-grey on close inspection. Then the rug rat turned around to look at Worsley and said, 'Where the hell have you been?', and he had a moustache, and, oh Jesus, it was David Moskowitz.

Worsley was lost for words, and started stammering apologies for having been delayed, at which the downsized publisher held up one tiny palm and, sighing, closed his eyes.

'Is Hector there again?'

Worsley could only nod, at which the Moskowitz-child shook its elderly head in exasperation.

'We don't know what's causing him. The specialist we spoke to thought it could be sunspots. I've got everyone in legal working on it, seeing if we can take out some kind of preternatural injunction, but it isn't looking hopeful. Anyway, we don't have time to stand around exchanging pleasantries like this when you're wanted upstairs. Please follow me.'

Though Moskowitz's transformation had been coming for a long time, now that Worsley thought about it, witnessing the final stages was no less bewildering. The voice and features were those of somebody in their early seventies, so this wasn't so much rejuvenation as reduction, a return to childhood that did not relinquish adult knowledge, power, or status. With the miniature executive running in front of him, he followed Moskowitz through the American mirage-maze, to a door that Worsley thought had once been that of Mimi Drucker's office.

'Wasn't this once Mimi's room?'

The old man's head on the child's body tilted to look up at Worsley chidingly, as Moskowitz reached out to turn the grown-up handle with his sticky infant paw.

'It still is.'

Drucker's office looked as if the former VP had just stepped out for a five-year restroom break. Atop the oddly shaped designer desk, a dainty cup of herbal tea was steaming on its King Bee coaster. Worsley was confused.

'Um, weren't we headed for the elevator? So that I could go upstairs?'

The pocket publisher allowed himself a smug grin, as if he was at his own tenth birthday party, showing his new toys to all his pals.

'Oh, no. This is a different kind of upstairs, so we use a different kind of elevator. It's behind the big framed picture, back of Mimi's desk.'

Still struggling to make sense of anything that he'd experienced since pressing 'play' on *Glenfield* season one, Worsley glanced up at the ornately bordered giant photograph that overpowered the office's rear wall. Its austere black and white contained in carven arabesques of painted gold, the shot of Mimi Drucker's dad and General Pinochet approaching the eleventh green had been the source of many raucous comics-business anecdotes – and

Worsley had of course seen it before – but there was something different this time. It was so unmissably apparent that he couldn't place it for a moment.

Then he could. There were three people in the picture now, upsetting Richard Avedon's masterful composition. On the clipped grey grass beneath a cold pearl sky, between a windswept and relaxed Senator Drucker and his merciless Chilean fascist golfing buddy, Mimi Drucker stood naked and beaming, one hand resting casually on each of the men's sleeves. Besides her clothing, the petite blonde also lacked for bodily hair, genitals and nipples. She'd have looked more like a plastic doll or airbrushed centrefold, if not for all the goosebumps that were clearly evident, raised from her white flesh out there on the chilly links. She looked more happy and fulfilled than Worsley could remember seeing her, and both of the old men looked glad to have her there. Casting a sideways glance towards Mimi's redacted breasts, Augusto Pinochet smiled thinly behind his untrimmed moustache. The three of them playfully coexisted in the captured pewter light of a gone afternoon, and Worsley didn't have the first idea what he was looking at.

'But this, this isn't Photoshopped. How did they work the photograph of Mimi into …?'

From beneath his pepper-and-salt brow, the grade-school publisher served Worsley with a warning glare. 'That's not a photograph of Mimi. Anyway, it's not important for our purposes.'

Approaching the impractical and lovely desk, lips set to a grim line, the moppet Moskowitz placed one diminutive hand on the King Bee coaster that was without herbal tea, and gave it a sharp quarter-turn. The huge framed photograph, and what looked like the whole section of wall that it was mounted on, purred smoothly to the left, exposing a bronze door beneath. A further quarter-turn caused this to open and display the elevator car itself, white-lit and big enough for two at most. Moskowitz stared at Worsley, his progeria-afflicted schoolboy face unreadable.

'Get in. There's two columns of eleven buttons each, and it's important that you only press the one marked with an aleph. That's the top one on the left side. Don't press any of the others, or you'll end up somewhere you don't want to be. That's how we lost Pete Mastroserio. As far as we can work out, he's a cattle rustler now, on Tzaddi.'

Worsley did as he was told, and occupied the box of light. Fixated fretfully on pressing the right button, he'd not really taken in the bit about Pete Mastroserio and cattle-rustling. Beside the door were the two rows of buttons Moskowitz had mentioned. There were twenty-two of them in all, each button black but marked with letters from the Hebrew alphabet in gold. The aleph, which he thought he recognised, was there at the top left as he'd been told it would be.

Through the open elevator door, he could see Mimi Drucker's office, with the Moskowitz-boy peering in towards him – somewhat anxiously, it seemed to Worsley.

'Porlock, can I say, the company wishes you the very best of luck in all of this. Remember, if the head is human, then you're on the wrong floor. And if Hector Bass's name comes up, I've told them that we have the situation in control, so don't say anything. Good man.'

While comprehending none of the instructions he had just been given, Worsley nodded reassuringly and pressed the aleph button. The bronze door slid shut, at which the Hebrew character there at the bottom of the rightmost column suddenly lit up, as if with a gold light inside it. Worsley didn't know which character it was, but thought it maybe marked the floor that he was on at present, which was twenty-eight. The elevator started moving.

The black squares beside the door announced the alphabet in Hebrew, backwards, with the gold light slowly climbing up the file of buttons on the right. The movement of the carriage was ambiguous: he couldn't tell if he was shooting up at speed, or if the elevator cable had just snapped and he was plummeting. At times, his overburdened inner ear told him that he was going sideways, and with each measured ascension of the golden light, his stomach felt like he'd performed a somersault. Still more unsettling, each new floor seemed to involve a sharp and noticeable change of atmosphere, moods so strange and specific that they came and went before he could articulate precisely what they were. As the gold light rose through the last few buttons of the left-hand column, he experienced a strong compulsion to do evil, a brief fit of childish giggling, and unbearable nostalgia for the 1940s. Finally, the lexical progression reached the aleph, and the sense of motion ceased. The feeling on this floor was one of Christmas morning excitation, shading into something else that Worsley thought might possibly be terror. The arrival at his destination was suggested by a solitary chime, and after a few seconds, the bronze elevator door withdrew, discreetly, like a waiter.

Disappointingly, outside was nothing but a field of diffused shades – bursts of soft pink, splashes of lemon, twilights of pale blue and green – that looked like babies had thrown powder-paint against a nursery wall, except it moved, crumpling slowly into new configurations. Supposing it to be some sort of high-tech lighting trick he hadn't previously encountered, Worsley Porlock drew a deep breath and stepped through the elevator door, into the beautifully tinted and psychotic pasture that revealed itself beyond the shifting candy lights.

It was a flawless summer afternoon in the Midwest, and far away, bare telegraph wires hymned the 1950s at each novel breeze. He stood on solid dirt below the sky's blue-glass sublime, and he was suffering respiratory difficulties, gasping the thin, perfumed air. Attempted screams, dilute and breathless, were all but inaudible in his own popping eardrums. Pouring midday light, that seemed to come from everywhere, was crystalline, was perfect, was entirely wrong. Here was the heaven for a foreign world, with him frightened and wheezing in it.

Labouring to assimilate impossible terrain, he saw that – from his shaking hands to gentle tumuli past distant fields – all shapes were bounded by thin lines of dark, as though overexposed at their scorched edges. A new Real, relieved of cluttering detail, ridded of distracting textures, a placatory simplicity that bordered archetype. He was in arid scrubland outskirting the small-town past, with boulders, weeds, a featureless grain silo left of background. Everything pared down to signal, prickling in its clarity.

Noisily hyperventilating, he perceived that even colour was here reimagined, brighter yet more limited, calm neutrals gemmed with sherbet primaries. Hues were at once more artificial and more true, but closer up appeared to be particulate, tinted mechanically so that his sleeves were dot-screened on their hanging folds, themselves reduced to pen strokes. Unsourced glare from all directions banished shadow, so that nothing looked to be with weight or volume, but in its own terms seemed right, seemed satisfyingly familiar. Visually, at least, it was a world less challenging than his.

Other than wind in weeds, the sound of open distance, or his straining lungs, it was likewise a minimal acoustic with no traffic, trains or other transport audible. Past straight-tilled land, generically Middle American, low hills plumped against graded cyan firmament near bleached at its horizon. Ocean, surely, was thousands of miles away, yet still he caught that redolence of a marine maternity, of seals, of aromatic bladderwrack, incongruous amidst these dusty latitudes. His skin crawled, wanting to be elsewhere.

Turning his much-simplified head, suffocating still, he noticed other figures in this shocking, charming landscape. Off in its right midground, one adult and several little boys and girls in fancy dress were standing grouped beside something he realised, haltingly, was forty feet of metal hourglass, shimmering hot in sunlight where no sun was visible. Rising up from perfunctory yellow wastes, it was faux silver, white with tremulous azure trickling on its wasp-waisted contours, outline crisped to hair's-breadth black. As with its mesmerising rustic backdrop, its aura was one of tantalising reminiscence, alien and yet insidiously familiar, singular but seen before.

Clustering at its base where umbra should have been, children in sugared-almond costume, perhaps twelve years old, conferred with their adult companion. Powerfully built, he faced away, presenting just a long gold coat with hunching shoulders as he solemnly addressed his festively attired young friends, there in their tingling, long-gone utopia. His hanging robe was decorated with an emblem of sharp TV monochrome, and in that dreadful moment, Worsley realised it was Thunderman – but when he turned, he had a tiger's head.

It was just how he'd looked, there on some half-forgotten cover of *Exciting Comics* sixty years since, freak effect of Felix Firestone's Random Ray, put right in the same tale, but now appallingly made manifest. The youngsters, it became apparent, were dressed up as various Tomorrow Friends, whose time machine was hourglass-shaped, if memory served correct. Dust Damsel in her smart grey uniform was present, Clock Kid in his enigmatic watch-face mask, with Indescribable Lass also there. They stared at the onlooking editor-in-chief, expressing cold indifference that seemed out of place on such cherubic countenances. Their beast-headed senior, lifting one giant honey paw in greeting, began his approach across the intervening half-tone dirt.

It was as if, in this uncanny place, time was a thing of discrete parcelled instants. Hideous or magnificent in aspect, Thunderman advanced towards him in disorienting lapses, fading out of sight after a pace or two then reappearing nearer, travelling through space-time by way of bewildering saccades: right background, centre midground, creases in his violet suit redrawing themselves with each step, until he jewelled into existence left of foreground, close enough to feel his burning exhalations.

He did not speak, instead bubbling forth spheres of pure meaning that would burst as wet words in his visitor's disintegrating consciousness. As with Thunderman's walk through hyphenated time, so too was information bundled into concise, separate packages, with some concepts expressed more forcefully, a heavier telepathic timbre.

{**Worsley**! Finally, we meet. Sorry about my **head**. Unfortunately, Firestone's **Random Ray** proved **irreversible**, although I thought it better to conceal that from your **readership**, as with my **executing** Firestone very soon thereafter.}

Thunderman's low psychic growl was gruff, was kindly, but his human interlocutor could feel identity itself unravelling, just from the creature's dread proximity. Oblivious to its own crushing consequence, this frightful gnostic demiurge continued.

{You're most likely wondering where you **are**. This is **World Aleph**, Worsley. This is the **real world**. Your Earth, **World Tau**, is a **control** where no one is exempt from laws of **probability** or **physics**. I know your life there is **hard**. That's why I want to **help**.}

Monstrously lovely, Thunderman's enormous head here nodded at him reassuringly. Wanting to weep, wanting to defecate, he let his flinching gaze stray to the costumed children standing by their hourglass, still regarding him with chill disdain. Catching his glance, Thunderman smiled engagingly, displaying three-inch-long incisors.

{Ah, yes! The **Tomorrow Friends**! They got your **message**, Worsley, the one that you **didn't send** when you were **five years old**. They're making you a **member**, Worsley.}

Everything he'd ever wanted, it destroyed him. Fondly, Thunderman rested one massive paw upon his shoulder, heavy as mahogany, and in those golden eyes were all the marvellous and terrifying things mankind must never, ever have.

AMERICAN LIGHT – AN APPRECIATION

BY C. F. BIRD

While Harmon Belner's shooting-star arrival in the literary firmament came with the publication of his controversial *Harlem Gold* in 1959, it would not be until *American Light*'s thunderous debut, two decades later, that he would accomplish what was thought to be impossible in US literature: a second act.

Acclaimed as Belner's masterpiece, *American Light* can be seen as having retroactively supplied a narrative for his career in poetry; this later work a vindication of the brilliance predicted by so many after *Harlem Gold*'s phenomenal reception. By establishing iconic start and end points in the Belner story – early promise and its late fulfilment – a less lauded middle period has, of course, also been reappraised. Collections such as *Radio is Burning* (1961), *The Coffee-Ring Mandala* (1966), and *Norton's Empire* (1970), initially reviewed as underwhelming, stand revealed as necessary stepping stones, developmental stages in *American Light*'s ultimate gestation. It seems that the radiance of the poem's title is sufficient for us to detect its bullion gleam in all of Belner's previous writings.

And yet, in the comprehensive dazzle of the work's accomplishment, it would appear that this belated reassessment of the author has become the only focal point of critical attention – what *American Light* means in terms of Belner and his place in letters, rather than addressing what *American Light* means. Perhaps intimidated by the poet's overnight canonisation, commentators have proven reluctant to attempt more than a superficial confirmation of *American Light*'s monumental stature, without any adequate investigation of the poem's content, context, or, indeed, its origins.

This timorous approach does great disservice to its subject, for, as will be demonstrated, Harmon Belner's magnum opus is a trove of San Franciscan and Beat culture that demands careful unpacking. It is the intention of this essay to provide an annotated excavation of the text, and, in the process, to unearth what Barthes would term its 'cultural code', which is to say those aspects of the culture from which any given work emerges, that inevitably will inform said work's construction.

In *American Light*'s instance, this would be the post-Beat counterculture that prevailed in San Francisco through the 1960s and the 1970s. This is the milieu in which Belner locates his poem, and from which *American Light*'s painted backdrop is contrived. The persons who comprised that 'scene' or movement are the often pseudonymous walk-ons that the poet presses into service as his extras or supporting cast. The poem's furnishings are those appropriated from the city's Mission District and its environs during those fraught and fertile years, and it is from that place, those times, that Belner gathers all his colour, incident and character. It might be argued that without a close examination of such backgrounded material, our understanding of this work and what it represents must necessarily remain forever incomplete. Amongst the multitude of celebrants come to praise Caesar, it should be remembered that there is, nevertheless, important spadework waiting to be done.

We do not, after all, define the Late Cretaceous as the Age of the Tyrannosaurus, recognising that the thing of interest is the whole environment which generated and supported this celebrity top predator. So, too, with art or literary movements, where, unless we would succumb to a 'Great Man' theory of history, we must acknowledge that no artist or creation can be properly considered without reference to the complex human systems that engendered both.

This is especially the case with a phenomenon as fluid as Beat literature, where for a previously controversial view to be accepted as cultural heritage, it must be simplified into one comprehensible agenda; trimmed of its rough edges and its inconvenient trailing threads. In this simplification, much of any subject's vital substance will be permanently excised and excluded. With Joyce Johnson's *Minor Characters*, we are made justifiably aware of an exclusion of the female from that famous gang and its hard-up beatitude, but that should not obscure the many names redacted from the legendary roster on grounds other than their gender. The intent of this appreciation, therefore, is to re-include all those floor sweepings from the cultural cutting room, and in this way to present Harmon Belner's most successful work fully contextualised and with the penetrating scrutiny it merits and deserves. Its hope, in short, is to succeed in casting light on light itself.

American Light

Born messy over Agua Vista Park the baby day kicked in my window,
scaring piss-hard dreams away and drenching me in time. American light,
up and at 'em,[1] jostled surly with flushed fishermen on the Embarcadero,
and slapped blear from powdered cheeks down Castro Street. He ran
through traffic on James Lick and yelled 'Tomorrow is relentless'[2] as they squinted,

[1] This, a reference to Egyptian solar deity Atem, marks a departure in Belner's work from his previous Buddhist stance, adopted after the spiritual beliefs of Belner's literary idol, the poet Allen Ginsberg.

[2] An allusion to Belner's partner, Paul Landesman, who sustained minor injuries when running into traffic on San Francisco's James Lick Freeway, as described here, shortly before his committal to a psychiatric institution in September, 1971. There seems to be the implication that at this stage in the poem, Belner is identifying the titular *American Light* with Landesman. This reference to an abstract American phenomenon as a character in the text may also owe something to Beat writer Richard Brautigan's novel *Trout Fishing in America*, although Belner was often openly dismissive of Brautigan's writings, another opinion he may have picked up from his idol Ginsberg.

swerving to avoid him, then set fire to the dead flowers heaped past Masonic.[3] It was him
smashed eggs across the Tenderloin, smooched dirty glass Madonnas in heartbroken churches
and welcomed the night shift out of prison, clapping backs, warm and congratulatory. He
bullied ruined men asleep in doorways, was first on the scene discovering dead bodies, dancing
in awoken fountains, buttering babies, stretching cats, evaporating puddles
just by looking at them, tempting sea-monkeys and turning overnight loves ugly. Checked
himself in every shopfront rear-view mirror broken bottle hubcap passing stranger's eyes, and
skinny as a teenage burglar slipped in through the transom, climbed
one at a time the stairs without a sound to make a glory of their dust, then tongued
my lids to peach translucence, kissed clean of unconsciousness. Whorous, he trailed
a finger long and bright through the igniting belly hair until I was all set,[4] whence I
retrieved the brain that had been hooked out through my nose[5] and throwing
off the Karloff-bandage bed sheets, in my resurrected flesh, I came forth into him.[6]

[3] 'the dead flowers heaped past Masonic' presumably refers to the Haight-Ashbury district, epicentre of the psychedelic movement and its attendant 'flower children' in the late 1960s, which, from a perspective of Belner's home address in 1979 – when *American Light* was written – would be just west of Masonic Avenue. Though Belner appeared to court the so-called 'Love Generation' in its 1967 heyday, the lack of a reciprocal response is perhaps the reason for the somewhat dismissive reference to that 'dead' generation here.

[4] Although this phrase seems to refer to an early morning sexual encounter, probably with lover Paul Landesman, the word 'Whorous' is an obvious allusion to Egyptian sun-god Horus, while the phrase ends with a lower-case mention of Horus's uncle, Set, god of storms and chaos. In one of the Egyptian mythological traditions, Horus is sodomised by Set, which may be the implication that Belner intended for these lines.

[5] Possibly a reference to Belner's much-publicised cocaine addiction during the 1970s.

[6] This, clearly a sexual allusion, also references the *Book of Coming Forth by Day*, the original title of the text better known in the Western world as *The Egyptian Book of the Dead*.

American light sluiced from the TV; sheened glossy magazines; was always
generous with boyfriends; stroked their profiles in dust-jacket photographs until
the gleam attracted moths, flattering, fluttering white wings of onionskin, left
glyphic corpses by the bedside lamp and nibbled holes in my best patience.[7] Arm in
arm I strolled with him into a Caledonian[8] dawn, its bagpipe breeze beyond a doorstep
coastally eroded by the lapping surf of pretty Micks broken against it.[9] We barged out
upon Nilotic morning to the plaint of thigh-bone car horns all along Van Ness, and turned
heads in a Hopper diner on 16th, where he fell from the street on to my neck and shoulder, while
I architectured hash browns into pyramids beneath the ketchup sun. He gestured
always at the western lands[10] beyond Guerrero and Dolores, where the dead
roamed mute in Celtic twilight[11] and on Prosper Street lamented absent shadows, raised black

[7] We note that by this second stanza, the American light now referred to would seem to be the light of fame and celebrity. The 'fluttering, flattering' moths, with their 'white wings of onionskin' would appear to be lesser writers, attracted by that celebrity, who leave onionskin copies of their manuscripts for Belner's perusal. Such manuscripts are evidently the 'glyphic corpses' left by the author's bedside lamp, and that he finds these bothersome is indicated by the description of nibbled holes in his 'best patience'.

[8] Between 1973 and 1982, Belner lived at 15 Caledonia St, off 15th St between Valencia and Mission.

[9] Not for the last time, Belner demonstrates aversion to physically attractive writers of Irish descent. While we cannot say who is specifically referred to here, candidates might include the aforementioned Richard Brautigan; the justly celebrated Michael McClure; as-yet-unpublished Beat novelist Connor Davey; or the underappreciated Kirby Doyle. Nor is it clear whether Belner dislikes them for their genetic background or their good looks.

[10] This continues the poem's Egyptian theme, the ancient Egyptians regarding the Western Lands as the kingdom of the dead, ruled over by the murdered-and-resurrected god Osiris.

[11] Referencing *The Celtic Twilight* as imagined by W. B. Yeats, this appears to announce a pejorative approach to the Irish that informs the poem's next lines.

pints of porter to O'Siris, long since gone to pieces.[12] But just then a
bouquet of bruised roses bowled past towards studded Folsom, dragged the red half of my needle
east behind them, and American light posed as a municipal employee, brushing
sidewalks clean ahead of us before the trail went cold near 12th and Isis.[13] Idling on the
intersection he applied rear indicators stop signs eyes of dime-store skull rings like they
were a lipstick and we went on, cornering at 10th then over Howard Mission Market unto
Polk's fell[14] fundament where my fourteenth piece[15] was too often found, too often lost.

Transfixed I was on that defile, in mid-stride friezed, a side-seen pharaoh in intaglio stood

[12] The writer Connor Davey lived at 12 Prosper St, just off 16th and Market, with his girlfriend, between 1969 and Davey's death in 1976. Davey may be the figure referred to as 'O'Siris', a comical combination of the poem's Egyptian stylings and its anti-Irish insinuations. Strengthening this association, the mention of O'Siris being 'long since gone to pieces' could as easily be a callous reference to Davey having suffered a psychological breakdown just prior to his death, or a reference to the god Osiris, slain and cut into fourteen pieces by his brother, Set.

[13] This passage, ostensibly detailing how Belner compulsively followed a 'bouquet of bruised roses' – presumably a group of young gay men – towards the 'studded' leather bars of Folsom St, is suspicious only in that Belner's pursuit terminates at Isis St, tiny and insignificant but the only street in the city to take its name from an Egyptian goddess.

[14] A not-inappropriate pun: at its bottom end, or 'fundament', the famously gay cruising strip of Polk St adjoins the far shorter Fell St, a place which at that time was as grim and dispiriting as its name suggests.

[15] In the mythology of Osiris, the god is murdered and cut into fourteen pieces by Set, who scatters his brother's fragments throughout Egypt so that they could not be found and reassembled. However, the goddess Isis, being both the wife and sister of Osiris, searches the land and recovers thirteen of the dismembered god's body parts, with only Osiris's genitals remaining undiscovered. It thus seems safe to conclude that when Belner refers here to his 'fourteenth piece', he is talking about his apparently errant penis.

sighting up the twelve hours of his seamy night at Foster's Cafeteria,[16] Restau hot for rant,[17]
where once were zoo-browed gods at table: sunflower-headed Ra with slender consort,[18] or
dandy McCool all Finn-de-siècle,[19] shaven yet forever troubled by his Beard,[20] quite
estimable if not for his would-BeBehan crew and wolf-eyed bride.[21] And there amongst them,
sparkling in spilled cola on Formica was American light,[22] hung on every word, on every
scribbled napkin, also upstairs at the Wentley leaning southerly in on LaVigne to flood his
canvas,[23] and across the street at Hotel Young on Fern while sol yearned pale through fog[24] or else

[16] Still in Egyptian mode, 'the twelve hours of his seamy night' references the Twelve Hours of the Night through which the sun barge of Osiris must pass after descending past the horizon into the underworld. The phrase possibly also nods to the structure of Belner's poem, with its twelve stanzas marking the twelve hours of the poet's day. The Foster's Cafeteria mentioned once stood at 1200 Polk St, and it was here that Allen Ginsberg would gather for coffee and excited conversation in 1954 with the painter Robert LaVigne, Ginsberg's future lover Peter Orlovsky, and poets Michael and Joanna McClure. Given that this branch of the since vanished cafeteria chain was situated near the corner of Sutter and Polk, many blocks up from Belner's Market St vantage, we must suppose that the famously astigmatic poet was 'sighting' the premises in his mind's eye only.

[17] This puns upon the name Restau or Re-Stau, land of the Egyptian gods, and the word restaurant.

[18] Amongst the animal-headed gods assembled in Belner's cafeteria pantheon we should be unsurprised to find 'Sunflower Sutra' author Ginsberg, with Peter Orlovsky presumably supplying the 'slender consort'.

[19] Here we find the always well-dressed Michael McClure conflated with Irish folk-hero Finn McCool.

[20] A reference to McClure's continually raided and closed-down controversial play, *The Beard*.

[21] Interestingly, Belner seems reluctant to openly criticise McClure, who was, after all, a senior Beat figure and a friend of Ginsberg's. Instead, he opts for the suggestion that the otherwise 'quite estimable' McClure was let down by the company he kept, namely his 'would-BeBehan crew and wolf-eyed bride'. The former is almost certainly the same coterie of writers alluded to earlier, i.e. Brautigan, Doyle and Davey, while the 'wolf-eyed bride' is a dismissive reference to McClure's wife, the fine poet Joanna McClure, whose first volume of poetry, published in 1974, was titled *Wolf Eyes*.

[22] At this stage in the poem's development, Belner seems to be identifying the origins of the Beat movement as a source of American light, or at least suggesting it as an inspirational presence at those first get-togethers.

[23] The painter Robert LaVigne, an early and enduring friend of Allen Ginsberg, had rooms at the Hotel Wentley, which was directly upstairs from Foster's Cafeteria.

[24] This refers to the Hotel Young on nearby Fern Street. If we assume that 'sol' is a continuation of Belner's association of Allen Ginsberg with the sun-god Ra, as in line 39, then the Hotel Young is where Ginsberg lived during a melancholy and yearning break with boyfriend Peter Orlovsky.

went down on the burned-rubber angel,[25] who cracked wise, who flipped his monkey wrench, who
finally ran out of road and pranks and heartbeats, boarded an ethereal train and left
his lovely body by the trackside like forgotten luggage.[26] Here, then, was death's country, great
stone heads in chiselled afterlife looming in reminiscence from rooms over half the shabby delis,
gilt sarcophagi in all the bookstores, our illustrious cadavers, jewel-boned skeletons hung
decoratively from the conversation and American light was their marrow. Shrugging reverie, I let
him lead me, Market Street my aisle and ghosts the fabric of my wedding dress dragged after me,
past gradually encroaching bums and rubbled movie houses where American light poured once from
big silver faces on to smaller ones upturned,[27] the hypnogogic drift of nations at the edge of
sleep, and we processioned up to Kearney when St Patrick's clock was striking ten.

Should this horology fail to convince, assume I fucked a boy with every other

[25] Ginsberg would later write that his stay at the Hotel Young had afforded him the privacy for an unrestrained sexual encounter with a visiting Neal Cassady, iconic Beat muse and Jack Kerouac's driver for *On the Road*, who is without doubt the 'burned-rubber angel' that Belner alludes to here.

[26] After his time on the road with Kerouac and subsequent stint as driver of the bus 'Furthur' for Ken Kesey and his Merry Pranksters, Neal Cassady finally died in February, 1968, after a solitary drug-fuelled overnight hike through the San Miguel de Allende region. His comatose body was discovered just feet from a railroad track.

[27] We note in passing that American light is now the mesmeric radiance cast by America's film industry.

stanza break.[28] So, wiping-zipping-looking up on Kearney Street
I saw the ugly inn of holidays
wherein were hearts and feathers weighed, where towered American light unrepentant in the
dock while Shig and Larry gnawed their thumbnails and the sun himself away in Mexico, in
telepathic jungle, waited his foregone conclusion.[29] Saw across the street on Washington pure koan
Zen Nam Yuen, name where a restaurant wasn't, Snyder's one-hand-clap a finger snap as he chopped
sticks, stuck chops with vanished Jack[30] who typed a highway fading ribbon grey that
ran to Florida and bottle-mom and nonsense about Vietnam, then the black jackal man.[31] Saw,

[28] If we ignore the unpleasantness of these lines, they appear to be a means of reinforcing the poem's central 'Twelve Hours of the Day' conceit, as remarked upon in note 16, while at the same time bragging of Belner's sexual prowess. Given that *American Light* has twelve stanzas, we are clearly meant to infer that the day described in the poem involved at least six sexual encounters. This may have been an invention or an exaggeration, but for anyone familiar with San Francisco's gay scene during the pre-AIDS 1970s, it is not by any means an impossible tally, nor even a particularly unlikely one.

[29] Looking up Kearney St from Market St, Belner is here describing the Holiday Inn that has replaced the Hall of Justice where, in the closing months of 1957, the poet Lawrence Ferlinghetti and his business partner Shigeyoshi Murao of City Lights Books underwent their famous obscenity trial over the publication of Allen Ginsberg's *Howl and Other Poems*. If the pair 'gnawed their thumbnails' it was not without just cause: as publishers, it was they who were facing the loss of their business, liberty or livelihoods, rather than the poem's author. During the trial, Ginsberg himself was in Mexico hunting for the fabled hallucinogen yagé, or telepathine, claiming to have always known that the favourable outcome of the hearings was a foregone conclusion, although Ferlinghetti and Murao appear to have a somewhat different recollection of events.

[30] The Nam Yuen at 740 Washington was the favourite Chinatown eatery of poet, Zen scholar and environmentalist Gary Snyder. It was here that Snyder introduced Jack Kerouac to both Chinese cuisine and the use of chopsticks when the latter was newly arrived in San Francisco.

[31] This line is a bleak summary of Jack Kerouac's later years. After the enormous success of *On the Road* seemed, at least to its author, to have reduced all later works to footnotes in the eyes of the literary public, Kerouac grew steadily more depressed and his drinking worsened. Moving back in with his co-dependent alcoholic mother, his conservativism and anti-communism became more pronounced, until his support for the conflict in Vietnam caused a rift with former Beat colleagues like Ginsberg who were fervently anti-war. Kerouac's cruel disowning of his biological daughter Jan was also partly based upon his aversion to her 'peacenik' hippy tendencies. Kerouac eventually died in 1969, aged 47, hence the allusion here to funerary deity Anubis as 'the black jackal man', in keeping with *American Light*'s Egyptian imagery.

up on Jackson, Mort Sahl and Dick Gregory concealing fists in punchlines, Lenny Bruce with
hungry eyes like blackened spoons, outside the hungry i, and such are the breath-taken
show bills of eternity.[32] Blue flame was in the holy lantern skulls hanging in
backstreets right across the city and American light gushing from quizzical sockets, spilling
poetry on hangovers, on love affairs, on tantrums, whiskey scribes bemoaning lost
papyri,[33] 'Love Me Tender' on a somewhere jukebox that hymned Memphis and the valley of the
king. Saw, too, the ectoplasm of deceased hotel rooms on Columbus, Paradise kicking his
shoes off, sleeping in a marinade of cars, of crockery, hep Negro script and Chinese
lullaby.[34] Crowned corpses shuffling after me, I trod a block just past the subway's
underworld mouth to Montgomery where I went up into a San Franciscan Book of Gone.

I hauled all nine perspiring bodies of my soul[35] through Sutter Bush Pine California Clay,

[32] The hungry i club at 599 Jackson was one of the key performance venues about which Beat society revolved, featuring socially aware comedians like Sahl, Gregory, and the drug-addicted Lenny Bruce amongst its dazzling roster of hip entertainers.

[33] This may refer obliquely to an episode in 1975 when Belner apparently lost a manuscript copy of Connor Davey's debut novel, *Coming Forth by Day in America*, that Davey had left with Belner for the revered older writer's consideration and comments. Possibly Davey's work was one of the patience-nibbling 'glyphic corpses' referred to in footnote 7.

[34] These lines are an evocation of the long-vanished Bell Hotel at 39 Columbus, mentioned by Kerouac in *Desolation Angels* as a favourite stopover on his San Francisco visits. The inclusion of 'hep Negro script' would seem to be a glancing reference to sometime Bell resident, black working-class writer Al Sublette. We will find that in *American Light*, women, people of colour, representatives of the underclass and those of Irish extraction all seem to merit no more than glancing references, unless exempted through being friends of Allen Ginsberg. 'Paradise' is, of course, a reference to Sal Paradise, the self-based principal character of Kerouac's *On the Road*.

[35] According to ancient Egyptian metaphysics, the human soul has nine separate components, or bodies.

beneath the tomb of interred Transamerica,[36] and kept my dwindling khaibit[37] to the left. Hawk with a
human head, alert for capon, the heart's spirit moved past Jackson,[38] soaring on the
torch-song updraft of a disappeared Black Cat, got trick-or-treated out of business 1963, still
filled by spectres and conjectures, by fine drinkers, problem writers, Steinbeck in mid-
werewolf-shift to Faulkner.[39] Here, queer fountainhead, Stonewall not yet a course of
brick, where Sarria padded out her falsie empire in a drizzle of dull Eisenhower, and
kohl-eyed queens nursed vipers at pretended bosoms.[40] O'er the way in onion-layers of purple
history were carven profiles conga-lining midst the dust of decades: Garry Goodrow's tragic

[36] Here, Belner playfully misprises the Transamerica Pyramid at Washington and Montgomery as the tomb of a buried pharaoh named Transamerica.

[37] The khaibit is the part of the human soul corresponding to the shadow.

[38] The ba or heart-soul, another division of the Egyptian soul, was depicted as a hawk with a human head. From Belner's reference to 'capon' here, along with the opening declaration of the fourth stanza, we should probably assume that the hawk representing the poet's heart-soul has a stated fondness for chicken.

[39] These lines celebrate the Black Cat Cafe at 710 Montgomery, closed down after a Halloween-night raid in 1963. Its clientele of hard-drinking literary figures included William Saroyan, Truman Capote and John Steinbeck, depicted here metamorphosing into the famously alcohol-destroyed William Faulkner.

[40] Aside from its reputation as haven for drunken literati, the Black Cat is justly recognised as one of the earliest flowerings of American gay culture. Long before the Greenwich Village Stonewall Riots of 1969 sparked the modern gay pride movement, the Black Cat was, in the 1950s, an almost unique meeting place for openly gay individuals, presided over by drag artist Jose Sarria, who performed as the Empress Norton, in honour of visionary San Franciscan eccentric and self-proclaimed emperor of America, Joshua Norton. Norton was the titular spirit of Belner's earlier San Francisco-based poetry collection, *Norton's Empire* (Nailhead Books, 1970).

grin and brothers smothering and blackbirds singing from their low-wage cage.[41] Not far, up on the
incline's right, was drama by committee where fair McAllure had his barb busted for a bogus
blow job, real ones in a dozen titty bars along the street,[42] and first-night Fenians fawning on that
eighth part of the self that is my name.[43] With ab in mouth, with double at my heels and shadow
trampled now below them,[44] I climbed into apple-blue noon[45] and, at Broadway, smacked by awe,
kneeled speechless to behold 1010 Montgomery in where the undefeated sun[46] squeezed an
American light out from hypodermic saints madhouses cock-suckers, squeezed Moloch

[41] Belner is here recalling the glory days of the Purple Onion, still there at 140 Columbus St. This quintessential San Francisco cellar club hosted the earliest performances of great entertainers and artists such as the Smothers Brothers and the Kingston Trio. Garry Goodrow, mentioned here, was a well-liked stand-up comedian and actor – his movie credits include 1973's *Steelyard Blues* – who also appeared at the Purple Onion. In the well-known group photograph of prominent Beats that was the cover of *City Lights Journal* #3, to which we will be returning, Goodrow is the figure standing on the far right with the comical hat and the admittedly 'tragic grin'. The reference to 'blackbirds singing from their low-wage cage' is a by-now-predictable side-lining of the writer Maya Angelou, author of *I Know Why the Caged Bird Sings*, who sang at the Purple Onion in the 1950s.

[42] The Committee Theater at 836 Montgomery was the venue at which Michael McClure hoped to present his play *The Beard* in 1966 after a previous theatre had been threatened with closure for the play's brief inclusion of simulated oral sex. In the event, the performance at the Committee Theater was shut down after one night on the same grounds, this on a block otherwise crowded with topless bars and strip clubs.

[43] The 'first-night Fenians' referred to here are, unsurprisingly, McClure's writer friends of Irish ancestry who were attending the play's first (and last) night. The mention of 'fawning' might be specifically directed at the writer Connor Davey: *The Beard*'s performance at the Committee was the first occasion that Davey had met Belner, who at that point was the younger author's literary hero. Belner may have interpreted this enthusiasm as mere fawning over a famous name – the name, or ren, being the eighth body of the ancient Egyptian soul.

[44] More divisions of the soul: the ab is the heart, the ka is the double, and the khaibit, as earlier, is the shadow.

[45] This is an inversion of the enigmatic phrase 'noon-blue apples', related to the Rennes-le-Château mysteries. Since this appears to have no relevance to Egyptology or the poem's other themes, we can only suppose that its inclusion is solely for the purpose of underlining Belner's one-stanza-per-hour structure.

[46] Since 1010 Montgomery was the address at which Allen Ginsberg composed most of *Howl* in 1956, we must assume that he is 'the undefeated sun', an Anglicisation of late Roman solar deity Sol Invictus.

from the Francis Drake,[47] squeezed from our blood-striped rag a starry howl, the ibis-word of Thoth,
then, sacred with profanity, birthed in this hepcat land his language of the birds.[48]

And with that wind of syntax at my back swelling my shirt-front sails, did I lean my
trireme to port on Broadway, bound for Orient and its curled dragon rooftops in cascade down
Powell and Stockton.[49] Put in to the far shore of Columbus by its bubbling ferlinghetto of
downtrodden paragraphs,[50] where once in intermittent diamond rain I stood amongst a pantheon, with
giant Bunford blocking out posterity;[51] meanwhile American light, blind drunk and promiscuous,
licked every other sainted face till they shone with his spittled phosphors. Here admirers sometimes,
tetra-shoaled, to tug the sleeve or zipper if in luck in vogue in stock,[52] but through its

[47] The Sir Francis Drake Hotel at 450 Powell, witnessed while under the influence of peyote, was Ginsberg's inspiration for the vision of Moloch that presides over one of *Howl*'s most memorable passages.

[48] Here, Belner equates *Howl* with an utterance of ibis-headed Egyptian writing-and-magic god Thoth, who was said to have created human speech after 'the language of the birds'. This phrase was also used by alchemists to indicate a particularly rich and symbol-laden poetry whereby profound alchemical ideas might be conveyed.

[49] A trireme is a three-mast sailing vessel of the ancient world, and the overall sense of these lines would appear to be that Belner turned left on Broadway and headed towards Chinatown.

[50] This is a less than celebratory reference to Lawrence Ferlinghetti's City Lights Books at 261 Columbus Avenue which, since its inception in 1953, has been the vital central pivot of Beat literature. In its thirty-two years thus far as a publisher, however, it is yet to publish any of the works of Harmon Belner.

[51] The front cover of *City Lights Journal* #3, referred to above, is a group photograph by Larry Keenan Jr of many leading Beat figures gathered in front of the bookshop, with Ferlinghetti at the rear. Between Gary Goodrow on the far right and the white-hatted Richard Brautigan next to him, we can see one eyebrow and the side-parting of a young Harmon Belner. 'Bunford' was Allen Ginsberg's contemptuous nickname for Brautigan.

[52] Apparently an admission that Belner has used City Lights as a potential pick-up spot for literary groupies, since the bookshop is as far as the poet gets from home in the course of the poem, this raises the possibility that the excursion described in *American Light* was conducted entirely in search of random sexual assignations.

front pane now was only my reflection interesting, new, in an attention-grabbing
jacket, who presided over the display's headstone octavos, half transparent, a Beat essence in
symbolic superimposition on that lexical necropolis.[53] Self-edited from
picture-window, I next loitered brief down alley through to Grant, pulp-dusted seam of gumshoe
dream and there in my all-seeing private eye was Hammett-dashing, lighting cigarettes I don't
smoke behind upturned collars that I wasn't wearing, and hot on some heartless mummy's gilded
case through the sand-blasted sockets of a city where the bigshots were all
animals from the neck up, and everyone got taken for a ride by noir dogs in the end.[54] Last-
glancing down the backtrack crack, with Gee almighty rolling thunder at the Hibbing

[53] Here we have Belner finding his own reflection to be the only thing of interest in City Lights' front window.

[54] An unusual passage, with Belner using the alleyway between Grant and Columbus as an excuse for this sudden veer into Egypt-inflected noir private-eye imagery. Interestingly, in 1982 and therefore six years after Connor Davey's death, Davey's widowed partner found a previously unsuspected draft copy of Davey's presumed-lost novel, *Coming Forth by Day in America*, to be published by the Hillwood Press in 1986. We may usefully compare Belner's lines here with the opening paragraph of Davey's absurdist Egyptian-noir Beat novel: 'The sun was a big Egyptian bastard that had finally caught up with Brendan O'Jaysus, after he'd been avoiding it for months. It came through his slatted blinds like gold planks, falling off of a delivery truck to bury the poor, nearly dead man as he slept there on the coffee-ringed sarcophagus that he was using for a desk. Startled awake, he came out fighting. "Up and Atem," he unfathomabled, taking wild swings at the glittering intruder. But the thuggish cosmic phenomenon was too fast for him, and anyway was made of photons through which Brendan's fists, made out of reinforced ham or the like, passed ineffectually. Still, he managed to punch almost all the other objects in his office, bedroom, kitchen and, if he was honest, sometimes bathroom, before giving up with a despairing cry of "How and why do I remain alive?" He sat on the edge of his fold-down coffin, located an unpunched cigarette, and bitterly accepted that he was a two- or even one-bit private eye in Ptolemaic San Francisco, where the bigshots were all beasts from the neck up. Sure, the whole city was a morbid Disneyland.'

kid who sang for homesick subterraneans,[55] I bore the jar that held my rumbling
guts on to Vesuvio, that I might hazard pyroclastic flow and out-eat the devourer of the dead.[56]

Ripe to a margin of solidity, tomato schists wore mozzarella pearls without compare and I
wound pasta bandage-wraps about my fork to whip-quick flick cream beads of topaz on my
constellated chin, then hot bread that bled butter, coffee custards, crystal wine
astringent in the coated throat.[57] Tables that echoed still North Beach Italian anarchists, fuse-eyed,
denouncing Mussolini; Kerouac, boozed and confused, missing his dinner
date with Henry Miller; Dylan Thomas in wet-run rehearsal for a Chelsea checkout and phantoms
diaphanous of burly girlesque belles from down the block swelling Lenoir's silk stocking
flock.[58] I, with a clavicle of alphabet, unlocked the mealtime mausolea and released their

[55] If we assume that 'Gee almighty' is a further reference to Ginsberg, and that 'the Hibbing kid' is Bob Dylan, born in Hibbing, Minnesota, then these lines refer to Ginsberg and Dylan being photographed in this same alley during the middle 1960s. Michael McClure, unmentioned here, was also present. The mention of 'rolling thunder' is a reference to the Rolling Thunder Revue tour that Dylan and Ginsberg undertook in 1975.

[56] Within the time frame of the poem, it is now approximately 1:00 p.m., and Belner has decided to have lunch at the Vesuvio Cafe, just across the intervening alley from City Lights at 255 Columbus. The Devourer of the Dead is an Egyptian funerary entity, sometimes depicted as a gigantic python arranged in intestinal loops and coils, that is said to ingest those souls whose hearts outweigh the feather of truth on the scales of judgement.

[57] While Belner's repast doesn't seem to derive from the regular Vesuvio menu, we cannot rule out that the establishment may have made exceptions for such a revered customer. Or he may have eaten somewhere else.

[58] Here we have a recap of Vesuvio's rich history: in the thirties and forties, the whole North Beach area was a haven for Italian anarchists. In 1960, a possibly nervous Jack Kerouac drank his way out of a dinner engagement with Henry Miller up in Carmel Highlands, while Dylan Thomas got ruinously drunk at Vesuvio during the same American tour that would end up killing him at New York's Chelsea Hotel in 1953. Henri Lenoir, the café's proprietor, had started out selling silk stockings to the neighbourhood's burlesque performers.

flavorous memories, American light winking lustful from my cutlery and dribbling down the
goblet's bulbous flank, shining approval on the sand-dance crypt-script in this
notebook, on this golden Parker stylus when the mortal bill is squared. Replete, I came
forth from that aromatic tomb by afternoon, prohibited names chiselled on its
threshold there, with foremost this coast's coarse Gregorian corsair and such of less
note as Shameless O'Sullivan, bards barred eternal with their appellations O'Zymandias dust
scuffed by my exit.[59] Once, the solar centre of his naked, starving generation sat and wrote here in the
twilight of his heterosexuality, waiting on girls who showed too late to bait him from queer
fate with soulmate Saint Peter the Great[60] and heaven's gate swung open on bohemian Pentecost, and
tongue fired with its sparks I cut back through to Grant, was down on Sutter Street before I knew.

Past its meridian, the Beaten soul's winged disc commenced descent, the movement of a
movement into afterlife, hearts quivering in their balance against Maat-black vulture truth; shied by

[59] Carven into the cement outside Vesuvio's front door are the names of those permanently barred by reason of their drunken behaviour. The 'coarse Gregorian corsair' on this list is obviously Gregory Corso, while 'Shameless O'Sullivan' is the itinerant San Francisco street-poet, Paddy O'Sullivan, to which we can only remark, 'Again with the Irish'. We would also draw attention to those names gouged into Vesuvio's doorstep that Belner does not make even derogatory reference to here, including the poet Janis Blue and the almost unique Beat writer of colour, Bob Kaufman.

[60] The café is also the place where, in 1954, Allen Ginsberg wrote 'In Vesuvio's Waiting for Sheila', about his then girlfriend Sheila Williams, whom he would soon thereafter break up with before commencing his relationship with Peter Orlovsky and writing *Howl*.

time's random ape of judgement.[61] Over Sutter, back in the before, stood a White House
department store whereat the Driving Force gypped his off-road fiancée with a Woolworth's five-
and-dime engagement ring, caught later naked basking in the risen Sun or triangled to his most
beatific passenger and O, O, O Osiris, let us of our tawdry salesman cheapness be
acquitted.[62] For our cruelties thefts deceptions vanities deliver us not to constrictors critical and
intestinal who digest remains of the remaindered, nor interrogate, by negative confession, eating
cakes left for the dead or putting out of fires before their time.[63] Freighted with crime the spirit

[61] Here, at approximately 2:00 p.m. in the poem's chronology, we see Belner's spirits and those of the whole Beat movement declining as if in sympathy with the gradually sinking sun. Certainly, *American Light* seems to take on a darker and more regretful tone as the poem moves towards its sunset. The reference to 'hearts quivering in their balance' alludes again to the Egyptian concept of weighing the heart against a black vulture feather, symbol of the goddess Maat. Sometimes, presiding over, or at least present, at this ceremony, we find the cynocephalus, otherwise the dog-headed Ape of Thoth, whose arbitrary and apparently senseless interventions are at least impartial. There is a sense here that Belner's concern is for how he – and by extension the Beat movement – might come to be judged by history and literary criticism in the fullness of time.

[62] The White House department store that stood between Sutter and Post had a jewellery department from which, in 1948, Neal Cassady had promised to buy a wedding ring for his pregnant girlfriend Carolyn, who would go on to write revealingly about her life with Kerouac and Cassady. Having arranged to meet Cassady and a friend of his outside the store, from her vantage, Carolyn watched Cassady's friend buy the ring at the five-and-dime Woolworth's outlet next door, then enter the White House by a side entrance to emerge from the front. This was the start of a difficult marriage, during which she returned home to find her husband in bed with swiftly evicted house guest Allen Ginsberg, and later found herself in a relationship with Jack Kerouac during those periods when Cassady was away from home.

[63] The 'constrictors critical and intestinal' is another reference to the Devourer of the Dead, perhaps in this instance seen as the literary critics who will digest and deliver their verdict on a writer's work after he or she is deceased. The rest of these lines are derived from a section of *The Egyptian Book of the Dead* known as 'the negative confession', in which the soul being judged swears not to have committed a long list of offences. Why Belner, out of this lengthy list, should feel particularly uneasy about the 'eating of cakes left for the dead', or the 'putting out of fires before their time' is perhaps a question best left for another day.

sank on its Ulyssean avenue, homebound for Ithaca and Paul's Penelope,[64] and crossing Post
thought of its ghost-house past Van Ness,[65] where Brakhage saw with his own
eyes, where Jess and Robert happy-coupled in their haunted ballroom[66] while down Franklin some
side-ordered Moriarty sweetheart hurdled throat-cut from a roof and into
gravity when horseplay played out the wrong way, so many bop wraiths in the sway of Duncan's
coffin dance floor now.[67] American the light, likewise American the dark shape cast, cut out from
sweaters, old berets, and neath my generation's yellowing penumbra I
veered over Geary, barrelled past O'Farrell, next, with head on backwards looking to the path

[64] Belner slips from Egyptian mode to Greek here, becoming Odysseus on his home journey, with Caledonia St now become Ithaca, while Belner's lover Paul Landesman transformed into Penelope.

[65] This alludes to the Charles Addams-style residence at 1350 Franklin, known as 'the Ghost House'.

[66] The above residence, formerly a palatial mansion, was home across the years to poet Philip Lamantia and his wife the photographer Goldian Nesbit, film-maker Stan Brakhage who made *The Act of Seeing with One's Own Eyes*, and long-term partners poet Robert Duncan and painter Jess Collins, who were the house's principal occupants during the Beat glory days of the 1950s.

[67] These lines present what is arguably one of the most ignoble and shameful episodes in Beat history. In 1955, Neal Cassady – *On the Road*'s Dean Moriarty – persuaded his girlfriend Natalie Jackson to impersonate his wife Carolyn Cassady and withdraw $10,000 from Carolyn's account. His plan was to multiply the money by betting it on a horse, then return the original sum to his wife's account before she knew it was missing. Inevitably, the 'horseplay played out the wrong way', and the horse lost. Natalie Jackson was distraught over her part in the crime, and though Cassady left her in the care of Jack Kerouac, on 30 November she cut her own throat and then ran across the rooftops adjoining her apartment at 1041 Franklin, pursued by a police officer who was attempting to help her, before jumping or falling to her death. On learning what had happened, the terrified Cassady and Kerouac both claimed not to have known Jackson. What is interesting is Belner's deployment of the tragedy at this point in his poem's narrative. Belner seems to be in a state of penitence and seeking atonement, but the Jackson story presents this as if Belner is seeking forgiveness for the generalised sins of the entire Beat movement, rather than for any that might be his alone. Is Belner attempting to bury the specific in the general? The final reference to 'Duncan's coffin dance floor' alludes to the above-mentioned Robert Duncan and the apartment that he shared with Jess Collins at the 'Ghost House', formerly the mansion's ballroom.

behind,[68] my mourning barque bumped Market's southmost
bank, whence west I went to boneland.

Crowded numinous were apparitions picketing the Palace, TV
interference patterns
crackling from 1963, Beat Amon holding his hand-lettered howl
at Bloody Mama Nhu, Vietnam
gestapo moll, and welching Lew with grifter grin joins in this
first of many Southeast Asian
interventions.[69] Parasoled in private shade I made my way by the
disfigured Federal Writers' Project joint in where did Rexroth
map our typewriter topography, a
dusting of Depression deco on its fenestrated upper case but
faceless otherwise,[70] and had my
hackles jackalled further down at 721, made monochrome, a
flicker of intruding future
mooching through a famed and faded fifties photograph where
there below the Market Street
marquee promising Tarzan Wild One Stranger Wore a Gun
hunks Tootin' Car-Man Cassady,
his Franklin suicide-blonde cheek to cheek, and we have
harboured such betrayals as I cannot

[68] This would seem to refer to the hieroglyphic figure of a god with his head reversed that is found in *The Egyptian Book of the Dead* and known as 'He who comes forth backwards'. In the context here, it appears to signify merely that Belner is in a reflective or retrospective mood as he begins to head back down Market St.

[69] If we assume that 'Beat Amon' is a further deification of Allen Ginsberg, then this passage commemorates the demonstration outside the Palace Hotel at 633–655 Market in October 1963, protesting against a visit by Madame Nhu, wife of Vietnam's secret-police chief, which was the first political protest that Ginsberg attended. Also in attendance was poet Lew Welch, who liked to present himself as a Beat confidence-trickster.

[70] During the depression, the Federal Writers' Project had its offices at 717 Market, where the poet Kenneth Rexroth worked as editor on the project's American Guide Series for California and San Francisco.

speak.[71] Now flailed and penitent progressed my pilgrimage a hundred
numbers on to the Pacific Building where, back in the woe-beat gone, there stood the Brotherhood
of Trailroad Rainmen from when On the Road jumped tracks to On the Rail and rode that
lonesome whistle down the wildly worded line.[72] Past 5th the psychic print of a Vic Tanny's in
tenebrous jockstrap steam, that motorbike Mike who nobody didn't like whereat mclured
musculatures into the limbs and language,[73] so side-walking styl-ised on a sun-stained
sidewalk up to 6th I stock-still stopped and saw American light blare like a delinquent radio
straight down Golden Gate and blinded thus by avenue I thought again of bridge.

Souls in suspension between blue and bay amidst a choral swell of wind in the soprano
wire, their unendurable complexities resolved as plain ballistics, unpowered objects in
trajectory and splash unheard above the Nile-wide waters. Ferrous tangerine are
hanging loops of gartered stocking steel, unwritten lines running away into a boil of purpling

[71] Moving a little further down Market, Belner here finds himself walking through the setting – at 721, where one of the street's many movie theatres used to stand – of Allen Ginsberg's most well-known photograph, showing Neal Cassady and the tragic Natalie Jackson embracing happily beneath a hoarding with the same show bill that Belner details here, just a few months before the events that would lead to Jackson's death. Again, Belner seems unduly penitent over generalised Beat 'betrayals' to which he was in no way connected.

[72] The old Pacific building at 821 Market housed, in the 1940s, the offices of the Brotherhood of Railroad Trainmen, during the period when both Neal Cassady and Jack Kerouac were working for Southern Pacific.

[73] Michael McClure, newly arrived in San Francisco in the 1950s, worked at the Vic Tanny Gym which stood at 949 Market. In his spare time, motorcycle-enthusiast McClure would work out using the gym's facilities or would be writing poetry.

vapour, off to next world Sausalito in the non-existent distance.
There we tremble on an edge of
balance and deliberation, scarcely light of heart or yet of feather
heavy, fixed by our conclusion neither we nor world were real
things at the last. Seeking in
hopeless fog a clarity we take our single long step from fictitious
history into the truth of
empty air, and in our breast is all beat and all movement ceased,
an end I please believe me
never sought, a misjudged rhythm that I cannot now correct.[74]
Of this mind, then, and
followed close by black bipedal dog, in self-wrought ankle chains I
shuffled on, and up at 7th's corner was arrested by the Greyhound
Station's unimaginable
absence, ghostly orchestra of throaty engine, sighing brake, echoing voice against a
roof celestially distant. Gasoline, piss, cigarettes, love in the

[74] This sudden associational leap from Golden Gate Avenue to the Golden Gate Bridge demands scrutiny. For one thing, throughout *American Light*, the locations that Belner passes through or even thinks about are chiefly employed as reasons to rhapsodise about the Beat history associated with those places, providing much of the poem's substance. Here, however, we have roughly half a stanza that seems to contain no specific Beat references at all, and which instead appears to be a meditation on the Golden Gate Bridge as a favoured spot for suicides, once more informed by the sense of penitence and ambiguous guilt that we have noted in the preceding stanzas. Nor, if we exclude the mention of 'Nile-wide waters' and a further allusion to hearts being weighed against feathers, does there appear to be the same density of Egyptian reference in this passage as we have noted previously. Nevertheless, the notion of Sausalito on the bridge's far side as a 'next world' can be usefully compared with this passage from chapter ten of Connor Davey's *Coming Forth by Day in America*: 'With a defiant yelp of pain, O'Jaysus drove the back of his head into the oncoming Egyptian ceremonial mace to show what he thought of it. A black pool of unconsciousness swallowed him, but very quickly retched him back up with a look of appalled disbelief. It came to him in depressing increments that he was in the back seat of a Ford Sarcophagus, tied up with sandy bandages, and being driven at ferocious speed across the bridge of Golden Fate by two dog-headed fellers who were jackaling his hackles fit to burst. "What is it with you underworld enforcers that you're always dogs?", he irrelevanted. "You've got Cerberus; you've got Anubis; you've got Pluto. I'd always thought the dog a relatively sunny animal. And where, might I ask, are you taking me, wrapped up as if I were all wound and damage?" His canine captors snickered their reply past flappy tongues and horrifying teeth. "Yer bound fer the hereafter, boyo, all the way to Sacred Sausalito and an afterlife that's more an afterthought in your case." Brendan haughted snortily, "Why, Sausalito's just a fairy tale made up by Catholics. It's an evasive metaphor for death, in my opinion." "Have it your way," gruffed the ruffians, and backed his head into another ceremonial mace. Darkness swallowed him again, but not without an apprehensive grimace.'

washrooms and American light jemmying the eyelids of Old Angel Desolation
fresh out of Seattle; winking in distractingly through dusty basement windows at shift
workers weary from beatitude, poetry's planetary pivot and deadeye Ed Dorn, slaves building
tombs from baggage, like us all, and O to be again there, blameless in our unstained morning.[75]

Dragging casket-leaded legs I, carrion, carried on to ford Van Ness, five o'clock
fingerings of opaque damp down distant boulevards, grey and vermicular. Filmy in after-
image stared a phantom Fillmore from forgetful murk, gratefully dead and crowned with
album-cover crania; with the anthems of its sons.[76] Desirous of a streetcar bier bearing this body
west, this gold-leaf rot to rest, I boarded there the bump and rattle of my
burial bed and from a left-side statue seat glanced off at lost Valencia as we crossed,
stalking a wounded sun to its aortal gush on the horizon's blade.[77] Down there was where the
wheelman's wife was made to wait, winter of '48, 109 Liberty but baby-bound until

[75] This passage resurrects the Greyhound station that formerly stood at 7th and Market, mentioned in *Desolation Angels* as Jack Kerouac's point of arrival in San Francisco after a journey from Seattle. Presumably, 'poetry's planetary pivot' is another heliocentric nod to Allen Ginsberg, who, in 1956, worked in the Greyhound station's baggage department when unable to find railroad work like Kerouac and Cassady. The wonderful Black Mountain poet Ed Dorn was working in the same department at the same time, but on a different shift.

[76] These lines seem to be recasting the Fillmore West at Van Ness and Market in an Egyptian light by alluding to the Egypt-referencing Grateful Dead, their *Anthem of the Sun* and their skull-festooned record jackets.

[77] Draped as it is in funerary flourishes and allusions to Tennessee Williams, we should infer that at this point Belner boarded San Francisco's historic streetcar line, that would take him to the western end of 16th St.

absconded dad drove home from Denver and beyond, with his besotted buddy Jack he
picked up on the track in back, and thus that hard Beat road begins, and here its point of
vanishing.[78] Down that way also the book sepulchre graced once by one gregariously coarse and a
bum-stumble dross of lesser drums, more muted beats, that shabby planet since
abandoned.[79] On a darkening incline slid my funerary chariot, caught in the burning solar
barge's wake, with each street passed some ritual stage McCoppin Pearl Guerrero of our mortal
process into afterwards Duboce Dolores and at 16th I dismounted to the gathering
crepuscule, American light some heroic punk who's dying on a fire escape, gone from that high-up
ledge where you just saw him, and as San Francisco Nuit bent to croquet-hoop under the misted
stars, then came a buried thunder of the coffin-boat, and Sunset underground at Buena Vista Park.[80]

[78] It was at Carolyn Cassady's apartment at 109 Liberty, referred to here, that Carolyn – demoted here to 'the wheelman's wife' – waited over the winter of 1948, with a newborn baby, for husband and father Neal to return from a trip to Denver and the East Coast. When he finally arrived home in early February, he had new-found friend Jack Kerouac with him, having just completed the epic cross-country drive that would become *On the Road*. In his suddenly melancholy mood, Belner seems to construe this area as the place where the Beat vision began and also, for reasons that are possibly clear only to the poet himself, where that vision finds its end.

[79] A reference here to the Abandoned Planet bookstore that once stood at 518 Valencia, a faintly shabby but much-loved and respected literary outlet that, amongst its clientele, may well have numbered Gregory Corso, as Belner maintains here, but was much better known as the hangout of the magnificent Jack Micheline. Eking out a hand-to-mouth existence on the streets, particularly in these later years, Micheline is an exemplary poet, painter, and early proponent of jazz–poetry who has performed with Charlie Mingus, and is regarded by many as one of the few genuinely authentic Beat figures, relegated to Belner's 'bum-stumble dross' in this passage.

[80] More Egyptian window dressing: Nuit is the Egyptian goddess of the night sky, usually depicted as bending in an arch across the heavens. The reference to the Sunset rail line that runs under Buena Vista Park is refitted here to reflect the Egyptian concept that when the solar barge has completed its journey across the daytime skies, it must next commence its subterranean passage through the underworld and the Twelve Hours of the Night; literally a 'Sunset underground'.

Last-miling home to Caledonia as onyx settled on a blotter district drinking ink and doorways
fat with black, American light blue in muzzle-flash, flypaper yellow in oncoming
headlight, waded Pond and on the street where nothing prospered after all, made haunted
halt.[81] Here ends the road, here where the bridge was out, here where we
broke off in mid-howl and pharaoh-hounds snapped bones for their jazz jelly. Here, our

[81] If Belner's day and poem are, respectively, twelve hours and twelve stanzas in length, then we can perhaps deduce that this Beat-encompassing walk took place around 16 March in 1979, when the sun would have risen at 6:18 a.m. and set at 6:18 p.m. The fact that Belner makes his 'haunted halt' on 'the street where nothing prospered after all' is seemingly a reference to Prosper St, which, as we have pointed out in note 12, was the residence of writer Connor Davey and his partner between 1969 and Davey's death in 1976. This may be a good point at which to examine the Davey story in greater detail, given that the young author, unnamed, seems to be a hidden undercurrent that runs throughout Belner's poem. Born 1941 in Chicago, Connor Davey arrived in San Francisco in the summer of 1964 as a good-looking young man in his early twenties, openly besotted with Beat literature and, in particular, the writings of Harmon Belner, whose poem *Harlem Gold* in 1959 had made a tremendous impression on the then teenage Davey. Davey, then living just off Filbert St in North Beach, soon became friends with Michael and Joanna McClure, and through them encountered many of the scene's other luminaries, notably McClure's friends Kirby Doyle and Richard Brautigan. It was during a late-night drinking session with this latter pair that Doyle had remarked on how terrible it would be to be a poet in ancient Sumer, having to carry clay tablets around to jot down inspirations on. This had evolved, by the conversation's end, into the notion of a similarly burdened private eye in the ancient world, providing the seed idea for what would, almost a decade later, grow into Davey's first book, *Coming Forth by Day in America*, and possibly inspire Richard Brautigan's delightful 1977 novel, *Dreaming of Babylon*. Davey met Harmon Belner in 1966 at the sole performance of Michael McClure's *The Beard* at the Committee Theater, as mentioned in notes 42 and 43. In 1969 Davey moved into his new girlfriend's apartment on Prosper St, which happened to be just a few blocks from where Belner lived with Paul Landesman at 15 Caledonia St. In 1975, after typing the first draft of *Coming Forth by Day in America*, Davey loaned it to Belner, eager for his literary hero's comments. When this commentary was unforthcoming and Davey at last plucked up the courage to ask the older writer if he had any thoughts on the manuscript, Belner at first claimed that he must have lost it, and then later questioned whether Davey had ever loaned him the work in the first instance. Believing the only copy of his life's work to be thus disappeared, Davey grew increasingly distraught and angry, at one point confronting Belner after a chance meeting on Kearney St, the incident referred to in note 33. Finally, in a spiral of depression caused by the apparent loss of his work, unaware that the careful longhand notebooks containing his original draft had fallen inside his writing desk where they would later be found by his widowed partner, Davey took his own life by jumping from the Golden Gate Bridge on 16 March 1976, which, strangely, would appear to be the date commemorated in Belner's poem.

cardiac weight, the plundered scrolls now firelighters in a
tumbled Alexandrian
library.[82] Night's ashes in my hair I rolled this dung-ball soul past
Sanchez, over Church in these
skull-sugar territories and so came at last upon Our Lady of the
Sorrows by her dried-tear creek,[83]
shining albino through impenetrable wino dark. Here dreamed
the dead, Miwok, Ohlone, hunting
happy in the ground; Mexican governors or commandants;
victims of
vigilance and other martyrs, where we were the dream that
clouded bone brows in their cobwebbed
sleep.[84] Here too, reviled was I, by Coghlan Catholics cast from
that dolorous basilica, flinted
hysterias stinging past my ears wherein that avian shrill rings
still, respects rejected and
atonement inadmissible, too late for truth's jet plume.[85]
Conscience away at war, I

[82] If 'the road' at the start of this section is the same Kerouacian road that Belner claimed had begun at Carolyn Cassady's apartment on Liberty, as per note 78, then Belner seems to feel that Prosper St is where the Beat dream reached its end point – or, perhaps more accurately, where Harmon Belner's Beat dream was concluded. Similarly, if the phrase 'where the bridge was out' refers to Connor Davey's suicide, as described above, then perhaps the young writer's death is not unconnected with Belner's sense of his personal Beat dream being extinguished here. The final line, with its 'cardiac weight' signifying Belner's heavy heart, seems to refer to the burning of manuscripts at the Library at Alexandria that became emblematic of the commencement of the Dark Ages, unless of course Belner is referring to some other 'plundered scrolls' that may have ended up in flames.

[83] These lines refer to the Mission Dolores and the adjoining Mission Dolores Basilica on 16th St, with the original mission being San Francisco's oldest surviving structure, originally named after a nearby creek, Arroyo de Nuestra Señora de los Dolores, or 'Our Lady of Sorrows Creek'.

[84] Interred at the mission are many prominent San Franciscans, including some thousands of the Native American Miwok and Ohlone people who helped construct the Mission Dolores; the first Mexican governor; the first commandant of the Presidio; victims of the Committee of Vigilance, and any 'other martyrs' Belner may be thinking of in these lines.

[85] Here, Belner somewhat disingenuously refers to the funeral of Connor Davey, held at the Mission Dolores Basilica on 11 April 1976. The reference to notoriously anti-Semitic Catholic broadcaster, Father Coghlan, seems to be an attempt to imply that Belner was excluded from Davey's funeral – which he was – by virtue of Belner being Jewish, which was certainly not the case: when Belner arrived at the event uninvited, Davey's widowed partner became volubly upset, loudly blamed Belner's careless indifference for Davey's suicide, and demanded that the poet be escorted from the basilica before the ceremony could proceed. Her condemnations possibly account for the 'flinted hysterias' and 'avian shrill' mentioned here.

soldiered past Guerrero and the Roxie where American light into *Female Trouble* or *Eraserhead*
contorts, and all my thoughts were lilies shunned, evicted eulogies and Frankie Feathers
ruffling at the grave.[86] Returned home to find love and lights both out, in my dead bed I came to
understand our names and days and dynasties as dust; our eras as contingencies of sand.

[86] This apparently refers to the event described above. 'Frankie Feathers' is Connor Davey's partner, who evicted Belner from Davey's funeral and who went on to rediscover Davey's lost book and prepare it for publication by Hillwood Press next year, Clara Frances 'Frankie' Bird.

AND, AT THE LAST, JUST TO BE DONE WITH SILENCE

‘Does not this wind what’s in the branches make a noise of unkind laughter? Those are, anyway, my best thoughts on the matter. What say you, now?’

‘ ’

‘Come, put not such a sober face upon it. I’ll allow we are in a bad way of things, but at the least we have each other’s company and chatter, do we not? To be alone at our ordeal, I think, should be a misery past all enduring.’

‘ ’

‘Well, if that’s your mood, I shall not press you further, though it seems to me a pity. We two are the last men left out of our party who set forth from Brackley. Was that truly not yet fourteen days since? I have lost sense of time’s passage, but I would have thought it as more like to months.’

‘ ’

‘You are not to be turned from your decision, I can see it. You are in no mood to talk, it’s plain, though if for my part I speak out, I take it that you shall not have objection?’

‘ ’

‘That is more the spirit! We shall make a pleasant outing of this yet, we pair of old companions. When I think what we have seen together, I am fair made giddy. What a day that was, when we were met in Brackley at the old church. Five or six of us, as I recall it now, though many more came out to watch the hanging, as is only what you might expect. It was, I think, October then, with spectacle scarce otherwise in those parts. There was an old man, not in his right wits by the look of him, who cheered and clapped along with the excitement of it, and a small boy with a green snot going up and down beneath his nose as he breathed in and out, do you remember? Now I think, there was as well a dog what only had three legs, who barked and limped about the edges of the gathering. That was a time, all right. They shan't forget the half a dozen of us in a hurry, I'll be bound.'

'Five. Five of us.'

'What? What was that? I thought to hear a sound, above the tree limbs and their oaken mockery.'

' '

'Pray, fellow, take ye no offence. Come, speak again, that there should be a fellowship in our distress. What was it that you said just now? I could not make it out. I'm not in good health, if I tell the truth.'

'Five. I said, there were five of us at Brackley church. Now, be quiet with your nonsense.'

'Five, you say? Ah, then it may be so. Myself, I'm nearly mad from punishment, and trust neither my recollections nor my senses. Things are shimmering or singing, and I can't tell which it is.'

'Well, I'm no better, am I? All things have an air to them as if they might do ill at any instant, like milk not far from the boil. Of mud and puddle, gate and nettle bed, I grow dismayed, disliking something spiteful in their character. We are the both of us not far from death, is my belief.'

'I am as sure of it as you. More sure, I dare to say. My thoughts are maggoted from woe. What of our comrades, who were with us at the start? There were then six of us, I thought you said.'

'Five, blast you. There were five of us. I said it not a minute since. Five of us at the church. Roger of Hinckley, he was bailiff. It was him as said we should go in, and him who was the author of our troubles. If I had him here beside me now, why, I should set our burden down, and choke him dead.'

'He is not one of us already fallen, then? There have been one or two done that, as I'm aware.'

'No. If it were that way, I should not mind so much. When he heard what our sentence was to be, he was made paler as the lily. He said it should kill him, and went straight on the King's Highway down to Dover, where he made for France. And yet, he were the one! He were the one who said we should go in and bring the rascal out. When I made protest, and said doing so should tempt God's wrath, he cuffed me, saying that if I did not, then it would tempt the Earl of Leicester's wrath the sooner.'

'You are right. It was the going in the church that did for all of us. I can remember thinking, 'it shall do me not a bit of good to come in here', but went and did it anyway.'

'Aye. Aye, we did, and there's no coming back from it. So, if you do not mind, I'd—'

'Ah, my memory is like a sieve that has big holes, where all my thoughts are small. So, when the bailiff Roger that you speak of had run off, there were then five of us, if I am understanding you.'

'Yes. What? No. No, there were only the four of us once he had gone. There was myself – John Halpen – come from Banbury, and Will Tite from that place also. With us there was Rob of Bedford, and Martin from Peterborough, who I did not know as well. Might that be you yourself?'

'Yes! Yes, it might! But, thinking of it, I have never been in Peterborough, and cannot remember if they called me Martin. I fear that my wits are, for the most of it, destroyed. Can you not have a look, then tell me who you think I seem like?'

'Fat good would it do, with my eyes being how they are. All that I see is half enchanted, as if viewed through spiderwebs that make a pattern over everything. Its bulbs and beads are big and slow at the outsides, but littler and more frantic in the midst. This hard and frozen path we tread is to me everywhere with swirls and currents, as though it was sluggish waters. It is frightening in its prettiness, and I would as soon drop our load and run, were it not for the pair that ride always behind us. They're still there, I'll wager. Can you spot them from where you are?'

'No. My eyes are all right, but I have a stiffness in my neck that will not let me turn my head. I hear them, though. They trot some way behind, as you suspect, and make complaint about the smell of us. But would I know more of these signs and wonders you behold. Are you a saint, do you suppose?'

'I had not thought it so afore you said, but now I cannot tell. Are not the visions of the saints more full of lambs and angels? Mine has only ugly creatures snarling out of tree bark, and up from the ponds we pass teem glistening beasts like bladders, or like soft and slimy beetles, or the pimpled bone of crab claws but with many hateful eyes. These masses over us, that I know to be but the winter clouds, are in my gaze made to great, tangled balls of giant worm that hang as big as towns from the bare sky. They writhe continually in and out from squirming knots, blind bodies thick like turrets, in plump, parcelled lengths, pink-grey, that have wet light wiped down their sides. The colours that there are in things would make your scalp crawl, all the world more intricate than snails. I cannot think I am a saint, but have not otherwise a reason for this starry terror that there is in everything.'

'I have heard say – though only by ungodly men – that when the saints would scourge themselves, with flails of leather what had not been cured, it would let plagues in where the skin was broke and that was why they saw the things they did. If that were so, then with you being flogged so many times by now, and with the pestilential weight you carry, I should say that in my sight you are as good a saint as any. It is my guess that the lambs and angels shall arrive in their due course.'

'There may be much in what you say. I have not heard that tale before, or else it was forgot. It would make cruel sense of our sentence and its stipulations, were it so. Old Bishop Hugh said as we should be stripped down to our britches and then took to Brackley, all in irons, to dig up the man—'

'This was the fellow that you dragged from out the church and hanged?'

'Aye, that same man. We were to dig him up, then carry him on our bare shoulders all about the churches in the shire, there to be scourged at every one before we could with bloody backs and stinking lich proceed. If what you say is true, then Hugh of Lincoln did as good as put us all to death, but saw to it that we should first be madmen. It is not so much a wonder that Roger of Hinckley ran away to exile how he did, although as I have said, he were the one insisted we breach sanctuary.'

'Ah, well, sanctuary. It's a thing that God is said to be particular about, or so his ministers would have it. In the ordinary run of things, I've found it better that the church be not upset about a matter, as they more than often take it bad.'

'That is made plain by our predicament. The church is over all, and not the Earl of Leicester nor his men shall come before it. Why, was not King Henry flogged himself, for murdering Tom Becket? It may be he was as well beset by visions, though they surely would be better ones than mine, to suit his standing. He would not have everywhere these turning wheels of skull, nor take the movement of the grass for landed birds all shivering in the chill. He should not see in each hill a despairing giant, sat for so long with its head between its knees that weed and bramble have grown up its spine. A king, I think, should see more of embroidery or lions, and as like to that.'

'Is it yet Henry who is king? I do not keep my ear to new events.'

'No, it has not been Henry for a ten-year now, but rather Richard, called Heart of a Lion, who battled heathen Saladin in the most recent of crusades. Our third, I think, that surely has decided the affair.'

'There have been three crusades? My oath, this is a world where there is always something going on, although I think men are so wicked it must soon be ended when we come at last to Judgement Day.'

'It is a certain thing. I am expecting it next year, when calendars shall be all twelves and not elevens. It is well known that the natural way of things contrives they should be done in dozens, as the months that go to make a year, so it is likely that the Lord would have that be the date where he was done with us. Twelve hundred, I am sure of it, shall be the midnight of the ages, although neither of us shall be still alive to hear its chime, not in my reckoning.'

'I can do no more than agree, for you seem a more learned man than I, whoever I might be.'

'Ah, yes. We did not settle on which one of us you were before our conversation made a turn, but it may be that we can put our heads together on the matter, and in this way come upon an answer to it.'

'That would be a pick-me-up. I think you have already said you are John Halpen out of Banbury, so that is one gone from our list, for I cannot be you when it is plain you are somebody else entire. What of the other Banbury man you talked about? Might he not be the sort of fellow who'd be me?'

'Will Tite? I should not think it. I would play on Banbury Green with him when we were boys, and even then he had a deeper voice than you have now. In any case, he's dead. I would not swear it, but it comes to me he was perhaps the first of us to go that way.'

'Oh … now I think I have him! Was it him tried running off when we were near to Wootton?'

'That were Will. He said he could not more endure the lash, and soonest would be dead.'

'That was a stern conclusion he had reached, though I cannot help but admire his pluck.'

'Well, it might be as he thought better of it. He was not far off the road when one of them what follow rode him down and struck his head in with a mace – that I would think a good sight worse than scourging. And it was not quickly done with, either. I heard what to me seemed an unfortunate number of blows afore Will ceased with his shrill protest.'

'You have said before he had a voice more deep than mine.'

'Aye. I suspect the hurt of being struck so many times was one not easily made plain in a low register. Still, now we are decided you are neither I nor yet Will Tite, are we not nearer to an end of your conundrum? I should think that— blast it!'

'What was that, now? Did you stumble?'

'Aye. I put my foot down in a rain hole, that I did not see for all this mazy air that's everywhere. I should not like to happen on the spider who has strung this gossamer all over things. It is a great impediment, when I and thee would both prefer as our ordeal were faster done with.'

'In that, you're not wrong. Is it a long way further, do you now suppose?'

'What, our return to Brackley? No, I do not think it can be. It is my belief I saw a milestone some way back behind us, else it were a post whose markings were but accident. That said as it were two mile or it might be three. The bottom of the number was not to be read for cow shit.'

'And so that shall be an end to our unfortunate parade, at Brackley?'

'Would it were. At Brackley they shall set us to reburying the fellow that we dragged from sanctuary there, so that at least we shall no longer bear our sorry load. Then they would have us walk to Lincoln and be scourged again before we are set free, though it is plain we shall be lucky if we make it to the top end of this hill what we are on. I am surprised that you do not better recall our sentence, for it made a terrible impression on us at the time.'

'I have a sense of most of it up to the hanging, although after that, my memories are vague things or not there at all. The next I knew, we were together on this journey and have been so since. How is it with your visions? Are they fairer and more saintly, so as not to play you up so much?'

'Should you compel me to be truthful, I would say, if anything, that they were worse. This ploughed ground that we pass seemed not a moment since, to me, to be an ocean all of soil where were the ridges and the furrows like to black and crumbling waves. And in this great deluge of dirt were swimming skeletons, that leaped and dived amidst the filthy breakers as though grinning fish. Fanned out their naked ribs like fins, they did, and breathed earth through their empty eyes. Not only men and women were there, but likewise the greater bones of horses, charging breast-deep in cold land, dead roots for manes, all snorting beetles. None of this seems saintly in my reckoning. If these be visions, then they are more noisome and yet more a burden than this falling-to-bits scoundrel that we lug.'

'Then you have seen no angels, from the sound of it, lest they were skeletons.'

'I should not think as angels may have skeletons, when they are surely made of naught save spirit.'

'Then how can they have brows, chins and noses what stick out, rather than all their faces sagging in like a wet sack? Why do their arms and legs not dangle ever in the breeze?'

'Put like that, I can see your reasoning. What I think proves my point is that an angel cannot die.'

'That may well be, but neither can a skeleton.'

'I ... can we not turn back our talk to fathoming if you should be Martin of Peterborough or else Rob of Bedford? I have not the strength nor yet the character to speak on the insides of angels.'

'If that is your wish. I have contrived a way that I might know the pair of them apart, by means that have but lately come to me: which one was it got sick and brought up all the black material, and which one was it broke his leg so that we left him in a ditch?'

'Why, you are right! That is a simple method that has stared us in the face this while. Now, let me think on it ... so far as I can tell, it would be Rob as did the dreadful vomit. What it was that he produced I could not say from looking, but he soon thereafter died from it. As for Martin of Peterborough, now I think, he looked to be the oldest out of us and was already frail. I am near certain it was he who tripped from off the road into its ditch, not very long after Will Tite was lost to us. The leg was broke on his way down, and those who follow said as we should leave him there. From what I can remember of it, he made loud entreaty, asking that he should instead be killed by some means that would take less time, and would not be so likely to involve wild animals. His argument to me seemed forceful and well-reasoned, at least to the point where he went from our earshot. Well, now! What about that? We have in between the two of us worked out an answer that will fit our riddle.'

'I am struck with wonder by the skill of our deliberation.'

'As am I alike. Though in hard circumstance, we have our wits about us still.'

'Aye, that we do. So, in the end, which one of us did I turn out to be?'

'Well, you are … did we not just now establish that?'

'I cannot think we did. Most of our talk has been concerned with who I'm not. I'm not Roger of Hinckley, when by your account he is in France. Neither am I John Halpen out of Banbury, for that is you, you have convinced me. Will Tite had his head done in, while old Martin of Peterborough begged that his should be done in the same. Rob, come from Bedford, did the vomiting. I'll own my adding up is very bad, and well it may be there is somebody I have forgot.'

'For my part, I can think of no one. Not unless it happened that you were the …'

'Yes? Unless it happened that I was the what? Have you cast light on our besetting mystery?'

'I … I would sooner that I did not say.'

'Oh, come now! Surely you do not intend as I should be left hanging?'

'I think … I think it is better that I do not further talk with thee.'

'How is that better, when I thought we were become fast friends and fellows in adversity?'

' '

'Say that we are not back to that again. To walk in silence, sure as anything, shall drive you mad.'

' '

'Well, then. If such be your reply, that is a game for two to play.'

' '

' '

' '

' '

ACKNOWLEDGEMENTS

First of all, I would like to thank Edgar Allan Poe for taking time off from the torment of his life to invent the short story – still the best form for a young writer to learn their craft, and still the most versatile vehicle when they're elderly and bent beneath the weight of all those words.

Of the yarns collected here, 'A Hypothetical Lizard' was my first serious attempt at short prose fiction, written in 1987 for the third of the *Liavek* shared-world anthologies published by Ace Books, for which I'd like to thank Emma Bull and Will Shetterly, who edited the series and provided the imaginary city in which the tale occurs. I'd also like to belatedly acknowledge the superb Lewis Furey, for a line in his song 'Poetic Young Man' from the album *The Humors Of*, which sparked off the tale's central identity-theft conceit.

'Not Even Legend' was written in 2020 for inclusion in the fifth volume of *Uncertainties* (Swan River Press, 2021), and thanks are due to the redoubtable Brian J. Showers as the weird fiction anthology's editor and publisher, keeping the myriad voices of Irish fantasy alive there in Dublin.

'Location, Location, Location', written in 2019, was originally intended for a science-fiction anthology issued by my beloved Northampton Arts Lab and edited by the magnificent Donna Scott. Admittedly, what with the appearance of Plague on his coughing horse and the (properly) chaotic workings of Arts Lab, this may never appear, but I still want to thank Donna and all my Arts Lab pals just for being there, wherever the hell we are.

'Cold Reading' was written and published in 2009 as a seasonal ghost story in the Christmas issue of my exquisite-but-ruinous underground magazine *Dodgem Logic*. I made the central character a fraudulent psychic so that my many atheist and rationalist friends could enjoy a tale of terrible supernatural revenge, despite their cheerless and depressingly evidence-based philosophy.

'The Improbably Complex High-Energy State' emerged from a single point in the quantum vacuum during 2019, and was written for the latest resurrection of Michael Moorcock's *New Worlds* from the estimable Pete Crowther at PS Publishing, to whom both gratitude and love are due.

The remaining four stories were all written for this current collection between February and August in 2021. Regarding 'Illuminations', based on a woefully misguided seaside holiday in 2005, I must thank my wife Melinda Gebbie for her tolerance, and apologise for threatening to set a blameless holiday-camp helper dressed as a cartoon animal on fire if he or she attempted to cheer me up. You know I didn't mean it, darling, and I was only waving the cigarette lighter for effect.

As for the tiger-headed elephant in the room, 'What We Can Know About Thunderman' exploded like a lanced boil between February and April, and I like to think it has an air of spring about it. Other than all those people in comic-book editorial and their unguarded moments, I must thank Addy Tantamed and Steven Grant for what I think they call 'additional material' concerning the much-missed Archie Goodwin, and a couple of intriguing rumours. I must also thank my dear friend of these last few decades, the immaculate Kevin O'Neill, arguably the finest comic artist of his generation and somebody who knows where all the restless horror-comic corpses are buried.

'American Light: An Appreciation' wouldn't have been possible save for, again, the assistance of Melinda with her intimate knowledge of her native city and her memories of its shifting counter-cultures. I'd also like to thank the splendid

Kevin Ring for his heroic *Beat Scene* magazine, constantly telling me new things about a literary movement I thought I knew. Subscribe now.

The collection's final story, 'And, At the Last, Just to Be Done with Silence', was also the last written, and is as good a place as any to express my enormous debt to my friend, collaborator, and indentured slave, Joe Brown. Joe hunted down ancient local newspaper articles and historical references for this piece, dug up investigative hearings for 'Thunderman', and provided me with uncountable obscure facts right when I needed them. It's almost as if he has some kind of unimaginable magic looking-glass for finding out this stuff.

My thanks go also to my first literary agent, James Wills of Watson, Little, for his astute and loyal labours, for his impeccable taste, and for the fragrant talcum powder he got us for Christmas. Thanks also to Paul Baggaley, Daniel Loedel and all of the wonderful people at Bloomsbury for their care, their enthusiasm, and for making this new experience such a pleasant and comfortable one.

As always, thanks to my fellow language-mangles, Iain Sinclair, Brian Catling and Michael Moorcock for their unending inspiration and encouragement; to the superb Michael Butterworth and the memory of Dave Britton; and to the modern world for managing to stay several steps ahead of my most ludicrous imaginings.

Finally, I am thankful to the people I love the most, and who provide my motivation for both writing and living: to my daughters Leah and Amber, who were around my knees while I was writing 'A Hypothetical Lizard' and who engaged with 'Thunderman' without retching. They, their husbands and our four unlikely European folk-tale grandsons are the illuminations of my existence. The same is true of the above-cited Melinda Gebbie, who as an eager initial audience for most of the stories here has been a first-responder at the scene of the catastrophe, and the warmest pandemic companion that anyone could wish for. I'd also like to extend my love and appreciation to Kirsty

Noble, who's apparently been looking forward to this collection. I really hope she enjoys it.

And thanks to the tiny percentage of you readers who have read to the end of these acknowledgements. To be honest I usually skip them, so your efforts are truly appreciated.

Alan Moore
Northampton
January, 2022

A NOTE ON THE AUTHOR

ALAN MOORE is an English writer widely regarded as the best and most influential writer in the history of comics. His seminal works include *From Hell, Lost Girls* and *The League of Extraordinary Gentleman.* He is also the author of the bestselling *Jerusalem.* He was born in Northampton, and has lived there ever since.

A NOTE ON THE TYPE

The text of this book is set in Bembo, which was first used in 1495 by the Venetian printer Aldus Manutius for Cardinal Bembo's *De Aetna.* The original types were cut for Manutius by Francesco Griffo. Bembo was one of the types used by Claude Garamond (1480–1561) as a model for his Romain de l'Université, and so it was a forerunner of what became the standard European type for the following two centuries. Its modern form follows the original types and was designed for Monotype in 1929.